HARVEST
of
ILLUSION

A Spiritual Adventure

George C. Wallach

HighSight Publishing

Phoenix, Arizona

HighSight Publishing
5102 East Cheery Lynn Road
Phoenix, Arizona 85018-6627
HighSight@cox.net

Harvest of Illusion Website: **www.harvestofillusion.com**

Printed in the United States of America

Cover Painting by Carole Wallach ©2003 George C. Wallach. All rights reserved.
Author Photo ©2003 George C. Wallach. All rights reserved.
Cover Construction and Graphics by Manjari
Text Formatting and Layout by Jamie Saloff
Fonts: Times New Roman, Gatsby, Stylus

The characters in this book are fictitious and any resemblance to any person or entity in any dimension is purely coincidental.

The quotation from Katha Upanishad is from The Upanishads, translated by Eknath Easwaran, founder of the Blue Mountain Center of Meditation, copyright 1987; reprinted by permission of Nilgiri Press, www.nilgiri.org.

ACKNOWLEDGEMENTS

Many friends have helped in connection with this book through encouragement, constructive comments and in many other ways. I thank you all and feel the need to mention the following in particular:

One Mind
My Angels, my Guides, my Higher Self and all the others in the Superconscious Dimension who love me and help me,

Tom Bird – A writing mentor who understands where the words come from,

Pamela J.P. Donison – Invaluable Editing Suggestions,

David Thalberg – Planned Television Arts,

Carole Wallach – Front Cover Painting (Yes, she's my wife),

Jamie Saloff – Manuscript Formatting and Layout,

Manjari – Cover Construction and Graphics,

Mark Peebler - All Good Things Website Design,

All those who read drafts and contributed their constructive comments – Carole Wallach, Kim Wallach, Amy and Tracy Wallach, Wendy and Sean Kirby, Kellie and Dan Jarman, Carol Colombo, Joe Martori, Cynthia McCoy, Michael and Sandy Martindale, Jean and Ev Mauldin, and Lois and Phil Paris,

Jim Zupancic for his unflagging good spirit,

and Robert E.B. Allen, Esq. – My law partner for his continuous generosity.

<<~>>

DEDICATION

This book is dedicated to my mother who taught me to explore with my right brain, to my father who taught me to explore with my left brain, to my wife who constantly encouraged me to write it, to my children, who did the same, and to my friends who were a continuing source of encouragement. Above all, it is dedicated to One Mind and the source of this novel, my Higher Self, my Angels, Guides and all the others in the spiritual dimension, which I refer to as the Superconscious Dimension, who love me and help me – you will certainly understand when you read it. All of the foregoing made the following pages a joy to write.

PREFACE

The adventure in this book contains terrestrial aliens, extraterrestrial aliens, spacecraft, interbeing procreation, interbeing love, abductions, alien induced pregnancies, interbeing offspring, fidelity, infidelity, appearing, disappearing, humor, healing, Particulating, Phase Shifting, remote viewing, telepathy, the Universal Connection, the seeding of Earth, crop circles, Foo Fighters, the Tesla Field, Rods, Greys, Blondes, government, humans, CEO's, Santa Claus, Paranoia Purveyors, relationships, fear of annihilation, suicide, life, beings who live below the surface of the Earth, people who live on the surface of the Earth, beings who live on other planets, space travel, the source of the Big Bang singularity, the Grand Illusion, the Material Dimension, Transpiration, ascension, souls who live in the Superconscious Dimension, Guides, Teachers, Overseers, incarnation, reincarnation, existence beyond the Superconscious Dimension, One Mind (the highest source) and other things of the foregoing nature. *But above all, it is about unconditional love, the nature of being, and the purpose of being.*

Interwoven throughout – this spiritual adventure details in a logical but uncommon way a belief system for:

* The source and nature of spirituality, consciousness and soul,
* The source and nature of the material universe,
* The source and purpose of material life in the Material
    Dimension,
* The nature and effect of death,
* The Superconscious Dimension,
* The Entrainment of worldwide thought and its resulting power,
* The process of mentally healing the physical body available to
    anyone,
* The process of ascension from the Material Dimension
    available to anyone,
* Which of the above are illusion, and
* The Truth about the nature of existence.

The message is here. You will understand it. It can easily be a template for the direction you choose to flow for the rest of your life.

Ignorant of their ignorance, yet wise in their own esteem,

these deluded men, proud of their vain learning

go round and round

like the blind led by the blind.

Far beyond their eyes,

hypnotized by the world of sense,

opens the way to immortality.

"I am my body; when my body dies, I die."

Living in this superstition

they fall life after life . . .

Katha Upanishad

HARVEST OF ILLUSION

PROLOGUE

Terrorist acts early in the twenty-first century accelerated the formation of a democratically structured worldwide governmental organization, the United Continents, with common humanitarian and peacekeeping goals. It was an outgrowth of the old United Nations and occupied its former headquarters in New York, but with significant differences. Each country's elected leaders were the representatives in attendance on highly important United Continents issues, a majority vote was binding on all countries on all continents, and significant global issues were determined by a world popular vote. Coincident with the development of this government, a system for the mass production and wireless delivery of both electrical energy and instant electronic communication everywhere on the globe was developed and perfected, accelerating democracy and the standard of living for even the most remote inhabitants. Those remarkable events occurred in an amazingly short span of years because they were assisted by "subliminal" help from a special group of Earth's inhabitants.

A useful byproduct of the increase in economic capacity on Earth's continents was the development of a worldwide monetary system based on "unicredits," but an unintended result was the focus on acquisition of material goods and wealth which overshadowed the elevation of spiritual awareness that was previously advancing on the surface of the planet.

As a result of the special subliminal assistance, the United Continents government, together with its peacekeeping force which was the dominant military power on Earth, had become firmly established while the twenty-first century was relatively young – young enough so that neither cultural memory nor technology advances had lost connection to the twentieth century. People still ate beef, fashions continued to cycle and the twentieth-century nostalgia craze had re-energized. Things hadn't changed that much, but they would, soon.

<<~>>

CHAPTER ONE

The craft swooped closer and closer toward the rocky New Mexico landscape, diving straight at the mountain which seemed to be flickering under the light of a full moon. What looked like so much gray started taking on more and more detail as the arid scene rushed to her. Hurtling at the ground, Mari's terror started in her toes, flashed up her legs and spine between her shoulder blades to the back of her neck, and exploded into her head. Just as she opened her mouth to scream, she felt transparently charged and saw all those little "electrical" dots again, just like the time she was a child of six.

The ground had disappeared and they were still in the air, but the sky was green! Underneath them appeared to be a large airport-like facility, except there were no runways and the craft all seemed to be circular, triangular or oblong – no wings. There were other craft in the air, seemingly moving in an orderly fashion. The one containing Mari came gently to rest on a vacant landing pad, making the same beating sound she had heard as a child.

~Lenaan and Minuum did that on purpose. They were also piloting the craft when you were six.~

Jenoor rose. Calmer now, she studied him more closely than she had earlier in the evening. Having assisted her parapsychologist husband, Murph, with his patients and session transcripts for the past several years, she had listened to and transcribed many descriptions of beings like this. Until tonight, they had been just words.

At about six feet, he was quite tall compared to most of the ones Murph's patients described and the few others she had seen on the craft so far. While slender by human standards, perhaps 145 pounds, his thighs were long with powerful-looking, smooth, sheath-like muscles. The same long, powerful musculature was repeated for the back of his legs and calves. His feet were slender, seemed a little longer than the usual "foot" size and shape and gave the impression that he was primarily supported from his toes and the balls of his feet, without the heel portion bearing any weight. She couldn't really see any toes, just what appeared to be their long outlines under either very tight fitting material of some kind, or his "skin." That was the way his entire body looked, outlines of form under seamless material, or his natural outer covering.

From the abdomen up through the shoulders and arms, he seemed downright scrawny, like a body builder with upper-body potential who worked only on his legs in the gym. Connected to his shoulders by a long thin neck was a head like a balloon on a guided string, proportionately too big for his body. It had an oversized cranial area that smoothed down to a very small chin, like a rounded three-dimensional gray valentine which evidenced three suggestions – ears, nose and lips. His eyes were huge. She had trouble looking at them long enough to keep her thoughts clear. She decided to inspect them closely some other time.

Mari was one of five children a year apart, an attractive girl sandwiched between two brothers on each side. They all did the same things, wrestled and boxed with each other, engaged in judo, karate, baseball, tennis, soccer, basketball, yoga (the really hard kind), tai chi, and almost any other physical activity. They played hard against each other, and with each other against the other kids, but never with animosity in either case. It was always with a love of the game. Winning was important, but the family understood that winning was not the only thing. It was a byproduct of deeper, more important values. The result of that mixture was a woman equally comfortable in polite parlor conversation or swearing like a trooper when the occasion arose. These days, Mari still hit the gym four times a week for strenuous aerobic workouts and had a supple, graceful body, rock hard when in action. Thus, at an extremely fit five feet, eight inches, 124 pounds, she felt more physically adept and faster than Jenoor looked to her, and decided she could probably kick the shit out of this top-weighted string bean if they ever got into it.

Some of her perceptions evaporated when, watching Jenoor come toward her, she realized that he was strangely agile and carried himself with command and grace. He extended his "hand" to Mari to help her out of the chair. Responding to this "gentlemanly" act, she automatically grasped it – and then froze. It was the first time – certainly as an adult – she had voluntarily touched one of them. His three "fingers" looked stiff and stick-like, but were flexible and didn't articulate at joints. They just bent continuously and seamlessly like thick annealed wire with a gray, almost soft, leather-like covering. She marveled that the feel was so much different from the look.

In addition to feeling like her hand was fastened onto his, she discovered it was. His fingertips – no fingernails – had little suction cups on the bottoms of them that were attached to her, but it felt okay. His fourth digit, a "thumb," had no suction cups and in a funny way seemed to be stuck onto his hand as an afterthought. It didn't fit with the smooth flow of its design. It interrupted the *gestalt*. She looked at the "females" that had helped her change clothes earlier and they had no thumbs.

As they continued to touch, her hand seemed to melt into his, as if they *should* be touching each other, the cosmic valences of each adding to a whole. She'd only felt similar to this with Murph. At that moment, she thought she detected the slightest hesitation in Jenoor's movement even though he otherwise deftly and effortlessly helped her out of the chair and onto her feet.

When Jenoor communicated again, he made no reference to any feeling when their hands touched even though he was confused by his own momentary hesitation, ~Your thoughts are correct, we did not have thumbs originally and our digits were quite stiff. That is why the suction cups evolved. In altering ourselves to be more like humans, we limbered up our digits and the 'thumbs' were genetically added to some of us over time. We concentrated on that rather than a fourth 'finger' because it seemed much more useful, and made us more like you than we had been before; however, we have been working on a fourth finger for quite a while now and some have it.

~We have also developed the ability to speak out loud although we seldom do, and to hear much as humans do. We are always trying to improve and, of course, long ago we succeeded in genetically altering ourselves so that the original physiological factors that drove our ancestors underground no longer affect us. However the remaining factor that drove us here still exists – our extreme concern that those we call the Harvesters, the arch enemy who brought us to Earth initially, will return.~

He released his grip, unwinding his long fingers from around her hand, steering her toward the door with a gentle touch of his thoughts on her mind. It did not take long to exit the craft, which was perhaps one-hundred feet in diameter and twenty-five feet at its highest point, although she had seen craft of all sizes while in the air. In the "air?" Looking up at the green sky she couldn't quite figure it out. Then it hit her. If Jenoor was telling her the truth, she had to be looking at the top of a cave so large it wasn't appropriate to describe it that way. This was a bubble in the Earth big enough that she couldn't tell from ground level where its boundaries were. The yellowish-green phosphorescent glow seemed a very familiar color.

~That is because it is phosphorus,~ Jenoor volunteered. ~We needed a source of light for the 'sky' and that material was plentiful to us. The biggest challenge was making it fireproof. It is a flammable material and we did not want a truly flaming sky started by a small accidental breach in the solidified magma. It would have been a conflagration the equivalent of some of the biblical stories that have developed on the Surface.~

Still at the Travelport, as the Mantid referred to it, they climbed into a much smaller but similarly shaped craft about the size of a car with four individual seats, functional enough but not designed for the human form. Between the two front seats was a small metallic ball on a pedestal. Jenoor put his hand on it and the craft rose and began moving. She had no idea of direction because there was no sun for reference in the green twilight from above, nor were there any mountains or other significant land features. At some point far enough in the distance to be indistinct, the green sky seemed to meet the ground in all directions in an enormous circle. Other than the eerie effect of the light, the structures below seemed like the rooftops of any large metropolitan area, but there were no streets, only round holes in the ground close to the buildings. The smallest hole was about thirty feet in diameter. Otherwise, the ground was covered with vegetation that seemed to glow slightly with a black light and, except for the airfield control tower, all the structures seemed to be one-story structures of varying sizes with a lot of air handling equipment on top.

The craft eased down one of the holes and came to rest in a fair-sized landing room like a large underground parking garage with similar craft parked there. There were a number of identical unmarked doors in the walls and Jenoor took her through one of them as she asked, ~If you hadn't been here before how would you know which door to go through?~

~We would just Connect with that portion of the Universal Connection specific to us and the persons we are trying to reach. Then the path to them would become clear. If there were a lot of humans like you down here, we would have to put up signs, at least until you collectively developed a greater ability to tap into the Universal Connection.~ Consistent with his demeanor earlier in the evening, he intended it to be explanatory. It was not the sign of a droll, though limited, sense of humor.

They went into a laboratory-looking room. There were other Greys working in there, much as one might observe humans in a laboratory on the Surface. She moved closer to see what they were doing. Jenoor did not stop her and the Greys moved out of her way when she approached. There were glass containers about the size of Mason jars with fetuses in them. She felt a wave of sadness that all these little beings died in their experiments, and thought it macabre that they would keep all of them in little jars. They didn't look quite like the pictures of human fetuses she had seen.

She leaned over to examine one closely. It moved! She instinctively jerked back. Then she examined the glass container more carefully. It had tubes going in and out of it. They all did. A little numb, she moved closer again, ready to spring away if it did anything weird, like fly through the side of the jar and attach itself to her nose. She told herself she needed to get a grip. She'd seen too many science fiction movies with Murph who was fascinated by them because of the abduction patients he had worked with.

The fetuses had slightly different proportions from the pictures of human fetuses she had seen. They were pink, but their heads seemed a little bigger. The dark places where their eyes were beneath the skin seemed to be larger and darker. Their bodies and limbs seemed to be lengthened and they – well, they were just *different* even though one couldn't swear it wasn't a human fetus. ~Are these, these – ~ Her thoughts trailed off.

~Yes. They are what I have been telling you about.~ She just stared at him. At his enormous eyes.

~How old are these?~

~Just over six weeks.~

The thoughts were whirling in her head. ~You've, you've . . . just taken them then!~

~That's correct.~

She couldn't think. My God! The stories these women were telling Murph *were* true! She wondered if some of these belonged to Murph's patients. So many had insisted that they *knew* they were pregnant and about six weeks later they weren't. No tangible evidence, just a story. She shook her head thinking it might organize her thoughts. It didn't.

She whirled, angry at what they may have done, "Where's my sister!"
He jumped at the sound of her voice shattering the relative silence.

~Please don't do that, Mari. You will meet her.~

~Well, let's do it then!~

~We will soon, but I think you should see a few more things first.~

Somewhat reluctantly, she went down a hall with him into another room. This room was like a nursery. There were many female Mantid sitting around and each one had a baby in its arms, rocking it and holding it close. The activity looked strange in comparison to the stiff forms of the females performing it. She moved closer to look at the babies. She got the same impression she did from the living fetuses. They didn't look *not* human, but there was just a feeling that it wasn't quite right. Their heads were just a little too big, not ugly big, just a little too big, but they were in proportion to their eyes. Their eyes were large, beautifully large. They did not seem to be without pupils as Jenoor's. They were deep with the purity of a baby's eyes. She leaned very close to one. Its eyes were an indescribable shade of baby blue. She had never seen such delicately large, amazing eyes on a baby. ~Wow! Wait till you're sixteen. You're going to drive all the little boys wild! Wait a minute.~ She realized she couldn't see if this were actually a little girl.

~Your Connection is accurate, Mari. She is a little girl.~

~Do you have little boys?~

~Of course.~

~Are they anatomically correct? I . . I mean like humans. I . . . I don't see anything on you.~ It must have been her Midwestern upbringing that made her feel a little embarrassed to be talking about this, particularly with reference to Jenoor. She was beginning to feel a synergy with him, no longer viewing him as just some sort of alien-like specimen. Jenoor had no clothing, but also had no visible male apparatus. For that matter the female Greys wore nothing and she could not see any signs of "femaleness," yet she knew which were the males and which were the females. Maybe she was tuning in more accurately to the "Connection" as Jenoor put it when making a shorthand reference to what he called the Universal Connection.

~You are getting better at it. Practice helps. But, to answer your initial thought, the hybrids, or 'Melds' as we refer to them, are humanly anatomically correct, in form if not completely in function.~

~What do you mean?~

~It is easier to start from an historical genetic perspective and turn your attention away from the Melds for a moment. In the Mantid effort to become more like humans, we initially succeeded with genetic male manipulation at developing a human-like penis; however, we soon discovered that when the enhanced Mantid males reached maturity, they could not achieve an erection, which of course, we think is essential if we are ultimately going to breed with human females in a 'normal' way and not in vitro.~ He didn't know why, but he really did not want to communicate with her about this subject.

~We are convinced that the ability to achieve an erection is related to human emotion – and emotion is exactly what we are trying to achieve, but we have so far failed in finding your emotion gene, your 'E-gene.' Thus, until we can, we have had to find some way of achieving an erection so that we might consummate 'normal' breeding if and when that should occur. We are hopeful that if the Mantid breed with humans in the normal way it will ultimately liberate and integrate the E-gene into the resulting Melds.~

Mari tossed out, ~Screw and it will come.~ He didn't get it. Apparently he hadn't intercepted and watched *that* many old Surface movies.

He continued, ~In order to accomplish this, we purloined from certain of your mammal species, such as the walrus, and developed a penis bone . . .~

Mari burst into hysterical, very *loud* laughter. They all jumped back and the babies became very agitated. Between gales and gasps she managed to get out, "Wait a minute . . . just a minute!" She cracked up again. "You guys . . . you guys put a bone . . . a bone in your . . . !" She was laughing so hard, she couldn't talk for a few moments. They stared at her in disbelief and pain from her shouts of laughter. "Wait! Wait! This is every girl's dream! Don't change a thing! Not a thing!!" She was helpless and almost falling to the floor she was laughing so hard.

The Greys were stupefied. They were literally thoughtless.

Still speaking out-loud, but under a little more control, "So . . . so where is this marvelous appendage?" She cracked up again. "I don't see anything on you. . . and I'm extremely curious by nature!!" Again gales of uncontrollable laughter. She felt like she had been having a few too many toddies with the girls and they had gotten into their hilarious comparisons of guys.

~Well, if you had spent any time studying the reproductive functions of certain of your Surface mammals, you would find in that sphere that this is a very common occurrence and a perfectly acceptable way of accomplishing what is necessary. It is particularly important to us because we cannot generate the necessary emotion to accomplish that feat.~ His thought tone seemed to her a little less Hal-like, even a little huffy. If Jenoor had understood what was happening to him, he would find that he was offended.

~We have drugs for that stuff, Jenoor. You haven't been watching the right digivision movies.~ She was still smiling broadly.

~They do not work on us.~

~Okay, okay. I'm sorry I laughed, Jenoor, but where is it?~ She couldn't allow herself to think about the possibilities, or despite her apology she would start cracking up again, and she really *did* think she had hurt his feelings even though, according to Jenoor at least, that wasn't supposed to be possible.

~It is there. It is in the right place, and I do not wish to communicate with you about it any more right at the moment.~

Well, maybe so, but she couldn't see it, ~Okay, let's get off 'pure' Mantids then and go back to the Melds. Did you put a bone in the little boys?~ She was still toying with him, but he didn't get it.

~No. Of course not. In our in vitro inseminations, we have activated as few of our genes and as many of your genes as we think appropriate. We are trying to create a joinder between our species that is as human in physical looks and physical function as possible. We want the Melds to be as human as possible physically, so long as they retain our mental development and potential, coupled with your emotional capacity.~

Reluctant to focus on the bizarre implications of her next flurry of questions, she just asked them. ~Have any of the male and female Melds reached maturity? And if so, do you allow them to fraternize? And if so, what happens?~ She thought she was beginning to sound like a combination of her dad and Murph's lawyer-sister.

~Initially, when we first started our insemination program and subsequently took the fetuses – and remember *always* with consent even though the mothers in their present Earthly incarnation usually do not remember that since the amnesia is also by agreement and design – and incubated them, we would carefully keep those fetuses in a sterile room after they became viable outside of our artificial-womb container. It was an excellently designed post-container environment that provided all the food and hygiene necessary, but despite our best efforts, almost all of them would waste away to nothing while still babies and, physically at least, would pass from this plane of existence.

~Then, we began to examine what human mothers did and it became clear that they had a great deal of physical contact with their babies. So we had our females imitate that physical contact behavior as much as possible and it worked to keep them alive and healthy, but we still have not seen any evidence that the Melds have developed emotion. Somehow, the Meld is not capturing the E-gene. As a result, and even though we have Melds who have reached maturity, including your half sister, neither the males nor females have had any interest in each other from a romantic procreational standpoint. Thus, we do not know what would happen if they 'fraternized' as you put it. Forcing the issue would not meet our goals.~

The mention of her half sister shocked her back on track. Her overwhelming curiosity had again caused her to digress. ~Hey! Where is she?~

~We are getting there. It will happen shortly, but first I want you to see what happens while the younger ones are maturing.~

~Look, this better be the last stop.~

~I assure you, it will be.~

They went to a room close by that Jenoor informed her was a classroom for Melds. There were perhaps thirty in the room, some standing, some seated, some at work tables scattered about the room. All seemed to be paying attention to the instructor who was communicating with them mentally about matters relating to Surface life. The Melds were all human-looking although some seemed closer than others to a mythical norm Mari visualized. She presumed it was because the gene manipulations were not always as exacting as the Mantid would like.

Some had stringy hair like a person going bald, their craniums were a little bigger than regular and their eyes were large and slightly almond shaped, with fingers that seemed very long in comparison with their palms, and they were very thin. But seeing them, one would still think they were human beings, albeit strange looking ones. People that looked similar to that on the Surface generally were treated as being weird and, as a result, they were weird – fringe people in society who did not fit into the mainstream, or perhaps any stream for that matter. Others looked not only "normal," but were very attractive. The Mantid had succeeded in pulling the best out of those genes indeed.

The class was over shortly and the Melds left the room, the care-giving teachers remaining behind, ~Jenoor, do the Melds talk?~

~They can, but not usually. We instruct mentally.~

She thought for a moment. ~Did I miss something here? If your goal is to 'meld' the two species, don't you think they should be prac-ticing speaking like Surface people? There are just a whole lot of folks up there who would be very put off by this mental business, not to mention 'melding,' which is a great idea to you, but will just scare the living hell out of people up there if you haven't figured that one out yet.~

~Our *ultimate* goal is not to meld the two species for eternity. It is to gain emotional capacity. After we succeed in isolating and inbreed-ing the E-gene into ourselves, the Surface beings need not particularly concern themselves with us. We will cause no harm.~

She paused with thought again. ~Well, isn't that incredibly short-sighted? Are you planning on leaving the planet? I don't think so. You've already communicated about the threat of damage that can be caused to the Mantid by what Surface people do. If I can think of a lot more ways humans can cause harm, you should be able to also. If you think you've got so much to gain from us, are you just going to take? Where is the *quid pro quo*? If you are as advanced as you claim, don't you also have a lot to bring to the table for us? Has it occurred to you advanced folks – it was a stretch, but that was the word she chose – to *share*? You could start out with your technology and your mental capacity. You could keep doing exactly what you are trying to do, only on a basis intended to help us also. If we are all going to live here, it would make a lot more sense to try to make it a better place.~

Her comments concerning the Mantid selfishness brought him up short. For the first time he realized that the Mantid vision had been tun-nel-like. Then it hit him. The Mantid self-involvement and shortsight-edness had been producing the effect of a systemic pesticide. How could they be so stupid, so mentally unevolved? In addition to getting what they wanted, the Mantid *should* protect themselves further. It was the intelligent thing to do, and the differences between the two species were so vast that they could not be bridged only intellectually. There had to be contact! Often and continuous. All of this secretive experimentation and manipulation would not accomplish what should be a goal equally as important as acquiring the E-gene, that of protecting their own environment on a cooperative and permanent basis so they would have a platform on – in – which they could enjoy their emotions. How elemental.

It also bothered him that he had matter-of-factly explained to her how deep and intelligent his mind was compared to hers. His focus was in the wrong place for this circumstance and it surprised him that there might be something to learn from the Surface. He wondered if not having emotion had anything to do with his shortfall in this regard.

~Where is my sister?~

Jenoor thought-motioned to one of the remaining caregiving teachers, who left the room and returned shortly with the most stunningly beautiful woman Mari had ever seen. Mari felt instinctively drawn to her and unconsciously started to move slowly toward her, staring at her, drinking in every detail, knowing without inquiry this was Xanthas, knowing her name, knowing they were part of each other. Xanthas looked like she was somewhere in her 20's, had her mother's virtually translucent white beautiful porcelain skin, a slender, graceful bone structure overlaid by marvelously athletically-proportioned muscles, and a face with the clear capability of causing civil war in the universe. Her stone-black hair was cut short. It appeared to have the texture of thick velvet, accentuating the biggest, softest, deepest violet eyes – with just a hint of blue, and shimmering points of green every now and then – that she had ever seen and couldn't possibly have imagined.

Her classic-movie-buff mind involuntarily blurted out, ~My God! A cosmic young Elizabeth Taylor to the thousandth power!~

~No, this is Xanthas.~ Jenoor somewhat innocently volunteered.

Xanthas and Mari extended their hands to one another at exactly the same moment. Xanthas' lovely, soft, long tapered fingers intertwined with Mari's and they simply looked into each other's eyes. Tears welled out of Mari's eyes and began running down her face. The same thing happened to Xanthas.

If Jenoor's jaw had been big enough, it would have hit the floor. If he hadn't been so surprised, he might have realized he was feeling something very strange indeed, perhaps an emotion, for the second time in a very few minutes. The other Greys in the room drew closer, their sizeable eyes fastened on Xanthas' tears. They were again thoughtless.

Xanthas and Mari put their arms around each other and just held on for awhile, rocking slightly back and forth with their eyes closed. The Greys were motionless. Mari and Xanthas simultaneously realized the origin of those thoughts which had been sifting into their minds for so many years. The feeling there was always someone just out of reach, the longing to know, ignoring it as just something self-manufactured indicating some unknown and unreachable wish or desire. It was real all the time! They hugged tighter. Each one embracing the visitor who had been waiting in the antechamber of her mind. There was nothing "half" about their sisterhood.

Mari stepped back, still holding onto Xanthas' hands, looking at her with Connected love. Chiding Jenoor, ~Wow! It's impossible to understand why you wouldn't have a bunch of hard-petered young Melds running around here with someone like this in your midst.~

Jenoor was paying no attention. ~Xanthas! You were crying like Surface people!~ He failed to recognize he was excited. ~Describe what has happened to you!~

~I . . . I . . .~

Mari interrupted, ~I can tell you. For the first time she is conscious of feeling love. A love we have always had for each other without knowing or understanding it. We may still not understand it, but we definitely have it. So, it looks like you have succeeded, Jenoor, at least in this case. Even if Xanthas doesn't know how to describe it, I can guarantee she's got it!~ Mari felt amazement and wonder generated throughout the entire room.

Jenoor's mind, operating at cosmic-chip speed, was trying to figure out why the E-gene was passed in this instance and not the others. He didn't know. He came to the conclusion that, in any event, this family was a very special gene pool. ~Mari, this makes it all the more imperative that you fulfill your original commitment and breed with me.~

~Leave me alone with my sister for awhile and then I'll give you an answer, but frankly, I still haven't come to a conclusion about which way I'll go.~

~As you wish.~

As Jenoor and the other Greys slowly began to leave the room, Mari's mind flew over the events of the last few days that culminated in her arrival here. Things had started to heat up several days before when Mari and Murph were in bed one night.

CHAPTER TWO

Just as his lips pressed the hollow between her breasts, Mari catapulted away, "Someone is watching us!"

Stunned for a moment at the sudden disappearance of his pleasure world, Murphy Bailey looked around in the dim light and somewhat irritably stated the apparent fact, "Mari, there is no one here!" Events like this with Mari seemed to be happening relatively frequently lately, not necessarily during sex, and they annoyed him. They shouldn't. He was an experienced psychologist and should be making an attempt to understand her. He wasn't. It pissed him off.

"Listen, there was someone watching us! Whether you believe me or not, they were *watching* us!"

They? He knew he should be making some sort of connection here, but *hornus interruptus* was not a conducive time.

A few nights later at the military base covering the region which included the Bailey house, "Shit! Another one." Captain Core hit the "danger yellow" security button to UniCom Headquarters down the hall. Colonel Janes came on the run. "It's still on the screen, sir."

"It sure as hell is. How can anything zip around like that?" The blip was moving all over the screen in amazing patterns at incredible speeds, defying all known theories of propulsion, gravity, structural integrity and known physics. Core turned and nodded at a communications corporal, "Try to talk to it."

"Unidentified flying object in Quadrant 43218, this is United Continents Protective Forces Regional Command Headquarters, please identify yourself." No answer. "We are assigning you the identifying sign 'Visitor.' Visitor, please respond." The message was simultaneously translated by computer into every language, code, word, music, electrical impulse, magnetic impulse, light impulse, and almost every other possible method of communication known to the United Continents of Earth, and sent by Big Boy to Quadrant 43218. No answer. Janes didn't bother to scramble any stratofighters. He knew they couldn't catch it.

Inside the craft, ~I do not know why they have not ascertained they do not have to do all the multi-translations, impulses and music gyrations with their big computer in order to communicate with us. All they have to do is think,~ thought Co-pilot Minuum.

~Well, in the twentieth century they got attached to radio, television and movies and have never let go of the idea that communication, particularly with unknown flying craft, should be primarily audible or visual. Of course, we have not given them much of a chance to figure it out, and we have made some very strong efforts to either confuse them or to cover our movements,~ replied Pilot Lenaan.

~At least they are getting smart enough not to waste time chasing us. Darting all over like this has its benefits since Jenoor wants to condition them to leave us alone. But I think we should not take any risk and just Phase Shift since we are supposed to protect our human visitors' safety as much as possible, particularly Marion. Ever since we started picking her up as a child, we have always had especially strict instructions from Jenoor to do nothing to unnecessarily put her in danger,~ responded Minuum. However, knowing Jenoor was in the craft's examining module with Mari, the co-pilot did not want to risk chastisement for failure to follow Jenoor's instructions to stay in phase.

Not having been privy to the communications that had just occurred with the U.C.P.F., nor to the thoughts of Lenaan and Minuum, Mari didn't know where she was, how she got here or that the room she occupied was darting all over the sky. But she knew damn well someone had been watching the last few days, somebody had kidnapped her and something awful was going to happen. She was very frightened and her mind started running through possibilities.

Since she was a child, Mari had been an avid fan of the old twentieth-century classic movies and television programs shown on the digivision channels dedicated to them. They called the medium DV these days instead of TV. She liked all kinds, but particularly fantasy and science fiction, both good and bad. She was a participant in the world-wide popular nostalgia fad which, incidentally, included the United States President. His favorite was reputed to be *Plan 9 From Outer Space*, considered for a long, long time to be the worst of the worst, but it had made director Ed Wood's name a household word among aficionados.

She wondered if she was dreaming an amalgamation of about ten of those old science fiction movies mixed together. However, she was reasonably certain, actually pretty positive, that it wasn't a dream –

simply too real by all the measures of reality she knew.

In any event, Mari was scared to death. She did not know how she got here, had absolutely no clothes on and could not move her body to get off of what seemed to be an examining or operating table, which was cold and certainly not comfortable. Lying on her back, her eyes moved in a panic around what she could see of the room. She'd had her appendix out once and this room looked like an operating room with strong moveable lights overhead and various medical-looking machines and equipment, some suspended from the ceiling. She couldn't really tell what they were, but one looked similar to a magnetic imaging machine.

There were people standing around. Then it hit her. Christ! They aren't *people*, they are . . . they look just like . . . they are *gray*! My God! They are the gray beings, the *Greys*! The ones Murph's patients are constantly describing to him! The ones in the session transcripts!

She wanted desperately to get off the table, but even her strongest desire would not translate into muscle movements of her choice. She could feel that their thoughts had taken control of her muscles. The only movements she could make were ones they allowed. Not being a shrinking violet, she was angry as well as being very frightened. She had little doubt it was clear to the Greys from her thoughts that she was very upset concerning this violation of her privacy and personal freedom.

Now that she was here, for some reason she couldn't put her finger on, she wasn't quite sure whether or not she had been in this situation before. She kind of thought maybe she had been. It was weird. It had a certain familiarity. *They* had a certain familiarity. How the hell did they get her here? The feeling that she was being watched over the last several days had been disconcerting and certainly hadn't been particularly conducive to an intimate relationship with Murph. Then, she went to sleep earlier tonight and woke up here! She was instinctively aware she hadn't been asleep long and that she *was* awake. She absolutely *knew* the difference between a waking experience and even the most vivid of dreams.

In the descriptions by Murph's patients of scenes much like this, a number of them woke immediately once the abduction started, or they were someplace other than in bed when they were taken. Sooner or later, most of his patients remembered substantially the whole experience, either spontaneously, under hypnosis or some combination of the two. Of course, if they had no such memory or nothing of that nature concerned them, he probably would never see them. Of the ones he did see, many of them were terrified, and she knew why now. Then again, some were not. However that might shake out on Murph's couch, she didn't like this at all. It seemed clear to her at this moment that the reason UFO sightings and reports of abductions and aliens had never died out was because they were true. She'd rather read about it.

There was a tall doctor-like Grey standing over her. At least she sensed he was a doctor.

~Mari, you should not be so upset with us. You *consented* to this procedure some time ago.~ thought the being. Just like in the patient reports, his mouth hadn't moved and no sound came from it, but in her mind she "heard" exactly what he was thinking.

"What the hell are you talking about?!" Mari was yelling from fear. Not the genteel behavior her mother would have expected from a college educated woman with two degrees from a conservative eastern university. But having grown up fighting for her own identity among her brothers, often when her parents weren't around, scrambling to protect herself and her space came naturally – particularly when she was as threatened as she felt now. But, at least they were letting her talk.

Jenoor took a step back. ~Mari, *I* am not talking, *I* am thinking, and that is all you have to do to respond to me. In fact we are so used to communicating in that fashion that it is painful to us, and somewhat confusing, when you shout. Please do not do it.~

Inside her head he sounded just like "Hal," that soft, soothing computer voice, HAL 9000, from that old movie, *2001: A Space Odyssey*. She wanted to kick him in the nuts and get out of here, but she couldn't see that he had any. "Listen, pearhead, I am not here by consent, I did not ask to come here, I don't know how I got here or where I am, but I do know I can't move, you look very, very peculiar to me. I don't like it here and I want to leave – *now!*" She was yelling louder.

He took another step back. ~Mari, if you will not stop shouting and start thinking your communications, we will do it for you. I know you would prefer to perform that act of your own volition, and you *are* here voluntarily.~

~Bullshit!~ She decided to try thinking it. Since her mother and father disapproved of salty language in their presence, she usually swore better thinking anyway. In any event, it was something she could control. ~What's voluntary about this?~

~Thank you, Mari. You see, it works, and although the fear and anger we detect by the language of your thoughts causes an unusual reaction in us, your choice is the reason you are here, and the reason we have allowed you to be consciously aware of it.~

The being's thoughts in her head were so emotionless, and presented so calmly, that they quieted her somewhat and also piqued her natural, nearly uncontrollable curiosity, even if she did feel extremely vulnerable lying naked on an examining table. Since it was clear they had her, and had her good, her survival instinct helped her decide to try a different tack. Information might help her plan her next move. She made an additional conscious effort to calm herself. Uncharacteristically almost pleading, ~Who are you? Can you explain all this to me?~

~I can and I will. But, I am going to tell you things that may seem very unusual at first.~

~Go ahead.~ She was wishing he would let her up off the table, but sensed he was concerned about her uncooperative behavior. She thought back to when her brothers would hold her down and give her bare-knuckle "noogies" on her head and forearms for sport. No matter how much those little welts hurt, she wouldn't react, except for just asking them a lot of questions as if a normal conversation were taking place, and they would finally give up and let her go. So she decided to concentrate on what this slender gray entity was saying as hard as she could and not get crazy again, no matter what.

~So long ago now that the time span is meaningless in modern human terms, our physical ancestors were brought here by beings from another place in the universe which is still unknown to us. We were deposited here on Earth with many other life forms in what is best described as a giant spatial terrarium.~

Still curious notwithstanding the situation, ~You mean Earth is a terrarium? Like some kid's science experiment?!~

~Exactly. We are certain a good portion of the physical life on Earth evolved only after it was intentionally put here at a point in time long after Earth was created, probably from time to time. We, and I am referring to our physical species and not yours, were originally what you know as praying mantis or, more accurately, an unusual type of them . . . .~

Her unshielded thoughts interrupted him. ~This is just *too* frigging absurd. When does the hidden camera come out to photograph me for the 1950's B-movie sci-fi promo poster – they'd have to air brush a few parts! But . . . he *does* have a mantis-like look. His body and limbs *are* stick-like in a way, yet have a human quality. His movements are jerky, maybe just quick, and smooth at the same time, and his head, his *head* sure as hell could have evolved from a mantis, yet at the same time, he seems imbued with a certain undefinable, intelligent dignity. She had always been fascinated by praying mantis, having kept them as "pets" in her room through most of her childhood.~

~Yes, I know. I have always been very interested in humans too.~ There was no chuckle; his manner was quietly matter-of-fact. ~It might be more convenient for you if we refer to ourselves as the Mantid while I describe our evolution. Our Mantid ancestors were a different species of mantis that found it very difficult to exist on the surface of the Earth because certain components of the sun's light spectrum had a very negative effect on them and, for our ancestors whose fluids and circulation were different from other mantis, it was very cold on the surface. So, our most intelligent 'insect' ancestors began looking for ways to get out of the sunlight and to warm up, no oxymoron intended.~

Her thoughts interrupted him again and he responded, ~Well, I do not know if Ed Wood's infant daughter could have written a better script, but you are right, our ancestor Mantid did make their way down to the Earth's mantle. Of course at a point, the further down they got, the hotter it got. But because they also felt driven, we believe by instinct, to protect themselves from the beings that deposited them on Earth in the first place, they did not stop at a level comfortable for them, but consistently looked for ways to go deeper without being destroyed by the heat. As a result, we believe through a process of natural selection from the genetic pool available to them, our ancestors developed the inherent ability all Mantid now have, the ability to Phase Shift.~

~Huh?~

~It is an ability to keep our physical configuration, from our perspective, but to shift its vibration so it is out of phase with what you experience as matter on the Earth. In that state, we are occupying the same area as Earthly matter, but we are unaffected by it. For us in an out-of-phase or, more precisely, an opposite-phase condition, you do not physically exist from our perspective. The reverse is true for you when we are at opposite phase; we do not physically exist from your perspective. We are both there, but invisible to and unaffected physically by one another.~

~Let me see if I have this straight. It's like parallel worlds and you have the ability to jump back and forth.~ This was too easy; she was beginning to get more upset again. This must be some kind of bizarre, giant joke.

~That is basically correct; however, this is *definitely* not a joke.~

She couldn't put her finger on why, but based on the way he communicated that thought, she was certain no one was joking around. Remembering her information-gathering tactic, ~All right, please keep going with this Phase Shifting stuff.~

He continued, ~Think of an S on its side with a horizontal line through the middle, the commonly illustrated sine wave rising and falling evenly above and below a center line.~ She thought of a tipped over dollar sign. ~Then think of the human atomic physical existence as being an atomic vibrational state represented by the highest point above the line, and the Mantid atomic physical existence, when in an opposite Phase Shift, as the lowest point below the line. Vastly over simplified, we are in the same oscillation, but out of atomic phase with one another.~

~Okay. I get it, but how do you get from one phase to the other, through worm holes and warp speed like those old *Star Trek* movies?~

~No. It is a process of changing the vibration of our atomic structure, our atoms and molecules, until they are vibrating in the phase opposite from the one we are in. It is like sliding down that S. In fact, we can stop anywhere on that slide and be partly in or out of phase with you. From your perspective, we would be partially invisible or transparent.

~When it got very hot in the Earth, we initially lived in a Phase Shifted environment, but it was not practical in the long run since there is nothing there except what we take there. So we ultimately learned how to create large Earth-phase living spaces for our communities under the Earth and protect them from excessive heat. We have lived that way now for a long, long time.~

She was becoming more interested, ~Is that how you come through walls like Murph's patients describe, by a Phase Shift?~

~We could go through a wall that way but we usually use a different process we call Particulation.~

~What is that?~

~Particulation is a process of momentarily changing our atomic structure from atoms and molecules into neutrino-like particles while we pass through a solid object, and then reforming them in the open space on the other side of the object. Neutrinos are subatomic particles so small that billions are passing through your body at any given moment. Our shifted atoms are not changed into neutrinos, but into neutrino-*like* particles which are actually much smaller than neutrinos. It is easy for either to pass through the atoms and molecules of 'solid' objects because atoms comprising anything are approximately ninety-nine percent empty space.~

Mari had always enjoyed the humor around the edges of convention. She got it from hanging out with her quirky brothers. It was another way to compete with them and get their attention, yet have fun in a nice way. She couldn't help it, ~Do you guys watch our classic movies? Specifically, *The Fly*?~ She figured he'd have to start asking her for information now. The thought of a bunch of praying mantis watching *The Fly* cracked her up. She laughed out loud.

Emotionless, his face seemed incapable of expression, Jenoor responded. ~We have studied many of your movies ever since you started making them, including that one.~

~Well, is that how you do it, with big machines that buzz and smoke?~ She was starting to have a little fun. The jousting-with-jest was just part of her makeup and, at the least, useful now as an escape mechanism.

~No, it is most likely genetic in origin. We just want to do it and it happens, whether it is Phase Shift or Particulation, the same as when you decide to raise your arm or your finger.~

~Can you teach me how to do it?~ She'd Particulate her bare butt right out of here.

~We have never tried with a human, but we do not think so. We believe the ability to cause it is genetically passed.~

~Then I could never go to 'Mantidville.'~ She was trying to be a little cute, with the hope of making friends with him, almost forgetting for the moment that she was naked on a table, although she was sure no woman in that situation could completely forget it, even for the briefest moment.

Still emotionless and non-reactive, ~Yes you can if we decide to take you.~ Mari was surprised, which did not register with him. Jenoor continued, ~Any physical being or object we touch, or which is inside, or in contact with any physical object we are inside or touching, goes into Phase Shift or Particulation with us unless we mentally exclude it.~

~Sorry, that was too much for me.~

~If we want you to go with us, you will.~

~Are you going to?~

~That is not our present plan.~

Fully reentering the reality of her current situation, she spoke, "What is your . . ." ~Excuse me. What is your present plan? Why *am* I stripped on this table? To get back to one of my basic original questions – *What the hell is going on here?!!~* Jenoor moved back slightly when she initially spoke out loud, reacting to the sound, but the emotion accompanying her subsequent thoughts did not register with him, other than intellectually extrapolated from their intensity and the language she was using. She was again obviously agitated.

Jenoor acquiesced to her insistence on knowing, ~Mari, we are going to *breed* with you. *I* am going to breed with you.~

As he did not feel the emotion flooding her thoughts and body, including her virtually uncontrollable fear, anger and sense of helplessness, Jenoor witnessed silence, flushing of her face and most of her body, widening of her eyes, a cold sweat and her physical struggle to move (she couldn't), and the one word exploding from her mind – ~R-A-P-E!!!~

Jenoor calmly continued in that *2001* thought voice. ~Mari, you have consented to this. We have been visiting you since you were a small child, and you have been known since long before that.~

Stupefied, terrified and horrified, she just stared at him. None of her usual and habitual ways of dealing with unexpected situations were working. Humor failed, intellect failed, she couldn't move to help herself. This seemed to be the absolute end of being protected. Who she was, what she looked like and the type of person she was flashed in some detail through her mind.

Mari had absolutely clear skin everywhere on her body except for three freckles on her nose. Her head was topped with natural, thick, tousled hair just a little shorter than collar length. It was somewhere between strawberry and flaming red, and Murph said it always changed colors depending on her mood. Some of it turned under and some of it turned out on the ends, casual looking, but definitely not unkempt. Her clothes – when she had some on, which was the normal case – matched the attitude of her hair, nice and natural-looking on her, sweaters, blouses, skirts, shorts, athletic wear. They were color coordinated and tasteful, but beyond looking nice, and fresh, she was not a brand-maven and didn't make a fetish out of it. She was the girl next door with just the right amount of tomboy mixed in.

Her hazel eyes, which definitely did change color with her moods, all gradations from sky blue to a very deep green according to Murph, looked directly at you when she was talking. He said he didn't know where to focus in those eyes, but he could look anywhere in them and he knew that she was talking to him and she was unmistakably *in* the conversation, not elsewhere. She was normally relaxed, funny, and a lot of other pleasant things, until someone did something that wasn't right. Then there was hell to pay, and the speed with which her hair changed from strawberry to flaming red and her eyes from baby-blue to burning-emerald – again according to Murph – was directly correlated to what would happen next, not much of which was predictable. Murph always maintained that he had fallen in love with Chameleon Woman.

All of the kids in her family went to Sunday School regularly. Her mother was careful to see to it and her father encouraged it. As a result of that and her father's strong sense of fairness as a judge in a small Midwestern county, when it really counted she had an embedded sense of right and wrong. In most situations, it pointed her toward doing the reasonable and decent thing under the circumstances, guided by a broad sense of love and respect for others and for herself. Thus, when faced with the helpless reality of being raped in this bizarre situation, she just couldn't understand it. Something like this just shouldn't be happening to a person like her. She started to cry uncontrollably, "I don't get it. I just don't get it. Why? Why?! Please tell me why! What is happening to me!? Why is *this* happening to me?" She was close to disintegrating psychologically.

Jenoor took control of her thoughts and, after a few tense moments, calmed her to the point she could think without overwhelming fear, ~Mari, it is important that you stay calm and allow me to explain, but you must concentrate and stretch your mind, let it float back and touch other parts of your consciousness. If you can, let other thoughts and memories float in as they may be triggered by what I convey, even if you think it is only fantasy or suggestion at first, for I promise you, I will only transmit the truth as we know it.

~Please pay attention. This is an important foundation for everything that follows. It will be the underlayment for all the important conscious decisions you make on the rest of this trip to Earth.~

Calmed by the being, she renewed her resolve to keep resisting. ~*This* trip?~ she thought. She also figured that the more he talked (thought?), the better chance she might have, ~Okay, I'm ready.~

~Yes, this trip. But first, you must *suspend your disbelief*.~ He turned his great cranium toward her. It seemed to her it might come loose from his comparatively thin neck. ~Will you do that?~

~Yes.~

Softly, ~Mari, right now your Earthly conscious memory consists of your present lifetime, and you believe that whatever makes up your persona is a product of your physical heredity and the experiences that have happened to you since you were born. You have some vague feelings that you have a soul and, hopefully, some kind of continuous existence after death, but you cannot accurately define it and you feel that concept is in the area of religion, which you try to follow but do not truly understand either.

~To describe it as you would, you figure you will find out for sure when you die, or there is nothing and it will not matter anyway. But you do have a basic sense that good is better than the alternatives and should be striven for. You believe that meanness is unnecessary, as are mean people, and the best evidence you have seen of a loving soul in the center of a person's being is when you look into Murph's eyes, whom you love very much. You have never thought much about where love comes from.~

The being's head was an earnest "conversational" distance away and his eyes were in a position to look directly into hers. She assumed they were doing that, but couldn't tell. They were huge in proportion to the rest of his head, black teardrop-shaped masses that looked like they were made of eye material, but had no pupils or, more accurately, appeared to be *all* pupil.

Staring into those vast eyes while listening to his thoughts, which were incredibly straightforward and accurate as if he were speaking from knowledge obvious to anyone who would be standing in the center of her mind, she felt as though she was looking fully into his soul, as opposed to the little peeks she could get looking into Murph's pupils, small by comparison.

Entranced by this experience, she actually did forget for the moment that she was chilly, naked, involuntarily paralyzed and threatened with something she didn't want to think about. She made no effort to move, nor was it necessary to tell him his description was right on the button since they both knew it.

But, she did it anyway, ~Okay. You nailed it. But how is that related to my consenting to any of this?~ She was hoping against hope that he would never be able to justify it and, based on what she thought she had seen in those eyes, he would just let her go.

~What do you believe makes up your mind? You are educated, you assist your husband and he is an accomplished new-thought psychologist, you must have some idea.~

~Well, I have a conscious mind, like I'm thinking with right now, and not only Murph, but any psychologist will tell you that you have a subconscious or unconscious mind that isn't readily accessible without help, but which contains a lot of thoughts and memories of things that happened to you since you were a little kid, which often motivate you or affect your behavior on a level that you don't consciously comprehend.~

Continuing with his thoughts flowing more softly, ~Mari, more than that, your mind is made up of other facets of which you are unaware or may have only slightly sensed. Each individual's mind, including yours and mine, has a non-material, and in your case non-human, aspect which, so far as we know, is the most important feature of all. We refer to it as the Superconscious Dimension. It is a spiritual dimension which extends far beyond the tip of that material mental iceberg you are referring to as the unconscious mind.~

~I've heard Murph make references to that dimension when referring to his patients' descriptions of the place they say they are between lives on Earth, and I've also transcribed some of those hypnotic regression sessions. Are you going to tell me that it really is true?~ She kept looking into those eyes and she didn't know what to think.

~The Superconscious Dimension seems to be the underlying fabric of existence for both of us, but it is not easily known to you in your human existence, and not easily known to us either; however, some of us, Mantid and human, have a more complete understanding of it than others. But most humans and Mantid do not naturally, that is without education, training, meditation and often hypnosis, have a conscious understanding access to the Superconscious component of mind.

~But, some Mantid, including myself, seem to be a little more advanced in this regard, and *so far as we know*, an individual's mind never ends. My more expanded consciousness, including that portion of the Superconscious to which I have greater conscious access than many, is what you sense looking into my eyes. The Superconscious has so much depth as compared to most Mantid, and certainly as compared to the material human mentality, that it exudes a substantially uncomprehended intelligence to one in your position.~

"One in her position" was right – naked on a table.

She had a dual reaction to all of this, and feeling two different ways at once was strange indeed. For not entirely explainable reasons, it felt natural for this being to call her "Mari;" however, she was also feeling very uneasy with the talk of consent, which he had yet to explain, and a never-ending mind. Reading between the lines, this could be the start of a proselytization by an Alien Latter Day Saint, an old-television Mork on a mission, pounding on the door to her mind. Except this was worse, he was already inside.

~Mari, I am not trying to convert you to anything.~ She obviously wasn't controlling or apparently able to guard completely, if at all, her personal thoughts. ~I am just explaining the facts of existence as I know them, as I said I would.~

~Sorry.~ No sense antagonizing him. ~Tell me more.~ She wondered if she were developing the infamous Stockholm syndrome of cooperating with her captors in order to survive. Murph had described it to her with reference to a sensational twentieth-century kidnapping case involving a media heiress turned bankrobber.

~Can you put a sheet over me?~ She had no idea why she hadn't asked earlier, probably parts of her thinking were just short-circuiting from fear and the strangeness of all this. The gray doctor-like being had been acting like this situation was not an unusual event at all. For all the emotion and interest he was showing in her unclothed form, she may as well have been a talking frog. Perhaps she should be offended that he hadn't noticed her body, wonderfully healthy with that clear skin accentuated by just those three freckles on her nose and, somewhat unusual these days, she was obviously a totally natural redhead. In any event, the being complied without thought or comment. She kicked herself for not asking before.

Jenoor continued, ~The Superconscious Dimension appears to be a part of what we have come to call One Mind. The Surface has many names for that concept. One Mind seems to be the *substance* of all things. It is constantly continuing, the substance of *all* 'individual' minds and, thus, the Connection of all of them with one another in an infinite group or network which we refer to as the Universal Connection, but this Connection is not necessarily on a conscious level for all materially-oriented minds. The human author, Carl Jung, touched on it ever so slightly with his 'archetypes.' Of course we are certain we are not yet aware of One Mind's full extent, but as Mantid we do know from experience that our understanding and consciousness is, as I stated before, more expansive in that regard than that of most humans.~

For some reason, her fear kept slipping away, replaced by fascination, curiosity and something tugging, sometimes jerking, at her mindstrings. ~What do you mean this mind is the substance of all things? I can see and touch a rock that has substance, but my mind doesn't have *substance*. I can't pick it up.~

~Perhaps you will see after I have finished. Mari, your mind did not commence when you were born as Marion Miles. It – *you* – existed long before that, but not in the physical form you now find yourself. We do not know when you – meaning your mind or soul – started. We do not know when we started. We just know that at some point we were conscious of being able to think, but have no real reference point to starting. We do know from our experience, however, that before you became the human Mari Miles, you *agreed* to help us.~

It idled through her mind that not only was it strange to her to be able to communicate in this way, but she instinctively understood what would be italics and punctuation, as if the thoughts were typed out. Then it dawned on her that they were back to the issue of her volunteering to ride his breeding wagon. She felt her blood pressure start to rise even more, warming her for the umpteenth time against the chill of the room, and she held her emotions back as much as she could, but not with complete success.

~What the blazes are you *really* talking about?!~ She knew he was thinking, not talking, but being that precise didn't seem to matter so much right now.

~Mari, we need help and we need it from humans. At a point in our evolution, we came to the conclusion that while we could think and we were very, very intelligent, we were not complete. After observing humans and their evolution for eons, one very important thing became apparent to us, *we could not express or feel emotion.* We could see from their behavior that it was something humans could do, and after they developed a sophisticated language, it was easier for us to intellectually comprehend from the descriptions, but we could not *do* it.~

~Holy crap! We're sliding down the Yellow Brick Road!~

He ignored the thought. ~Once we realized we could not do it, we naturally tried to find out why. After much discussion and research, we concluded it was genetic – a gene humans had and we did not. Of course there were many genes you had that we did not, and vice-versa, but this one quality and ability seemed to be most basic and fundamentally important. Even though we tried very hard, we could not identify, much less isolate in your species, the emotion gene, the 'E-gene' as we refer to it.

~Thus, as a last resort, we, the Mantid race, made the collective decision to genetically manipulate ourselves using human genes, by advance consent of the Mantid involved this time, to become more human-like in the hope of fortuitously achieving our goal. The Mantid now are the result of an incredible amount of such manipulation – beings who are much more physically humanoid now and, in any event, no longer insect. We would have stopped the manipulation earlier and would now be more like our original physical selves, except no matter how much we manipulated our genes, we did not succeed at feeling and expressing emotion. We do not know what it is actually like, but we are certain we will know it when it happens, to analogize to an old decision of the human U.S. Supreme Court concerning their ability to recognize pornography.~

She tried to resist the thought that this had degenerated into a C-movie, and she didn't think she wanted to know the answer to the question she was about to ask, but it seemed like the logical line in the script, ~So what did you decide to do next?~

~It became apparent the only chance we had of acquiring it was to interbreed, to ultimately meld our two races.~

Almost uncontrollable fear welled up in her again.

Unrecognized by Jenoor, he continued, ~We concluded that, in the long range view, it would be very beneficial to both races to meld them, humans acquiring our intellectual capacity, and probably our Phase Shifting and Particulation ability, and the Mantid acquiring your capacity for emotion, all voluntary on the part of humans of course, as we would not force ourselves sexually or reproductively on any other beings.~

She began to relax slightly.

~At a point in time while we were still trying to create melded beings in test tubes, we started experimentation with interbeing in vitro fertilization. At that same time, we also formed the parallel goal of consciously-voluntary interbeing breeding between humans and Mantid. In that connection, we concluded that interbeing breeding would be much easier for humans to accept, and it was more likely that they would agree on an Earthly *human* conscious level, if we were physiologically and physically more like them from a reproductive standpoint. In that regard, we spent a lot of genetic-manipulation time making our sexual and other reproductive organs compatible with humans, even though we have not yet succeeded in getting them identical, particularly in the Mantid males. As you have surmised, our efforts and research continue.~

~Great. Let me out of here. I'm not buying into the voluntary part.~

~As I advised, you already have.~

~Run through that again will you?~ She wanted an explanation concerning the how and why of her consent and didn't hold back her slightly cynical manner bolstered by her confidence in his "voluntary" comments.

~Mari, I told you a short time ago that before you ever began your physical existence on Earth this trip, you agreed to help us with this endeavor. Your soul has been in existence since long before this temporal existence on Earth in your present 'lifetime.' You considered this prior to each of the last several of your Earthly incarnations. You declined to do it when planning previous physical lifetimes, but for the purposes of the improvements to be made to your spirituality through the lessons of this particular physical lifetime, you consented to help us so your 'being' could, very simply, assimilate the experience of making a monumental effort in order to help others.

~You do not remember it because in order for the lessons on Earth to be most effective, to 'take' so to speak, it is generally necessary that a being's Superconscious memory prior to each physical lifetime experience be blanked out as much as possible, unless an exception would be beneficial. This is done by a conscious decision and willing effort on the incarnate's part prior to becoming physical, whether it is you or us.~

~This is too much, just *too* much. Okay, what is my name while I am 'mental' between lives?~ She was gaining more confidence.

Being intent on imparting information, he did not recognize the exasperated tenor of her thoughts. ~Well, often those of us who have shared incarnation experiences call one another by the most recent name used in an incarnation, or by a favorite name used in one of them. We also have a Superconscious name if we wish, but it is just for casual convenience and familiarity. The reality is that you do not need a name in the Superconscious Dimension. None of us do in that dimension. We just *are*. Each soul's signal is different from every other because its experiences, development and unfoldment are different. Yet, all are Connected to one another by the Universal Connection, each with an individuality, or constellation of thoughts, that is recognizably different from every other. So, in the Superconscious Dimension, our *substance* is *mind* and names are actually superfluous.~

~If I consciously and willingly consented, prove it, because I'm sure not conscious of it now, Jenoor.~ How in the hell did she know to address him as Jenoor? He'd never said his name. Why wasn't she grilling him about the reincarnation aspects of what he communicated? Murph's practice specialized in parapsychology, in "new age," "paranormal" and "abduction" patients. She could ask a million intelligent questions about it on both sides of the issue.

~Well, we do not have one of your digivision sticks so you can see it. That is neither possible nor necessary in a pure non-physical state, but I can help bring you back into conscious contact with portions of your Superconscious status prior to your present Earthly experience. Because of the filter of your present material 'human' state, you may not fully understand it, but what you do understand, you will know happened.~

~Will this knowledge unhinge me?~

~Because your Guides in the Superconscious Dimension will always monitor any important mental contact with the Superconscious by you as an Earthly material incarnate, whether through hypnosis or otherwise, they will not allow you to gain information if they think it will substantially interfere with the effect you desire from your present Earth trip as Mari Bailey. Any knowledge you are allowed to acquire should help you to achieve your goals with respect to the overall developmental evolution of your spirituality and consciousness. And, Mari, we desperately need your help. We are hoping you will be the Jackie Robinson of conscious human cooperation in this venture.~

She couldn't explain to herself why she saw no ironic humor in that historic reference to the ground-breaking baseball star. Having played a lot of baseball with her brothers, normally she would, but she had the odd feeling that . . . . She didn't want to articulate it to herself, even in her thoughts.

More nervously now, probably because she didn't want the answer his confident manner indicated was coming, ~Okay, show me my consent. How do you do it? It must be by hypnotizing me. How do I know you won't plant whatever suggestion you want if that's the case?~ In Murph's work on prior-life regression she knew that he was extremely careful not to do that with his patients. Then it dawned on her that up to now, she thought prior lives and the Superconscious realm just applied in the context of some of Murph's patients. It hadn't occurred to her that it could have relevance to just a "regular" human being like herself, that is, to everybody. Resisting the idea, ~In fact, you've probably already implanted the suggestions! I'm a patsy. This is a set-up!~

~Mari, I have not. After you are in contact with your Superconsciousness, you will *know* that what you do understand *did* occur. You will simply know. Just as you are certain that your present circumstances, which to you at this moment are an extremely bizarre event, are not a dream but actually occurring, you will be certain beyond thought of contradiction that the things shown from your consciousness prior to this Earthly experience, *happened*. You will *know*.

~After you see these things, if you wish to be released from your agreement, I will deposit you back into your present Earthly circumstances, but without this memory as anything more than a dream. In short, if after this you still think we are a combination of the Lion, Tin Man and Scarecrow crammed into gray stick-like bodies, all you have to do is click your heels.~

Damn. She needed to learn how to protect those thoughts. Strange, but she felt a slight twinge that she may have hurt his feelings. What feelings? That's what this is all about. She quickly developed a plan, which she hoped she'd shielded, to let him hypnotize her and then tell him she wanted to leave. It's all she had left.

Resignedly, ~What the hell, let's go for it.~

~Mari, I am going to let you put on a robe and sit up in a chair so you will feel more comfortable while we do this. Just promise me you will not try to physically attack any of us or otherwise become violent.~

~I promise, but what good would it do me if I did? If you got me into this room, you could certainly stop me.~ It dawned on her that she did not know where this room was. For all she knew, she might be *in* Mantidville.

~You are not. You are in a spacecraft.~

She should have known. One of the other Greys, significantly smaller than Mari and whom she distinctly felt was female, helped her off the table and into a warm, comfortable white terrycloth-like robe and green slippers. All were a little too small, but very soft. After lying on the table for what seemed like an eternity, she was extremely grateful for these small pleasures which seemed like kindness. At the same time, what Mari perceived as two male Greys, smaller than she but larger than the females, moved some equipment aside, produced a comfortable overstuffed easy chair seemingly from nowhere and moved it over to her. She sunk into it and Jenoor sat quickly and rather stiffly in front of her in a longer, narrower chair better designed for his structure. That chair had also been produced "a la carte" so to speak.

~Mari, I am going to help you remember through human hypnosis in much the same fashion as your husband has done on patients many, many times. I could do it other ways, but I believe this will cause the result to be more acceptable to the human facet of your mind. Is this agreeable to you?~

~Yes.~ She noted he was allowing her to make a decision. But, comfortable and warm in the chair while staring into his large dark eyes and listening in her mind to his Hal-like voice which now seemed to have gotten about two octaves deeper and noticeably slower, she felt she might respond in the affirmative to anything he suggested.

~Mari, I will not suggest anything to you. I will not do anything to you. I am doing this *for* you. I will merely help you to focus your attention so you can remember. I will do this by taking you back to two occurrences. First, I will take you to a time when you were a little girl in this lifetime. You will remember it and experience some rather concrete revelations in connection with it. That will help you move back to the other occurrence which was immediately prior to your present life here on Earth.~

Jenoor paused, ~Mari, your thoughts seem to be jumping around a great deal. Please try to keep them focused.~

~Well, what the hell do you think your thoughts would be doing if this were happening to you?~ Emotionally stressed despite her best efforts otherwise, she suddenly became indignant at his reference to her inability to concentrate.

Jenoor had achieved his goal to make her determined to concentrate on the task at hand, and his thoughts again were slow, deep and relaxing, ~Now, make yourself as comfortable as possible and place your right hand open and palm down on your right thigh. Stare at your hand. Take a deep breath and breathe deeply and regularly. Keep staring at your hand and listen only to my voice. If other thoughts or sounds come into your mind, they will quickly leave and your attention will return to my voice. Keep staring at your hand, staring at your hand and listen to my voice. Feel the heat of your thigh on your hand and keep staring at your hand.~

Her focus, vision and concentration were continuously drawn more and more tightly onto her hand until it seemed almost surreal, suspended in space, except she could feel the heat of her thigh on her hand.

~Keep staring at your hand and listen only to my voice. Soon you will see movement in one of your fingers. Imperceptible at first, but the movement is there and will become greater until one of your fingers raises from your thigh and points upward.~ Her index finger moved slightly and then pointed upward. ~As your finger points into the air, your hand will become lighter and lighter, as if it were filled with helium, and it will slowly start floating up into the air toward your face. Lighter and lighter. Lighter and lighter.~

His "voice" seemed to fill all the space there was in her head for any sound or thought to be, and she watched her hand slowly float upward into the air. She wasn't certain if it were still attached to her wrist, but there it was, just slowly floating up into the air toward her face.

His dream voice continued, ~You are feeling very relaxed now and very good. Very, very relaxed, and as your hand floats upward, you are becoming sleepier and sleepier. Very relaxed.~ Her hand kept coming. She was aware now only of her hand and her head, both of which seemed to be comfortably detached and floating in space. ~As your hand rises higher and higher, you are sleepier and sleepier and your eyelids start to close as your hand gets closer and closer to your forehead. When your finger (which was still extended) touches your forehead, your eyes will completely close, steel bands holding them shut, and you will be deeply asleep. Deeply, deeply asleep and feeling very good.~

The moment the finger touched her forehead, her eyes snapped shut, no thoughts were in her mind, she felt very, very good, her breathing was deep and regular, and her hand remained at her forehead as if sewn there.

~Let your hand fall slowly into your lap.~ It did. ~Mari, you can communicate to me without waking up. You can even open your eyes if you like and you will not wake up. I will communicate to you from time to time and you will not wake up. But at any time, if you decide you want to wake up, you can. Or if I want you to wake up, you will if I count backwards from three to one. Once you are awake, if you decide you would like to come back to this sleep state for more information, we can do it by my just communicating the words 'In hoc signo vinces' and you will immediately return to this relaxed sleeping state feeling very good. Can you do all that?~

Her answer slid quietly out, ~Yes.~

~You will be very alert and very interested in everything that follows now. How do you feel?~

~Very good.~

~Mari, let your thoughts go back to when you were a little girl about six years old. Back to the night just before Christmas when you thought Santa Claus came in his sleigh from the sky. You know, the story you tell Murph with amusement and nostalgia. You have always consciously believed you were so excited about Christmas that you fantasized Santa lighting the sky with Christmas lights, visiting you to tell you what a good girl you had been and leaving you a small present.~

~Yes, I remember.~ She smiled.

~Mari, go back to that night as if it were happening now, except if you experienced any fear or unpleasant emotion then, you will not experience it now. In such an instance, you will not experience negative emotion any more strongly than you do when watching a movie, and you will be able to understand the situation and deal with what you remember in a rational and constructive manner, and in particular, just because something you remember experiencing is different from what you have usually experienced in this Earthly lifetime, it will not frighten or upset you for that reason. Can you do that and still describe it to me with an adult vocabulary?~

~Yes.~ Her eyes opened as if seeing and experiencing the scene in front of her. ~It's very late at night on Christmas Eve. I'm awakened by a lot of lights outside my window. They seem to be flashing around and changing colors. I can't see them directly because the venetian blinds are closed, but I'm certain it's Santa. I'm very excited and happy. I can hear, and to some extent feel, a 'beating' sound. The best I can describe it now is its kind of like the sound a person hears over those antique short wave radios before they're adjusted right. Kind of like machinery and kind of like energy; it's hard to describe. I'm sure it's the sound of the reindeer hooves beating through the sky toward my house.

~I run to the window and pull the chain that opens the slats in the blinds. So much intense, revolving, changing light comes in from outside that I feel propelled backwards a few feet. This is an amazing experience, one that fits the arrival of Santa Claus in my life. And outside he's coming toward me from out of the light! It's hard to see him with all the light behind him and I'm thinking that I need to get the window open somehow so he can get in. We have no chimney and my mother has told me how Santa will just come in through a window or door, but I can't get it open far enough and he just walks right through it! Inside the room it is much easier to see him because he is not back-lit even though it is very bright. But he's *not* dressed like Santa Claus, he's dressed like . . . like . . . . My God! It's *you*!~ Her eyes were wide now, looking directly at him.

~Yes. Relax and recall how you are going to deal with these memories.~

~Yes, yes.~ She was fascinated, not upset. Her focus changed back to the scene. ~I *know* who you are. I can't place where or why, but I know you and I'm not afraid. We are well acquainted, but I don't remember why, and it doesn't seem important to me to remember. I accept you naturally, but I *am* expecting Santa Claus and I'm surprised, a little confused and very disappointed for that reason. I ask why you are there because I want it to be Santa.

~You are very nice and explain that you haven't visited me for several years and want to make sure that I am healthy and all right. I say I feel fine but I want to see Santa. You ask if I will go with you for a few minutes so you can make certain I'm all right since your machines have Magic Glasses that can look inside me. I say sure, but I should tell my Mom because she could wake up and worry, particularly with all the lights and the beating sound, and I want to be sure she has Santa stay in case he comes while I am gone. You assure me that neither she nor my father will wake up before I get back, and that I will be back in plenty of time to see Santa. You ask me to touch your hand. I do, and I have the strangest sensation that I'm electric and turning transparent. We seem to disappear for a moment into little electrical dots, and then we reappear in a room very similar to this!~

~It is this room. It is the same spacecraft you heard as Santa's reindeer. We made the noise on purpose.~

~You ask me to take my pajamas off and lie down on this table which looks cold, but isn't, not like today. You bring a machine out of the ceiling which seems to scan up and down the entire length of my body, but doesn't touch me. You tell me those are your Magic Glasses. Then a thing comes out of the wall that looks like a big hollow gingerbread man's glove and you ask me to put my hand into it. I do and before I know it, it has pricked my finger and I try to jerk my hand out, but can't. I start to cry and get scared. I'm also very surprised because I didn't think you would hurt me.

~You tell me you are sorry you did that without telling me what would happen first, but feel that was better than scaring me before it happened. I'm not sure that makes a lot of sense, but you tell me that to make up for it, you will give me a little present when you take me back to my room. That seems pretty good to me, particularly because the pricked finger surprises me more than it hurts, and I feel *somehow* that I'm supposed to do this anyway.~

~Mari, you felt that way because you previously agreed to do it, as I will show you later. Also as you can see, the memory of your agreement was, reasonably successfully, erased for this Earthly trip, even though it is often very difficult to completely erase all prior memories, particularly memories of the agreements like yours because they are usually the last thing to occur before one's physical journey and are very important developmental milestones. But as you have been experiencing, any memory that remains does tend to fade, or perhaps more accurately to be layered-over as time passes while one accumulates more and more physical life experiences. Please continue. ~

~I put my pajamas back on, you take my hand, that funny electrical-dot thing happens again and we are back in my room. You take a praying mantis out of a little box and it hops onto my finger, the same one that got pricked. It cocks its head and looks right at me. I'm fascinated by it and love it immediately. You tell me that when I wake in the morning, I will know I saw Santa come from the Christmas lights in the sky and know he gave me my new little friend. I wake up Christmas morning and very excitedly tell my parents that Santa came to see me in the night and left me my new pet, which I promptly name 'Jen.'

~My parents think it's a sweet story generated by the Christmas excitement of a six-year-old's imagination; however, my mother is horrified at the 'present' Santa has left, thinking it got into my room during the night through the window that I somehow managed to get part way open. She allows me to keep Jen even though she has always been absolutely and irrationally terrified of insects, praying mantis in particular for some reason. She instructs my father to fasten my bedroom window screen tightly, immediately.~

~We apologize about your mother's fear. We are constantly

improving our techniques, but because we cannot feel emotion, we cannot 'empathize,' as humans call it, with you. We have to do it all from an intellectual basis and it is often not satisfactory. Because of our work with your mother, she absolutely hates praying mantis. They remind her of us. But, you are fond of them and that shows improvement in our techniques. In your case, instead of inserting a small monitor pellet somewhere into your head, we modified the praying mantis pet instead. It was the first time we used a pet and we thought that particular selection clever. It only worked when the pet was with you of course, but for the purposes then, that was sufficient and you did not have the trauma of the insertion.~

She popped out of the trance and drilled him with her eyes which were rapidly deepening in color, ~What do you mean, the 'work' you did with my *mother*?!~

Not being used to humans staring directly into his eyes and interrogating him, he was taken slightly aback, ~Well . . . but only with her consent prior to incarnation also, although she has never had the benefit of our improved techniques or the illuminating recall experiences you are having now. Thus, from a human standpoint, she has many repressed experiences that have affected her in a less than a positive way – so to speak.~

Sitting up in the chair and leaning toward him, ~So to speak! In a lot of ways the woman is an emotional wreck! *What* did you do to her?!~

Wanting to soften the explanation, ~As I started to tell you before, we first started our melding efforts long ago by taking sperm or eggs from humans and either fertilized a Mantid egg with a human sperm, or a human egg with a Mantid sperm. We did this in a test tube as you call it. We also started the other programs I mentioned, and it has taken many experiments over many centuries not only to achieve viability, but to transfer the fetus to larger and larger containers until it reached full term. Our experimentation in all areas continues. That is why there are still reports by individuals of having a small amount of material scooped from their legs, backs or some other area. We are constantly looking for the E-gene, and yes, they have all given consent prior to incarnation.

~While those who have 'visited' with *us* all consented prior to their tenure on Earth, we have done our best to cause them not to remember during their Earthly experience as it simply does not fit well with their normal experiences nor with their psychological development at the time. We are not always completely successful, and those who do remember, either spontaneously or with hypnotic assistance, run the reactional gamut of dismissing it out-of-hand as a very realistic dream experience, accepting it as an unbelievably interesting experience if it really happened, accepting it as an unbelievably interesting and exciting experience that actually did happen, being emotionally tense and upset even though they cannot remember on a conscious level, being emotionally tense and upset because they do remember on a conscious level, thinking they are crazy even though they are able to carry on with their lives, becoming so emotionally disturbed they can no longer function with any semblance of normalcy, and any and all variations and combinations of the foregoing.~

She just continued to stare at him. He found himself wanting to look somewhere else and talk about something else, but he dutifully continued his explanation.

~In any event, during the period of this experimentation, from the beginning up to now, we have experimented all over the world and caused great consternation on Earth when our craft have been sighted. The more bold among you have written or talked of the sightings, usually in terms of objects with which the observer is familiar at that time in history, for instance Ezekiel seeing the wheel in your sixth century B.C.

~While some people have spoken of the craft they have seen, until fairly recent times, very few have spoken of the examinations by us or the other 'procedures' for fear of being ostracized or viewed as mentally unbalanced. Although some, such as in Japan for instance, began to speak and write openly and publicly somewhat sooner than others, it has only been in the years since the middle twentieth century, after we had the unfortunate accident at Roswell, and incidents such as that encountered by Betty and Barney Hill, which was not a contact with us by the way, coupled with the subsequent publication of books by pioneering human authors such as Budd Hopkins who did much investigation but never visited with us, and Whitley Strieber whom we have closely observed, that those on the Surface, particularly those in your country, have begun to communicate openly about what many have termed the 'abduction' phenomena. 'Abduction' is a misnomer in our case because with us, since it is consensual, humans are simply experiencing 'visits.' In fact, some just call themselves 'Experiencers' and refer to us as the 'Visitors.'~

She was about to blow up again, ~Look, I recognize stalling when I see it. What did you do to my mother?!~

Still attempting to mitigate the effect of the explanation, ~I am getting to that. As I said before, during our period of test-tube experimentation, it seemed a logical step to also experiment with in vitro fertilization. For convenience, we tried it first with human sperm fertilizing a Mantid ovum and implanted into a genetically altered and evolved female Mantid. That produced some very unfortunate experiences because we are, on average, significantly smaller than humans and the fetus simply became too large for our females' bodies prior to full term. It is not necessary to go into details . . . . The next logical step . . .~

~. . . would be to stop!~ she interrupted. Her hair seemed to be turning a deeper red and her eyes an even deeper green.

~No, no. Remember, all the interaction with humans or Mantid is consensual.~

Her emotions were getting the best of her again, ~That seems like a bunch of horsecrap to me. If they don't know it, how can it be consensual?~

~I have started explaining that to you, and I am confident that if you will allow me to finish, when you leave here, you will *know*.~

~Okay. Okay. What's the deal with my mother!~

~As I was relating, the next logical step was fertilization in vitro using a human female. During that experimentation, which still continues, your mother was one of those who assisted us in that regard.~

She could feel the blood pressure expanding the arteries in her neck and head. ~Shouldn't you be putting 'assisted' in quotes?~

Jenoor did not hesitate, ~Only from your immediate perspective. In any event, we first took an egg from your mother, fertilized it in a test tube with sperm from a Mantid, as well as performed certain genetic manipulations on the fertilized egg, and then replanted it in your mother for about six weeks. Of course we were not certain it would have been feasible to allow her to carry it to full term because we could not be positive of the outcome, and humans might not be able to bear that result through natural childbirth. So in your mother's case, and actually in all cases since as an ultimate caution, we removed it at approximately six weeks and brought it to full term in one of our containers developed for that purpose.~

Mari went into a slow stun as the import of his explanation sunk in. ~Wh . . . what are you saying?~

~Yes Mari, your half sister lives with us.~

They may as well have paralyzed her again, because she was. She was blank – too much of an emotional slap. In any other situation, she would have either laughed at the joke or leveled him with the pungent language of which she was quite capable, always to her mother's dismay and her father's embarrassment, but also one of the things that had attracted Murph to her. Be that as it may, somehow she was beginning to believe that this bizarre conversation was accurate.

~I . . . I . . . I'm having some trouble with this. Is she here?~ Her eyes were welled with tears and she could not quite understand it.

~No, Mari, she is not on the craft. She is in 'Mantidville' as you call it.~

~I want to see her and talk to her!~

~You can, Mari, but we have other things to accomplish first.~

~What?~ She was petulant.

~Showing you that you consented to be here.~

~Then let's get to it.~ It was a command. She wanted to meet her half sister. And at some point when things settled down, she wanted to talk to her mother about this, maybe with Murph's help.

~To go forward, we must return to the trance and move backward. Please sit back in the chair and release your mind.~ He communicated the trigger-phrase, ~In hoc signo vinces,~ and she immediately slipped back into the hypnotic trance. ~With every breath and every passing moment, let present thoughts flow out of your mind, let anything having to do with your conscious experience in your present lifetime flow from your consciousness. Flowing........flowing........~

His Hal-voice in her head continued until her consciousness was totally separated from her body, existing only elsewhere, or as a Buddhist might say, "centered everywhere, with a circumference nowhere" – not thinking, just being, Jenoor's thoughts floating in from everywhere, nowhere.

~Think now of the periods when you were not in the physical body called Mari, when you were just *you*.~

Her mind flooded with Superconscious experience, no body, no Earth, no stars or physical universe, no space, no matter! Just consciousness which has no perceivable limit. It is the stuff *being* is made of. It is the *substance* of being! She is simply herself. An awareness like none other.

She was surprised she could recall a number of events in which she participated since her soul began in the Superconscious Dimension. Her experience had literally been a journey to develop herself, her consciousness, that is, her soul, toward higher and higher levels of spirituality and understanding. She knew this clearly. She also knew she had a long way to go.

During this period of developing herself, which is continuing, she has communicated with many other souls in the Superconscious Dimension, all Connected, with thoughts mercurially flowing from one to the other when each wishes to communicate. She recalled that an important part of the Superconscious development process is participation in thought communication groups structured by more advanced souls, including the Guides who lead the others in structured thought exercises, lectures or group thought interactions. It is training, schooling in thinking, caring, being. Most of her classmates in the Superconscious Dimension aptly refer to it as the School of Thought.

She also recalled that another important part of training for some souls that need it, or believe it would be beneficial for them, is to go to the "matter-based" training environment. Individual souls can participate at these material training locations through role-playing experiences that operate on them only or which cause them to interact with others there. The experiences include making decisions, carrying them out and experiencing the results. These material training grounds were created by the Teachers, who are certain highly advanced consciousnesses among the Superconscious Dimension educators. The Teachers are souls in development, but are so far advanced that it is *natural* for them to develop teaching programs for those who are less advanced.

Mari remembered that the artificial material teaching environment the Teachers created from their Superconsciousness *is* the physical universe and the physical laws that operate in it, the Material Dimension. They did this by first creating, entirely from their collective consciousness, the basic energy vibrations of matter. Then, through a process that is analogous to a magnetic field influencing the arrangement and density of metal filings on top of a piece of paper, their collective "mental magnetism" influenced the arrangement and density of the material energy vibrations into the many different, often seemingly solid, states of matter and types of energy which comprise the Material Dimension. In conjunction with this creation, they also made up basic rules concerning how the matter and material energy in their physical universe training ground would operate – the laws of physics.

It comforted her to recall that the marvelous thing about the training is that because it is role-playing that takes place in an artificial environment created entirely from thought, the experience in the Material Dimension only *seems to be* reality which sometimes causes great harm, but no harm is actually done. The Material Dimension events serve only as discussion and learning devices back in the Superconscious School of Thought in order to advance the continued development of the spirituality of souls. Thus, the role-playing exercises always lead toward a positive result.

It came back to her that a soul in the Superconscious Dimension can agree to incarnate on Earth, or at some other place in the physical universe, and take any form that helps teach the lesson that particular soul needs to learn at that time, or more properly, that *stage* of development, since time is a physical concept that exists only in the Material Dimension.

Now Mari was clearly recalling that in order to have the Earth illusion mistaken for reality, she had agreed each time to enter the "classroom" devoid of that Superconscious knowledge, either completely or partially in varying degrees, by being "blanked" for the purpose of the exercise. Of course, the blanked result is her "material mind," as opposed to her Superconscious mind. Mari remembered that for most the "amnesia" is complete at the beginning of any "life" trip, but sometimes when the Guides allow it, the knowledge seems to spontaneously "leak" through in varying degrees, or is recalled through hypnotherapy or is learned from the more enlightened thinkers on Earth, many of whom acquire their knowledge through the first two methods.

Thus, it can be specifically intended that Superconscious knowledge be retained from the beginning in some degree by the individual involved. And, on a very few occasions, individuals are sent with very little "blanking" and they consciously retain much or all of their Superconscious knowledge, or "develop" it within a very short period of time, so they are able help others in seemingly incredible ways. It was clear to Mari that Jesus and Buddha were included in that group of beings.

As with all souls, Mari's Earthly exercises, and she had experienced a large number, were planned by educators on many levels of development in the Superconscious Dimension, but her Guides had first-line responsibility for her supervision and training. After Mari would view several possible proposed-life sketches at the area designated for that purpose, Mari would select one and discuss the proposed exercise with her Guides and the other principal players in it, to include setting it up for the occurrence of common synchronous events involving those participating. However, the exercise is not completely structured or controlled in every detail, which assists the learning process, forcing the participants to be responsible for the choices each makes, leaving the ultimate outcome to be determined by their actions. The Guides always keep a watchful "eye" on the exercise as it progresses and many times make adjustments or provide needed assistance along the way.

This deep hypnotic state which put Mari in touch with her Superconscious also helped her to remember that those who elevate and expand their human consciousness, that is their material mind, after their incarnation commences begin to understand that synchronous events in their lives are not accidental. The trick is to recognize a synchronicity when in human form and take advantage of it. Whether one succeeds with that recognition or not, incarnation experiences are always ultimately beneficial because they are examined completely after exit from the physical classroom for the lessons learned or missed.

Having followed her thoughts and maintaining Mari in a hypnotic state, Jenoor asked, ~What is your reaction, Mari?~

~Wow!~ More than a little stunned at these recollections, that was the only word that came to her. ~I had completely forgotten that all physical matter, and even physical consciousness, is an illusion, a monumental illusion. It's all make believe! It's like a vivid dream. It seems real while it is happening, but when you wake up, you understand that your mind made apparent substance from your thoughts.~

Jenoor added, ~On the larger scale, the Teachers did exactly the same thing and made the universe from their thoughts, from 'mindstuff.' And even though it has no more ultimate reality than the dreams a material mind creates, it is for a serious purpose, Mari. It is not a dream game in the sense of children's 'make believe,' and if you just walk away from it, you learn nothing, your spiritual development stalls. That is why we are pressing forward, and you must, also. This opportunity is a major synchronicity in your life and you must take advantage of it in order to progress. That is why your Guides are allowing this to be shown to you now. So you do not waste this opportunity.~

Still incredulous at these memories, ~You know, I can remember some of the other times I have been on Earth. I was a rock once for hundreds of thousands of years in universe time.~ She noted she was careful to make the physical universe time distinction now that she recalled the concept of time has no meaning in relation to eternity, which is without beginning and without end – an aspect of One Mind, which simply *is*.

~Yes. Yes, I remember. As that rock, I waited and waited and finally developed patience. It involved an understanding, or at least a feeling, that One Mind was constantly expressing itself, and all I had to do was be patient, *without doubting*, and things would change, or more accurately would unfold in a positive way. As soon as I did that, I wasn't that rock any more. I was *me*, my consciousness flowing from One Mind, evaluating the experience with my Superconscious 'classmate' group and my Guides. And that's right, even the rocks are physically sentient, physically feeling on a certain level, perhaps similar to the mechanism the author, Aldous Huxley, referred to as 'physiological intelligence.' It's very interesting to remember that, and also the discussion of that experience afterward in the School of Thought. It seems very normal right now.~

~Exactly. And of course, to the Mantid, the rocks are very fortunate to be able to feel.~

~I also remember that in the beginning of my visits to Earth, I wasn't a very nice being and I arrived as a male. I was very angry all the time, constantly striking out at others and didn't understand why. I was just an unpleasant, abusive person on Earth. Ultimately, I was the victim of a senseless and brutal murder by someone who was much worse than I. I was terrified when I was the recipient of the abuse, and furious at the injustice of it all. That was a very necessary basic learning experience for me, learning empathy, compassion and respect for others. I remember a number of other times, but I guess you know them already.~

~No, Mari. Mantid are souls operating in the physical universe just as you, but in the Superconscious, we are souls *without distinction from you* except for the individuality and particular level of spiritual advancement inherent in any soul. While as Mantid incarnates we are more advanced than humans in some ways, we have been blanked also and have been allowed to remember only those Superconscious aspects that are beneficial to our current learning exercises.

~But now that you remember this basic underpinning of your existence, I want to return the focus to why you are on Earth in this 'life.' Do you recall?~

~I think so. I discussed this with my Guides while I was in my normal Superconscious existence and I agreed to help you in what, for both of us, would be a very important way that would, hopefully, help not only you in your spiritual development, but would help me to make a highly meaningful sacrifice from the standpoint of my development in order to move toward an unconditional willingness to help others, but I don't remember a lot, even now.~

~Of course not, or the lesson for *you* would not take. It would merely be a rote exercise you had thought about in advance and agreed to 'get through' because you said you would while preparing in the Superconscious Dimension for this particular life experience. The same is true for me. You and I are amnesic in varying degrees depending on the lesson for each of us. And because, currently, we are still very much in the Earthly-consciousness state with all of the choices and conflicts that entails, the Earth experience is still extremely real to both of us, even though, as a result of this hypnosis for you and other factors for me, we both have some memory and knowledge of how we got to this point.~

As Jenoor brought her out of the trance, he told her she would remember as much of what occurred as would be beneficial to her, and he finished with the admonishment, ~What you do in response to this Earthly challenge will have a significant effect on your ultimate learning and spiritual development.~

Out of the Superconscious Connection and back in the Earth "reality," she immediately concluded that the part about Earth consciousness seeming extremely real was absolutely right. Even though she could remember some of that Superconscious stuff, right now she could *see* herself and Jenoor, and at least *she* looked and felt human as hell, and she sure seemed to be *here*. While she did not doubt that she was remembering, it wasn't penetrating in any way that took her out of her human experience. While she could follow it as an intellectual exercise and even understood that she *was* remembering it, she believed and felt that what was happening right this moment in her human state – *is* what is happening.

Mari thought that while she might be equivocating, her current reality is that she *is* a human being who would much prefer to be right back on the surface of Earth with Murph, with the nice comfortable life she enjoys, instead of lounging in nothing but a robe chatting with Dignified Stick Man, and on a spaceship at that! She could write a book from this. Sure, every decent person is trying to improve spiritually, but *come on*!

~Actually, your thinking right now helps underscore my point with reference to your own development. We could just make you do what we want even though you would not consent; however, we can intellectually appreciate that it would be a negative in our overall spiritual development because our end would be selfish only, without regard for how you felt or how it affected you. What we would like you to do is realize the same thing, that is, even though just going back to Murph would be the easiest and most comfortable thing for you to do, what you can do for us – for another physical species of beings – while a monumental sacrifice for you, could help us in equally monumental ways, and, as a result, assist your spiritual development in an exponential ratio equal to your act. But the decision is necessarily yours, and as I promised, we will send you back to Murph if you want and not insist that you do it.~

She wanted desperately to go back and just be "normal," but somehow she knew she could not simply dismiss this out of hand. No longer afraid of being involuntarily violated, she felt she had a little negotiating power, but wanted some time to think and gather some more facts, ~Look, I'd like to see my half sister in Mantidville.~

Recognizing his chances were still viable, ~As you wish. Would you like to watch the occurrences outside the craft while we travel?~

~Of course, but could I at least have my panties and nightgown back? I think you got me out of my bed didn't you?~ With her regained confidence, she managed to be a little indignant.

~Yes. Perhaps you would be more comfortable in this.~ Along with her panties, one of the Greys in the room handed her a bluish jumpsuit made out of a very soft, light and pleasant cloth-like material, but it didn't seem to be woven or even that seemingly extruded, aerated synthetic material with which she was familiar. She idly thought she would call the color "dimensional blue." In addition to feeling more comfortable with the apparent turn of events, she had been hoping for a bra, but from the appearance of the females, wasn't surprised to learn that none were available.

In response to Jenoor's thought commands, Lenaan activated the viewing factor of the examining room wall and suddenly Mari could see through to the outside, but no mechanism had moved. ~How'd you do that?~

~It is just a matter of readjusting the atomic structure into a different pattern. It is a function of our computer technology combined with the recognition that one's thinking can affect, and effect, one's environment. In our present state of development we are far short of the Teachers' ability and have not mastered it, but we have developed some aspects of it and have been able to create computer programs that help perform some functions of it. Our pilot, Lenaan, merely places his hand, as you would call it, on a small sphere containing the craft's computer, thinks the result desired and the computer's 'thinking' effects that result. Of course, our computers are somewhat more advanced than those on the Surface.~

~Hell of an understatement, Jenoor!~ She didn't know that she understood it, but it was a pretty impressive kind of a *Star Trek* deal, except it wasn't a viewing screen. She was looking outside as if no wall were there. She hoped she couldn't fall out.

~You cannot.~

She was looking at Earth from a height that seemed similar to the pictures she had seen taken from the Space Shuttle, except that it was fading in and out, sort of flickering. A little anxious, ~Is there anything wrong with your computer?~ Until now, it hadn't occurred to her that something could go wrong with all this magnificent technology and she could become so much space dust – instantaneously. Flying in the face of what she had just remembered under hypnosis, she was still afraid to "die."

If Jenoor were human, his eyes would be twinkling and he would be chuckling a little with his reply. Instead, his eyes remained large, limitless and, to Mari at this juncture – starting to look kind. ~Everything is all right, Mari. The computer is functioning normally.~

Still anxious, ~Why are things flickering then?~

~To the people looking at us, if they are and can see us, we are flickering.~

Her red hair, seemingly a lighter shade now, flipped back and forth as she quickly looked from the outside to the inside of the craft several times, ~You mean it's not the computer, the Earth is actually flickering!? We're flickering!? What the hell is going on!?~

~Look at yourself. You are not flickering and neither is the craft. However, because we are currently in a continuous, rapidly-altering Phase Shift in relation to Earth's vibrational plane, that is, we are rapidly going partially in and out of phase with the Earth, it seems to you the Earth is flickering, and on Earth it looks like our craft is flickering, but no one is actually flickering. It just appears that way to whoever is doing the looking at the other. We do not 'flicker' when observing ourselves because we are always in phase with ourselves and vice-versa for Earth.~

She stared at him as if he were feeding her "word pills" in order to calm her down.

~If we were completely in the opposite phase, we would be invisible to Earth and Earth would be invisible to us. So, in order to see where we are going and not rely totally on our instruments, we often stay slightly in phase with Earth or we go in and out rapidly, we 'flicker' like now. It is helpful to be close to out-of-phase, not only to confuse people as to what they think they see, but in order to get completely out as quickly as possible if someone would foolishly direct a missile, destructive laser or similar device at us. Although by flickering in and out, your radar usually does not pick us up, but it depends on the length of in-phase vibration we choose since the longer we stay in Earth-phase vibration, the better we can see too.~

Still somewhat incredulous and half kidding, ~I think I'm beginning to get it. That's why on all those UFO programs I see on DV, the UFO's are never in focus and a great deal of the time seem to be flickering on and off in a very fuzzy sort of way. The problem isn't related to the technology limitations of those 'blinking' digicorders.~

Missing the play on words and not realizing she was kidding around, Jenoor was getting into the subject. ~Yes, certainly when they have *us*. Unless you are very interested in military or UFO history, you probably do not know of the 'Foo Fighters,' as they were called, that military pilots from several countries started seeing during your World War II. They looked like bright balls of flickering light in differing colors, with somewhat indistinct edges because of the phase flicker. They generally seemed to come up from the ground, follow military aircraft in particular, 'zip,' as you would call it, around in rapid and strange patterns, and then disappear, usually back toward the ground.~

~They were actually unmanned probes we sent up to view what was going on, and we still use them from time to time. We were very concerned that your foolish conflicts, which ultimately resulted in the development of nuclear destructive capability, would cause great harm to our inner-Earth environment, and as you might imagine, we became deeply concerned when underground nuclear testing started.

~We normally would not interject ourselves to the extent we ultimately did, but it was extremely threatening to us, and it subsequently took a great deal of effort and time on our part to subliminally condition the minds of your world leaders, scientists and the Surface population, including the minds of your television and movie script writers, and science fiction authors, to bring about some acceptance, perspective and thought-conditioning on many levels in order to produce the relative governmental and economic stability, and the minimization of nuclear testing, that has existed for some time, although much needs to be done.~

Ignoring the implications of his last thoughts, ~Wait a minute. You said, 'when they have *us*?' Do you mean there are others?~

~We are certain there is at least one extraterrestrial species that has visited Earth, although we have never seen them. They are the ones who brought us here. We call them the 'Harvesters.' We cannot even claim to have been abducted by them after they brought us here, but, even though we cannot produce 'hard' incontrovertible physical evidence to support our beliefs any more than Surface inhabitants can about extraterrestrials or us, we are certain the Harvesters exist, have been here and will return.~

Her eyes, back to sky blue, sparkled and she almost laughed out loud. ~Let me see if I have this straight. You folks live here and are not extraterrestrials, but everybody thinks you are. You are careful to flicker around so no one can get a really good fix on you. You abduct people and fool with their minds so they can't be sure, and even if they are sure, they can't irrefutably prove it because everything you do can also have another explanation, to include just dismissing people with those experiences as crackpots, which of course a few of them are, so that only helps your cover. But – *but* – YOU believe in extraterrestrials and are certain of their existence even though you have never seen them, don't even have anyone who claims to have been abducted by them and have absolutely no incontrovertible evidence that they exist! No wonder you want to be more like us. You're crazier than we are!~

Clearly unmoved, ~We are also a lot more developed mentally and do not need the same kinds of evidence most humans seem to need.~

~Sure, pal.~

Under co-pilot Minuum's guidance the craft began to move toward the ground, toward a bald-looking mountain Mari surmised to be in the Southwest somewhere.

~New Mexico,~ Jenoor responded. ~One of your psychic remote viewers some years ago was certain he 'saw' Martians under this mountain, but it was the Mantid. He came relatively close to getting it right, but mainstream Surface people dismissed him as just another societal 'fringe person' because, again, there was no hard verification, just the remote viewer's own internal verification based primarily on being able to correctly identify targets usually known to some other person, but not to himself. That is easily explained away by the skeptic as either a telepathic communication with the person who knows the target, blind luck or a partial fabrication based on getting a few things right that can be tortured into claiming there was an accurate target hit.

~Depending on how well a remote viewer can tune in to the Universal Connection, the viewer can be very accurate, but of course the only way humans can prove there are beings under the mountain is for us to let them find us if they can dig that far; however, unless we were ready for that to happen, we would just Phase Shift our entire complex so that from their perspective, we would not be there.~

Mari's curiosity seldom deserted her, ~So why were – are – you concerned about nuclear weapons harming your inner-Earth environment if you can go out of phase. Why don't you just live out of phase all the time?~

Jenoor pedantically replied, ~Because everything we have, including us, comes from an in-phase Earth environment. Although our ancestors initially tried to live out of phase, they ultimately discovered that we were more comfortable from a homeostatic standpoint in phase with the Earth. That was because we found nothing in the area which is out of phase with the universe, except for what we may cause to be taken there. And, of course, that would come from an in-phase Earth. We do not have the understanding which would allow us to create our own matter from thought as the Teachers have done with their collective mental magnetism. We can mentally alter and rearrange it to a certain extent, but we cannot create it mentally, at least at our present stage of development.

~In any event, it seems there would be no point in extricating ourselves permanently to a different phase since we recognize, intellectually at least, that the only reason matter exists in the ultimate scheme of things is as a training ground, a school. We are learning and developing mentally and spiritually on our level just as you are on yours, and in order to do that properly, it is necessary for us to interact with you. Thus, if we went out of phase as a usual state, it would be like going to a self-contained resort that was a microcosm of our material existence, but also limited to itself, in a way a cosmic Club Med with little point but to lounge around.~

~You have space travel, why don't you go to another planet?~

~Several additional reasons. If you were able, how quickly would your Surface civilization pick up, bag and baggage as you say, and move off to another planet? You would only if it were absolutely necessary. This has been and is your home. It is familiar, you like it, you want to keep it intact and constantly improve upon it. You may explore other places, but there is no place like home as Dorothy would say in your old *Wizard of Oz* movie. It is the same with us.

~Further, while we have the capability of space travel, we have never developed it beyond our immediate needs in relation to the Earth. Even though we have some mental and technological advantages over the Surface population, we operate from the same physical resource base as you do, and because we have a better, even though not complete, understanding than you concerning the true nature of things, we are not nearly as curious as you with regard to space exploration, preferring to direct our collective resources toward a better understanding of other areas of development, particularly spiritual ones.~

~So, do all of you live under New Mexico?~

~No, we live in several places around – actually under in our case – the world. We initially started seriously going underground eons ago at the place you currently call Turkey. If you go there now, you will find perhaps two hundred subterranean cities in a region one still can reach from the surface. There are semi-round passages connecting the parts of any given city, some of which are eighteen stories or so deep. When we started, the passages were small. We enlarged them as we grew and developed so that now they are large enough for a human to traverse them. Even today there is a tunnel approximately five miles long connecting two of the cities.

~At the point when we expanded a great deal further into other parts of the Earth and abandoned the tunnels – having developed our Phase Shifting ability among other things – there were about thirty thousand Mantid there. Of course humans eventually moved into those tunnels and now the Surface speculation is that they were created by humans three or four thousand years ago.~

In the direct manner she had picked up from dealing with her brothers, ~Normally, I would think this is a bunch of bullshit, but I'm flying around in this thing.~

Uncharacteristically casual for Jenoor, ~Take a vacation to Turkey. See for yourself.~

She knew she didn't have to. ~Where else do you live besides New Mexico?~

~It is not important that you know everywhere we live, but one you will be familiar with is Mt. St. Helens in your Washington state.~

~That's a little tough to believe, it blew to smithereens back in the twentieth century.~

~Exactly. We needed the room. We had originally chosen that underground site as one of our settlements and when we first started, the expulsion of material harmed no one because there was no one there to be harmed. However, the Surface population in that area commenced and continued to grow until the last time we needed to enlarge, it was dangerous for them. We did not want to unnecessarily injure anyone; thus, we started mentally implanting the seeds of prediction technology into certain of your volcanologists until they acquired enough expertise to predict that an eruption was imminent. Unfortunately, perhaps, there were some newspeople, curiosity seekers and old Mr. Truman who just would not leave and they – physically only – expired in the undertaking; however, I presume it was also part of their ultimate developmental lessons. Collaterally, Mr. Truman is an apt illustration of 'love of home.'~ Jenoor seldom missed an opportunity to reinforce his point.

~Where else?~

~Well, I am still not going to disclose them all, but we have a 'bubble' city under Mt. Rainier, also in your Washington state. Some interesting myths have arisen in your UFO folklore as a result of our crafts' ingress and egress from it. In fact it was some of those craft, seen in the summer of the Surface year 1947 by your Surface pilot, Kenneth Arnold, which were ultimately described as 'flying saucers' by the Surface media. Others have speculated that there is a secret civilization of dwarf-like beings under Mt. Rainier, which is not far from the truth, and not all speculation.~

As the last of the Greys finally left the room, Mari's thoughts returned from her "abduction" earlier in the evening to the events of the moment.

Mari and Xanthas were alone.

They sat facing each other, holding hands, knees touching, looking deeply into each other's eyes, violet into blue, soul into soul. ~Somehow, I always knew,~ thought Xanthas. ~I just always *knew*.~

~Me too. It was always there. I always felt there was something, no some*one*, who was *part* of me, who was *Connected*. I simply couldn't figure it out. So I didn't think about it much. This is wonderful, unbelievable!~

It was not necessary for Xanthas to respond. Having made this Connection, they each knew what the other was feeling. Xanthas was overwhelmed by the feelings of love she was experiencing. It had never happened to her before. She knew they were searching for the E-gene, but didn't think she had it. Until now it had never manifested itself. They had high hopes for her from the beginning because she was such an ideal Meld specimen who seemed perfectly human, and with Mantid mind power.

The Mantid females had held her from birth, closely like human mothers. They had played thought games with her and even physical human games parents played with their children. She was very good at them and knew *Mother Goose, A Child's Garden of Verses* and all the Dr. Seuss books by heart as well as thousands of other Surface books.

But she had never demonstrated any emotion until now, nor had any other Meld, much less any Mantid. It was wonderful. She knew there were other emotions. She wondered if all emotions *felt* like this. She wondered if at some point it just popped out if you had the E-gene, or if you had to be in the proximity of a Surface relative, or a hundred other possibilities she could think of.

~Mari, this is so wonderful, you *have* to help us find the E-gene for everyone. Mantid are so intelligent and peaceful and have such perception. This would make them complete. If our two species could fully blend, it would be marvelous for both of them. They each have so much to give one another! I know! I'm part of each. I can see now that I am the beginnings of what they are searching for.~

The power with which she felt this conviction was simultaneously transmitted to Mari who was deeply moved by it as though she had thought it herself. In certain ways she had – her Connection with Xanthas was that strong. Xanthas' conviction was her conviction. There was no way she could refuse.

Mari made her decision, ~Xanthas, how do we get Jenoor back in here?~ She felt Xanthas' thought message go out to Jenoor and realized they had been communicating with each other in a way that shielded their thoughts from anyone else. Hey, she was getting pretty good at this!

Jenoor returned to the room.

~Okay.~

~Okay what?~

~Okay, I'll do it with you.~

~Do what?~

His uncharacteristic confusion, particularly in view of his telepathic abilities and after the evening's events, caused some second thoughts about her decision, plus some feelings of rejection which she thought very strange in this situation, ~I'm willing to *screw* you for crying out loud! You've got one of the most original pick-up techniques anywhere on, or in, Earth and you've been making a serious effort to get into my panties for *quite* some time now. I finally tell you okay, and you act like you're a freshman in high school!~

Always wanting to help, Xanthas interjected, ~ Breed with you, Jenoor. ~

Jenoor went blank for a moment, trying to comprehend that what he wanted, what he had planned for, what he had thought about since before his and Mari's current lifetime was actually going to happen. He didn't realize that for the third time that day, he was feeling emotion. He was surprised and stupefied. Now that it was going to happen, he was not sure what to do. He had never done *it* with a human before. He had only *thought* about it. He was, essentially, a virginal Surface high school boy! He had taught human sex-education classes to selected Mantid, but had no practical experience. He had formulated the curriculum, but had not done it! If thoughts stammered, his were about to. If his gray outer covering could have blushed, it would have. He took a deep breath – unusual because he never did anything but breathe normally – and took a moment to collect himself.

Trying to think something that wouldn't sound stupid, ~W. . . well,

M . . . Mari that is very gratifying that you will help us . . . . Help everyone that is, Surface people also.~

Xanthas looked at him curiously.

Mari began to sense he was a little nonplussed and started to smile. Here was a Mantid main-mind for who knows how long and he was starting to choke at the thought of getting a little. She was beaming. Xanthas looked at her curiously. Mari loved this control. She started to press.

~Okay, Jenoor, let's get it on.~ She reached for his hand.

He quickly pulled it out of reach. ~I . . . I am not certain I know what you mean by putting something on.~

~Come on, Jenoor. Don't chicken out on me. Now I'm getting all ready and you act like you just hatched. I mean get - it - on. Dooo it. Do they have motels here?~ Her thoughts were gently chiding, but soft and seductive. She caught his hand this time and gently pulled him toward her.

Jenoor was trying to analyze why he found himself drawn to her in more than an experimental way. She was spontaneous, irreverent in a genial way, responsive to him, had emotions, was intelligent, and pointed things out to him that even with all his intellect he did not see. She was many things he was not, coupled with an intangible factor he couldn't articulate. The analysis delayed his backpedaling only momentarily, ~I . . . well . . . I . . . I thought the breeding would take place in the examining room so the others could document how things occur . . .~

~No way, Jose – that's how I pronounce your name in Spanish. I don't breed with an audience. If you don't have a nice private room here with a nice big, soft bed and a little wine, music and candlelight, let's go back to the Surface and rent one. We can hit a Quick-Stop on the way for the wine and candles. You stay in the saucer. I don't want anyone to get suspicious.~

She was close to laughing out loud again and she shot a glance at Xanthas who, feeling the amusement transmitted from Mari for the first time and enjoying it even though she didn't truly understand it, was smiling a slight little smile, particularly because she also sensed Jenoor's now unguarded consternation.

With only his logic to fall back on, ~But they will get suspicious if they see the craft,~ Jenoor protested.

Mari couldn't help it. She did laugh out loud again. She felt like she was seducing someone who had been living in a cave all his life. Well, actually . . . . She could see he was going to need a little help with his project and, having graduated from high school and college with a little experience under her belt, she felt qualified to do it. While clearly mischievous, she was also kind and felt if she pushed this much further, Jenoor's libido wouldn't develop properly. This was wild, she was starting to feel a responsibility for his sexual development – or as he might put it, his breeding technique. She realized it must be coming from Xanthas who was very concerned that melding advance between the two species.

She pulled harder on his hand. ~Come on Jenoor, let's find a quiet place, just you and me. I can't do it in front of all these beings.~ She was again surprised at how soft his skin was. She took both his hands and pulled him toward her, looking directly into his eyes. While she had intended this to be a seductive move to draw him into her, she found herself being drawn into him, into his eyes. She was falling into them, she . . . . ~Wow, Jenoor. Let's just find a room to ourselves with a normal bed and a door we can lock and see what happens.~ She was starting to get a little excited. She didn't care about his gray body or anything else. It was those eyes, just what she could see through those eyes.

~You can use my room; it's like that!~ volunteered Xanthas, childishly happy to be of help.

Mari didn't have to ask where it was. Xanthas put it into her mind and Mari led him there and locked the door. The other Mantid knew their minds were not invited and acted accordingly. But Xanthas, of course, was curious.

Alone in the room, Mari knew what she would have done with Murph, but this guy wasn't exactly built like Murph and her bravado started to give way to puzzlement concerning what to do next. Murph! My, God! Murph! What the hell was she doing! She'd never cheated on Murph! She was certain he had never cheated on her. She had gotten so caught up in this, she had begun to think this was the main program for her existence and was starting to sweep her Surface life into a closet. Holy moly! She had really gotten herself into it now.

Ordinarily, she would just wake up at this point, but she knew this wasn't a dream. She'd try it anyway. Didn't work. She felt that she should just bail on the whole deal. Jenoor told her she could at any time. But she sensed Xanthas in the back of her mind, ~Please don't, please don't, we need you so badly.~ She knew Xanthas was Connecting with her thoughts and was pleading with her to go forward. Her Midwestern upbringing told her she should stop, but Xanthas' pathos was literally pulling her heart out. She looked at Jenoor, ran her hands up his arms and Connected through his eyes – Xanthas was pushing her into them.

She felt a million miles away from Earth. No one would ever know. No one would ever believe it anyway. This was just the first step in interspecies "communication" through "natural" conception. They would take the baby at six weeks. It would never show and no one would know. It was pioneering, it was . . . She felt herself flying into his eyes, being drawn to a point in the middle of smaller and smaller concentric circles, like reverse waves on a pond.

She no longer had on her blue jump suit and her panties had been slipped off. She didn't know if she had done it or if Jenoor was smooth enough to accomplish that. She was groping his body, which didn't have any clothes on to start out with, and she was so excited there was clearly evidence of it. His body was sooo soft; it was amazing. Like the softest gray glove leather she had ever touched or could imagine. Jenoor didn't know what was happening to him, but he was groping her too, wrapping his long, strong fingers around her hips and pulling her into him. It flitted through her mind that she was grateful for her religious attendance at all those Jazzercise classes. Her butt was so firm that the legendary jazz drummer, J. L. "Happy Beat" Hammertune, could do a one-handed drum roll on them. She had no clue if Jenoor cared – he wasn't concentrating on that right then.

As Jenoor's hand slid around the front, she noted that his fingers were not only long and strong, but extremely supple. She was panting and she thought he was too. If she wasn't making so much noise, she would have been able to tell one way or the other. She was frantically searching for his penis. Just as she started to focus on the fact that she couldn't see anything remotely resembling one on his unclad body, nor even the telltale signs evident under every male ballet dancer's tights, it happened.

Out of a normally imperceptible orifice in his form, right where it should be, there emerged, coming out like an extruded rod – the only thing she could think of at the time – looking just like it should, this marvelous, big, long . . . . Wow! She stared at it for a few moments, marveling at it and how it had presented itself. Then her eyes, now smoky blue, slid up his body, fastening onto his prodigious and transcendental orbs as she went backward, pulling him over her as they fell onto the bed. He may not have done this before with a human, but he clearly knew exactly where it should go.

True to the juvenile nature of his experience in these matters, he completed the biological portion of his mission almost immediately. He definitely was panting. "Oh no, Jenoor," she moaned softly. She had almost started to laugh at the irony of the entire situation when she realized that . . . it was still there! With joy she remembered . . . the bone. The penis bone she had laughed so hard about! Great day! She vowed never to make fun of anybody again, grabbed his hips (?), and controlled the rhythm from then on, at least until she totally lost control.

Simultaneously, while waiting in a room with several of the Mantid caregivers for Mari and Jenoor to return, Xanthas made a multitude of unintelligible sounds, loudly, as Mari reached the apex of her delight. Startled at the first audible sounds they had ever heard from her outside of the practice in class, and having become increasingly apprehensive at Xanthas' agitated behavior and shortness of breath, the caregiving Mantid rushed to her as she cried out and bent over in her chair, seemingly with some type of convulsions.

Xanthas' curiosity had gotten the best of her. She knew she probably shouldn't have tuned in to her sister, and she was very confused about what had just happened to her physically, particularly because it seemed she'd had a little accident, but she felt great! Never having experienced embarrassment before, and not wanting her caregiving teachers to know she wasn't as proper as they in tuning out any unguarded thoughts – and, gracious!, were Mari's ever unguarded, not to mention Jenoor who totally lost it too, he'd *never* been like that – she spent some time assuring them she just had a brief coughing spell and was fine. Seeing no indication of a problem, other than the beautiful pink hue that had infiltrated her porcelain skin, they accepted her rambling explanation.

Mari lay on the bed with Jenoor still on top of her. There had never been a moment when she had stopped looking into his eyes, from the beginning till now. She usually closed her eyes, but she couldn't. She hadn't felt the motion of their bodies. She just kept flying through those eyes. It was not describable. She was in his soul. At least that's where it seemed like she was. She didn't know where she was. She just knew that she felt complete, and completely without tension, stress, strife or any other negative thing right now. Perhaps she had hit Nirvana through those eyes. They just looked at each other. Not saying anything. Not wanting to say anything. Both in a state of pleasant shock at what they were feeling, and neither was certain what it was.

Finally, Mari's attention returned to her surroundings.

~Jenoor.~

~Yes.~

~Does it retract?~

~Well . . yes.~

~I think you should.~

Mari gave a little "whoops" and a giggle as Jenoor complied. It gave Xanthas a start too.

Mari and Jenoor returned to the room containing Xanthas and the Mantid caregivers and tried to act as if they had simply been professionally engaged in a medical procedure. The caregivers bought it, but Xanthas definitely knew better. Mari was regaining her composure and, in a very businesslike way, they discussed that she would go back and carry on as usual and Jenoor would check on her from time to time to determine her progress. Then, presuming it "took," at six weeks they would remove the baby and place it in one of their containers until it was full term.

They discussed other details as they traveled back to the main craft. She was returned to the bed she shared with Murph, just before he woke up. Actually, he was not able to wake up until she returned, which occurred just before the alarm was set to go off. It seemed to Mari that she had been gone much longer than the time of a long night's sleep, but that hadn't been the case and she wasn't tired. In fact, she was excited. Blown away would be a better way to describe it.

<<~>>

CHAPTER FOUR

"Man, the sleep of the dead. I don't think I moved all night," Murph mumbled as he knocked his rimless glasses off the nightstand trying to answer the phone, ultimately realizing it was the alarm. He rolled over to look at Mari and she looked fresh as a daisy, staring at him wide-eyed. He stared back trying to remember what had happened before *el sueno del muerto*.

"What the hell happened last night? The last thing I remember, we went to bed early and then you started bouncing around claiming someone was watching us again." He simply couldn't remember anything after that. Shifting from his inability to remember, "Mari, you've been saying things like that a fair amount lately. Do you think we should discuss it? If you're under some type of pressure, you need to talk it out. We should because, frankly, your behavior is becoming a little paranoid and we ought to catch any problem in the beginning."

She debated disclosure with herself. He was not only a highly competent and experienced psychologist, but most of his practice, almost since the moment he finished his Ph.D. in clinical counseling at Stanford, had been with patients who experienced all manner of "psi" related events, who evidenced parapsychological abilities or who were 'Experiencers.' This wouldn't be anything he hadn't heard before. He'd just never heard it from her.

"Well, to make a long visitation short, I've been taken into a spaceship by Greys, not only last night, but since I was a little girl and they have asked me to help them with their problem."

He was staring at her blankly, primarily because he could tell she was serious. He had heard similar lead-ins from many patients who were intelligent, normal, reasonable, highly-believable people, except that they were saying things like this. But, despite the fact that there was not one shred of undisputable physical evidence, any existing physical evidence being capable of interpretation in at least two ways, and one of those being totally nonsupportive of the UFO premise, he was fundamentally convinced they had experienced something real in their lives.

But now his *wife* was saying it. This was different, very different. It hit home that at some very deep level, he may be a great deal more skeptical – hypocritical? – about his patients' revelations than he had ever been willing to admit to himself. All of this threw his thoughts into reverse, scrambling back to how he became interested in paranormal psychology in the first place.

Murph's mother had always been metaphysical. While she had now "passed back," to put it in her terms, she was always interested in why we were here and the nature of the grander organization, being convinced by her intuition that her mind did not originate with matter and was not dependent upon it. She would close her eyes and simply feel her mind outside her body. She spent her lifetime studying and contemplating "what the deal was," as Murph would put it.

It percolated into Murph who, combining it with the influence of his father's engineering background, wanted to investigate in a more systematic way what he couldn't see, what was beyond the edges that influenced people to do whatever they did. As a result, he ultimately became a clinical psychologist who studied paranormal behavior and experiences, conducting therapy with those who said they were negatively affected by them. That held him up to some ridicule by his peers, but Murph was the son of an engineer who calculated exact parameters and results, and who believed that everything he thought on any subject was as correct as his computations. Consequently, Murph's dad didn't give a damn what anyone else thought.

That mental toughness, but not the rabid irrationality of always being right, washed over Murph who was generally unaffected by the opprobrium of others, except to examine why they felt that way. And he had come to the conclusion that it made them uncomfortable to consider any reality other than their own – even if the alternatives might be better – so they refused to expand their thinking. It was their choice, and also *their* problem.

During those few reflective moments, he continued to stare blankly.

"Murph . . . Murph?"

He snapped out of it and started collecting his thoughts. He didn't want to be an insensitive jerk, but he was having trouble viewing this in the detached way he did with his patients. Why was he able to be detached with them? Was it proper professionalism or was he just not into it? No, he found it fascinating. Perhaps it was just that he had never experienced it for himself. He would love to make sure. That was it. He loved this work. It was just that he wasn't *sure*. Well, this was a marvelous chance to find out close up, and he'd better work hard at it because he didn't want to come to the conclusion that she was nuts. He loved her too much.

Calmly, "Tell me about it. This is my 'admin' morning and I don't have any appointments."

They dressed, ate breakfast and Mari explained everything in detail from the time she was a little girl. Her mother, Xanthas, the Universal Connection, the Greys' need to find the E-gene and develop emotion, and so on. She just left out one teeny-weeny set of details. That they wanted to breed directly with a human, that she was the one Jenoor wanted to do it with – and that they had.

Murph asked the same question he would ask a patient, "Well, why do they need you?"

There was a pregnant pause.

Thank God for those brothers and thinking fast to survive them. Her sky-blues were a little wider than normal, "Well . . . they would like to work with a Surface professional on this problem, but they can't just knock on somebody's door and engage them to do that, soooo . . . because I'm Xanthas' half sister and you are a highly skilled psychologist who is familiar with these kinds of matters, they thought I might be able to talk you into delving into Xanthas' psyche concerning emotion, and you wouldn't freak out or blabber it all over the place."

When she saw that it was taking, she congratulated herself on how fast she thought on her feet. She was only telling these little fibs because she didn't want to take the chance of hurting him. It would all be over in six weeks and he would never know, and that would be the end of it.

He was trying to put this together quickly in his mind and all of a sudden it hit him. Proof! This would be the proof! I can get them to take me there to see her and then I'll *know*! He was very excited. Fourteen years of doing this and now he was going to have his proof! – or he would find out his wife was a little squishy in the reality department. Hey, she's the one who said she could bring all this about, and up to now in their lives there hadn't been a squish factor.

"Mari, this is my work. You know I'll be happy to help. I'm excited to help! Wow, this is unbelievable! So what do we do next?"

"I, uh . . . well, I . . . uh . . . I guess I'll have to . . . try to contact Jenoor and see how to arrange it, but I'm not sure how to do that.

Perhaps if we just wait for him to contact me."

Accustomed to pressing his patients to explain every event in their paranormal chronicles, "Well, if the whole purpose of this was to have me work with your half sister, wouldn't it have been arranged for a 'yea' or 'nay' response?"

Dammit. He could have been a lawyer if he'd wanted. "You know, I just can't remember. I'm sure Jenoor will contact me soon, though."

It wasn't computing, but he was so excited at the prospect and so bowled over by the circumstances that he just let it slide. Besides, he had a lot of work he had to get at today no matter how excited he was. "Okay, but let's hope it's soon, and tell me right away no matter what." Then he controlled himself. He didn't want to get too excited in case his own wife turned out to wacky.

Later that day, Murph was in his office at home and, a few rooms away in the study, Mari sat quietly in a chair with the blinds drawn, trying to communicate mentally with Jenoor. She got Xanthas.

~Oh, Surface sister, I've missed you already. I do not think Jenoor can perceive you because you are not well practiced at this and are trying in a way that is not conducive to creating a good signal line, but we are Connected, as you can tell, even though you are a little 'scratchy.'~

It was wonderful to feel her thoughts, ~Sister beneath, I need to communicate with Jenoor. I think I've gotten myself into a little jam. Can you tell him I need to see him?~

Xanthas was confused concerning Mari's need to see Jenoor because she had placed herself into a food item, but she communicated the message to Jenoor. ~He will come see you tonight.~

~What time?~

~Do not be concerned. He says it will work out like it did before.~

Of course it would. What an idiot. They would put Murph into a paralyzed sleep and she and Jenoor would carry on their business.

That night she heard Jenoor's thoughts telling her to walk outside. She looked at Murph and he was definitely out. She shook him just to make sure. No movement. She pulled on her robe and slippers and went outside. Nothing was there. She looked around and realized the stars overhead were blocked out in a triangular pattern. About that time a dimensional blue beam came from the middle of the dark patch, she saw the little electrical dots and she was with Jenoor, presumably in the triangular craft.

~You are,~ he responded to her thoughts. ~We were coming tonight anyway to look at you with our 'Magic Glasses.'~

She smiled at the reference to her childhood and thought it curious that Jenoor would offer that somewhat tender and nostalgic reference. She wondered if he would have smiled when he said it, if he could. Maybe he could for all she knew. He was certainly amazing in other ways.

He led her to a comfortable room where they were alone. She told him all the details of her conversation with Murph, including the details she failed to disclose as well as the disingenuous reasons for the Mantid desire to work with her.

~My God! I did not blank you before you went back!~

~You said, 'My God.'~

~I thought what?~

~'My God.' You said 'God.'~

~God, One Mind, whatever. Perhaps I have started to identify with the Surface more than I realize. It is all the same thing you know. Just different terminology depending upon where one lives.~

He was looking directly at her with those endless eyes and she started to move into them. Her hands reached out and started to move over his body. Jees! So soft. She still couldn't believe it. He made no move to resist. His strong fingers came up around her back and slipped off her robe. As her hands went down she noticed that he was already "coming out" so to speak. Everything she wore to the spacecraft was now on the floor of the spacecraft, as were Mari and Jenoor.

Neither had any idea how much time had gone by or how many times each had reached that delightful "space between thoughts," but they both felt marvelous. Poor Xanthas had a great deal of difficulty going to sleep that night and didn't understand why.

Mari stuffed what had just happened into a little logic-tight compartment in her mind and asked Jenoor what he thought they should do in relation to the story she had told Murph, who seemed so excited about it. On reflection, Jenoor thought it would be an excellent idea for someone with Murph's credentials, experience and apparent mindset to examine Xanthas and contribute what he may be able to determine from a Surface viewpoint concerning her emotional ability and development. He also decided he would like to have Xanthas live at their house for awhile so they could see how well a Meld might adapt to Surface life, yet she could also be protected by Mari and Murph.

Further, he determined that he would need to examine Mari on a fairly frequent basis with his Magic Glasses to keep tabs on her progress. Mari did not object. He ultimately did examine her that night with the Magic Glasses and determined that their union had been successful the first time and she was doing fine.

CHAPTER FIVE

Murph was excited about Xanthas coming to live with them, but then it dawned on him that he wasn't going to be in a spaceship, the home of the Mantid or perhaps have any other hard evidence except Xanthas. He wondered if this was some type of misdirection by Mari in order to support what was actually her delusion. Presuming it wasn't, the girl *can't* be just like us. Mari hadn't spent a lot of time describing her except to say she looked just like a human being and not a gray grasshopper – but there must be *some* physical characteristic about her that would be proof positive. He'd certainly make it a point to find out along with inspecting her psyche.

But then again, they'd *have* to bring her in a spaceship. He wanted to be certain to be around for that, but Mari didn't know exactly when they planned to bring her, other than "soon." He couldn't stay awake twenty-four hours a day, and he was going to be pissed if he was asleep. But they couldn't just drop her here. Of course he'd see them bring her. He felt like a little kid waiting for Santa's sleigh. He made Mari promise to wake him if it was at night.

The following Sunday he awoke from another *sueno del muerto* and Mari was not in bed. It was 9:00 a.m. Mari heard him floundering around and came into the bedroom.

"She's in the study."

"Who?"

"Xanthas. She's nervous about meeting you."

"You didn't wake me! You said you'd wake me!" He felt squished.

"Shhhh. You'll scare her. I tried to wake you. Honest. But it was like you were dead. Jenoor said it was better that way anyway."

He was *really* feeling that he had been had.

"Clean yourself up and come meet her."

He showered and shaved and resolved to make the best of the situation, including having faith in Mari. Besides, there just had to be some distinguishing physical characteristic in a cross between an insect and a human. There had to be. That's it. Mari hadn't described her in great detail because she didn't want him to chicken out. She probably had big multiple spurs coming out of the backs of her legs, long feelers on her head, a mouth like a cootie-catcher and vice-grips for hands. He steeled himself and quietly went into the study to meet her. Mari was seated with her back to the door, across from Xanthas who was facing Murph. He involuntarily sucked air. Mari turned and Xanthas looked up, focusing her violet eyes intently on his. He was unable to speak. He was paralyzed by those incredible eyes, the green points shimmering everywhere in them.

"Murph, this is Xanthas. Murph . . . Murph . . . !?"

His mouth was moving up and down, but nothing was coming out. They both looked at him waiting, but nothing happened. Xanthas, having never seen a Surface male in person before, looked at Mari for some explanation.

"Murph, snap out of it! I know she's beautiful, but stop acting like you're in the eighth grade and say hello!"

"Hello."

"H . . hello," ventured Xanthas.

Her voice was as soft as her eyes were beautiful. Murph had thought he was going to regain his composure, until she spoke. Mari was staring in disbelief at the extent of Murph's schoolboy paralysis. Murph was trying to remember why Xanthas was there and why he was in the room so he could muster something reasonably appropriate to say.

It came to him in a flash and he stated with genuine enthusiasm, "Xanthas, I'm so happy to meet you! I'm looking forward to speaking with you at length as the days go by. I hope you will be comfortable here."

Xanthas sensed immediately that Murphy Bailey was a nice man and meant well, but she had no understanding whatsoever concerning the way she looked or sounded to humans, particularly males. In fact, speaking with Mari before Murph woke up was the most extended talking-out-loud practice she'd had since her younger days in the Mantid school, where they stopped practicing after the children learned how to do it.

"Thank you very much. This is all a very new experience to me, but I want to help as much as I can. Even though I'm a little apprehensive, I'm also very inquisitive." Her mental training for communicating Surface-style clicked in automatically, including grammatical contractions and politeness, the latter being natural anyway.

"That all sounds wonderful," Murph half stammered. Realizing he needed to get his act together, "Look, it will take me a day or so to collect my thoughts concerning how I want to approach our inquiry into the matters Mari has explained to me. I think that time will also help you acclimate here and get a little more used to things. Does that sound okay?"

"I think it will help you too." Mari chuckled the words and solicitously gave Murph a little pat. He was slightly offended she could read him so well and was rubbing it in, although in this case a gorilla could have figured it out. Xanthas just watched, smiling pleasantly, and beautifully, without guile, secret, artifice or hidden agenda.

CHAPTER SIX

Murph had been giving Xanthas various psychological tests for ten days, compiling results and talking to her for hours on end. The more he talked to her, the more he was drawn into her. He could not believe that such loveliness could be combined with genuine innocence, purity of thought and intelligence.

This was a beauty and innocence written about only in fairy tales, untouched by the avarice of humans. His tests had no meaning other than to underscore that conclusion. If every person were this lovely inside, the world would function without the problems generated by many of the "intelligent" beings in it.

He was losing his focus. All he wanted to do was simply spend time with her. He was supposed to be contributing to the Greys' pool of emotion\no-emotion knowledge, but his tests were useless because her experience wasn't human experience and her emotional development wasn't human-based.

Suddenly it hit him. There *were* parallels here. From the way she described her development and that of other Melds, she was reared by *handlers* doing their best, but who had, or at least expressed, no emotion themselves. Surface – he was working into the lingo – psychologists had often seen similar, though more drastic, results in unwanted children all over the world who were just handled, but not loved. Children who had only their biological needs met, but nothing else. Of course, those children were usually neglected in every other way also, with no meaningful education or positive contact with others. The latter had not been the case with Xanthas.

Xanthas' contact with her caregivers was positive in every way except there was no emotion expressed by those who reared her, even though they had held her and the others of her generation a great deal. Thus, she seemed wonderful, except for something he couldn't quite put his finger on, a certain non-responsiveness to physical touch. Not a withdrawal from it as might occur in someone with bad emotional experiences relating to others, just a seeming non-awareness or non-recognition that touch is, or can be, emotionally meaningful, although he sensed she had a hunger to respond.

It was either a genetic or a cultural phenomenon going back to the beginnings of the Greys' known history. If it was genetic as the Greys believed, he didn't know how much he could do about it. But if it was cultural, that would be a different story entirely. He decided he needed to determine whether she could be taught to respond emotionally to meaningful positive touch.

Keeping the emphasis on "positive," he automatically determined that he would not try to evoke fear or anger by striking or threatening her. Looking at those beautiful, innocent, shimmering eyes and that porcelain skin, making the decision to see if Xanthas could be taught to respond to kind, loving touches was incredibly easy. His intent – at least consciously – was a few gentle touches, perhaps some hugs, to see what happened. He didn't want to scare her or make her fearful.

"Xanthas, will you hold out your hands please." She was seated next to him on the couch in the study and unhesitatingly extended her hands to him. He gently took them in his. It was the first time he had touched her other than inadvertently and he was struck by how soft, gentle, warm and pliable her hands were. He just stared at her hands against his. Those long, tapered, beautiful, malleable fingers. Her touch was a soft nexus he had experienced only when touching Mari's hands. His eyes traveled up to hers. She was looking at her hands in his. She looked up at him softly and questioningly, having come to expect a gentle answer concerning things she didn't understand.

He exerted a loving pressure on her hands and very gently and slightly massaged each of them in his as he continued transfixed by her eyes and her touch. Her mouth opened slightly and she involuntarily took a little extra breath as she continued to look back at him, confused, but not unpleasantly, not understanding how she was being affected. Without thinking about it, or perhaps not being able to help himself, he raised both her hands to his mouth and lovingly kissed them, easily and gently. Her breathing quickened slightly and she cocked her head a little, first one way and then the other, reminiscent of a curious kitten, all the while looking directly at Murph and knowing the gentle answer would come.

Recovering a little and determined not to compromise his professionalism, "Xanthas, what are you feeling right now?"

"Feeling?"

"Yes . . . ah . . . describe what's happening to you – inside, not what I did."

"I . . . well I . . . I don't know how to say it."

"But something did happen to you inside?"

"Yes."

"Was it unpleasant."

"Unpleasant?"

"Did you want me to stop?"

"No."

Her directness caught him by surprise. He didn't want to stop either. She hadn't taken her eyes off his and he wasn't capable at that moment of looking away from hers. His eyelids fluttered, perhaps a nanoinch, as he realized his own confusion about what was happening inside himself. These were the types of feelings he had when he first held Mari's hands. He'd never experienced them with anyone else. Recognizing the slight break in adhesion, Xanthas head again cocked a little to one side, but relying on his years of professional demeanor, Murph moved forward smoothly, "You wanted me to continue?"

"Yes."

Still trying to control his composure, "Xanthas, please do the best you can to describe what happened to you inside. In your education, you've seen movies made by Surface people that demonstrate and talk about emotions they have, haven't you?"

"Yes, but except for the strange things that happened with Mari because she is my sister, I don't have any with anyone else. I don't know what is supposed to happen. We've never seemed to be able to get it right genetically, even with me."

"Do you know that is true for certain?"

"Well, they wouldn't tell us if it wasn't so."

"Xanthas, if something happened to you inside just now that has never happened to you before, do your best to explain it to me some more."

"Well, something happened inside, I just don't have any words for it because it never happened before, but it did happen and I didn't want it to stop, or the way I was inside to stop, and I know you were that way and didn't want it to stop either, and that made me want it to keep going even more and . . ." Her soft, low voice almost made him crazy.

"Xanthas, that means you liked it."

"*Liked* it?"

"Yes, you've seen people in the Surface movies talking about how they liked something and, depending on what it was, they would react in different ways, but they always wanted it to continue if they liked it.

Xanthas, that is feeling emotion, that is feeling good, that is being happy!"

"*Feeling* emotion? That's *emotion*? I can feel emotion with *anyone*!!?" Her voice rose and her hands trembled. Tears started down her face. Her eyes were wide with wonder and discovery. "Can I do this all the time?"

"Come over here to the mirror!" He was also very excited now at this discovery. She looked at herself, the tears streaming down her face, she stared at her trembling hands and concentrated on the way she felt inside. She looked back at him, knowing an explanation would come. He took her by the shoulders and spoke directly at her. "Xanthas, you *have* emotion! This *is* emotion, and it's not related to your sister. This is what you have seen in the movies *feels* like! Look at your tears!" As she saw herself in the mirror, her epiphany overwhelmed both of them. He pulled her close, squeezing very hard. She did likewise, alternately crying and laughing – now that she knew she could at any time.

"Oh, my goodness! I've got so many emotions to learn about and to feel! Please help me learn about all of them!" She was so happy and excited that he just stepped back and looked at her with joy and love. He didn't realize that the last few minutes had commenced the construction of Murph's very own logic-tight compartment.

CHAPTER SEVEN

In the previous ten days while Murph was testing Xanthas, Jenoor had come to the Surface twice to examine Mari with his Magic Glasses, always while Murph was "asleep." Everything was progressing so satisfactorily in all areas that Jenoor suggested Mari spend a week or two "Below" in "Mantidville," ostensibly to help the Mantid understand Surface people better, while Murph continued to work on the Surface with Xanthas.

Due to some inevitable chinks in her specious reasoning, coupled with being an amateur liar, Mari could scarcely talk when she relayed the suggestion to Murph. Much to her surprise, he didn't seem to notice or question what, clearly to her, were obviously spurious reasons for her departure. Instead, he said he thought that might be a good idea since he was extremely busy sandwiching Xanthas in with his other professional duties, and he was certain Mari could probably be of great assistance to the Mantid.

Murph didn't notice the pragmatic failure of his own reasoning when it never occurred to him to request that they all go together so he could put his doubts firmly to rest once and for all. Nor did he tell her any more than he believed he was making "some progress" with regard to Xanthas' emotions, in addition to the testing. Stated another way, both Murph and Mari busily busied themselves elsewhere than with each other.

<<~>>

CHAPTER EIGHT

Having thought about his "squish concerns" a little more, Murph decided he was going to see the spaceship, Jenoor, the blue beam and everything else he wanted to see upon Mari's departure. He made Mari promise that if he were asleep, she would wake him up or make Jenoor do it, and that she would not leave until Murph had talked to Jenoor in person and Jenoor had consented that Murph could watch her being beamed into the spaceship and see it fly away.

It didn't happen. He awoke early the next morning to find Mari gone, a note that she wasn't sure what day she would be back, but that he should take good care of Xanthas. He felt like he was on the short end of that game where you look for a pea under one of several shells, but its never under the one you turn over.

But, perhaps it wasn't all sleight of hand. He hurried to Xanthas' room to see if she were actually there. The door was not latched and he pushed it open slowly. She was asleep in the loose, semi-transparent, lacy nightgown Mari had given her. It was the middle of March, warm in the house and unseasonably warm outside. The window was open and Xanthas had thrown the bedclothes back from the upper half of her body.

Murph knew it was impolite and invasive in a certain way, but he just couldn't help himself. He stood in the doorway staring at her. With a slight breeze rippling the curtains, which seemed to be made of the same material as her nightgown, he started to think about . . . . He *had* to get ahold of himself. He was thinking about doing some things that could be really, really stupid, not to mention possibly blowing Xanthas' mind, alien or otherwise. While he had absolutely no proof she was anything Mari said she was, he couldn't think of why Mari would lie, and she certainly seemed in contact with reality to him. Neither could he think of any reason Xanthas would involve herself if Mari did happen to be delusional.

And if it *was* a hoax, Xanthas was a marvelous actress – in fact she should be a mega-star by now if she was acting, based on looks alone, not to mention the fact that she had him convinced. But still, no spaceship, no Jenoor, no nothing except Xanthas, who didn't have the slightest appearance of anything insect-like about her – and that was a pretty thin nightgown. He almost had to slap himself to stop thinking and looking. He took a deep breath and quietly pulled the door to its original position.

How could he get some information about what was going on? If he just had some way of following Mari, but he was always out like a light. If he could just . . . Shit! Of course! His pal, Pralit Lofler! While the mainstream had giggled Pralit out of any serious credibility, presumably because they were threatened in direct proportion to his abilities, the facts were that, time and again, he had proven himself to be perhaps the most gifted remote viewer on the planet.

<<~>>

CHAPTER NINE

Pralit Lofler was puzzled by Murph's mysterious and extremely vague narrative, but at his good friend's request, he wasted no time getting to Murph's place. They had been interested in one another's work for years, with Murph often acting as Pralit's monitor for a remote-viewing session.

Pralit was a native of the Republic of India. His mother was a gifted Indian psychic and his father was one of those strange, brooding, inner-searching, Indian artists whose work made sense only to him as a statement of the true meaning of life and spirituality. No one else could figure it out, and he wouldn't explain it. That combination perhaps had something to do with Pralit's unique talents. He seemed very accurate at seeing what was happening elsewhere without physically being there, but usually wouldn't explain how or why, at least not in great detail. Only within the last few years had Pralit explained to Murph that even though he was Indian, he had adopted the surname "Lofler" because no one seemed to be able to pronounce his real name and his business often came through word-of-mouth.

Murph had busied Xanthas in the living room watching digisticks on the DV, designed to elicit various emotional reactions which Murph intended to discuss with her later. Pralit settled his small, slight form into the chair at the desk in Murph's office with a pencil in his hand. His dark skin, shock of thick, straight black hair neatly combed back, and bushy deftly-trimmed moustache were a stark contrast to his white nylon shirt and the stack of white paper in front of him. The chair was set for Murph's six-foot one-inch frame and Pralit's head and arms barely poked over the top of the desk.

To avoid injecting any preconceived notions into his mind, Murph had deliberately not told Pralit why he wanted him to come over. He told him only that he may find it one of the most interesting sessions of his life. Pralit understood why he was being given no facts, and the "teaser" from a respected friend was all that he needed. Murph handed him a sealed envelope with Mari's name in it on a folded piece of paper. Pralit did not open it. He cleared his mind and sent it down into a zone that excluded everything except his consciously-unknown target, and Murph's guidance as his monitor when it was necessary, the latter being determined by Murph from Pralit's responses.

"Whew! I get the impression of being down. Not in a basement, but way, *way* down. Like – have you ever seen that old movie *Journey to the Center of the Earth* or whatever it was called?" He drew a circle with a dot inside the circumference as he was speaking, rather semi-mumbling in a moderate trance-like state. He stared at the circle.

Murph, in remote-viewing monitor's jargon, "No aesthetic overlays. Don't conclude. Just tell me what you see."

"In the ground, in . . . way in . . . under the surface . . ."

"All right bring yourself above the surface five hundred miles. What do you see?"

"Earth." He was drawing a circle with the outline of the North American continent in it.

"Where on Earth?"

"United States."

"Be specific."

"New Mexico. Under a bald mountain in New Mexico. This can't be."

"No emotional overlays, please. Go back under the mountain now. Just tell me what you see under the mountain. Just what you see. Don't make judgments."

"It's . . . it's like a big bubble, a *huge* bubble under the mountain. Square shapes – buildings, round shapes – holes, greenish fuzzy shapes – trees. It's a city! A city under the mountain!" Pralit had been scribbling this information and his impressions on a matrix he had drawn on the paper in front of him.

"Have you concluded that, or is that what you see?"

"I see it. No doubt about it. I can smell the trees."

"Place yourself in the bubble at the top of it. How far is it to the buildings and the trees?"

"Two to five thousand feet or so."

"Can you be more specific."

"I can't. This is strange. No sun, but light seems to come from the inner surface of the bubble."

Wondering if he was injecting these thoughts into Pralit's mind from the descriptions Mari had given him, Murph concentrated on the color red emanating from the inside of the "bubble." "What color is the light?"

"Green. Yellow-green."

Continuing to test Pralit, "Draw a picture of the streets."

Pralit's clear brown eyes searched the space over the desk with a longer pause than usual. "There aren't any. No streets. Just a lot of low buildings, fairly large round holes in the ground and lots of trees and vegetation."

"Do you see anything else?"

"An airport facility."

"Is that an aesthetic overlay? What do you actually see?"

"There are craft flying through the air and coming to rest at this facility which has a tower-like structure sticking up, and . . . wait . . . there are no runways! The whole facility is round, with smaller circular pads on it that the aircraft are landing on. They must be helicopters."

"Don't guess. Draw a picture of the flying craft you see."

Pralit drew pictures of round, triangular and cigar-shaped craft, all with no wings, rotors or visible engines or propulsion systems of any kind.

"Move down one of the holes you said you saw. What's down the holes? Pick a hole and go down it."

"It's a room full of round craft, smaller versions of the ones I saw flying around."

"What else do you see?"

"Doors."

"Go through the doors until you find a living being."

"Holy shit!"

"Curb your emotion. Draw what you see."

He drew and described a room with a series of clear containers that had varying sized objects in them, with tubes everywhere, and stick-like figures with large heads and eyes also in the room.

Despite his best efforts to remain calm and objective as if this were just another professional exercise, Murph was starting to get excited. Up to this point he had filled his head with responses that were totally inconsistent with what Mari had told him, but Pralit's responses were totally consistent with what she had said. He was as certain as he was able to be that Pralit was not picking the responses up from him telepathically. "Who are the beings you see?"

Pralit drew a deep breath and his head went back as if he were going to another, deeper level, communicating with something. His eyes shut and moved as if he were in highly active rem sleep – but he was definitely not sleeping. He let out a sigh and came back, staring at the desk. "They are, no, used to be, insects, praying mantis. But they aren't now. They are highly evolved. In many ways they are beyond us. They communicate telepathically. They have spacecraft, but they live underground and don't use them to explore space. They, they're . . ."

Pralit was becoming visibly nervous and upset. Murph instinctively sensed that he was emotionally resisting whatever he had learned and he quickly shifted the focus of Pralit's attention. "That sounds like an aesthetic overlay to me. You couldn't have seen all that. You concluded it. How is it you know it?"

"I can't fully explain it. I tried to do a deep-mind-probe on one of them, but I seem to be communicating with a collective fund of knowledge. It's like a collective of ideas or intelligences that flow the information into my mind. It's very real. Tapping into this on a larger scale is how I view remotely in the first instance, finding signal lines, but this collective of consciousnesses is like a subset specific to these beings. I do not doubt for a moment the veracity of what was communicated."

Murph was in a certain state of shock also. All of this was right on the money with what Mari had told him. At this point he was amazed, but still not one shred of tangible proof, notwithstanding his respect for Pralit Lofler's ability, which he had seen astoundingly demonstrated in a number of other contexts. He pressed on. "Are there any *human* beings down there?"

Pralit's eyes searched the desk top as if he were looking through a three-dimensional projection of the underground city. Suddenly they stopped. His jaw dropped a little and his face registered surprise, "Its, Mari!"

Murph's heart jumped a little. "What is she doing?" Pralit didn't answer. "Who is she with?"

Slowly, "One of the beings."

"Does the being have a name?"

"Yes." His answers were extremely stilted now and he appeared very uncomfortable.

"What is it?"

"His thoughts are very . . . busy. I . . . I can't get it from him."

"What is he doing?" No answer. "*Dammit Pralit*, what is he

doing!"

The strength of the monitor's command overrode Pralit's hesitation. "He's screwing your wife."

Murph was struck dumb at the thought. Then he smiled. It was as inconceivable to him that she would be unfaithful as it was to her that he would be. Their bond, their love, was too strong to entertain any realistic possibility that could occur. It simply was not conceivable. Not with a human and *certainly* not with an alien evolved from a praying mantis, assuming *any* of this bullshit was true. No evidence. Not one shred. The only possibility here was that Xanthas was some type of a giant test, or joke.

That was it! April 1st was not too far away. This was colossal! Mari had outdone herself on the April Fool's joke this time. It was one of her family's long-standing traditions, started by her mischievous brothers when they were teenagers. Someone in the family got it every year and he was finally getting his. They got along well and he knew her brothers liked him, but he had finally arrived! They all must have had a blast thinking this up. What an effort. He couldn't figure out how Mari had talked Pralit into participating. His little seer friend must have more of a sense of humor than he realized.

In any event, it wasn't all that much of a stretch to consider the various reactions Murph might have to the entire affair. He chuckled at his pun. She obviously had contacted Pralit in the event Murph called him, or they had planned to work Pralit in some other way, and Murph fell right into his lap! Xanthas was an even bigger coup. Where in the hell did Mari get such a gorgeous girl!? And how did they get her to do it? She had to be an actress. She was just *too* good at this. One of Mari's brothers must have known her. Matt was still a bachelor and a great-looking guy with lots of unicredits in the bank. It was all beginning to make sense.

He was wondering how much Mari's participation in this joke was going to cost him. But it was probably worth it, particularly if he didn't bite. He could turn the whole thing around. He reveled in his new-found knowledge. He wouldn't even have to think of and plan a pay-back joke – and it would be very, very hard to top this one. He almost jumped up and down and clicked his heels, but he didn't want to give himself away. He needed to play it out and then send Pralit on his way to report to Mari.

"Why is she doing that?"

"She wants to."

"Why is the being doing that?"

"He wants to."

"That's it?"

"No. He wants to interbreed with humans so his kind can learn how to complete their development, and she has agreed to help him."

"When did she do that?"

"Before she was born this time."

Damn. Pralit was good and thinking fast. He and Mari had the story down pretty pat. Pralit was going to have to remember how all this went to clue Mari in though. Murph decided he would extend this to give Pralit a good workout and also give Mari a lot to remember, if Pralit could remember it all to tell her.

"Pralit, that's a new concept to me. Perhaps you could explain that and elaborate in detail on how it is my wife has come to screw a grasshopper." It was everything he could do to keep from bursting out laughing. He considered turning on his digi sound recorder, but it would cause too much commotion. Pralit would notice and he didn't want to tip off the payback.

"Mantid. Not grasshoppers." Pralit was following Murph's request and, after lapsing into communication in much the same manner as he had before with the "collective fund of knowledge," he described in great detail everything that had occurred, commencing with Mari's agreement with Jenoor prior to her birth up to the present.

Murph was kicking himself for not having figured this out sooner and having his sound recorder ready. This was unbelievable. After he had his fun turning this joke around, he was going to have an award ceremony and give Pralit one of those fake Oscars on a "best actor" plaque. This was going to be the greatest backfire in the history of man! He wanted to get Pralit out of there so he could make notes before he forgot the sequence of events. Cheez! It could even be the start of a great novel.

He terminated the session, thanked Pralit for his time and told him to be certain to send a bill. Pralit seemed confused at Murph's calm demeanor and said that under the circumstances, he wouldn't feel right sending a bill and he told Murph he would always be there for him and to call any time he felt he needed to talk. Murph said he was just more or less in shock and needed to think about things. Pralit said he understood, but he was there if needed, and he left.

Murph pounded the desk with glee after Pralit left and busily started making his notes. He peeked in on Xanthas who gave every indication of dutifully watching the digisticks. She was playing it to the hilt. He had plans for her. He'd take it right to the wire until she ran for cover. Boy, they almost had him. He was falling for the whole deal, hook, line and sinker, and was very close to making a monumental ass out of himself, from which he could never recover. If he had, they'd have ridden him till the end of his days. In many ways it could have turned out to be a very cruel joke if not carefully controlled. But he was sure no harm was intended. It was a fantastic effort with great planning; however, they'd have to get up awfully early in the day to catch "Ol' Murph" asleep for long. He smacked his fist into his palm with joy.

CHAPTER TEN

Jenoor stopped abruptly. His large head swiveled on his small neck as he rapidly looked around the room, ~Someone has been watching us!~

Shocked out of whatever plane she was on, ~Jenoor, that's my line, there is no one here. We're alone.~

~No we are not. Someone was here, watching us!~ Jenoor didn't like the reversal at all.

Mari was not only surprised to see him agitated, but very surprised to see him this agitated. ~Jenoor, look around the room. We are alone. The door is locked.~

~No. There was a consciousness here. It used the Universal Connection to find us. It was actually looking for you and came upon me more or less by accident. It also extracted information about the Mantid from our collective mind. It was so unexpected and I was so . . . busy, I didn't consider blocking it until after it left.~

This was the first thing Jenoor had done since they had "Connected" (in more ways than one) that Mari considered a little loopy. She thought it very curious and out of character. *She* hadn't sensed anything, not that she had a chance in the state she was in.

<<~>>

CHAPTER ELEVEN

Murph went into the living room where Xanthas had been watching the digisticks. He was still stupefied by how incredibly gorgeous she was. How in the world could she still be undiscovered?! Unbelievably beautiful and a great actress – she sure had him fooled. After he'd had his fun, perhaps he should give some consideration to becoming her personal manager/agent. He could learn how to do that. If he didn't, it was just a matter of time until someone else discovered her. She must be from a very small place that no one has ever heard of. What a find! He wondered if Mari or her brothers were having the same thoughts.

"Hi Xanthas, if you're finished watching the digisticks, we can start the tests if it's all right with you."

"That will be fine. Why was that man Connecting with the Mantid?"

Boy she was good! Now she was going to tell him she sensed it instead of disclosing she was eavesdropping at the office door. "How do you know that?"

"Well, he wasn't blocking his thoughts while gathering information about the Mantid. My consciousness is part of the Universal Connection and well-tuned into that part of it which is the Mantid Connection. While I am not tuned nearly as well into Surface thought, I knew right away he was searching for Mari, and I was very surprised he was able to make some contact with Jenoor, although I didn't pick up what they were doing because I was concentrating on these movies. You know, I'm not sure why Jenoor wasn't blocking contact from at least Surface thoughts. I think he has been acting a little differently lately."

God she was *excellent*. But she probably didn't have to listen at the door much. She, Pralit and Mari obviously all had the basic story line down pat. Of course they did. "Xanthas, when you saw the digistick about the boy and the girl kissing after seeing a movie together, how did it make you feel?" He moved very close to her. She smelled wonderful.

"Like it did when you hugged me. Like it does when you are very close to me like now." Her breathing increased very slightly.

Murph slipped to her side and then behind her with his arm around her waist. The top of her head came to just above his ear. His lips brushed the nape of her neck, right where the little black velvet-like hairs stopped and the soft translucent white porcelain skin was completely unprotected. Her breathing noticeably quickened. As his other arm slid around her waist and he gently pulled her back into him, burying his lips in her neck, he quickened in several ways. She did not resist and melted into him, making small noises as she did so.

The only thing keeping him from losing it was the thought in the back of his mind that Mari and Pralit had to be ready to burst into the room at any moment. If they did, he wondered if he would have a tough time convincing them he had figured out the joke. His brains had started to drain out of his head. But not completely.

When they didn't burst into the room at what would have been the appropriate time, Murph went back to his original plan. Since they weren't there, he'd just have to push this so far that the woman playing Xanthas would quit. That would be the best anyway, because then he would tell her he knew all along, and she would tell them, etcetera, etcetera.

This would be rough – he smiled inwardly at that thought – but he was going to beat them at their own game. Certainly the actress couldn't complain. After all, she was in on this and they were trying to convince him that his wife was doing it with an alien. The idle thought popped into his head that the grasshopper was not an alien in the usual extraterrestrial sense.

His hands slid upward as his lips continued to caress her neck and ears. She was breathing so hard now and squirming against him so much, he was starting to get scared. It wasn't working. His moves were so smooth – well okay, maybe he wasn't completely acting – she was going out of control, or she was double crossing Mari.

No, wait. Of course! A woman this beautiful hadn't just fallen off the cosmetics truck. She was not going to have any interest in him, particularly a married "him." This gorgeous young woman was an actress and sportingly intent on pressing him to the limit. She was going to make *him* crack and run for cover first.

Well, he had the ace because there was no way she was going to let him get her clothes off of her. His hands went to the buttons on her light blouse. He started at the bottom, undoing them slowly, one by one. She had on no bra and he knew the last one would never get unbuttoned. His glasses fogged up. He tossed them someplace. He wasn't sure exactly where. Her moment of truth. Her beautiful white skin was moist and flushed now, her breath coming harder, not to mention his, and she was making no effort whatsoever to move away from his excitement of the moment and the pressure that moment was creating. In fact, she seemed to be playing it up quite a bit. The last button. This was it.

He undid it *very* slowly. She was acting very excitedly now, but he knew that just before that last one came open, she would whirl and that would be the end of it. He would break into hysterical "gotcha" laughter. She would be in disbelief as to how he figured it out. Then he'd lay it on Mari and Pralit, she would confirm it and he would have his Great Day!

The button came out of the buttonhole. She didn't stop. *But*, the blouse was still covering her breasts. He was tempted to slide it back, but that was too easy. He dropped his hands and gently came up under the blouse, which had not been tucked in from the beginning, until his fingers rested lightly on her stomach. It was so smooth and soft and moist, with just the tiniest, finest soft hairs coming up from it. He imagined how white and softly muscular it must look and wondered if the little tiny hairs were blonde or black. Oops. Brains draining out again.

He caught himself and very, very slowly slid his fingers up toward her breasts. She was good. She was staying with it right up to the end. He felt like he was a sophomore in high school. He, knew he'd never make it, but he wasn't going to chicken out. It was going to be Xanthas that cried uncle. She cried out, but it certainly wasn't "uncle." Xanthas moved a lot, but it wasn't to get rid of Murph. Somehow the blouse had come completely off and Xanthas, who had started out the warm day barefoot, was facing him with only the little shorts on that Mari had given her.

If he were able to write down what he saw and felt, he would be arrested for violating every standard of free expression known in the world. He was virtually paralyzed with awe. Mari had a great body, but Holy Tamales! How could a union of two human beings produce such a perfect specimen as Xanthas!? He'd sure like to see her mother and father.

In any event, Xanthas, did not stop. She felt like she had when she was Connecting with Mari when the latter was alone in the room with Jenoor. And she liked it a lot. She attached herself as one writhing, virginal, crazed mass to Murph, and now he was *really* scared. She wasn't quitting. He'd lost. She'd *won* the game of chicken. Soon she would have *his* shorts off. While she might be impressed that so much of a human being's blood could get to one portion of his body, that's where *he* was drawing the line. He was proving the old adage wrong that the human male had only enough blood to operate either that part of his body or his brain, but not both at the same time. Oh, well, at least he'd have the satisfaction of having figured out the ruse, and they'd all have a good laugh for many years to come, *and* he was damn well going to sign Xanthas to a personal service contract – movies, DV, you name it.

"Okay, okay, you win. I quit. But I figured it out. You are just a better chicken-player than I am, and by the way, a great actress." He pulled her off and held her away at arms length, taking one last, long wistful look as he spoke.

Stunned, Xanthas didn't know what was happening to her for a few seconds. Then she was even more confused when she heard what he was saying. Wide-eyed, breasts heaving, "I . . . I don't understand." She was totally unable to comprehend what was going on. "Are we playing a game?"

"Look. It's over. I've figured it out. You're a beautiful woman, and part of me – he resisted the temptation to look down – would like to continue, but I'm married, I love my wife very much and I don't want this joke to go too far. So, where are they? Call 'em up and tell 'em to come back. Great job though. You had me for awhile and, I've got to give you credit, I chickened out in the end."

He was laughing now as he tossed her the blouse. "By the way, I've got to say this. Not taking anything away from the fact that I do love my wife dearly, you are the most beautiful woman with the most incredible body I have ever seen, and ever will see as far as I'm concerned."

Xanthas just stood limply, staring at him with the blouse in her hand. She didn't know what was happening, but she knew it wasn't good. Enormous tears welled out of her wide, very confused and hurt violet-blue-green eyes. They rolled down her cheeks, slowly at first and then in cascades as the racking sobs slowly built while she stood there looking at him. The blouse, like a wounded butterfly, fluttered to the floor.

Murph had only seen that look once before in his life. He had been chasing a small fawn through the woods on horseback, just for fun. He meant no harm at all. The little fawn's leg got tangled in some brush and broke. Murph got off his horse and rushed to it. It was unable to move and extremely frightened as it lay there, chest heaving from the effort, eyes wide from the confusion and the pain. He looked into that fawn's wide eyes and stared into a soul that didn't understand, a soul whose beautiful innocent eyes continually asked him "Why?" – they slowly closed as the helpless little bundle died from the shock. Murph wept uncontrollably in the woods for a long time as he held that little fawn.

CHAPTER TWELVE

Below, Mari had actually sensed something was wrong with Xanthas before Jenoor did. They couldn't tell what was happening, but they both knew she was in terrible distress.

Mari was amazed at how rapidly the saucers could travel. They didn't wait to take the smaller saucer to the Travelport and transfer to the larger one piloted by Lenaan and Minuum. They just rushed to the smaller vehicle piloted by Jenoor, Phase Shifted and shot through the crust at hot-rod speed toward the Bailey residence. Jenoor knew the Mantid Command Center would recommend a Level 5 Inquiry because he hadn't bothered to get the proper clearances, but he also knew he had the clout to pull it off when he got back, particularly because it was Xanthas who was in danger.

Popping slightly in and out of positive phase so he could see where he was going, Jenoor landed the small craft in the back yard, setting off every dog and cat within a half-mile radius. He put it into a complete negative phase and, with Mari holding onto his hand, ran through the walls of the house to the living room. Murph, who had managed to get the blouse back on Xanthas, was sitting on the floor with her cuddled in his arms. She was sobbing like a child who had just seen her pet run over.

Mari let go of Jenoor's hand and materialized right in front of Murph's eyes. Murph was speechless for a moment, then decided he was so upset by the behavior of Xanthas, the actress, which confused the living hell out of him and rendered all of his psychological training and experience useless, that he had just not seen Mari come in the door.

"Okay, what's the deal? I figured all this out, but when I did, Xanthas, or whoever she is, just went to pieces. The joke isn't funny any more." He was irritated and a little self-righteous.

"What did you *do* to her?!" Mari's hands were on her hips, her face was flushed, little darts were launching at Murph from those burning-emerald eyes and she was *irritated*.

That irritated him more. "What do you mean, what did *I* do to her? You, your brothers and Pralit play this giant joke on me about you screwing a grasshopper, but I figured it out and got your actress' number here in the process, and I guess she is so into the whole deal that she just couldn't take it when I told her I got the joke. *I* didn't do shit! You guys did it, and you and Matt should have gotten somebody more stable to play your alien sister!"

Mari was now almost as completely confused as Murph, except she was a little nervous about the grasshopper screwing part. Jenoor had been positioned behind Murph from the beginning since it was necessary for him to stay slightly in phase in order to maintain contact with them. To someone looking directly at him, there would be a fairly clear question of whether an apparition were present. Connecting with Murph's consciousness, it became clear to Jenoor just who Pralit was, and with a quick pass through Murph's and Xanthas' thoughts, Jenoor realized what had happened. Xanthas was in a terrible state and she needed badly to know that Murph's treatment of her was a sad mistake that was none of his doing.

Jenoor stepped in front of Murph and shifted into full phase. ~Mr. Bailey. I am Jenoor and this is no joke.~

It was Murph's turn to go into a state of shock. He shook his head as if his eyes were stuck. Jenoor was still there. He looked at Mari who was now holding Xanthas. He looked back at Jenoor to see if it was a costume. It clearly wasn't. He wondered if he had clicked off and gone crazy.

~You haven't,~ Jenoor responded. ~Yes, you may touch me.~

Murph gingerly touched him and even poked him a little bit in what he presumed was his abdomen. He'd never felt anything like it on a living being, and he had certainly never seen a living being like this. He looked into Jenoor's massive eyes. For an instant, he thought he saw the fawn's soul, but without fear. He slumped into a chair and just stared at Jenoor, but not his eyes. Everyone stared at Murph. Mari noticed he didn't have on his glasses. Xanthas explained to Mari as best she could what had happened.

It slowly became clear to Murph that this was anything but a giant joke. In front of him was clearly the non-human being Mari had described, that Pralit described, that had been described to him many times by his patients.

~They weren't all me,~ Jenoor corrected, ~. . . but those from our civilization were all like me, and doing the same work.~

Murph had to be absolutely certain, "I want to see your spaceship."

~Please step to your back window. I will not let you see it for long or it will cause great consternation if others see it.~ Murph thought that perhaps Jenoor may be the master of understatement.

As Mari slapped his glasses into his hand, Murph avoided the look that stated his behavior had placed him somewhere between a lunatic and a jackass. Jenoor looked out the window and a thought flitted through his mind. The craft momentarily appeared and then disappeared, but Murph clearly saw it. It fit one of the descriptions he had heard from his patients many times, as well as what Mari and Pralit had described. He wondered if any of his neighbors could see Jenoor in the window.

Then it hit him and Murph swung around to face Xanthas, "Oh my God! Xanthas! Can you ever forgive me. I didn't know. I *really* didn't know." He was pleading with the fawn.

Still involuntarily taking in gulps of air as if to sob, Xanthas replied as calmly as she could, "Murph, it is all right. Jenoor has given me a thought constellation that has helped me see you didn't understand. It is all right – really."

Murph wasn't truly satisfied that she actually was all right. But, he was so relieved he had been forgiven by the fawn that he was close to tears. He hugged Xanthas. She hugged him back – hard.

CHAPTER THIRTEEN

Jenoor took Xanthas back below the Surface, without Mari. Even though she had initially given assurances to Murph that she was all right, Xanthas was extremely and uncontrollably upset. She was unable to deal in any constructive way with what had happened, no matter how much she tried. She had never been harmed, even slightly, and the incredible shock to her fledgling emotional system ultimately resulted in a state of catatonia. In addition to Jenoor, the other Mantid doctors and the Mantid caregivers were consumed with anxiety. Without recognizing it, they demonstrated that they were capable of at least that one emotion. Actually two, since they were furious with Jenoor for leaving Xanthas alone and allowing this to happen to the shining star of Manticon.

Xanthas was little more than an uncomprehending doll. She simply stared into space when upright and closed her eyes if they laid her in bed. She would eat if they fed her and walk if they assisted her, but her beautiful eyes comprehended nothing. No one could have been more in despair than Jenoor. He ached. It didn't register with him that these were emotions, but he knew he would give anything to be able to do it over.

The Mantid did not know they need not be concerned for long. Upon becoming aware of this unexpected blip in the general plan that had been developed for Xanthas' current incarnation, Xanthas' Guides conferred with the Teachers, then intervened and directed the focus of her Superconsciousness back to the Superconscious Dimension. They had determined that it would be beneficial to reveal to her some educational information related to her presently intended lessons for this lifetime and also make it available to her Earthly material mind. They did not want her to get off track due to the inevitable indeterminate variables in Earthly incarnations. She was truly a shining star and had some important goals to accomplish.

When they had finished, her Superconsciousness returned its focus to her Earthly material body and she evidenced all the earmarks of simply snapping out of her catatonia. She knew she was a much more knowledgeable and mature, but certainly not perfect, being. Knowing the Mantid thoughts had been blocked from what had occurred, and at her Guides' request, she offered no explanation and assured them all that Jenoor should not be held responsible and she was perfectly fine. All the Mantid examinations confirmed the latter. Jenoor was not only personally relieved about Xanthas, but also relieved to be off the hook.

CHAPTER FOURTEEN

After Xanthas' departure from the Surface, Murph spent a lot of time listening and talking to Mari about One Mind, the Universal Connection, consciousness in general, the nature of apparent physical existence and all the other things Mari had learned from Jenoor, and which Murph's patients had described or alluded to. Unbelievable! His patients were not hallucinating, but telling the truth!

Murph sat in his study thinking about these things for hours, what had happened, the fact the Mantid were real and the E-gene problem. From what he had seen of Xanthas, he didn't believe the Mantid emotion-problem had anything to do with genes, but everything to do with Mantid culture. They simply had never, ever, expressed emotion within their culture, presumably due to their markedly different development from humans, and had raised all the Melds without any significant exposure to emotional behavior beyond holding them as infants and not treating them harshly. They'd created a bunch of little Spocks.

Judging from Xanthas, Murph thought they primarily needed close-up exposure to humans. That, coupled with a meaningful Connection with human thoughts, should open the door to emotions, which were readily available to them. After all, if everything flows from One Mind, all the qualities of it should be available through the Universal Connection for the taking – so what they need is to interact with humans and *participate* in the Connection with *human* thoughts. That's the catalyst for the realization and understanding necessary to fully utilize what is already here. Just as the principles of mathematics and music are here and it's a matter of discovering and practicing in order to properly utilize them.

So, this whole business of having to meld with humans in order to acquire the E-gene was a red – gray? – herring, and totally unnecessary in Murph's view.

He shoved his rimless glasses upward on his nose and while his finger was still on that little connecting piece of metal, it hit him. He had been pushing it to the back of his mind for a couple of weeks because it was too bizarre a thought for him to deal with. He didn't want to deal with it. He didn't want to pursue it because he didn't want to find out if it were true. But he had to and he knew it. It would dominate every waking thought he had from now on, and probably his dreams too. He was having a lot of difficulty bringing himself to talk to Mari about it. He would need some more assurance before he brought the subject up with her.

His own fidelity in their marriage had been unblemished. Not that there hadn't been temptations, even offers from some very attractive women, but Murph had always felt that his commitment to Mari was sacrosanct and that, above all, he always wanted to be able to look into her eyes with absolute faith, love and integrity. It had never occurred to him for an instant that she felt any differently, or would act any differently, no matter what.

He still could not believe that anything else could be the situation. He didn't want anything else to be the situation, but he had to know. He called Pralit Lofler.

He met Pralit at the latter's home and explained to him everything that had occurred, which in turn was an explanation to Pralit concerning why Murph's previous reaction had seemed so bizarre and out of touch with what was actually happening. None of the explanations seemed unbelievable in the least to Lofler. His psychic gifts and abilities had been highly and continuously utilized over the years, becoming extremely well developed, and he had come to trust what they revealed to him. Based on his experience and entirely consistent with it, the explanations of One Mind and the Universal Connection made absolute sense to him.

Murph was hoping Pralit would tell him that he was not sure about what he told Murph he had seen in the remote-viewing session that day. After all remote viewers had far from a one-hundred percent success rate, and it wasn't necessarily unusual for them to misinterpret what they saw. Unfortunately for Murph, that was less true of Pralit than anyone else in his line of work.

"Murph, the figure I saw was exactly as you describe the being named Jenoor. Some of the craft I saw underground were exactly as you describe the one you saw in your backyard. Everything else I saw was exactly as Mari has described it to you. If you want, you can refuse to believe the additional activities I told you I saw. I am as deeply distressed now as I was then to tell them to you, but that is what I saw. I was *there*. I believe you should consider going home and discussing this with Mari."

Pralit had become the counselor and Murph had become the

patient.

Murph's heart was sinking. "God, Pralit, I don't want it to be true." He was leaning forward in his chair, head in his hands, elbows on his knees.

"You have the option of not asking her."

"If I don't, I'll never be able to look in her eyes again without searching for the answer I don't want."

Pralit said calmly, acutely feeling his close friend's despair, "I can't make that decision for you."

CHAPTER FIFTEEN

Mari knew Murph had gone to talk to Pralit and, based on the remote viewing session Murph had described when she and Jenoor had come through the wall of the living room, it was not difficult to guess why. In the two weeks that passed after Murph's visit to Pralit, she and Murph had conversations about everything except her fidelity. Mari was dreading the possibility of the question, hoping against hope that it would never be asked. Coupling that with the guilt which forced her to pry open the logic-tight compartment she had constructed in her mind, she felt discovered – without escape, plan, misdirecting explanation or remote hope if the question were asked.

When Murph looked at her from behind those rimless glasses and finally asked, her eyes turned to gray and she admitted it instantly.

Seeing Murph's body deflate and the total, almost uncomprehending shock on his face, her heart physically ached as she began to realize the depth of the loving trust she had broken. As she tried to explain how it happened, instinctively she did not – could not – tell Murph what had happened to her and how she felt when she had looked into Jenoor's eyes. What it had done to her. That she had fallen in love with Jenoor's soul. It didn't matter what he looked like physically.

If the cornerstone of their relationship had been crushed into at least identifiable fragments by the admission of infidelity, the revelation that she had fallen in love with Jenoor would grind it beyond recognition. It would be in an irretrievable negative phase, so to speak. She found herself flying blind, grasping at anything to keep from a fatal crash.

"I . . . I just felt compelled to help."

"Why?" Murph's pleading face was white in the valleys, with red tinges at the peaks, like someone who has just lost limbs in a horrible accident and is in incredible pain, but still conscious and able to speak. He wanted desperately to hear some explanation he could accept. Some explanation that would make it okay. Somewhere inside he knew no explanation of any kind could have the effect of unringing that bell.

"I . . . I don't know. I . . . guess it was because of Xanthas, because she is my half sister and my mother's daughter, because of the Connection I felt to her." She thought she was picking up steam. "Xanthas was an in vitro baby and they needed a consciously willing subject and . . . well . . . I just thought that . . . and, well I *had* consented before this life and . . ."

It just wouldn't work. There was no way she could give any kind of a satisfactory explanation. All she could do was keep the even more painful aspects of it for him – to herself. She didn't know what would happen now. She wished that somehow it was okay to love two people, well, two *beings*, at once. She knew that there were others in the world who did do that and it was all right with them, but that just wasn't in her value system or in Murph's either. She was beginning to wish it were. She loved Murph deeply and she loved Jenoor deeply. She couldn't figure out whether she loved them both in the same way or for the same reasons, but she loved them and she didn't want to have to choose, didn't want to hurt anyone, and wished she could have her cake and eat it too.

Murph didn't feel anything, except like someone had kicked him in the stomach, punched him in the face and literally, physically torn his heart from his body, leaving him as walking dead. No matter how many times he asked himself why, he couldn't construct an answer. He felt absolutely powerless, as if he had been physically violated.

Didn't she care about me? How could she love me and voluntarily do that? He'd had no opportunity to defend himself. What was wrong with him? What had he done to deserve it? He finally understood the feelings of the rape victims he had treated. Why was it done? There was no helpful answer as to why. Why me? Is there any way to make it not have happened? Oh, God, if there were just a way to make it not have happened. Is there any way not to be this way? Is there any way to feel *something*, instead of hopeless and empty? Is there any real sense in going forward?

He knew he needed help promptly or he could become irrecoverable. But where? Whom could he trust who would believe him and treat the problem instead of an apparent hallucination about alien beings?

<<~>>

CHAPTER SIXTEEN

Below, after her "recovery," Xanthas had not been able to get the experience with Murph in his living room, before Jenoor and Mari showed up, out of her mind. She had made a Connection with Murph which was much more than casual. His current intense pain was transmitted to her with clear force. She felt deeply sorry for him and loved him so unconditionally that all she wanted to do was help him.

~Jenoor, the effect on Murphy Bailey of what you have done with Mari is unconscionable. How could a being of your understanding and Connection fail to foresee the result? I'm still learning many things, but *you* should know by now.~

~Why are you so concerned?~

~Because I love Murph.~

That comment brought him up short. That was the type of thing they had been working for a very long time to get Melds to spontaneously feel and say. As he thought about it, he was astounded. She certainly must have the E-gene!

Her thoughts compelled him to focus on his own peculiar behavior lately. He simply wanted to be with Mari without knowing why. He *needed* her. He needed to share his thoughts, experiences and *feelings* with her. Astonishing himself further, he suddenly realized the answer. She created in him and drew out *emotion*! It wasn't because he wanted to complete the experiments at all. He was in love with Mari! At the moments those clandestine and forbidden events occurred, he didn't give a bug's ass, as humans would say, about the experiments. He was simply lost in Mari, as she was in he. But how could he be? He didn't have the E-gene.

Then it struck him. It was instantaneously so clear. The common meld he had with humans was one of mind, not matter. It wasn't to be found in matter at all, but in consciousness, in his soul. And since that was the case, it was there all the time! Except in a highly restrictive laboratory-like setting, he and the rest of the Mantid just had not Connected with it, presumably because they had spent so much effort isolating themselves from humans and their consciousness. They had failed to simply interact with humans and let it flow. They hadn't trusted in the protective and obviously loving nature of One Mind to unfold the way for them through the Universal Connection.

In deciding *they* knew the best way, instead of "listening" for the way, they blocked it. Incredible! The tail was trying to wag the dog, as those humans said. The answer had been there all the time and was so simple – as all answers seem to be once realized. All they had ever had to do was open their consciousness to the Universal Connection, instead of limiting themselves to the Mantid consciousness, the "great" Mantid intellect, which was obviously finite and existed only for the purpose of the universe school, just as everything else seeming so solid and permanent did. He had paid no attention to the lessons he taught Mari about her, and his, true origin. The Mantid had been working on this lesson for so long, they had trapped themselves in the basic premise.

Before he could think on it further, Xanthas' thoughts interrupted, insisting on an answer concerning his behavior with Murph's wife.

~Well, Xanthas, I . . . I . . . I am in love with Mari.~

Hearing his thoughts stutter was most unusual indeed, and she seized the opportunity, ~ I want to help Murph, and you should comprehend a similar obligation. I want you to let me go to the Surface and help him as much as I can.~

Overwhelmed by the recognition of his own emotions, and assaulted by those he felt, including a great sadness for what he had caused for Murph, he consented. It would soon be time to bring Mari Below anyway in order to take the baby and place it in a development container until it could sustain independent life.

So it seemed that the timing of events might work out to mutual advantage, if there was an advantage to be had in the current situation.

<<~>>

CHAPTER SEVENTEEN

Jenoor had instructed Lenaan and Minuum to take Xanthas to the Surface and return with Mari. Then, determined not to make the same mistake again – and making a mistake had never happened to him before – he instructed them to go back to the Bailey back yard and stay in the craft, primarily out-of-phase but adjusted enough to tune to thoughts of danger from Xanthas, in which case they were to utilize any means necessary to protect her and return her Below. In the event of such an emergency, if consciousness-control was not effective, Jenoor authorized them to use Quantum Photon Weapons at their discretion. The only latitude available in connection with their discretion was that if so much as a molecule of her was harmed, they would be digging the space for the next Mantid underground city by hand. Such an authorization to use Photon Weapons was unprecedented and few in the Mantid structure were authorized to give it. The Mantid soldier-pilots were impressed by the seriousness of their task and confident they were equal to it.

Mari was relieved to leave. Her burden of guilt and sadness at seeing Murph's constant pain was sending her into episodes of despair concerning what to do. She hoped Xanthas would be able to help. She also fervently hoped that, while Below, she could find some way to deal constructively with everything that had happened and the emotions and desires she felt. They just didn't fit into the normal way of dealing with things. They sure didn't. There just *wasn't* any normal any more, at least from her perspective.

Not knowing what to do next, and in many ways not caring, Murph felt his burden lighten with the appearance of Xanthas, and for the same reasons, he did not object to Mari's leaving. Xanthas was kind, loving and caring, as was Mari, but Xanthas had never harmed him, and right now, he desperately needed someone near who had never harmed him. It was a bonus that she wanted to help him, though, unaware of her recent Superconscious experience, he could not see how she could do that.

Xanthas spoke softly, "Murph, I'm sorry about everything that has happened."

"Believe me, I am too. And I'm particularly sorry about what a jerk I was with you. You're the only one who hasn't hurt me and I'm afraid my conduct was less than sterling."

"You don't need to explain. We're Connected. I know how you feel. We are all learning. That's one of the reasons I came. We can work together to understand what it means. I know you are the therapist, but I have acquired some tools that may help you, and help me in the process. Is that all right?"

"Of course it's all right. I don't know what else to do anyway."

"Well, maybe we can start in much the same way that Jenoor explained it to Mari."

The reference made him flinch. "Okay, whatever."

"Do you remember, when Mari was telling you what happened to her, that Jenoor hypnotized her and took her back to an explanation of why she was here?"

"Yes."

"Do you believe that?"

He adjusted his glasses on his nose while he thought for a moment, "Well, even putting aside all that has happened, I'm pretty sure I do. I've had a lot of patients allude to that in one way or another. But, to tell you the truth, I've never had my own personal epiphany on the subject."

"You will. Lie down on your own couch." She smiled lovingly and he complied as she sat next to him. She removed his glasses. He loved the touch of her fingers as they brushed against his cheek. "Close your eyes and just think about relaxing your whole body." He had conducted sessions starting like this with his patients many times, but it was strange, the effect it was having on him when he was the recipient. "Start with your toes, relax your toes." He thought he had relaxed his entire body, but with the specific instruction, his toes relaxed even more and felt like they were just hanging off the end of his feet.

"Now, let that relaxation move slowly up your legs, relaxing everything as the wave of relaxation moves slowly up your legs." Her voice was so soft and soothing, and it was like there was an energy wave of relaxation surrounding his entire leg on each side, maybe extending out an inch or more, just traveling slowly up his legs, relaxing everything in its path. As it reached his knees, he felt his knee joints relax as if they came apart a little bit. The same thing happened with every part of his body as the wave moved toward his head. Everything seemed to expand and loosen with relaxation as it passed.

As it reached his head, she said softly, "Relax your jaw, let the wave completely flow around to the top of your head, relaxing your neck, your eyes, your head to the very crown and to the very core." He felt almost as if he were floating in space. Like he was not touching the couch any more. It was very pleasant.

"You feel very good, very relaxed. You can easily hear and follow my voice, and you feel very secure and safe. If your attention wanders, it will always automatically come back to my voice and what we are doing, right away and without effort."

He no longer had a sense of time and was floating pleasantly. "Now, I want you to sink deeper and deeper into the levels of consciousness, into your own consciousness, diving into the pool of your consciousness, going in deeper and back farther, without apprehension, but with wonder and joy. No matter what happens, you will be an observer, as if you are watching a movie. You will see and understand the events and emotions, but you will not experience them directly as if they are actually happening to you at the moment if they will cause you present harm or anxiety. You will not be frightened of, nor be harmed by, anything you see or experience. You will only learn in a positive way. Can you do that?"

Very slowly and softly, "Yes."

"You will be able to talk clearly to me and easily and instantaneously follow my instructions while you are doing this, no matter what happens, and all without waking up. But, you will wake up if I tell you to, no matter what is happening, particularly if I count backward from three and tell you that you are awake. After you are awake, you will continue to follow my instructions as they relate to anything that may have just occurred. Can you do that?"

He responded more quickly, "Yes." He knew he wasn't asleep. She was just using that term as a shorthand way of describing what was happening.

He was floating down and down into consciousness. The consistency of what he was floating through wasn't like water, it was more like energy or mind that had substance, holding him up and letting him gently and pleasantly go down, surrounding him, being careful not to let him drop too quickly. Each little mind bit seemed to hold onto him or his consciousness for an instant before passing him to the next one. "Down," "mind bit" and "him" were finite terms trying to describe the infinite. He could actually be floating up. It didn't matter. His consciousness was floating into, and was actually part of, infinite consciousness, infinite mind, the Universal Connection, One Mind.

"Do you understand that your consciousness existed before the experience you are having on Earth in this lifetime?"

He did. Not only had he learned it in connection with his patients' past-life regression therapy, it seemed he had always sensed it. He remembered clearly waking up in the middle of the night when he was perhaps three or four years old with the incredible revelation that he was alive! He had never forgotten it. He could see it and feel it. He was in his bunk bed at home. He had been asleep on his back and vaulted upright with the revelation. It was as if he had been someplace else for awhile and was very surprised to find himself back. He had looked around the room as if he were experiencing it for the first time, then lay back down and thought about it for a long time before he went back to sleep. He was too young to communicate it effectively to anyone, but the dialogue he had with himself and the thoughts he had then, the thoughts that had always stayed with him, were not the thoughts of a toddling boy. They were the thoughts of a mature sentient being, marveling at having returned.

Now, lying on his own couch and without knowing the details, it seemed clear to him that his childhood experience had been the natural result of events that had preceded his present lifetime. He responded in the affirmative to Xanthas' original question and waited, breathing slowly and deeply, knowing instruction would come.

"I want you to recall the times you were on Earth before your current incarnation. You will skip the events between incarnations. You are going back to your prior incarnations now and they are opening up before you. The important events that are the reason for your coming back for this Earthly lifetime are unfolding clearly. What do you see?"

Murph hesitated. Then, animated, "Hey! I'm an asshole! I'm a womanizing sonofabitch who just bullies other people around, treats my wife and everyone else like shit and generally doesn't give a damn about anyone or anything and won't help anyone for any reason, except myself of course."

He was mortified and astonished. "Wait a minute. What I'm seeing isn't just one appearance here. I've been here a number of times as a human. I pretty much started out a butthead, but each time I have actually improved a little, even though I'm still a long way from perfect.

"Last time, I wasn't too bad of a person, comparatively anyway, except I was still a womanizer and did not treat my wife well at all, being particularly unfaithful to her and not caring how she felt about it. Actually, being totally insensitive to how she felt about it. She loved me very much and it basically destroyed her.

"My God! This is it! I'm learning the other end of the stick! I deserve this! Son-of-a-bitch! It's the payback!" He was flabbergasted.

"Payback isn't the right concept, Murph. These experiences are not for retribution. They are for learning, for the full appreciation of the meaning and application of unconditional love. They seem like they are all that is going on at the time, but they are instructional tools. They are important ones and it is necessary to participate fully in this experience or it won't be as meaningful as it could be, which is why you are blanked as much as practicable before you come, but it is not reality. It is an arbitrarily created environment, a classroom environment – a 'clinical' instructional situation created by the Teachers and Guides you heard Mari speak of from her sessions with Jenoor."

"Mari also described consenting to do it. I don't remember consenting to anything. Did I consent to Mari's relationship with Jenoor?" Even though his eyes were closed, he habitually tried to push his glasses further up on his nose, not noticing they weren't there.

"Well, let's go to that point and you tell me. Free your attention and direct your consciousness to move to the events directly related to any determination concerning your present visit to Earth."

He gave himself that instruction and let go. He felt the movement of his mind in the Superconscious Dimension to the stage between his last "life" and this one. He witnessed communicating with his Guides concerning the fact that he still needed to acquire a full appreciation of how the wronged recipients felt in the situation of a breach of absolute trust and faith, even though he had been working on that and related concepts in a number of earlier "classroom" exercises.

He noted that his Guides and the others there did not appear as material beings, even though he sensed they could project themselves as such if they wanted. They just seemed to be energy or consciousnesses who radiated certain colors. He wasn't "Murph" at that point of course. He was simply his identity. They all just *knew*, naturally and without effort. The communication was one of love, assistance and development, not ruler-on-knuckles for failure to learn.

In his Superconscious classroom, he, his Guides and his classmates had mutually agreed that he needed an experience on the receiving end down in the Earth role-playing clinic to help him fully appreciate the concept he was to learn. He subsequently floated to the incarnation preview area with his Guides and reviewed several alternate possible general life situations, including his choice of parents, for his next incarnation on Earth. He was shown some of the general scenarios in each of those several alternative-life situations which would lead toward the objective of the lesson, but he was not shown exactly what would happen or to what extent the result would be successful, since nothing was planned to that extent and it was up to him to fully participate in the experience.

After thought and discussion with his Guides and classmates, he made his choice of life situation, knowing that he would be participating with others, some of whom would be from his Superconscious classmate group. The latter had also made their life-situation choices and would be there for their own developmental purposes too, not just for the sole purpose of participating in his. They would all be interacting with one another in the exercise, the ultimate intention being a positive learning result for all, and all being well aware that the exact unfoldment of the projection, and thus the result, was not intended to be predictable in advance.

Even so, the Guides, their Guides and the Teachers were highly experienced at this and knew that if he and the others made the effort, the ball should end up close to the hole, if not in it, for all participating. They blanked him with his cooperation and the next meaningful thing he remembered was waking up in bed that night years ago, astonished he was back, but not knowing, or connecting it to, anything else.

Xanthas returned Murph to his Earthly material consciousness, instructing him to remember all that had transpired. The entire experience was helpful to her as well.

"Well, we can both see now that you didn't specifically consent to Mari's relationship with Jenoor any more than you consented to the interaction with me, nor, based on what I've recently learned, I with you. But, you did consent to come here for a specific purpose which appears in progress toward its goal and, right now, you are in the middle of it with both feet, as you humans would say. Do you think you are learning anything?"

"Xanthas, not only am I learning, but it certainly doesn't seem like a classroom exercise to me, even taking into account what I just realized and experienced. What I'm feeling and experiencing right now seems real, *is real* so far as I'm concerned at this moment. To tell you the truth, knowing and feeling all this right now, I'm ripped in two ways. I'd kind of like to junk the learning experience until another trip here and just spend the rest of this one with you."

Lying there looking up at her, looking into those loving violet eyes radiating from that luminous porcelain skin, she was the most beautiful, irresistible and desirable physical being he had ever seen. Totally open and vulnerable at this moment, he just wanted to reach up and pull her to him, kiss those beautiful soft lips covering those flawless heavenly white teeth, and get lost in whatever came next.

Recognizing his thoughts and being pulled in the same direction, but trying to concentrate on her purpose and new-found role as therapist, "Well, as I understand it, if you don't get it right this time, you just have to keep coming back and back until you do or you won't 'graduate.' If you and I make love, from what you just told me, you'll be repeating exactly some of the behavior that got you here in the first place. I've only recently been shown a little of why I'm here, but I instinctively knew before that the ultimate object of it all is to learn to think right and do right. There is nothing wrong with loving each other. We should. How we should is the issue. Clearly that's part of the exercise for you, and I can't believe it's not part of it for me also."

"Shit, you're so damn logical!"

"I am not necessarily enjoying it."

"Well, can I just give you an unconditionally loving kiss then?"

She looked into his eyes. "Okay, but just be sure it is."

They did and, as their unconditional love continued, neither seemed sure of anything, particularly Murph.

<<~>>

CHAPTER EIGHTEEN

Concurrently Below, it was time for the removal of Mari's baby to the development container. Jenoor had done this many times before, but now he was concerned about making a mistake and harming either Mari or the baby, their baby. Each new emotion he experienced affected him a great deal and seemed often to trigger another emotion. He was continually boggled at everything that was going on inside of himself. The flood gates had been opened.

Being worried, he was nervous. He'd *never* been worried or nervous. They were strange emotions for Jenoor. They made him concerned he would fail at something that he had done so many times, he should be able to do it without thinking. In addition to the anesthesiologist, Marntaiin, he felt the need of precautionary assistance and asked Largeen to stand by during the procedure. Largeen thought it peculiar, but always complied with Jenoor's requests.

Inside the medical facility, the Mantid assistants were preparing Mari for the procedure. Although she had an entirely different understanding of the Mantid now than she had before, she could not help becoming apprehensive at being naked again on a table with a lot of medical equipment in a sterile room. At least this time, in addition to her red hair being tucked under one of those terrible looking hospital caps, she had a small hospital gown covering her from the waist up and a sheet covering the remainder of her private parts, and she was aware she had consented to be here.

She had been educating Jenoor, and thus indirectly the Mantid, concerning certain customs and niceties in the treatment of humans. Additionally, most Mantid were beginning to become aware of their emotions as a result of Jenoor's educational communications to their collective consciousness. Lettee, one of the assistants, sensed Mari's apprehension and was able to empathize, transmitting reassurances to Mari.

~Do not be frightened. We have done this many, many times and everything is entirely safe~

~If that's the case, why does Jenoor have another doctor standing by?~

With a certain comprehension of her new-found emotions, Lettee replied, ~Because he has very strong feelings for you that I do not fully understand, and he too is afraid, afraid he will make a mistake and harm either you or the fetus. It is very peculiar. Jenoor does not make mistakes and has never been afraid, only careful.~

Mari smiled within. Of course, she knew exactly the problem, but did not want anyone other than Jenoor taking the baby. She laughed inside. The first Mantid medical conflict of interest.

She made all that clear to Jenoor while her feet were placed in the stirrups. Lettee gently placed an oxygen mask on her face and the procedure was started. Jenoor explained that while surgical procedures on Mantid were customarily done with cooperative thought-control anesthetization, that had proved more difficult with humans, particularly under these types of stresses, so they were going to give her a spinal block until the baby was out and then a light anesthetic mixed with oxygen through the mask to help her rest. Jenoor was worried, but his years of skill and experience, coupled with his true inner belief that it was only possible that he perform properly in this situation, resulted in his worry having no effect.

The physician anesthesiologist, Marntaiin, administered the anesthetic and the fetus was skillfully and quickly removed, as always, and placed in the development container which had been prepared with the appropriate pumps, circulation tubes and fluids to duplicate the mother's womb. The procedure was done through the birth canal so there was nothing to stitch and only a minor amount of intrauterine cauterization, which was almost entirely undetectable. The group busied itself with insuring that the fetus was correctly positioned in the container and that its umbilical cord was properly coupled with the tubing.

They finished that task and turned to remove Mari to a recovery facility. She was as gray as they. Jenoor had never moved so fast as that leap to the table, but he clearly sensed on the way that her Earth consciousness had stopped. He thought the feelings inside of him would tear him apart. His mind was literally screaming instructions to the assistants, but all knew she was dead.

Jenoor did not know he was able to cry until then. He looked pleadingly at Largeen, and accusatorily at Marntaiin, not believing for even a moment that he, Jenoor, could have made an error. He had not. Marntaiin, experiencing as many new emotions as most other Mantid since Jenoor's communications on the subject, and not knowing how to deal with them effectively, had been concerned that he would make a professional error in front of Jenoor and Largeen, being particularly aware that this human was extremely important to Jenoor.

Not recognizing what was well-known to many Surface people since the popular twentieth-century Surface book, *Psycho-Cybernetics*, by the famous surgeon, Maxwell Maltz, pointed out that the human mind functioned like a computer which could be programmed for a positive or negative goal, Marntaiin's worry focused on what he was trying to avoid, instead of what he was trying to accomplish, unconsciously programming himself for the negative result and automatically getting him there. That human principle obviously worked in the Mantid mind too. Focusing on his fear, he had caused the wrong valves to move for the wrong amounts of time and, in accord with medical laws, Mari's consciousness passed from the Material Dimension. His recollection of his actions Connected with Jenoor and no further explanation was necessary.

They all stood, with identical feelings of helplessness in their midsections, staring alternately at Jenoor with tears streaming down his face and at Mari's lifeless form.

Jenoor's mind screamed at them, ~Leave me! *Leave* me!~ They all scurried from the room, in shock from the events and in shock from the overwhelming emotion pouring from Jenoor, and themselves.

Jenoor reached down and touched Mari's face. Sobs that came out like guttural chirps now racked his body. He had seen this in Surface movie transmissions and realized that intellectual studies and descriptions of emotions were meaningless when compared to experiencing them, but he did *not* want to find out this way. He fell to his knees with his eyes closed and his hands instinctively coming to a praying position, Connecting to his ancestral Universal Connection with the Teachers.

~Oh, great Teachers, why? *Why*?! She *cannot* have finished her learning cycle here! Take me! Leave her! *I* must have learned what I came for in this cycle by the way I feel right now, so take *me* but not her. There *must* be a random error in the training!~

Even knowing everything he knew, he could not separate himself from the apparent reality of the physical universe, though he new intellectually that it was a temporal, artificial training medium and not the timeless reality of existence. On his knees in supplication he pleaded to the Teachers, ~Oh, Teachers, please tell me there has been a random error in these events that will not efficiently produce the intended result. In so short a time, Mari cannot have accomplished what she came here to learn, but I have learned emotion. You know I have by what I am feeling now. I have learned to feel it well, because as you can tell, I am so upset and distressed now that I cannot plan and control what will happen. I can only plead with you. Take me. I have learned my lesson for this cycle. There are many things left for Mari to do.~

<~~Like what? She has unselfishly allowed the first physical conception between your species in order to help the Mantid. Isn't that what she came for? In fact, now that you make the point, you do have emotion and we should probably bring you back also.~~>

~No, no! That is fine for me. Absolutely fine. But leave her. She has a little Meld baby to rear after it reaches full term. What is learned will be of great assistance to the Mantid. She has *not* completed what she came for. She also has to accomplish certain interactions with her husband who most likely will not be able to complete what he came for without them.~ Jenoor had never had to think under emotional stress before. He was now wringing his hands with those long annealed fingers, grasping at everything he could think of, and he was so upset that he was not able to evaluate whether it truly made any sense. He only knew that he desperately wanted her to "live." It didn't matter what happened to him.

With love in their thoughts, the Teachers gently responded, <~~None of you has yet achieved what you are to accomplish in this cycle. The passing back was indeed a random error resulting, from time to time as you are aware, from the way the training platform is structured. But, all of you are learning and we are pleased. Mari is presently in the Superconscious Dimension with us and we have communicated with her. Her Superconsciousness will again be focused on her Earthly form. She feels she has more to learn and accomplish during this cycle and wants to return also.~~>

~Oh, my God! Thank you! Thank you!~

<~~Jenoor, that is the second time in the course of events that you have used the term 'God.' Your incarnation also continues.~~>

On his knees weeping, Mari's legs swung over the side of the table and stopped in front of Jenoor's eyes. ~Jenoor, what are you doing?~

To the extent his mouth was able to break into a smile, it did. ~I .

. . I think it is what humans would call praying.~

He couldn't move at first, he just knelt there and looked at her. She was *restored*! She was alive! He sprung up and clasped her close to him, rocking back and forth, loving, feeling their physical vibration intertwine, their energy passing one to the other. He probably would not have let go except that Mari, though appreciative of and enjoying the embrace, asked him if her baby were all right, why he was acting that way, why he was crying and where everyone else had gone.

~Our baby is fine, it is developing wonderfully and is right over there. Everyone is gone because there was nothing else for them to do.~ He was holding onto her tightly, as one would assist an infirm person, while she walked over to the development container.

She was slightly disoriented and even more perplexed by his tears, ~Jenoor, you don't need to hold onto me like that. I feel just fine, I think. Why were you crying and praying?~

Not being certain how much he should reveal, ~Well, to tell you the truth, events were a little 'touch and go' there for awhile as you might say, and I was frightened.~

~You know, I had the oddest dream while I was under. I floated through this long tunnel into a very bright white light. It seemed like I was leaving this world for some reason, like maybe I died, and there were these very kind and loving beings in the light. I couldn't see them clearly, but we were talking. They seemed a little surprised that I was there and asked me if I wanted to go back. It was very nice there, but I told them that I felt like I should go back, like I didn't think I ever should have left, that I felt I had a lot of things left to do, not the least of which was to raise my baby. They were wonderful and said they loved me and would help me go back. Then I woke up . . . Actually, I'm not so sure it was just a dream. The more I think about it, it was like it really happened.~

Looking at the tears still wet on Jenoor's face, she asked him ~Who were you praying to?~

~Well, *you* might say they are guardian angels. I might say they are interior designers.~

She thought she saw those magnificent eyes twinkling.

A high-level Mantid governmental aide suddenly burst into Jenoor's thoughts with an urgent message. She was certain she saw his face change expression, and then he communicated, ~I am sorry Mari,

I am being asked to go to a government meeting that I have been advised is urgent. I must excuse myself immediately.~

Mari told him not to concern himself with her since Mantid governmental affairs were certainly more important than the nature of being. Even in his rush, Jenoor caught the humor.

CHAPTER NINETEEN

At the same time as Mari's near death experience, Xanthas had become so occupied with Murph during, and after, the "unconditionally loving kiss" that she did not catch an inkling of what was happening Below with Jenoor and Mari. Normally, with thought energy that strong being generated, and her Connection, she would have. But, she was generating some pretty strong thought energy of her own, particularly as Murph was literally tearing open her light blouse again, which wasn't easy this time since it was made from Mantid material. They fell from the couch to the floor as if their lips were super-glued together.

Once he had the blouse off, he began kissing her everywhere he could on that amazing, soft, white skin above her waist, and with her last ounce of effort and common sense, she got one hand on his shoulder and a handful of his thick brown hair in the other and propelled his upper torso away from hers, keeping him at arm's length. It was a supreme effort because his shirt had come off somehow too – she preferred to think she had not torn it off – and, having never felt someone else's wildly hot, moist, incredibly desirous skin, lips and tongue on top of her like that, she was surprised – when she thought about it later – that she was thinking clearly enough to do that. Actually she wasn't so sure she was thinking then, it was literally as if someone else had provided the thoughts for her to do it.

"Murph! We can't do this! You can't waste this trip! Neither can I!" It didn't seem to her like she was really talking, but the words came out. What she actually wanted at that moment had nothing to do with those words.

Murph had been so absorbed and driven, he wasn't sure for a few seconds what had happened. He had the stunned and confused look of someone who had just been startled awake from a deep sleep. Xanthas took advantage of it and shoved him the rest of the way off, slipping from under him and back up to the couch, sitting there staring at him, half pleading, half lecturing. All he could do was stare at her breasts from his position on the floor. Those magnificent, perfect, snow white . . . He shut his eyes, trying to get a grip. He opened them again only to see them rising and falling with her rapid breathing. He shut his eyes again.

"If we are going to get ahold of ourselves, you've got to put your top back on." She looked down at herself. Unembarrassed, she slipped it back on, buttoning the buttons that were still intact. That helped; however, the vision was indelibly burned into Murph's mind and he thought he could see right through the material.

In a certain way though, he was glad she had helped – forced – him to stop. He looked at Xanthas, "Okay, where do we go from here?"

"I don't know. Let's wait until Jenoor and Mari return."

CHAPTER TWENTY

When Jenoor and Mari did return, they burst through the wall, advising Murph and Xanthas that they needed to discuss a very serious subject vital to all of their futures. The sudden appearance scared more than a little something out of Murph. Xanthas knew they were about to appear, but didn't get a chance to say anything.

Even though he understood infinitely more about himself now and why he was here, he had been feeling so sorry for himself that he had not spent the necessary time to collect his thoughts and formulate a plan or direction concerning what to do *vis a vis* the interaction of all their future relationships, but he had the feeling that the discussion of that subject was imminent. He steeled himself. He wasn't certain, but Jenoor seemed a little more pale than the last time he had seen him, probably nervous about this too.

"Murph, Xanthas, the Harvesters are coming!!" Jenoor's tone was extremely urgent.

"What the fuck are you talking about?!" Irritated, Murph couldn't help himself. He'd been surprised at their sudden explosion through the wall, had instantaneously braced himself to tackle a deeply emotional subject he wished he didn't have to discuss, and Jenoor says something that makes absolutely no sense whatsoever. There was little reason for him to like Jenoor anyway.

Mari, having had Jenoor's concerns explained to her, was taken aback by Murph's response, but then realized it was a normal reaction – the perpetrator has returned and is talking nonsense.

She turned her now blue eyes directly at him, "Murph, I know you have a lot of other things on your mind and I don't want to minimize them, but in many ways they pale in comparison to what Jenoor is about to explain to you and Xanthas."

She seemed serious enough. Maybe that's why Jenoor looked pale. "Okay, go for it." Murph's manner had become somewhat aggravated, disgusted, bored, recalcitrant and resignedly martyr-like. He was trying not to act like a child, but seemed to be regressing to that reaction because he didn't know what else to do, wasn't ready for any confrontation at all, and this nonsensical confusion was upsetting. Some psychologist, he thought.

"Our Mantid government has an organization you would analogize to your United Continents Intelligence Agency, only ours not only monitors Surface civilizations, it also monitors, as best it can, thoughts coming from elsewhere in the physical universe. We are very interested in the latter activity because we are certain that our species was placed here by beings, tall blonde aliens, whom we call the Harvesters."

Still irritated, but somewhat relieved that he had misread the subject matter of the conversation, Murph began to take a little interest. Many of his patients, in addition to describing the "Greys," had described tall, blonde, Scandinavian-like beings, often referring to them as the "Blondes."

"We call them the Harvesters because we are also certain from our early recollections that they put us here in order to grow and develop us and then at the right point, come to take us back – that is, to *Harvest* us. We have picked up that they are returning, we think within the next year or two. We don't know what form the Harvest will take or exactly what they want with the Mantid; however, based on our early recollections – the only ones we have about them are passed down from eons ago and these are the first thoughts we have picked up from them since then – we are positive it is not good. We are certain they intend to take us away from Earth to use us for their own purposes and not ours. We are also certain it will be horrible for us."

"So, why should we care if they come to take their bugs back?" Still being childish, Murph was consciously arrogant, cavalier and insensitive.

Offering a piece of advice commonly given to the petulant siblings in her family, Mari interjected, "Murph, stop being so 'baby.' "

Jenoor ignored his attitude and trained his huge eyes directly on Murph – who did not look directly back, "Because after the very early human-like species they put here did not adapt and develop well, they later put what you call '*Homo sapiens*' here, and our intelligence tells us they are coming to Harvest *you* too. We deduce they will either use you for food, slaves or both. You are of no other use to them because they are much more advanced than your species, and always have been. We presume they block all of their thoughts from us and we are surprised these slipped through. But then again, we have our best at the task."

He had Murph's attention, but Murph was still not in a mood to be polite or diplomatic. In fact, he was getting just a little more pissed off all the time, and Mari's admonishment that he was acting "baby" didn't help his disposition. "So now that all four of us know this, the deal is that the psychologist, his wife, the alien that's been screwing her, and her beautiful half sister who lives in a bubble beneath the Earth, band together to save the world from being devoured by hungry Nordics from outer space, just like in every 1950's science fiction movie I've ever seen! Shit!"

Jenoor continued earnestly, "I know how this seems to you, and I clearly sense your emotional state in connection with recent events, but acknowledge that just a short time ago, you felt that my existence was easily preposterous. *Believe me, these beings exist*! This problem *absolutely* transcends any personal problems among us. Let's try to solve this problem, and then you can break my stick-like body into tiny toothpicks like you want to do right now."

Because of his recent experiences, and even though that sounded like a speech from a movie in which Murph mused he might be stuck, he knew he had no plausible reason to doubt what Jenoor said about the Harvesters. He probably ought to get off his high horse, stop being infantile and start seriously thinking about it.

"All right. What do you think I can do? What do you think *we* can do? The movies are just that, you know, movies. What are the four of us supposed to do, collectively think them off?" This time, the sarcasm was intended in order to make the point.

Jenoor, sensing Murph's change of attitude, "Of course not, but you are an excellent psychologist. You know Surface beings well and how they act and react. There must be a logical approach here."

Continuing to put aside his personal pique and after some thought while he pushed his glasses higher on his nose, "Well, in a lot of those movies, the army comes and does battle with the alien invaders, reacting impromptu when they show up because that's the only time the government actually believes something like that is happening or might happen. Since there is no superhero here to fly in and save us, the best shot we have is to rely on our own government to do the job. We have to get the serious and undivided attention of world leaders, starting with our own President. Have the Mantid ever had contact with the U.C. or U.S. government or any other country's government?"

"No. We've avoided it."

Mari felt an increasing hopelessness.

Murph's eyes were twinkling now, "Well, we'll have to start by the four of us walking through a wall into the President's office and convincing him."

They all knew he was serious and that there was no other viable plan, but Jenoor interrupted, "Why would it be necessary for Mari and Xanthas to possibly jeopardize themselves by attending such an event?"

"Have them take a sample of Xanthas' DNA, they'll crap. Mari should come just because that's the way it always works in the movies. We're a team, right?" This time he did look directly into Jenoor's eyes, and smiled.

CHAPTER TWENTY ONE

The President of the United States of America, Bronson Freeman, was alone in the Oval Office at about 10:30 in the evening when he heard Murph's voice behind his desk chair. Murph spoke quietly, "Mr. President, please do not be alarmed, we mean you no harm in any way."

The President was a big savvy ranching man in his fifties from the Southwest. Dressed in his usual cowboy shirt with rolled-up long sleeves, blue jeans and cowboy boots, it was his standard uniform, even for important diplomatic meetings. He'd often stated, "Hell, if those other folks can wear turbans and robes because that's the way they like to dress, I can wear my cowboy hat and boots. It's the same deal." If he didn't have it on, his big white hat was never far away. Many wouldn't recognize him in public without it. If a state occasion was particularly important, he would add a bolo tie to his outfit, fastened with the United States Seal made from silver, gold, turquoise and other natural materials by Native American artisans. The big belt buckle on his blue jeans was constantly rotated among the many given him by his constituents.

Startled, he spun around in his chair and saw Murph, Mari and the most beautiful young woman he had ever laid eyes upon. Out of an abundance of caution he should have pushed the panic button within reach of his fingers curled under the arm of the chair, but he felt no danger from the bizarre appearance of these three – and he just wanted to look at the young woman a little longer before he decided what to do. She was astonishing!

When Murph saw what was happening, "She's unbelievable, isn't she?"

"Amazing!" Continuing to stare at Xanthas, the President didn't bother to look at Murph when he spoke.

"Mr. President, I know this is highly unusual, but we came here to tell you a story that is as unbelievable and amazing as what you are seeing. A story that is important not only to the security of the Country, but to the security of the world. We came here in this way because it is the only way you will believe it."

In his down-to-earth way, "How in the *hell* did you get in here?!"

"That's part of what we are going to show you, sir. You will find it more astonishing than Xanthas." Murph turned his head toward her.

"Ain't possible." The President caught himself. Controlling his Southwestern drawl, "Look, son, I don't feel you mean me any harm, but I ought to push this button by my finger and get someone in here before I listen to your story, just in case."

He was wondering who's head he was going to roll for allowing this to happen. He could not conceive how it happened unless they just came through the wall. At the same time, he wanted to hear what the beautiful young woman's voice sounded like. Never one to miss an opportunity, maybe he could sign her to a personal service contract. With her, he could control the entertainment industry when he got out of office. After all, one of the reasons he got here was because he never missed seeing the possibilities in what he called "those fortuitous, but golden, moments."

Referring to the security button, Murph said, "Go ahead, sir."

The President's finger would not push the button, no matter how hard he tried. He looked quizzically at Murph and began to realize there was something more going on here than was evident from the face of it. He couldn't make the rest of his body do what he wanted it to either, like jump up and run out of the room to kick ass on the security.

So that their visit would seem even less threatening, Mari stepped forward, making her sky-blue eyes appear as innocent and straight-forward as possible. Parroting Jenoor's thought prompting, she said, "Mr. President, I want to reiterate that we mean no harm whatsoever. In fact after we are done, I'm certain you will agree that we should have done exactly what we are doing. We are aware you cannot move and we do that only to demonstrate the believability of what we are going to tell you. Please do not become anxious. If we wanted to harm you, we could have done so already. There is no circumstance whatsoever under which we will harm you, but you would not listen to us or believe us if we did not do this. If you don't believe what we are going to tell and show you after we are finished, we will leave very quietly in the same manner as we came, and you can call the guards in here and see if they believe *you*."

Not arriving at his high office because he was stupid, the President realized that they had him. If they could get in here like that, they could leave like that, and he would look like a fool, or an hallucinatory cuckoo, trying to explain it to someone.

"Okay, I'm not dumb, and besides, it doesn't appear that I have any choice."

He smiled that great cowboy smile that was one of the things responsible for getting him elected in the first place. It was fortunate for the electors that he also did an excellent job as President, being sincerely dedicated to the task, even though not a perfect human being. He felt no apprehension whatsoever. He was a risk-taker and had always loved the challenge of riding those broncs on his ranch. For a second, out of the corner of his eye, he thought he saw someone standing over by the curtains, but when he looked directly, no one was there.

Murph resumed, "Sir, you might want to put on your cowboy hat, because what I'm going to tell you is going to be quite a ride."

"Well, sit down. Would it be too much to ask to have this beautiful young lady tell me?" He'd get to hear her voice no matter what came of this.

"Tell you what, I'll have her jump in at the right moments."

"Good enough, pardner. I'm all ears." Looking at Xanthas, he contemplated adding that he was all eyes too, but he had learned the hard way that, when in doubt, political correctness was the byword, not to mention learning to avoid a boorish tack-room, macho-man come-on.

Murph, Mari and Xanthas spent some time narrating and explaining to the President all the salient points concerning the history of the Mantid, what had transpired and what they knew about the Harvesters. In the process, the President asked many questions, but never for proof, and by the time they finished, they all felt comfortable with one another, to the point Murph was calling the President by his nickname, Bronc. Not once did the President make any attempt to push the button – and he'd gotten to hear Xanthas speak. He had to concentrate very hard on what she was saying as opposed to just watching and listening to her say it.

"I don't know how you got in here, and I don't know why I couldn't push that button. I think it had something to do with the way this young lady looks, but you are movie people, right? You know, this would make a good script for a science fiction movie if this young lady starred in it. How about us making a deal to where I get the financing for this movie, and in return for that, I sign her to a personal service contract?"

Realizing why the President had not asked for any proof, "Bronc, I'm about to show you something that's going to make you have an accident in those jeans."

"Son, you already have."

"No, I mean it. If I can prove to you in the next few minutes that we aren't movie people and what I've been saying is absolutely true, will you get as serious as we are?"

"Son, if you *can* prove it's true, I *will* have that accident in my pants and get *real* serious, but if you can't, I get the personal service contract."

His twinkling and mischievous eyes hardened into little beads, and it was clear to all why he was able to control the Congress with an iron hand when it was necessary, and why he had also been elected United Continents Coordinator, the most powerful political position on Earth.

"Deal."

"Okay, shoot, pardner."

Jenoor materialized, standing next to Murph's chair. Murph was not sure if the President was having a stroke. He seemed paralyzed as his eyes widened and his normally ruddy face flushed even more. He trembled slightly as he stared at Jenoor. Finally, he moved, looking down at himself. "Well, I sure peed in 'em. Damn! And I thought I was a good poker player!" He looked back up. Jenoor was still there and no one was smiling. The dread that this preposterous story might be true started creeping over Bronc. He looked at them, hoping Jenoor was a movie prop, "Make him talk."

"Mr. President, they have explained to you that my name is Jenoor, and it is not necessary for them to make me do anything. Would you like to touch me?" Jenoor stepped around the desk.

"Oooo shit! What'll happen if I do?"

"You will have touched me."

"You must be a lawyer." Never one to fail to see the humor in almost any situation, no matter how grave, Bronc couldn't resist and chuckled at himself. Murph caught it and smiled. Xanthas looked puzzled, and Mari didn't care. She was more than a little put off that the President of the United States *was* a human being, and acted like it. The President looked at Xanthas, "Honey, the joke is that he answered only the question I asked him, was absolutely correct and the information is useless." Xanthas was still puzzled, but had learned enough about Surface interaction to nod as if she understood and smile politely. Bronc loved that smile and he beamed even more with self satisfaction at producing it.

He reached out and touched Jenoor. "Man, I thought all you guys were supposed to be little, tough and leathery, but you are soft as a baby's butt! Sonofabitch!"

Incredulous, he looked at them all again, "Okay, how are you doing this. Just tell me. I won't get mad. This has got to be the greatest gimmick known to mankind and I want a piece of the action. In fact, you just promised me a piece of the action. Everyone has to be in on this or the guards and everyone else in this building would have checked on me by now, just as a matter of routine."

Then it hit him. "My God! It's after midnight. It's my birthday! GeeWillieWhackers! You got me! You really got me!" He roared at the joke. Even Jenoor could not control him enough mentally to get him to stop laughing. "God, I love a good joke!" He roared again. Tears were coming out of his eyes. He was slapping the desk and stamping his boots up and down so hard on the floor that Murph was sure he'd end up with shin splints.

Bronc knew only his wife could have arranged this with the security. She got him every year with something on his birthday. Bronc yelled toward the door, hardly able to speak he was laughing so hard, "Okay, okay, Mo, you got me. Come on in!"

Nothing happened. No one else was smiling. "Okay, Maureen, come on in!" Nothing. The dread crept back again that this was no joke. Murph, with a feeling of déjà vu, made a mental note that thinking it is a joke must be an archetypal reaction when grappling with the reality of other beings.

Jenoor said quietly, "Mr. President, no one is coming, they won't. They are not paralyzed, they are doing everything they are supposed to be doing, and they think they have been checking on you. Mr. President, please stand up, move to the window and look out."

"You won't laugh because I peed my jeans?"

"Mr. President, I assure you this is as far removed from a laughing matter as any situation could possibly be."

As Bronc stood up, Mari tried not to, but her red hair started jiggling first and then she started giggling almost uncontrollably. "Damn, little lady, this is really embarrassing and you said you wouldn't laugh."

"No, they said it," Mari smilingly responded. He grumbled under his breath that she must be a lawyer too as he went over to the window and pulled the drapes slightly aside.

Jenoor was at his side. "Mr. President, the spacecraft we told you about is out there on the lawn."

"I sure as hell don't see anything." He was starting to get irritated. They should have ended the joke back when he was laughing.

"You will." Jenoor gave a thought command and the craft materialized just long enough for Bronc to see it.

"How'd you do that? I've seen those guys on DV make planes and elephants appear and disappear. That don't prove nothin'." The joke was getting old and he was trying not to get genuinely pissed because he didn't want to ruin it for Mo when she finally popped through the door.

"Mr. President, will you please take my hand, Xanthas will take your other hand and the others will form a string on her side." He had Bronc for the moment, knowing he would not pass on an opportunity to come into contact with Xanthas. "Mr. President, please look at your watch and note the time." Bronc saw those little electrical dots and the next thing he knew they were inside the spacecraft looking back at the White House. "Mr. President, will you please note the time." Only seconds had passed.

Bronc was so shocked that he forgot what it felt like to touch Xanthas. "Gol dang!" Mari could scarcely believe that a person who actually talked like an old Western movie had gotten elected and was running the country, but she believed he was about to accept that he had a bronc by the tail for real. He agreed to go with them, if Jenoor would go back for his cowboy hat.

By the time they reached Manticon, Bronc was in awe. He took off his hat and ran his hand through his closely trimmed salt-and-pepper hair, "What do you call this place?"

"Home," Jenoor replied.

<<~>>

$\int$itting in the briefing area of Manticon's governmental head-quarters after his extensive tour of the "bubble," it was clear Bronc had become a firm believer in the Mantid, their abilities and that the Harvesters were definitely coming, with bad intentions. Bronc had been hard to convince until Jenoor assisted Bronc with very brief, incomplete glimpses of Bronc's own Superconscious existence and his purpose on his present trip to Earth. It didn't provide him with much metaphysical information, but it put the President over the top on his journey toward becoming extremely serious about a United Continents global defense against the Harvesters.

Not quite idly, the President offered, "You know, we have not been completely in the dark about the existence of you extraterrestrials."

Jenoor gently reminded him that the Mantid were not extraterrestrials, that the Mantid ancestors inhabited the Earth for a long time prior to the placement of *Homo sapiens* on it by the Harvesters, and that the Earth's future meant as much to those Below as to those on the Surface.

Focusing on the concept of being "planted" by the Harvesters, the President good-naturedly mused, "You know, I guess that's right. Just like that Steven Wright fella, or was it that little George Carlin guy, on the old DV reruns, I always wondered why if the humans we have on the Surface – he noted silently that he was even beginning to talk the jargon – evolved from apes and monkeys, why we still have apes and monkeys!" He was clearly pleased with his purloined humorous obser-vation and looked around for smiles.

There wasn't a high probability of seeing one on Jenoor, although he had secretly been practicing since he discovered he was capable of experiencing humor, and with a little effort, he could get the corners of his little mouth to turn up slightly. Now the trick was to let it happen spontaneously, just as soon as he learned to react to humor without analyzing it first. In any event, Jenoor politely refrained from a recita-tion of all the scientific and genetic possibilities of evolution, while thinking to himself that regardless of his reasoning, the President had come to the right conclusion.

Bronc returned to his original extraterrestrial theme, "While our government has tried to cover it over through the years for fear that the folks would totally panic and run amuck with fear – Big Daddy knows best y'know – our government has had contact with . . . ," he paused and looked at Jenoor and the other Mantid officials in the room, ". . . other beings, starting with the twentieth-century crash at Roswell, but none of them lived long enough to give us any information, or at least they wouldn't."

Jenoor turned slightly toward the other Mantid in the room and, almost imperceptibly, they all seemed to bow their heads. The President continued, "Over the years since then, we've tried to reverse engineer what craft, or the parts of them, we recovered from time to time. It's a tough process because the technology, even from the early Roswell craft, is so far in advance of ours, but we have been able to do some things with radar cloaking, electronic components and such. People sure did get curious about that old Area 51. We, actually my predecessors, finally had to move the critical parts of the operation to Utah. And the news media, particularly those gol darned DV people, they sure have been an aggravation. And we can't figure out how some of those fiction DV writer fellas, and book writin' fellas, have been able to get so close to the mark sometimes, starting way back with TV. We're jus' pos'tive we didn't, and we don't, have any leaks."

It gave Jenoor a chance to do his little smile and practice opening with a conversationally clever line, "Not from your end, Mr. President. Mr. Bailey has advised that we be completely candid with you, and now seems the right time. In connection with the point you just raised, the fiction writers, DV and otherwise, have been able to get 'close to the mark' because we put the basic thoughts for their stories into their heads, transmitting them subliminally you might say, 'starting way back with TV.' Further, referring to our desire to voluntarily meld our two species, which we have explained to you in some detail, it has been part of our program to prepare Surface minds to more readily accept the basic reality that other beings exist. We have been reasonably successful, even though your fiction writers often embellish the facts in a way we had not intended. Conversely, many writings and reports are not fiction and report actual events, or at least the Surface participants' perception of those events. In either case, the results generally have moved in the direction we intended as a first step. That is, a significant portion the Surface population either believes the idea of other beings is true, or believes in the *possibility* that it is true.

"Separately from that, it has been our long-standing policy not to interfere either in the governments or the hostilities of Surface inhabitants due to our sincere belief it would not be consistent with the primary purpose for Surface inhabitant incarnation. However, starting sometime after the middle of your twentieth century we became very concerned that the testing, proliferation and hostile use of nuclear weapons would jeopardize not only our underground cities, but the continued existence of all sentient beings on the planet, if not all life on the planet. As a result, but with an absolute minimum of interference, we undertook a long-range program to accomplish several things with which you are now very familiar. Initially, we subliminally transmitted to your scientists minds the ideas for just enough continued advance in military technology to keep you ahead of other countries and organizations that did not practice values of peace and human rights, or more accurately *being* rights. That was coupled with complimentary subliminal transmissions to key individuals in governments that had nuclear weapons capability, all toward the end that nuclear weapons would be controlled or eliminated."

"That was damn good thinkin', Doctor."

Jenoor continued, his politeness exceeded only by his professorial tendencies, "Thank you, Mr. President. Later as part of our program, because of the increased intensity of terrorist activity at the beginning of this century, we subliminally transmitted to the appropriate scientists' minds the ideas for the technological development of what you have named the Tesla Field. We believed the creation of an economical and universally available source both of electric power and of unblockable electronic communication was extremely important since most of the oppressions and hostile dissatisfactions on the Surface were interwoven with the lack of the basic necessities and comforts of life and the lack of universally available uncensored information. As you know, the Tesla Field remedies that by continuously and affordably providing wireless electric power and unblockable wireless communication, everywhere on Earth, which in turn has been the wellspring for global democracy and economic development."

Bronc was looking at him intently. His informational antennae were definitely up.

"Concurrently, and as you can readily appreciate, Mr. President, it was clearly vital to the accomplishment of those goals that they be drawn together under one umbrella as you might say. Thus, the rapid development of the United Continents government was imperative to bring about and insure the stability and continuance of those goals on a worldwide basis. It was, of course, our most extensive and intensive subliminal-idea transmission effort and, fortunately for all, it was successful and resulted in a unanimous vote for creation of the United Continents by every recognized government on the Surface."

More than casually, Bronc asked, "Doctor, do you folks have any more subliminal plans for us?"

"In line with the current parameters of our non-interference policy, any further thoughts you receive from us will not be subliminal. So the answer is absolutely not, even though the unintended consequence of economic prosperity and governmental stability throughout the Surface continents has been the obsessive acquisition of material goods and services at any price, including an environmental price. But acting on that is within *your* control, as is dealing with acts of terrorism or abuse of human rights that, from time to time, may still be undertaken by those whose motivation ignores the rights of others. In that respect the United Continents made a wise decision to continue a strong military protective force after the bulk of terrorist and abusive human rights activity was eliminated. However, other than the paramount threat of the Harvesters, my judgment is that the greatest problem facing the Surface population today is the rampant neglect of spiritual development. I am certain Xanthas would agree."

"Well, Doctor, you probably don't know it, but I read my family Bible most every day and I do believe those Harvesters could benefit by doing the same thing."

"I am certain they could, Mr. President. By the way, that craft at Roswell was ours. It was one of the very few accidents we have had."

Bronc didn't miss the opportunity, "It sure would be nice if you folks would show us your propulsion systems. We can't catch you, not t'mention those dang Foo Fighters – you say they are just probes? – man, from what I've been told, those things can move around!"

"Mr. President, we are going to give you and the rest of the United Continents governments as much help as we can, in as short a time as possible. If we are to stand any chance against the Harvesters, it must be a united effort. They are obviously much, much further advanced than we are."

"Yep, they must be. Sightings come from everywhere in the United Continents security system, but we can never come close ta catchin' one of 'em, er even communicatin' with 'em, or you for that matter. In fact, since none of 'em will talk to us and we can't catch 'em, except for the few that have crashed over the years, we don't know who's flying 'em in any given instance. Our remote viewin' boys have pretty much fallen down on us there. But we've had lotsa reports 'bout those big Blonde folks. They must be scouts fer what's comin' – Wahoo!"

When Bronc felt at ease with the company, he started lapsing into his native cowboy speech even more than usual. His campaign and public relations advisors had worked mightily to keep just the right mix so it would be cute and boyish, but not make people think it was a sign of lack of education or intelligence. Whatever his manner of speech, and Bronc could sound as stiff as they come if he wanted, he had two degrees at the top of his class from two prestigious American universities. He was gutsy, fun-loving and many other things, but he was not stupid.

It instantly occurred to the Mantid in the room that not even their best thought communicators had picked up the Harvester scouts' visits the President had referred to, yet *now* the Mantid were picking up thoughts from the Harvesters that they were coming *en masse*. The only thing they could ascribe it to was a sadistic arrogance, cutting off the Mantid from their thoughts until now, then feeding them only a few transmissions, yet allowing the Surface people to have seen them from time to time. It was logical. Any being that would "plant" other beings for later Harvesting must be that way.

Not wanting to fuel apprehension beyond its current state, Jenoor replied to Bronc's comments concerning the U.C.'s inability to communicate with the Mantid or the Blondes, "Mr. President, from what you have seen, the U.C.P.F. communications men should have just come together and tried sending thought, instead of all the multi-linguistic electronic transmission machinations in which they engaged."

"Well, that sounds good, Doctor, but how do we rely on the message back from you if you do send us your thoughts. I know damn well you haven't tried, at least with the government, because you said so. But anyway, how do we know its *you* thinking and how do we know we got the message right or the receiver isn't a nut? I wouldn't act on it, even if that Lofler said he got the message."

Murph knew it, he just knew it. Pralit Lofler, that sonofabitch. He probably hadn't even told his wife, mother or grandmother he had done work with the government. He tried not to jump up and down with glee at the President's slip of the tongue. Jenoor put it together immediately, filling in the cracks from the President and Murph's minds. He had to train these Surface beings how to block their thoughts, or the Harvesters would get them if they chose to focus on them.

"Mr. President, you have a point, but you should have more confidence in developing remote viewing and related programs in an organized way, instead of quietly using gentlemen like Mr. Lofler from time to time. There are some very gifted Surface beings whom you should give more of an opportunity."

"Well, most of us like to get reelected, or at least have some credibility. The 'giggle factor' about using 'psychics' is a very powerful deterrent to the government's organized use of those alternative means when gathering intelligence. Notwithstanding whatever their private beliefs may be, much of the voting public laughs about it, and those who develop government budgets and worry about government credibility are scared to death of that laughter. We tried an organized program last century and had to abandon it because of that. Besides, how do you tell the good psychics from the bad psychics?"

Jenoor had another opportunity to practice his little smile, "You didn't have any trouble recognizing Pralit Lofler's talent did you?"

"Sheeeit! Point taken, doctor."

<<~>>

CHAPTER TWENTY THREE

Some months later on the Surface, Jenoor and a number of other Mantid scientists, government officials and military personnel were seated in the Pentagon's huge main "War Room" along with their governmental, scientific and military counterparts from the United Continents.

Assembling these representatives from the various countries of the United Continents had not been easy, even though their governmental fund of knowledge exceeded that of their respective constituent populations. While some governments had been more candid with public information than others, they all knew and concealed much more than they released. Stretching back into the previous century, their governments had experienced, and continued to experience, many incidents similar to those occurring in the United States with UFO's and other reported alien encounters. However, their collective fund of secret knowledge was very limited compared to what they would learn.

At first, they agreed only to the seemingly endless conference calls, then interminable staff meetings, then meetings of every conceivable kind, external and internal, a government could think of. But one by one, the various leaders of the United Continents governments had become believers. After witnessing the same incredible demonstrations and participating in the same astounding tours as Bronc had, their belief was compelled.

As a result, without exception, all of the United Continents' leaders had come to believe the Mantid and to perceive the Harvesters as the final, terminal, nihilistic threat to current world civilization. They were firmly committed to expend every resource at their disposal to neutralize that threat. All were convinced there would be no compromise and no second chance.

On the main screen in the Pentagon War Room, there was a three-dimensional virtual model of a typical Mantid spacecraft configuration, emphasizing the propulsion system. The system was round, and looked like three balls, one inside the other, freely suspended and not touching. There was also a moving cutaway model of the same thing in the middle of the room. The outer ball was stationary in the craft and acted as a container/shield for the other two, each of which was capable of spinning independently, the third spinning inside the second.

The outer ball-shield also had what seemed to be some kind of an exhaust system to the outside of the craft.

A Mantid scientist with a slight pot belly and a deeper voice than his Mantid peers, who reminded Murph of a purebred Siamese cat Mari once owned, spoke. "Ladies and gentlemen, my name is Raama – his communication training was working – this is effectively a multidirectional, gravity/antigravity, machine. The two inner balls can simultaneously spin independently of one another in any direction at any speed and in a variable non-concentric manner, although they never touch. Depending on the spin combination, and the possible combinations are infinite, the craft can travel in any direction at any speed, almost up to the speed of light. We believe that at some point we can achieve speeds faster than light, but our macro technology is not yet that advanced."

United Continents scientist Diobelys Belcastro, "Do the Harvesters have technology in advance of yours?"

"Without knowing for certain, we presume they do. As they have come here, left and returned in order to 'plant' and then physically check on the progress of their work a number of times so far as we know, and taking into account the probable distances they would most likely have to travel in the known universe, light speed would not be fast enough to be consistent. They either know how to travel faster than that, 'warp speed' according to your dictionary and classic digivision reruns you know as '*Star Trek*,' or they have mastered travel utilizing the effect of your amazing Dr. Einstein's gravity wells, that is, through 'worm holes' in space as your scientists have called it."

Raama knew he was talking to non-scientist military and government officials as well as scientists and was trying to make the discussion as palatable as possible for the former, having prepared extensive scientific materials he would distribute to the latter.

United Continents Protective Forces General Vice-Commander Thulane Larsen, anxious to get back to the possible, "How does your propulsion system work?"

"The outer ball-shield is made of Maanturium. The two rotating inner balls are hollow and made of Praaydonium. Those are two elements you have not yet discovered. There are samples for you in your packets. They are not radioactive. The balls are analogous to two independently rotating gyroscopes, but with propulsion capabilities. As I stated before, the second ball is freely suspended and freely rotating inside the ball-shield, and the third ball is, likewise, freely suspended and freely rotating inside the second. The visual effect is as if a metal ball were vertically suspended in air between two opposite magnetic poles. You have all seen that effect in school science classes and 'executive' toys.

"While each of the two inner balls appear to have solid shells, it is all relative, and if a particle or other item is small enough, it can pass freely through them, just as billions of neutrinos are passing through each of us as I speak. A certain kind of energy in the so-called vacuum of the universe flows through, and is processed by the balls."

The non-scientists were still with him and became more attentive as he intimated that the vacuum was not truly a vacuum.

"Surface scientists have begun to discover what we have known for some time, that the vacuum, any vacuum, is not the absence of 'filling.' A vacuum is actually filled with what might generically be called, simply, energy. Stated another way, there is actually no such thing as a vacuum as many of you have traditionally thought of it. Space is 'filled' with all kinds of things that are not solid, or even extant to you. While many of them have not been ascertainable by you, there are those of you who have discovered some of them or theorized they exist, but only relatively recently. We have discovered many more properties of the vacuum and, more importantly, how to utilize some of them, even though we are not completely certain how all of them work."

The United Continents Protective Forces General Commander, Payson "Det" Menard, was impatiently rolling his cigar from one side of his mouth to the other. No one could ever remember seeing him without it. It looked like it had been smoked halfway down, stubbed out, then chewed on continuously, starting long, long ago. No one had ever seen him smoke it down or seen him with a new one. It was as if he had been born with that particular indestructible cigar in his mouth. At five-feet ten-inches and two-hundred-thirty hard pounds, referring to him as "sturdily-built" would be a gross understatement.

Menard's father, a military man and military history fanatic, gave him his nickname while Det was playing fullback on his high school football team, called the "Sharks." Their helmets had large pointed teeth painted on the sides, giving the impression of a shark's open mouth. He was immensely stronger than most of his opponents and when he carried the ball, he seemed to devour everything in his path. His father remarked to the coach that Payson looked like a "death eating tractor." It was printed in the local paper and Det's teammates perpetuated the name because they thought it accurately described his approach to life. It was ultimately shortened to "Det" because he made it clear to them, in his personal style, that he did not want to be called "Tractor," "Track" or "Tor." Prior to that his father had once referred to him as "Tank," making reference to the famous World War II tank commander, General George Patton, with whom he believed his son shared certain personality traits, but Payson wouldn't stand for it. Why he let them call him "Det," no one knows and he never explained. It would be fair to say that Det has always been a very private person.

In all events, his direct, humorless, intense black eyes make it clear Det is a prototypical "no-nonsense" commander, always driving toward getting the task-at-hand done in the simplest, most direct way, wanting immediate answers and immediate results. Det growled, "Well, how the hell does it work!?"

"Forgive me General, I want to give as complete and non-technical an explanation as possible, yet at the same time be certain that I have connected all the dots." Raama mentally patted himself on the back for weaving Surface colloquialisms into the conversation.

The highly respected world scientist Tua Rahman offered quietly, "Please do continue, Mr. Raama, I'm sure we can all be patient in such a grave matter."

Det knew he was slightly impolite, but he was thoroughly military, always knew his mission and had no other purpose in life. In fact, he never thought of his own life. He never married, had no children, definitely was not gay and didn't care if you were, so long as you successfully completed the mission, whatever it may be. He was donning his fighting persona, which was no different from his normal persona, to remind others why they were in the room.

Det bit into his cigar while Raama continued, "The vacuum, that is, space everywhere, is filled with an inexhaustible source and supply of energies of different kinds which have different qualities, some of which you are familiar with. You have discovered and measured physical vibrational energies such as radiation of various types in the vacuum, including electromagnetic energy, and you have also investigated some things you understand even less, dark matter and anti-matter. We know you have been working for some time on zero-point energy fields, concentrating on a coupling between electromagnetic and gravitational forces, trying to create an antigravity with no combustible or fissionable byproducts – but there is something else there."

Everyone except Det was fascinated. He was so damn curious how those ships could jump around like that, he couldn't stand waiting. Det was a new phenomenon to many in the room, but those who were acquainted with him knew that his cigar could draw its own attention, to the point that what he said or the way he felt would subliminally invade their minds. That cigar would ramble all over his mouth. One second it would be clenched on one side between his back teeth, the next it would be rolling to the other side while he was talking, yet every word would be clear. Then it would be suspended in mid-air, seemingly for several seconds, then clamped by his front teeth, then glued to his tongue, then protruding from his pursed lips, and so on ad infinitum. His colleagues always got his message, but could never take their eyes off that cigar. They also wondered if he had a mother, and in the unlikely event he did, whether the poor woman breast fed him as an infant.

Raama ignored his impatient cigar and continued, "So far as we know, that 'something else' in the vacuum is the basic fabric of being from which everything else emanates. Perhaps the best thing to call it is the *substance* of cosmic Superconsciousness – 'mindstuff.' "

Det drew back his lips in exasperation, revealing his two square front teeth. They had a slight gap and were stained from constant manipulation of that cigar. The military dentists had long wanted to properly whiten them, which they could do in less than an hour with a special solution and a certain laser light, but he wouldn't sit still long enough to complete the treatment. If he didn't absolutely need it to stay alive, he couldn't waste the time. Presently, he was making a monumental effort not to bellow, "Get – to – the – point!"

Despite the General's continued chafing, Raama knew his explanation was important, and continued, "Some of your Surface scientists have conducted fairly primitive experiments with shielded charged plates close to one another that modify electromagnetic energy in the vacuum in various ways depending on the proximity of the plates to each another, the Casimir Effect I believe you call it. Also, in very small ways in the laboratory, you have begun to control the emission, or its lack, of energy particles, specifically photons, and the timing of those events. You can slow them down or speed them up. Your theory is that when control of those photon emissions is fully developed, along with other concomitant technologies, you will be able to manipulate the forces of gravity and inertia in relation to a space vehicle and its travel, direction and speed."

Det had earned an excellent university education, then enlisted in the military and "came up through the ranks," following the example and advice of his father. The mix of education, practical and tactical experience, and success, earned loyalty from those whom he commanded and the sheer force of his traditional military personality propelled him to his present position as the top military commander in the world, except, of course, for Bronc who was the Commander in Chief. No person under his authority ever questioned his orders or would not go to the last measure for him.

His vocation was his avocation. He'd never studied the works of Joseph Campbell, but was following his "bliss." When he went home at night, his relaxation was thinking about how to better accomplish the mission of the moment. Right now it was finding out how those damn spacecraft worked and Det had started muttering "C'mon, c'mon, c'mon," under his breath.

Raama calmly stated, "We can do that."

In a first meeting, the uninformed might mistake Det's personal quirks and colorful military personality for a carefully nurtured caricature of a commanding general. An observer might mistakenly assume that what he had done during his career was to blindly follow orders and "charge the hill" against terrorists and pockets of human rights violators, fortuitously surviving and luckier still to be rewarded with all those stars on his collar, in order for the United Continents public relations agency to present the world with a "bona fide," easily identifiable military hero.

That would be wrong on all counts. The world at large scarcely knew him. Concentrating only on his duties, he shunned publicity and didn't give a damn about it. He had skillfully and quickly accomplished the military engagements he commanded with intelligent and clever planning, coupled with the best military technology available at the time. Det was the "genuine article" and few outside government circles knew it. Those who did couldn't get access to him. He was more than satisfied to let others have the credit and the resulting attention; thus, contact with the public through the media was left either to his aides or high government officials. He had never written a book and had never been interviewed beyond thirty-second sound bites. Almost no one in the general public had heard of him before Bronc had appointed him as United Continents Protective Forces General Commander, and Det was content to let the media concentrate on Bronc whose colorful character kept them busy indeed.

Det had also been the valedictorian of his university class, and he understood in every necessary detail exactly what Raama was talking about. When Raama stated, "We can do that," he finally had General Payson "Det" Menard's full attention.

Raama continued, "We have found a way to control the forces of gravity and inertia in relation to a space vehicle and its travel, direction and speed, but not by the means Surface scientists have been examining. While our rotating balls are somewhat analogous to the Casimir charged plates, the energy we affect in the vacuum is not electromagnetic or atomic, it is that 'mindstuff' of consciousness, the non-physical energy of One Mind according to Mantid perception.

"The speed and direction of the rotation of the second and third balls in relation to each other, coupled with the non-concentric center position of each of them in relation to one another and to the stationary shielding ball, generate the direction of the craft through the variations effected in the mindstuff energy passing through them, which in turn, for any given direction, create an antigravity behind which pushes, and a positive gravity in front which pulls. As the balls can change their center location, rotation and speed almost instantaneously, the changes in direction and power of these forces are instantaneous for all practical purposes, resulting in what you view as phenomenal changes in direction and speed."

Det got it. "Sonofabitch!" The cigar almost flew out of his mouth.

Tiozzo Cardona, a tall South American general with small eyes and a thin moustache, who always seemed to gratuitously and enthusiastically take the negative of any position, understood what Raama was saying, but was sure he smelled a rat. In his generally annoying and accusatory tone that annulled any pleasant quality to his Latin accent, "Wait just a minute, just a damn minute! If you folks don't want to tell us the secret of your propulsion system, fine. Just give us the engines to put in the ships and teach us how to fly them. If that was yours at Roswell, we can't reverse engineer it anyway. But don't treat us like a bunch of idiots and tell us that because there is *thought*, you can fly!"

Raama turned to him full face. His huge dark eyes seemed to paralyze Cardona as well as the rest of the room. Instead of speaking, he transmitted, ~ But *everything* starts with a thought, General. ~

The impact of that thought transmission was finally broken by a growling Det, "Tiozzo, get your head out of your butt! These people – he wasn't sure that was the right word – can do things we have only dreamed of, and some we couldn't even imagine before they showed themselves. Did you see the way they flew those ships! He put his *hand* – he guessed it was a hand – on a little ball and apparently just *thought*! That fuckin' thing turned every way but loose. Judging from the way *you* think, if you put your hand on that ball, assuming we *ever* got off the ground, we'd be back in it face first in a pissosecond!"

Raama responded before Tiozzo could retaliate, "You are correct in principle, General Menard. We are not certain we could train Surface personnel to fly the craft, certainly not quickly enough if we could, although we could start trying in our flight simulators. However, I believe it will be necessary for a Mantid pilot to fly every craft for the mission of which we speak, if we wish those craft to perform at the maximum of which they are capable."

At a loss for an intelligent response, Cardona barked, "So you think we are too dumb to do it?"

Tua Rahman, ever the diplomat, gently interjected, "No, our 'Surface' minds have just developed in a *different* way from the Mantid. As you can see, most of the Mantid cannot cock a 'six-shooter' using only one hand, but that does not mean they are impaired any more than we. All of us have simply developed with different attributes and skills."

In the back of the room Bronc roared, visualizing grasshoppers in cowboy hats with no thumbs trying to cock six-shooters in time for the shootout at the O.K. Corral. Cardona grumped around for a minute, then decided not to spar with Rahman further and possibly incur the President's wrath. Jenoor caught the humor in Bronc's thought picture and his little mouth smiled, but then again, he had thumbs.

"Forgive me, Mr. Raama," said U.C. Scientist Calzaghe Vanderpool, "but our science tells us that the faster an object goes, the more its mass increases, so that at speeds approaching that of light, it would be almost infinitely heavy and nearly impossible to propel without an infinite source of power equal to the task. You know, the irresistible force and the immovable object, not to mention going *faster* than the speed of light. Is your 'mindstuff' that powerful?"

Tiozzo Cardona smirked. Now the gray bastard would be smoked out.

"We don't know . . ."

"Yah!" Tiozzo yelled as he impulsively jumped up and pointed his finger at Raama.

". . . how powerful it is, because we can alter mass. We haven't tried to maximize the process because it has not been necessary for our purposes to date. However, we do think the power of consciousness is infinite."

Every scientist in the room visibly reacted to the words "alter mass." Cardona's pointed finger wilted as he fell back in his chair and the scientists began asking questions, all at once.

Raama winced at the pain of their collective voices and quickly raised his hand to silence them, answering in a way he believed the non-scientists would also understand, "Recall our explanation of Phase Shifting. When we travel through air or space at extremely high rates of speed, for all practical purposes, we enter into a partial Phase Shift which alters our mass in relation to the phase of the medium through which we are traveling. Thus, the mass of the craft and its contents automatically become very light, that is, much less dense, in correlation to the craft's increase in speed through that medium. As a result, since the craft has almost no *relative* mass, it can travel at very fast speeds free of the infinitely dense mass and its attendant power requirements Dr. Vanderpool suggests."

Reading the next question in their thoughts concerning the effects on the craft's occupants, human or Mantid, of extremely sudden changes in a craft's direction or acceleration, "Recognizing that the occupants are always in the same phase as the craft, we have needed to counteract sudden acceleration or changes in direction which would otherwise imbed an occupant into its interior walls due to the laws of inertia.

"In our early flight development, we would either Particulate or further Phase Shift until the change in speed or direction was stabilized, but we have since developed miniature propulsion systems in a matrix in the walls surrounding the inside of the craft, which briefly create an opposite 'mindstuff' energy field to the direction of a sudden motion of the craft, but only affecting its interior and not its movement from a perspective outside the craft. Analogize it to your noise canceling devices that meet the noise with an opposite noise, the noise source isn't gone, but it no longer has an effect on the user of the device."

General Thulane Larsen spoke as politely as his training and temperament would allow, "Mr. Raama, Doctor Jenoor, I don't mean to be rude, but we'd better get rolling with this project or those Blonde bastards will be roasting us for dinner."

<<~>>

CHAPTER TWENTY FOUR

In the following months, the Earth's leaders pulled together like never in its known history. The world's peoples took note of the unity and urgency of their leaders' single-minded apprehension and determination. However, that was more than counterbalanced by world population skepticism concerning the validity of the digistick and digivision programs showing what the world leaders claimed they had experienced first-hand.

The professional suspicion-mongers among the talk show hosts and the media ferreted out every conceivable enkindling person with an agitating opinion, engendering an initial and substantial flurry of inflammatory panic in the never-ending quest for ratings, viewers, listeners and readers, doing their best to convince the world's populace that the United Continents' leaders were engaged in a collective conspiracy to enslave the world's occupants for their benefit, and above all, people should not drink the water, and if possible not breathe the air, because that's how the U.C. leaders would ultimately control their minds.

Legitimate journalists were also having a lot of trouble with it, simply because the U.C. story was so bizarre. Those journalists were genuinely concerned that some unknown, collective and evil force had somehow acquired control of the worlds' best governing minds.

As a consequence of the communications activity generated by the Harvester threat and the "coming out" of the Mantid, the distributor of all Earth's energy needs, the Tesla Field which surrounded the Earth up to a distance of approximately one-hundred miles, was so active that some swore they could see a reddish-blue glow covering the night sky. Though the technology was markedly different, the field was named after Nikola Tesla, the early pioneer of its basic concept, and had replaced satellites, land lines and cables, and for all practical purposes the "airwaves," for the transmission of digivision, radio, personal and commercial communication devices, and the world wide web, the latter now called the "Tessie." A popular address suffix was ".ola" in Nikola Tesla's honor. Interestingly, because there never seemed to be any need to refer to it differently, "radio" had been the popular name retained for non-visual audio transmissions, and "broadcast" was still the most popular word for most kinds of audio and video communications.

Jenoor, Murph and Bronc, planning certain elements of the preparation for this materfamilias of all wars, decided to defuse the explosive media coverage by inviting five hundred of the continents' most influential Paranoia Purveyors, as Bronc disaffectionately called them, "PP's" for short, including all of the influential paranormal talk show hosts, plus five hundred of the most respected legitimate journalists from all media, to visit Manticon by means of the largest Mantid space vehicle, which would pick them up in Arizona at Phoenix International Raceway, landing at the infield with the passengers embarking from the stands.

The PP's immediately jumped on the invitation as a genocidal plot to eliminate the cream of the watchdogs of the world by duping them into gathering at one place in the desert for a "pogrom." Bronc, no novice in the art of spin, didn't bother to look that word up and immediately countered with a campaign designed to make the PP's look like paper tigers if they didn't have the guts to risk all for their point. Each PP, with single-minded purpose, quickly evaluated their collective alternatives. If they were blown to smithereens as most of them believed would happen, the ruse would be over and the world saved because of their courage and martyrdom. If they succeeded in calling the U.C.'s bluff without being annihilated and Manticon didn't exist, the courage of their convictions would be demonstrated, they could shout from the mountaintops that they were correct and knew it all the time, *and* their ratings would go up. Conversely, if the U.C. leaders *were* telling the truth, the PP's would have an experience generally unknown to most of the modern world, *and* their ratings would go up. As Bronc knew full well, ratings were more important to them than human life, even their own, and they bit.

The Phoenix metropolitan area was a catastrophonium of activity on the scheduled weekend. Its residents could do only the same as the rest of the world – watch on digivision. The U.C. security was so tight and so controlling that Mamadou Bennajem, U.C. Chief of Security, declared that a nematode would be unable to pass without proper authorization. The metropolitan area had been blocked off at every conceivable entry point starting three weeks prior to the event, now popularly known as the "Visitation."

Only authorized U.C. ground vehicles and U.C. aircraft were allowed to enter the restricted area or to pass into its airspace. No private vehicles nor any other aircraft were allowed to exit or enter. Mantid, paired with U.C. security personnel, patrolled the streets twenty-four hours a day examining the mindwaves, so to speak, for thoughts planning to interfere with the Visitation. As a result, the security forces took several groups totally by surprise, confiscating their terrorist materiel and incarcerating them. In the holding cells, the unsuccessful disrupters immediately started an eradication campaign against their members suspected of being the leak.

The Mantid also succeeded in directing the minds of all the curious private pilots who were contemplating ignoring all the clear government directives and warnings, so that they turned and flew away from the restricted airspace. That is all but one. Concerned about his ratings, a PP who failed to make the Visitation 1000 list tried to enter the restricted airspace in a small civilian jet aircraft, broadcasting as he did so, and unfortunately for him, he was not readily amenable to mind control or verbal direction. Consistent with his orders and as a last resort, the pilot of a Mantid security spacecraft leveled a blast from one of its Photon Weapons at him.

Raama briefed several U.C. officials concerning the incident and the nature of the weapon, "The photon 'modules' shot from a Photon Weapon are comprised of top quarks 'stuck' onto the streaming photons by manipulation and amalgamation of strong-force gluons. They enter the molecular structure of the target through, and by occupying, the 'empty space' between the atoms of each molecule. Then, they rapidly expand to several times their original size, similar to a burst of light from a light bulb in the center of a dark room, only each photon/quark module is an individual lightburst.

"They vaporize whatever they have entered, in this case the pilot and his aircraft, a molecule at a time, but simultaneously – without sound, other than the sound molecules make when they violently tear apart due to a technology based on a combination of electromagnetics and nuclear physics. But, it is not a fiery nuclear explosion with which the Surface is familiar." Raama analogized it for Tua Rahman as what happens to a drop of water in a microwave just as it bursts into steam, or perhaps a potato just as it explodes with that dull "whump."

Clinging tenaciously to their government conspiracy theory, and with great outrage, the PP's described the elimination of one of their own as being heartlessly blown out of the sky by U.C. Marine stratofighters stationed at the base in Yuma. The small Mantid patrol spacecraft seen flying around were dismissed by the PP's as unveiled technology of the U.C., probably developed at bases like the historically infamous former Area 51. Those on the streets who saw Mantid in ground-based patrol vehicles with the U.C. security forces strained hard to determine if it were a clever fake, having been conditioned by the PP's to think it probably was.

Everyone waited for Visitation Day to find the answers for certain.

It arrived. The PP talk show hosts were broadcasting with their portable communicators as they sat in the raceway stands awaiting the arrival of whatever was coming, most had their portable digicorders, digicameras and their equipment bags hanging from their necks and shoulders. Digivision media from all over the world who were not invited to go on the craft were either in the stands or ringed the perimeter of the raceway. There could have been twenty times as many, but the U.C. limited their numbers to five thousand non-traveling media. Bronc, Jenoor, Det, and other U.C. officials were in the pressbox – the name a popular remnant from outdated terminology.

The reigning king of paranormal Paranoia Purveyors began his broadcast, "Ladies and gentlemen, this is Eastman Foster of KUFO Radio. My fellow digivision, radio, print and Tessie media journalists and my fellow talk show hosts have been sitting in these stands for slightly over an hour now, having passed through the most extensive and incredible security check that certainly I've ever been through. We started at 4:30 a.m. this morning and it included a strip search, magnetic imaging and also magnoscopic imaging of our bodies and all our possessions, fingerprints, voiceprints, retina imaging and other extensive identification and credential checks by the U.C. Security Forces.

"The Greys just looked at us, almost as if they were listening for something. I'm told they can read our thoughts with no problem if they direct their attention to us. That is probably what they were doing. I still can't make up my mind if they are real or just clever Hollywood fakes. I hate to call the doctors who have examined them untruthful, but I think they are most likely liars. It's the greatest job Hollywood has ever done. Hollywood is very clever. I'll be amazed if any real proof materializes today. Of course, these could be the last few minutes you may be hearing my voice. I was one of the first to smell a rat and I still believe we will all be annihilated today, but by our own governments, not by aliens."

Actually he thought it less and less likely they intended to kill them all, because of the strict security measures. He didn't think they would go to all that trouble if they were going to blow them up, unless they simply wanted to be certain of whom they killed. Then again, maybe the U.C. gave them all a lethal radiation dose disguised as magnoscopy, so they would all go away and die slowly like rats in their holes without such dramatic attention called to their deaths. By the time anyone concluded an investigation, the United Continents' conspiracy-coup would be firmly in control.

He opted for the approach he believed would produce the most immediate boost to his image and ratings, just in case they were telling the truth. Starting again in his abrasive, whiney voice, "Well, if they do kill us today, however they do it, I'm willing to give my life so that you may know the truth. If they don't do it, you can count on first-person journalism from me." The technicians in the KUFO Tessie truck looked at each other and fought the desire to hurl the contents of their stomachs onto their equipment.

Almost all of the other PP's were rattling on in much the same fashion when, precisely at 10:00 a.m., a gruff authoritative voice came over the public address system. "Ladies and gentlemen, this is United Continents Protective Forces Commanding General Payson Menard. Please direct your attention to the stationary black dot you see in the sky almost straight over your heads and slightly to the west." His words were clear, though the cigar never left his mouth.

The crowd strained and it took a few moments for everyone to locate the dot. All the stationary perimeter digivision news digicameras and digicorders trained on it. It was so far away and so small that Eastman Foster didn't even bother to get his portable digicamera out of his pack. He figured it would be a waste of time anyway. As Foster droned on about the meaningless and almost indistinguishable dot, it became clear that it was not just dropping like a stone from a great height, but accelerating directly at them at great speed. In fact, it was becoming dramatically larger at incredible speed. So much so that it scared Foster in the same proportion.

"My God! It . . . it's coming directly at us. This is how they are going to kill us! It's going to crash directly on us!" His voice was terror stricken as it became clear the craft was approximately the size of a triangular football stadium, hurtling directly toward them with a deep beating sound growing exponentially louder as it prepared to terminate their present life experience with a monumental and instantaneous splatter. It seemed silly, but the last thing that went through his mind was empathy with the fly under a swatter in the last terrible moment of its life.

Reflexively and in unison, the crowd threw their hands over their heads to protect themselves from the inevitable impact and launched a collective death scream. The tremendous craft instantaneously stopped about one hundred feet over the Phoenix International Raceway infield. Everyone with a microphone had fallen silent from fear and shock. The perimeter digicameras were still running and locked on the craft, but their operators were on the ground in the "duck and cover" position. Many present, male and female, had soiled their clothing. More than a few of the spectators had lost consciousness. All of the conscious were ecstatic to be alive, exceeded only by their incredulity at the monstrous black triangular craft, hovering silently over their heads now, only a few yards away.

Det clamped down on his cigar. He had intended a dramatic entrance display with his last-minute decision for the dive, but he hadn't anticipated this effect. If he'd had that Bailey fellow here instead of off working with that Lofler guy and some of the grasshoppers trying to come up with some kind of a psychological profile of the Harvesters, Bailey probably could have given him some clue as to the possible extent of the crowd's reaction.

Sitting in the pressbox, he didn't want to turn and look at his Commander in Chief, but he did. Bronc shoved his big white Stetson back on his head and broke into a big grin, "Ya know if this wasn't so goddamned pathetic, it would be hysterical. But, hell, these people are sure starting to *believe* now!" His smile got wider. He turned to Jenoor. "Doctor, do you have any of those jump suit things in your craft? I think a lot of these people are going to need to change clothes."

Jenoor did not comprehend any humor in the event. He could feel what all in the crowd were thinking and feeling, and felt sorry for them. He noted the rapid development of his emotion and empathy. Apparently once unleashed, it expanded like an inflating balloon. "We have enough for those going on the Visitation, Mr. President. They were to be a surprise gift from us. Now, of course, they will be a necessity resulting from the surprise."

Eastman Foster was stammering into his microphone now, trying not to cry with relief that he was not dead. The reality of an uncontrollable fear of death in him was almost overwhelming as he tried to describe the scene before him, and he quickly became blubberingly incoherent. The fanatic paranoids in his listening audience sensed immediately that their hero had feet of clay. However, many in his audience who were not paranoid fanatics, but actual Experiencers of visitation/abduction events, knew his terror.

It took about an hour and a half for security and medical personnel to restore the crowd to a reasonable level of collective functionality, removing to medical facilities those who were unable to continue. Det's voice came over the P.A. system with no apology whatsoever. He wanted true believers after the day was done. "Ladies and gentlemen. This is Commanding General Menard again. Will you please either look through your field glasses, at your personal digicommunicators or at the large digivision monitors that have been erected for your convenience. Most of you know the United Continents Coordinator, President Bronson 'Bronc' Freeman, either personally or very well by sight. So you will understand the level of our sincerity and concern about our purpose here today, the President will come into the stands so that you can be assured it is he. We are doing this because the President will be the first in line to enter the craft you see above you. Please speak with him only to the extent necessary to convince yourselves that this is the President. Do not attempt to interview him. For those not boarding the craft, there will be a media conference later this evening after the Visitation is concluded and the Mantid craft returns to this facility."

Bronc's election to United Continents Coordinator by the United Continents Council had made him the most powerful figure on Earth, not only politically, but literally. The last thing anyone expected was the leader of the world to be present. It began to dawn on those in attendance that if they had been killed, he would have been too. They realized the primary reason for the intense security, and at least the legitimate broadcast journalists articulated it to their audiences. The crowd was buzzing as he entered the stands. There was no mistaking Bronc and his hat. For those not close enough to see him clearly, his face and voice were picked up by the roving digicamera and was broadcast to those present as well as viewers around the world.

A sense of relief enveloped the assemblage, as well as a sense of their own humanity – it was a warm Arizona day, but at least the Visitation 1000 had been assured fresh clothing aboard the craft for those in need. As the regrouping concluded, those authorized to board began to form a line out of the stands behind the President.

They waited for the craft to come lower, or a set of stairs or an escalator or elevator to come out of it. But nothing happened and the President and several U.C. Generals continued to walk toward and under the craft. Just like in the science fiction movies, a bluish beam came from the bottom of the craft. The President walked right into it and was gone. The crowd gasped and the line stopped. Then the President's voice came from the craft, urging the crowd to continue into the beam and join him.

The Paranoia Purveyors and the legitimate journalists were jabbering away into their microphones, with their portable digicorders and digicams humming away. Those at the front of the line, feeling they had survived what was probably going to be their only death scare of the day, simply decided "What the hell" and filed into the blue beam. The feeling went down the line like the ripple in a snake as, one by one, they disappeared into the dimensional blue shaft.

The huge craft shot away as fast as it had come and the world watching the Visitation was starting to believe.

<<~>>

CHAPTER TWENTY FIVE

After those of the media in need of a change of clothing had done so, all marveled at the maneuverability demonstrations of the large craft. They were flabbergasted at the way its walls became transparent so they could see out. Only about eight hundred of them had come through the initial appearance of the space vehicle at the raceway in stable enough condition to board it. They were invited to either file past the main control room or watch the piloting of the craft on the wall monitors. They couldn't believe what they saw. No dials or gauges in front of the pilots, just a smooth metal-appearing 'egg' on top of a stick-like base between the pilot's and copilot's chairs. At least one of them kept his (her, its?) "hand" on it during any maneuver. Their digi-corders and digicameras hummed away electronically. They were allowed to photograph or record anything or any activity on the craft.

They wanted to see the "engine room." Raama led the delegation to the propulsion deck. All eight hundred fit easily into one end. Raama explained that they saw several hundred round geometrically-arranged bubbles in the deck because, instead of one huge propulsion engine for a craft of that size, there were two hundred thirty smaller engines, which improved stability and operational reliability. They all nodded knowingly.

They were given the same model demonstration and explanation as had been given the scientists at the Pentagon, along with the accom-panying scientific materials for those who wanted them. Raama invit-ed them to put their ears to the deck to see if they could detect any sounds coming from the engines. Some believed they could; others were not certain. Finally one asked why some of the ships seemed to make so much noise and different kinds of noises at different times, at least based on the experience at the raceway, the previous U.C. DV programs and as reported by her viewers who said they were Experiencers.

Raama answered, "While in several of our earlier models, some of which are still in use, the engines did, and still do, make noise under certain circumstances, the functioning of the later model engines does not make noise. There is no meaningful friction, and no combustion, that would produce noise. However, those Mantid in the Manticon defense forces who developed our craft thought it would make sense psychologically, as a defensive weapon, if the craft were capable of making many different noises, and light shows, depending on the situation and the effect desired, primarily to confuse or frighten the enemy if there ever did happen to be an enemy. There never has been one except the Harvesters, whom we have never had the opportunity to encounter.

"As that has been the case, its primary use in recent years has been to confuse and mislead those who have sighted us on non-military flights. There have also been times when our 'jet jockeys,' as you would call them, simply got carried away – not a usual Mantid trait, but it happens."

"Well, what about the instances of radiation, either measured on the ground, or, for example, those two poor ladies who suffered radiation poisoning."

"There have been times when we introduced measurable radiation onto the ground or other surfaces in small quantities, either for the same purpose as the noise and lights, or as an experiment to see your reaction, but the harmful radiation as in the instance of the two women you refer to – was not us and never has been."

Immediately, the crowd sank into thoughtfully stunned silence as the implication of his comment penetrated. At that moment, there was a dreadful collective shift in focus from being there just for "proof" or to get a story for increased ratings. For almost all of them, it converted to an instantaneous and overriding purpose to bring the public to the realization that the Harvester threat could be the last threat that the world would ever have to worry about, if the world did not win.

While almost all of the PP's got it, the exclusions from that group included Eastman Foster. But of course, quite a few of the paranormal broadcasters did not need a wider focus to the larger view because many of their listeners had been telling them similar things for years, and a number of the PP's had genuinely believed them and believed their accounts true and important. Those broadcasters were right on many counts and had always felt the "Paranoia Purveyor" label unfair as applied to them just because they were interested in something unusual. And, as a result of the present Visitation so far, many of the "highly respected journalists" were being forced to grudgingly reevaluate their opinions of those PP's. Based on the evidence, they had to.

As the craft traveled to different points on the globe, primarily for demonstration of its capabilities and public relations purposes, many of the world's media "science editors" from digivision, Tessie, radio and print, gathered in the craft's auditorium to ask questions of Raama and other Mantid scientists. Initially, the questions continued to revolve around the propulsion system, Particulation, Phase Shifting, Mantid history and culture, the Harvesters and the notion that abductees or Experiencers had actually consented to their experiences when a lot of them certainly didn't seem to feel that way.

Regarding the latter, the contingent seemed to have great difficulty focusing on the metaphysical aspects of the nature of existence. If their scientifically oriented minds couldn't measure it, or theorize it through general or special relativity, quantum mechanics or string theory and the like, the idea of "mind as substance" was not within the parameters or their thinking. The Mantid did not force the issue, recognizing that individuals would become open to advancing their level of understanding only after the first step of acknowledging the possibility.

Most of the media had in the back of their minds that the Mantid simply did not want to reveal the source of their propulsion medium, and collectively the media did not press the issue feeling it would be a waste of time, all being familiar with governmental "slippin' 'n slidin' and peekin' 'n hidin'." From their viewpoint, that principle was most likely common to all cultures, human or not. So, they thought they would direct their efforts toward getting answers to what they perceived as more conventionally profound scientific questions related to how the universe and its inhabitants got here, such as inquiries about life, physics and the Big Bang. Their questions shot out.

"Sir, can you tell us if the Big Bang theory is accurate?"

"Why do the physical laws exist? Only infinitesimal changes would prevent physical life."

"Why is the universe amenable to living consciousness."

Being bombarded with these and other questions and knowing his time was limited, Raama replied, "I will try to answer your questions in a general way as briefly and informatively as I can because we are scheduled to arrive at Manticon soon and I do not want you to miss observing the approach." He had been working on trying to recognize emotions in himself and thought he felt a little inward smile at how they would react to diving into the ground. The craft's storeroom was almost out of jump suits.

He continued without hesitation in his usual authoritative manner, "Part of the difficulty you may have in understanding the nature of your being is that you are the created trying to understand creation. It is like Frankenstein's Monster trying to figure out how he came to exist without seeing it done, or having the background and belief system that would accept it if it were explained to him, or even believing it applicable to him if it were demonstrated.

"A number of your scientists have theorized that there were so many Big Bangs that at least one of them got it right by happenstance. But they still don't know what preceded that singularity – he was pleased with himself for using a contraction in conversation. Others have introduced into the Big Bang a concept that is somewhat analogous to what happened in terms of creating the physical universe. Preliminarily as you know, a popular concept is that the Big Bang came from a singularity, essentially a 'seed' suspended somewhere in all space. It blew up and everything proceeded from that. But other folks – pleased this time with his colloquialism – theorize that *all space* was *also* contained *in* the singularity-seed. Those folks are closer to the mark; that is, prior to the creation of the physical universe, there was no concept such as space."

Looking at each other, "Well, what was there then?"

"Let me continue a wee bit further – he was getting carried away with his colloquial conversational training – before I answer that, but for now, for purposes of a *physical* answer – nothing was there. Not one single physical thing. Nothing. Note that there are those among your scientists who do believe matter can be created from nothing. They have detected very small particles materializing from voids. Back in the twentieth century, your Surface astronomer Rees remarked that it was mysterious how energy, remember all matter is physical energy, can come from emptiness. There still are no Surface scientists who have determined how that can occur, or even theorize it, because the answer I am describing will not fit their logic of the creation of matter, and is not provable by scientific methods as you know them. Your scientific laws will not allow you to accept that the primordial building block of matter is mind.

"The unknown goal of your science is to discover that, in the real nature of existence, you do not exist – physically. Matter is an illusion, the '*Grand Illusion*' as we refer to it. As your Surface writer, Ambrose Bierce, perhaps alluded to it, 'Brain, n. An apparatus with which we think that we think.' "

"So, as a physical being, my goal is to scientifically prove that I don't exist physically?" asked a somewhat incredulous science reporter.

"More properly stated, your goal is to *understand* that your real *natural* existence is not, and never has been, physical. You are familiar with unpredictability in quantum theory. A particle can be in two places at once, it is not predictable where or when and the very act of observing it changes its behavior, or the attempt to observe can even create the particle. The reason for this uncertainty and unpredictability in subatomic particle physics is that the Teachers who created the physical universe and its physical laws from mind did not create or 'program' it much farther than that level of detail, intentionally, so that at some stage of development, scientists would finally stop chasing their quantum-mechanical tails, stringy or otherwise, finally stop trying to discover certainty were it does not exist and was never intended to be – unified field *theories*, string *theories*, what-physical-event-started-the-universe *theories* – and turn to other solutions for understanding the origin and nature of existence."

"Sir, from the statements in your materials, what you are telling us is that even if string theory, or some other theory, is 'proven' at some point, it will be because the collective minds of the Earth scientists literally 'programmed' it to a further level of detail and created the physical solution. But in terms of absolute reality, it will be meaningless."

"Exactly. One will never be able to prove or explain the nature of existence with physical science because physical laws are part of the created, not *the* laws of creation. Those physical laws mistakenly view matter as real. They will ultimately be known on this plane of existence as a failed attempt to describe the dynamics of consciousness. The illusion trying to describe reality."

"You mean it's all that stuff you've been telling us about how this is a training ground and many of us have been here before, often reincarnated in groups because we are from the same classroom, and the Teachers just created the universe *deus ex machina* from their minds, excuse me, from their collective mind, for a school-yard role-playing exercise and everything that goes with it? That's the analogy to the

'Big Bang-all space is in the singularity' example?"

"Fundamentally, yes. The singularity was a collective single thought."

"That's garbage!"

Never flustered, Raama responded calmly in his deep voice, "Freely translated, I think that means it is not within your belief system, your paradigm, including the realm of things you believe *might* be possible. Contemplate explaining the following. First, how did matter, even in its smallest form, which so far as you theorize may be strings of energy, get here in the first place; for example, what created the singularity? Second, how does a thought, which is consciousness, affect matter; for example, how does it cause a material physiological chemical reaction in the human body?"

And it was time to observe the approach to Manticon.

CHAPTER TWENTY SIX

The eight hundred Visitation observers in the Mantid craft were not certain whether the announcement from Raama's unmistakable voice came from inside their heads or over some kind of a speaker system. ~Ladies and gentlemen, there is plenty of room for you to observe what occurs outside the craft as we descend to Manticon under the state you call New Mexico. Please do not be frightened as the craft descends toward the ground at great speed. We would not like to repeat the incident that occurred earlier today at the raceway. While this type of descent is not customarily within your experience, we guarantee that you will not be harmed. We do this all the time and, as you can see, we are still here.~

There was a semi-nervous giggle from the crowd, with a failed mass-attempt to make it sound like an amused and confident chuckle.

~Think of it as a thrill ride at an amusement park. You become apprehensive and exhilarated, but you don't get hurt. You will experience Particulation, a sensation of little electrical dots in front of your eyes just before we move from the outside to Manticon. That is normal and part of the transition process.~ Raama believed it best not to make it clear that they would *be* tiny particles at that time.

There was a collective "whoop" just before they dove through the surface of the Earth. Then, collective exclamations as they saw Manticon from above for the first time. After a brief air tour of Manticon, they landed, disembarked and the ground tour began.

Even though they were acutely interested in the breeding experiments between the Mantid and Surface beings because of the many reports of abductions and other experiences which the Mantid had candidly admitted had occurred, the Visitation 1000 – now reduced to the "Diaper Rash 800" as some jokingly referred to themselves after their earlier experience at the raceway – were not given a tour of the rooms with the fetus development containers.

The U.C. and the Mantid knew they had to deal with intense interest in the subject, but did not want the breeding activities to become the main focus of the reporting and direct attention away from the primary goal of convincing the Surface that the Mantid and their technology were real and, more importantly, that the Harvesters were a real and terminal threat. Thus, the media were given highly softened sketches of those "development room" activities, with the explanation, which certainly was not without substantial justification, that the commotion could impair the development of the "babies," and that was, of course, the paramount consideration.

The media would, however, be allowed to see the "children" from the ages of about three on up, but only those who were most human-like. The Mantid did not duck questions about the ones the media would not see, but spun the answers a bit at the U.C.'s insistence pursuant to the psychological policy primarily being formed by Murph who had never been to Manticon, but who knew Surface people.

To further assuage their curiosity, the media was assembled in a large auditorium in a Mantid education facility in order to see demonstrations of the children's training. The narrator of the presentation was Xanthas. They had all seen photographs of Xanthas, but had never seen her in person.

There was a collective gasp when she walked on stage. The only sounds were the humming of their digicorders and digicameras, coupled with exclamations such as, "My God!" "Jesus!" "I wonder what she puts on her skin." "Where in the hell did they find someone who looks like that?" "She must be from down here. There's no way a person could look like that on the Surface and not be in the headlines damn near every day! People's lives would hinge on what she had for breakfast every morning."

There were also cruder thoughts from some members of that elite band of media, male and female, all of which would have shocked Xanthas if she had understood what they meant. Many were skeptical that she was a "Meld" as had been described in the handouts.

While Murph wasn't there, he had anticipated their skepticism, and Bronc, flanked by Jenoor and Mari's mother, walked out on the stage. At the sight of the President, the crowd fell silent. Bronc spoke, "I know you all are wondering if this beautiful young woman is for real. This is Xanthas and the woman on my left is her mother. This gentleman on my right is the Mantid doctor, Jenoor, who has furnished us with the DNA patterns of Xanthas' Mantid father from the Mantid medical records." A murmur went around the crowd even though they had been told the same thing in the handouts.

"I know, it was as hard for me to believe as it is for you. But I give you my personal word that the DNA test results in your packets are from Xanthas whom you see before you, and they conclusively show that this human woman standing next to her is her mother, and that a Mantid male supplied the sperm for the in vitro fertilization, at least to the extent that the resulting fertilized egg was not genetically altered. This young being, Xanthas, is a monument to fertilization in vitro, with genetic manipulation following immediately thereafter. As you can see, what a manipulation it is. Also, I can assure you, her beauty is exceeded only by her intelligence and kindness."

The reason Bronc had been elected United Continents Coordinator by the U.C. leaders was that the peoples of all the continents basically respected and trusted him as a world leader due to a long record of being perceived as impeccably honest and forthright when it counted, even though he wasn't a perfect person. As a result, no questions were voiced from the crowd on the subject of DNA, and no one was interested in the whereabouts of her father, figuring if you've seen one Mantid, you've seen them all.

Thinking there would be questions, Bronc was looking over the sea of faces when Xanthas communicated mentally with him. He leaned into the microphone, "Where's Eastman Foster? Come on up here, son."

Foster had no clue that Xanthas had advised Bronc that Foster believed the President was a liar and full of "crap," whatever that was. Foster, thinking that he had lucked out and was somehow going to become the star emerging from this elite group of world media, began making his way up to the stage, his happiness exceeded only by his arrogance. Bronc leaned over and whispered something to Jenoor and then to Xanthas. Foster jumped up on the stage and said expectantly, "Yes, sir!"

"Mr. Foster, you are one of the most vocal and skeptical of all the paranormal media broadcasters in the world. Take a moment to formulate your thoughts and then tell these folks what you think about Xanthas' parentage."

Foster started to beam. With all these digicams going, as soon as their contents were aired upon the return to the Surface, he would be resurrected from his blubbering collapse at the raceway. He began formulating his diatribe concerning the fraudulent presentation of Xanthas by the President of the United States. Then all of a sudden he went ashen, composed himself, stepped up to the mike and stated,

"You know I am the most skeptical of the skeptics. There is no doubt in my mind after what I've read, and after what I've seen here today, that the information about Xanthas' parentage is absolutely genuine and correct. Further, we must not lose sight of the fact that neither she, nor other genetic adaptations of the Mantid, are the main issue. We must join hands around the world to keep ourselves from being exterminated by the Harvesters. That should be the only focus of our efforts."

Jenoor turned away from the audience and actually laughed a little croaking, chirping laugh, as did Raama. The audience was very quiet, except for the slight electronic hum of the digicorders. The last smattering of skepticism had disappeared from their collective thought. If the unconvincible was convinced, they were convinced.

Mari's mother, whose general mental state had vastly improved after learning what had been troubling her all these years, leaned over to Jenoor and asked him what had happened. ~Mr. Foster is an influential professional conspiracy finder. He was not convinced and intended to make an inflammatory negative statement. Xanthas advised the President who in turn communicated with me. When he arrived on stage, I communicated with Mr. Foster as I am with you now. I told him his deepest, darkest secret and asked him if he would like me to share it with the audience. Then, utilizing some helpful thoughts from the President, Xanthas mentally suggested to Mr. Foster what he might say instead. You heard the rest.~ Jenoor was again smiling, although it may not have been apparent to the uninitiated.

The rest of the educational presentation was predictable and tame, with very human-like, bright children. It didn't matter much. The media scarcely comprehended a word. They were photographing Xanthas from every permissible angle and so busy with how she said it, rather than what she said, that Xanthas could have been reciting *Mein Kampf* and they wouldn't have known the difference.

After the educational presentation, Jenoor and Bronc asked if there were any further questions prior to the return to the raceway. A number of the truly serious journalists who had not lost sight of why they were there began asking questions about weapons systems to be used against the Harvesters in the anticipated spacecraft war, and the ground-troops war they believed must certainly follow since the Harvesters intended to take away those whom they wanted for whatever purpose they had seeded Earth in the first place.

Raama spoke. They had become comfortable with his unusual deep and reassuring voice that was at odds with his appearance, "Well, you are all familiar with our Photon Weapon system that 'expanded' the small jet aircraft that invaded the Phoenix restricted air space. It was well covered in the media and I presume you have a basic under-standing of that system. We have other systems that we would prefer not to disclose at this time in an effort to prevent the Harvesters from learning of them, or at least minimize any details they may be able to gain."

Actually, there were not many other systems, nor did Raama have confidence that the Harvesters would be unable to intercept informa-tion about them despite the Mantid best efforts at blocking their thoughts, but it was important not to demoralize.

"However, I can tell you about our Rapid Oblong Destruct System, or 'Rods' weapons system, which Surface observers of our early testing independently, and aptly, called 'rods' because they look very similar to the simple rod bacteria of the same name. However, Rods are not microscopic and can range in size from a few inches to several hundred feet. I believe that many years ago it was a Surface observer in New Mexico just above us, named Jose Escamilla, who coined that description after discovering our Rods which he acciden-tally caught on video tape medium in the late twentieth century. As they can fly through the air, many skeptical Surface media of that era claimed they were little more than fast flying insects accidentally caught on camera. Because people tend to interpret the unfamiliar in terms of the familiar, we understand why they might believe a Rod was an insect. If you do not know, rod bacteria look and act like a flexible, living sausage."

Trying to be clever, one of the PP's tossed out, "So you feed the enemy poison hot dogs?" No one laughed, not even the other PP's.

Recognizing the group's reaction as an appropriate penalty to the boorish PP, Raama ignored him and continued, "They look like rod bacteria because they are." This put the scientific element of the crowd in a state of amazement, and having learned to expect amazing things, they waited eagerly for Raama to continue. "We have altered the bac-teria in several meaningful ways." The scientific reporters had collec-tively learned that the Mantid were masters of the understatement.

"First we can quickly grow the bacteria in large numbers to almost any size. We just need very large petri dishes for the hundred footers." At least some of the scientific reporters chuckled, and Raama was very proud of himself. "We have succeeded in giving them a certain intelligence, together with not only the ability to fly, but to Phase Shift and Particulate."

A Brazilian science reporter, Pensativa Colon, spoke up with a lovely Latin accent, "Sir, that is a truly astounding thing to do to a bacterium, but how does that make it into an offensive or a defensive weapon?"

Raama didn't miss a stroke, "As you know, we have made great strides in the development of genetic manipulation, and in computer science. Almost every cell in a Rod's body has been genetically manipulated to be a very small *living* computer with a specific purpose. Many of those cells have been altered to be very small living microcosms of the engines in our spacecraft. Their tiny rotating engine spheres are cell walls containing atoms that are computers composed of living tissue, somewhat analogous to your brain cells.

"They know which way to spin, and how fast, depending on the instructions from the internal guidance system, which is also composed of living computer cells and is programmed to operate with a certain amount of memory, perception and logic, including the ability to make some decisions and the ability to receive the thoughts of a Mantid controller, who can reprogram them instantaneously. In short, it is like a little Mantid brain that can follow instructions and make certain observations and decisions in carrying them out."

Pensativa Colon spoke up again, this time with a slight tinge to her voice, "Sir, that is astounding, but *how* does that make a sausage-like object into a weapon of war?" A number of the scientific reporters were starting to get as restless as some of the serious journalists had already become, but the paranormal PP's were listening with intense interest. They had seen photographs of, and heard reports about, things like this, particularly from New Mexico.

"The Rods can fly with intelligent purpose at great speeds that can reach tens of thousands of miles per hour. Because they can Particulate and Phase Shift, they can effectively become invisible or move through solid objects without damage to themselves or the object. In addition, because we put certain amounts of a compound we created called 'biagra' into their petri-dish diets, they can become as solid and hard as necessary to penetrate anything in order to get the job done. Ladies and gentlemen, we have created the ultimate guided missile. We can even implant photon modules or other charges in them that, of course, Particulate and Phase Shift right along with the Rod, and don't go off until they are told.

He enjoyed the sound of hundreds of amazed jaws dropping open at once.

"Think of it. At the size of bullets, they can roam the terrain in any number necessary until they identify an appropriate target. Then, and only in the numbers corresponding to the number of targets, accelerate at great speed, penetrating the target as a projectile would, or instead, Particulate and enter the target, re-forming inside it. In the latter event, the damage to a physical being is obvious, particularly if it did so in the being's brain, but more to the point, it could Particulate and enter a building, a vehicle, a spacecraft or anything you can imagine, and either then explode, or seek out the operator and terminate him or her." Raama's training included being politically correct as well as informal. "The possibilities are enormous."

Sam Pearson, the Roswell correspondent, could not contain himself, "Well, I'll be damned! That's why there have been so many sightings of them in New Mexico and it seems like they come up from the ground! They do! Originating from Manticon!"

"Exactly."

Pearson continued, "Is the speculation true that if you injured one of them, it would get mad and try to hurt you?"

"No. If it were programmed to defend itself, that could be mistaken for anger, but, presuming you would be able to catch or harm one, all of our Surface test Rods have been instructed to go out of phase the instant that would occur."

Having read a lot of reports from hunters, fishermen, hikers, spelunkers and rock climbers in wilderness areas, and having interviewed some, Pearson beamed with enlightenment, "Well, all this explains a lot. The Rods must fly around almost out of phase which is why they appear very light and almost transparent. And on the very few occasions when it seems something has happened to one of them, basically nothing is left and nothing can be located."

"That is correct." Raama kicked himself for not using a contraction.

"Are they playful? They have been seen entering people's heads and other parts of their bodies, but with no damage."

Knowing that the professional offense takers, fault finders and problem seekers would probably jump on it, even though it had proven not to be a problem, Raama replied candidly anyway, "They aren't playful. It was just part of the testing in which we had full confidence."

Sure enough someone piped up, "If you had such confidence, why did you test using us as guinea pigs?"

Someone with a wider view of the necessities of the moment shot an appropriate retort over the heads of the crowd, "Oh, shut the fuck up!"

Bronc, who would have preferred that Raama had said he was not aware of any such incident, took the opportunity to end the meeting with the promise of food before the return to the raceway.

CHAPTER TWENTY SEVEN

When the immense craft hovered over the raceway late that evening, it bathed the racing facility in light, and the media waiting there covered the bottom and sides of the Mantid craft with their lights. At night, lit against the background of the starry, black Arizona sky, it was a truly phenomenal sight. To the viewers on digivision, it looked like something straight out of a science fiction movie. The viewers were relying on the reporters' narration that it was not science fiction, but reality, and the reporters who had remained behind were convincing. They were witnesses to this portion of the Visitation and they were not only convinced, but astounded.

The craft again emitted the beam, and the passengers started pouring from its bottom as if perhaps being extruded from the mind of a Teacher. From the instant they hit the ground, the Visitation 1000 began jabbering away into their portable communications equipment, telling their stories live on the air, the digivision reporters simultaneously broadcasting their digicorder video, all coordinated through their employers' remote Tesla setups at the site. Their collective listening and viewing ratings had never been so close to one-hundred percent. Once the commotion died down and they were all seated again at the raceway on that pleasant desert evening, Jenoor appeared on the digiscreens at the raceway and on digivision screens everywhere on Earth.

"Ladies and gentlemen, not only here at Phoenix International Raceway, but throughout Earth, you have all preliminarily seen what occurred on the Mantid craft today and at Manticon. I clearly sense that you now believe. Because of that, I want to try two experiments with all of you, right now. I want to do it right now because all of your minds are presently collectively focused on the subject of why we are doing this, to protect the inhabitants of Earth from extinction at the hands of the Harvesters. To protect you from ceasing to exist on Earth."

A collective chill went up the spines of every inhabitant of the continents as they listened on all parts of the globe to the instantaneous computer translation in the language of their country or of their choice, but retaining the sound characteristics of Jenoor's voice. Jenoor also directed his thoughts to the Mantid.

"The experiments I want to try are of collective 'Entrainment,' and collective entrained thought communication to the Harvesters. Entrainment is the process of harmonizing thoughts between two or more minds. In this case, your minds, billions of minds. It is a collective mental and emotional Connection that can have the effect of transcending the usual results of a set of circumstances, effecting a change of those results, all by thinking. Entrainment can be positive or negative and, of course, you should always strive for positive Entrainment.

"When enough of us direct our thoughts, our mental energy, toward the same goal, that energy can Entrain the thinking of others to be in harmony with that goal. It is analogous to a tuning fork setting other tuning forks into sympathetic vibration. It sets up a collective, harmonized empathy which can affect the thoughts of all within the sphere of that vibration's influence. With enough mental energy applied, the effect can be universal."

He sensed his pedantic approach was almost too intellectual, and too boring, for a worldwide audience mix, but they were scared and the tuning fork analogy did the trick.

"So, I want all of you to get as comfortable as you can and not only listen to what I have to say, but to feel and believe it, together. This Earthly crisis has led us all to focus on and to understand that the most important thing to us is the freedom for each to pursue his or her own goals without interference from others, so long as we do not interfere with others when we do so. In short, the most important thing to us right now is universal harmony, and I do not use the derivative of that word 'universe' lightly. The threat to that harmony comes from somewhere in the universe."

He definitely had the world's attention.

"Now, what I would like all of you to do is think about harmony with others, not only on Earth, but in the universe, how important it is and what a lovely place the Earth and the universe would be if we could 'all just get along,' if we all treated others as we wish to be treated. Think of this *now. Imbue yourself only with the feeling of harmony. Feel this now! All* of you! Billions of you at the same time! You feel it now. I can feel it. Make the feeling so overwhelming it is as if it is a physical force!

"Along with this feeling, send this thought, this universal message to the Harvesters. 'Let us all live in universal harmony, not only in thought, but in deed, in *each* thing we do, *all* the time. Please leave us alone as we wish to leave you alone.' Relax, but hold that thought and feeling. Send it without hostility. Send it with earnestness and sincerity, all of you, now. Let no other thought enter your consciousness. Let us Entrain the Harvesters to this thinking and feeling."

Jenoor felt the entire world entrained with that thought, feeling and effort to send the message of harmony to the Harvesters. It swelled. Everyone on Earth felt it and knew it. In the nighttime part of the world, the night sky took on a slightly reddish-green northern-light type of hue. It was a first-time experience for many, but not for others who had been tuned in to the power of mind for centuries. Jenoor simply let it happen, participating to the fullest himself. He had no idea how much time had elapsed when he, and everyone on Earth, received a return message.

<~Do not worry. Love is the immovable object of being. Expressing unconditional love is the irresistible force of reality. The immovable object and the irresistible force are harmonious because they are one and the guiding principle of everything that flows from One Mind, which is the spirit of all. This is the truth of life and the substance of soul. Do not worry.~>

If collective shock of billions of beings could have made a sound, it would have been loud and unique indeed. If Jenoor's eyes could widen and he could appear visibly shaken, it happened, right there on worldwide digivision. There was no doubt in the mind of any being on Earth, including the Mantid, that the message came from the Harvesters.

Jenoor recovered quickly and his intellect snapped into forceful action. "Ladies and gentlemen, we all know that message came from the Harvesters. Do not be deceived by the message. It can only be designed so that we will lower our guard. The Harvesters *are* coming and we must be prepared. Entrain your thought for that result!" Billions did so.

Still on world digivision, Jenoor addressed the audience at the raceway and around the world, "We haven't much time. Each of you here go back to your countries; each of you at home stay in your countries. Listen to your governments as they cooperate with the United Continents' leadership. Do whatever they ask. Pull together. The

Harvesters *are* coming."

As the media in the stands scrambled for the exits, again thinking only of themselves and their stories, a young female reporter, less familiar with the piranha-like ways of her journalistic family, was not protective enough of her own person and, helpless with her arms entangled in her digicorder straps, was knocked about seventy-five feet down the steps of one of the aisles, skidding on her face all the way. Her bumping slide was stopped when one of her legs became entangled in an aisle seat stanchion, snapping like a small branch. She was in excruciating pain and unrecognizable compared to a few moments before. Her face looked like a skinned snake, with the broken bridge of her nose exposed to the world, devoid of flesh. A bone was sticking backwards out of her calf, dripping vital fluids. Some of the reporters witnessing the incident threw up for the second time that day.

Digivision cameras immediately trained on the commotion, exposing the young woman's plight and her condition to the world. Crushing in to get a better look, the crowd was impassable for the medical service personnel since everyone was trying to see or get a picture. Suddenly Jenoor materialized next to her, having Particulated in order to get through the crowd. The world-wide audience was transfixed. He knelt and put his "hand" three or four inches above her face and she stopped screaming and writhing, staring straight up with the one eye that was still visible. He began speaking in a soft voice to her and several microphones were shoved down next to his small mouth.

"Relax. Think this deeply with me as I speak it to you. 'I rearrange my atoms, molecules and energy for perfect form and harmonious function without pain or injury. I *direct* that my atoms, molecules and energy be rearranged in this way, now'."

As he spoke, his hands, perhaps now two inches above her body, moved up and down it, slowly and continuously, from head to foot. She seemed to relax more and more. She closed her eye. "Visualize this with me now. Move your consciousness away from your physical body and think of your body as a simple drawing or computer-generated-like form that is created to show a simplified version of your present injuries. A gaseous cloud is enveloping this form. What color would you like it to be?"

She spoke softly through skinned lips, "White."

"This white gaseous cloud, composed of the healing power of One

Mind, is now penetrating the form, every atom, molecule and space of it, removing all pain as it does so. The cloud is now being drained away, like smoke sucked up by a vacuum cleaner, taking all pain, tension and negativity with it." She clearly relaxed even more. "Another substance, is descending on the form, including its face and legs. It is also composed of the healing power of One Mind. It is thicker and will work its way into the surface. What color would you like it to be?"

"Pink," she whispered.

"As this substance is descending onto the face, legs and all the other parts of the form, covering it where there is no covering, a ray is being projected through it into any broken bones underneath it. This ray softens the bones so that they become pliable and amorphous, and they go back into their original shape, strength and structure. As this is occurring, the pink substance covering the form softens and pulls everything, skin, muscles, eyelashes, blood vessels and anything else, back the way it was, changing as necessary and amalgamating with it, covering, assuming and replicating the original form and function, unblemished, perfect and operating in every perfect way. Do you see it happening on the form? Do you see the result?"

"Yes. I see it. It is repaired as if nothing ever occurred."

"Know the form you mentally created is you. Give the previous command, 'I direct that my atoms, molecules and energy be rearranged in accordance with the concept of this form, perfect and functioning perfectly and harmoniously in every way – now.' Relax, *knowing* that you are, now, this perfect projection and expression of Superconscious *mind*."

The crowd and the digivision audience were so absorbed in the mental process they heard Jenoor narrating that they did not realize exactly when she had changed. But they saw the young reporter arise, whole, just fine, absolutely normal, except that she seemed to radiate something from within – a little more than the usual person.

<<~>>

CHAPTER TWENTY EIGHT

A few days later, back at United Continents Headquarters, Mari, who had become the Communications Liaison Coordinator between the U.C. and the Mantid, asked Jenoor during a moment alone, "What did you do?" She did not need to tell Jenoor she was referring to the injured reporter – who had since received much more than fifteen minutes of fame and media attention. Mari was a little apprehensive, not sure if she should probe into the matter because she wasn't certain she was ready for the answers. But she had asked the question anyway, figuring she would understand what she was ready to understand.

"I did nothing of myself. I asked One Mind to amplify its power, amplify the understanding by another of the real nature of being, through me as a conduit or catalyst."

He went on without the necessity of another question, speaking aloud so he could continue to develop his proficiency, "It is very logical, even though in practice it is difficult to keep separate from the confusion caused by the *apparent* reality of being in the physical universe, because we certainly seem to be here, and for the moment, it is *our* reality, but not *the* reality.

"To do what happened last week with the reporter, one must focus on the truth of being, not on the Grand Illusion, and recognize that mind is not generated by matter, but matter is generated by mind. Carrying that concept to its logical extension, matter will be whatever mind wants it to be. Thus, we can change material manifestation just by understanding that fact and thinking in a different way, a way that takes into account that matter *is* created by mind."

"You are what you think."

"That's certainly correct, but the extension here is that you can *intentionally* demonstrate mind's principle to the extent you understand it. With her cooperation, I helped the reporter change herself physically by changing the way she thought about herself. It was a combination of understanding on my part and entraining her thoughts to mine, commingling our thoughts if you prefer, with the higher or stronger thoughts controlling and educating the weaker, in a positive way.

"I helped her to help herself. She was in such a disorganized and frightened mental state that she was willing to give herself over and try anything, at least after I calmed her at first by mentally paralyzing her, much as I did with you in the spacecraft during the trip when you first consciously learned the general purpose for your present incarnation. But with her I numbed her pain, so she could concentrate on considering her alternatives. She could have been calmed by more conventional means such as pain killers. The reporter was surprised that it worked. I was not."

Mari was still having trouble with what he was saying. It was just too foreign to her "matter-based reality" as he would put it. "Jenoor, you sound like a lot of college professors I had. They kept telling me there was a forest, but never described that it was made up of trees. I'm trying to get out of you, exactly what in the *hell* did you *do*!?."

"You are appealing to the wrong level of the illusion, too low." Somewhat proudly, he thought his little joke about the underworld was pretty funny. Mari looked at him with some exasperation, not responding. Getting the message, he tried to explain as briefly and in the most practical terms he could muster, as he wanted to get on with saving Earth.

"After calming her so I could get her to focus her attention, I helped dissociate her concentration from her physical body since her current belief system would not allow her to think of it as changeable by thinking. In fact she was thinking of it as permanently damaged, with a long imperfect healing process. She didn't need to be a doctor to know what physical science and medicine has taught us all – that matter in that condition can only be repaired by material means. Her thinking, as with most, has been entrained to that physical-science system of thought. As a result, her condition would continue to be the case, unless she changed her thinking.

"I made it easier for her to change her thinking by transferring it to a 'play' counterpart of herself, an alter ego she could create, manipulate and control. It's very similar in principle to what Murph does with children when he has them work out their problems with dolls in therapy. She literally healed the doll in her mind and in that process transferred that thinking, and thus the result, to herself. She changed and controlled her core thought of herself physically, and as result she changed physically. It's actually logical and simple, except for the fact that few understand that is the way it works – and fewer can accept it on a core level and practice it as reality even if they understand it intellectually."

Jenoor's last phrase took him by surprise. He suddenly realized he was so focused on the problems of his present physical life that even though, metaphysically, he could do some of the things he was doing, and understood some of the things he understood, in many ways he kept them separate in his mind, or just ignored them, and did not always practice them, and never practiced some of them, because he was so immersed in the Grand Illusion. Even now, this was just a side discourse from the main task of protecting Earth from the Harvesters, instead of being the main discourse of existence. He tucked that thought into a mindfold, and told himself that maybe he would think about it later.

Mari, ever curious, brought him back to the subject, "So you can't do it unless the other person participates?"

"At least to a minimal extent. It could have been done with only a mere willingness or desire by her and no other participation on her part. I am still learning, but my understanding has developed to the point where my thoughts are strong enough that if she had not been able to cooperate, but had been willing to let my thoughts commingle with hers and control her thinking, and also *desired* on a very basic level to change physically, they would have changed her unconscious and automatic thinking, and that would have changed her physically to the necessary extent. She wouldn't accurately know why, thinking it was some ability I had, and that she did not possess – not understanding that it was a form of positive Entrainment of her unconscious thinking.

"In any event, that is not what happened in her case. With my coaching, she consciously assisted and directed her thinking to the end result, and she knows it. That demonstration has changed her material thinking by elevating her material consciousness for the rest of her journey here. Because she has actually demonstrated the principle herself – a mind-based scientific demonstration instead of a matter-based scientific demonstration – she has started to believe in its truth and is curious about the Truth that is the nature of being. She has a new level of understanding and will seek to expand it.

"That is what it will take with others – demonstration. For those who have not experienced a demonstration of the principle in some way, but who are familiar with the evidence of the demonstrations of others, there will develop a sincere belief that it is possible and they can learn to demonstrate it. Then with the proper thinking and practice, belief will change into the understanding that leads to demonstration."

Mari wished she had a digicorder so she could study all of the things he just said. In any event, she was going to study the digisticks of what he said to the reporter at the raceway. Then she half stated a conclusion and half asked a question, "So, you are not a Messiah?"

"I am a Messiah only to the person who does not understand that I utilize a principle of One Mind that *anyone* can demonstrate. The *principle* itself is the Messianic Deliverer, not me. I am a messenger. The principle is the message. Anyone who understands and demonstrates the principle is capable of being its messenger.

"So if anyone can do it, how do *I* start?"

"You can start in smaller ways and work up. The next time you are injured or hurt in some way, even just a little pain, muscle pull or cut, and even though you have a physical explanation for it that you know is correct according to physical theory and practice, try it. You can make up almost any scenario. Be creative in the ways your schematic alter ego is healed if you would like. Spray paint skin tones with a golden sprayer. Inject exotic healing agents with a magic infuser. Change things with an 'intelligent' ray. You can be as detailed or as cartoon-like as you want, but accomplish the job mentally on the schematic of you and always see your schematic self as perfectly healed and perfectly functioning.

"Then complete the transfer of it to yourself by mentally directing that your atoms, molecules and energy be changed consistent with the healed concept you created. Use words and concepts similar to those I had the reporter say at the raceway. They don't have to be exact, but everyone has access to a digistick of it now, and that video is also readily available on many sites on the Tessie. Program your mental computer for the perfect result and direct 'Enter.' Actually say in your mind, 'I *direct* that result, *now*. I push the 'enter' button, now.' You should be surprised at what happens. It may not heal almost instantaneously as was demonstrated at the raceway, but it will transcend your ingrained physical expectations, both as to the time it takes and the result that is manifested. Repeat the process as often as you feel is necessary. Your thinking will control the result. Once you have demonstrated it, there is nowhere to go but up. With the right thinking, anyone can do it. Matter is a *servant* of mind, *not* its master."

Mari's thought process was rising higher than she had realized,

"Well, taking the concept beyond physical healing, why don't we just all think and change the world then?"

"With increased levels of understanding, I'm sure we can and we will. I tried that in a limited way, positively entraining the worldwide digivision audience at the raceway. You saw that we reached the Harvesters and are otherwise beginning to see the results of that positive Entrainment in worldwide cooperation. But you have also seen how powerful the Harvester consciousness can be. Mari, the Earth needs to make great strides in its thinking, or I do not think we can survive this onslaught."

His last statement scared her. She had never heard Jenoor take a negative view of the situation and she had been listening intently to what he had just said. Her eyes turned from the color of a summer sky to a much darker blue, "Jenoor, if that's the way you think, isn't that what's going to happen?"

"We have to be realistic, Mari."

She flushed with anger. It seemed to Jenoor that her hair was turning a deeper red as it started bouncing with the fervor of her point, "Just a damn second! One minute you tell me you *are* what you think, which I translate to mean that what I truly think *is* what will happen in my life here, and the next minute you wimp out on the whole deal and start spouting a bunch of negative thoughts instead of practicing what you preach, and there's no joke meant there." She was getting so upset, she tossed in the gratuitous shot, "Are you made of clay as well as looking like it!?"

A few months before, it wouldn't even have registered, much less have bothered him, but it hurt his feelings and Mari was sorry the instant she said it.

"God, I'm sorry, Jenoor. I'm just upset at that attitude because this is so important, not only to me, but everyone, and I'm afraid."

Recovering, "No, no, you are absolutely right. I must be becoming human in more ways than I realize." Catching himself, "No offense intended, of course."

"Well, let's just drop it, but *I* think *you* had better change *your* thinking. My being afraid doesn't help either. I should never doubt, and should have confidence in the outcome. Who said it? 'Nothing is either good or bad, but thinking makes it so.' That has a new and different meaning for me now."

CHAPTER TWENTY NINE

Murph had been exhausting himself working on the psychological aspects of war with the Harvesters, spending at least eighteen hours or more each day with Pralit Lofler. The two of them also spent a lot of that time with the most telepathically and behaviorally gifted personnel of the Mantid. Murph flopped into an easy chair in the furnished Washington apartment supplied to him and Mari, courtesy of United Continents, and wondered if it made any sense to think about his personal life. He might not even have one in a few months, depending on when the Harvesters decided to attack.

Mari would be here soon. She had been working equally hard on her facet of the problem, which included working closely with Jenoor. Neither her relationship with Jenoor, nor with him, had been overtly mentioned or even subtly alluded to after their initial discussion. That silence was a transparent and uneasy cloud between them, scented with broken trust, a mist through which they communicated every time they were with each other. Even though they did their best to ignore it, it was always there. Its invisible odor and distortion of vibrations of all kinds were not, as each had foolishly hoped, diminishing through mutual silence nor evaporating with the passage of time. "This too will pass" wasn't cutting it.

It was all he thought about when he wasn't forcing himself to concentrate on saving the world. Classroom exercise or not, learning experience or not, it was the most real thing happening to him right now and he could not get it into a different perspective. He felt empty and wasn't certain he cared. But certainly he must care or he wouldn't be thinking about it. In any event, he would talk to her about it so, hopefully, he could get his mental tire out of this particular groove. He desperately needed to turn his wheel in some direction because his current path was a road to nowhere.

Mari came in, kissed him hello perfunctorily and flopped into the other chair. Having been a perpetrator, she felt guilty about the harm she had inflicted on Murph and their relationship – notwithstanding what her feelings on related matters may be – and she had also thought to the point of having no more thoughts. She would be just as happy never to think or talk about it again. But Murph started.

"Mari, I know you are tired. I'm tired, but I have to talk about this with you, even if the world ends tomorrow."

She was hoping the subject wasn't IT, but it was.

"I don't even know where to start, but it is all I think about when I have time to think. I know all the things Xanthas and Jenoor have told us about why we are here, which I fully grasp in an intellectual sense, but that doesn't make me *feel* any better. I was hoping for the rest of this life to have a deep and abiding relationship with you that would be unblemished until the end. I wanted to be able to look in your eyes at any time, and you in mine, with that deep and unconditional love reserved for two people who have never broken trust, with a look that is not imbued with that horrible pale tint of disingenuousness."

She might have accused him of being overly dramatic, but she had seen, daily, the pain in his eyes and felt the hopelessness in his thoughts, "It's not possible for that to be the case now." She had thought about it so much, she could only be direct and tell him exactly what she was thinking at that moment, letting whatever the effect may be – be effective.

He had known the answer. He just didn't want to hear it. He wanted her to say, and prove, that the whole thing had been a giant bad joke or dream. She didn't say that, of course. She had accepted its reality. There was no way to fix it. It seemed so unfair. He'd done everything right. He just looked at her, but not with any particular emotion. He was almost out of them. He just looked, knowing that whatever happened, he would have to accept the facts.

"It can only happen from *now on*, Murph."

Acknowledging the only way to meaningfully discuss this was to be direct, "Do you want it to?"

She didn't answer.

"You're not answering."

"Murph, I love you."

"You know that's an avoidance. What *do* you want?"

"I . . . I don't know. I . . . guess I want to be able to love two people – beings – at the same time in that way and have it be okay. Isn't there enough love to go around?"

It flashed into his mind to say that it would be okay if he got Xanthas as *his* second, and that's were they would cut it off – nobody else, ever. But somehow he just couldn't bring himself to agree that was the correct thing to do. Something about a house divided against itself he guessed. It would never work for him. He must have been a penguin in a former incarnation. They're monogamous. He asked her, "Would you be comfortable with that?

"Somehow, I don't think so."

Delaying whatever the result of this conversation was going to be, Murph mused, "*Trying* to look at a bigger, more long-range picture, I wonder what people, 'er consciousnesses, do when they are in the Superconscious Dimension and not here?"

Mari was just as content to participate in the delay, "I don't know, I guess they all just get along. Just love each other and get along. They don't need money, cars or a bigger house or anything. I think it's a cinch they can't screw and foul things up. I don't even think in that state there is any such thing as a hard and fast division into male or female. They, we, are just comfortable with manifesting the full aspects of being."

Murph returned to the immediate, "Well, much as I don't want to face it, what are *we* going to do, here, now?" He pushed his glasses up a microscopic distance on his nose.

"Do we have to do anything? Can't we just go along sticking our heads in the sand? Who knows, we could be dead in a few weeks."

"Then what? We wait until our next life to work it out? Maybe we won't be dead in a few weeks, 'dead' being a relative term, of course."

He shouldn't have answered his own question rhetorically. Mari slipped her own question through the opening, "Okay. What do you want to do?"

Damn! She had maneuvered him into suggesting first. He'd try her trick, "Oh, I don't know, what do you want to do?"

"Out of order, I asked first."

The negotiation continued without hostility, but not without tension, "Well, look, I'm not the one who claims to be in love with two beings at the same time. I didn't start this. I'm the victim. So you should suggest first." His dad wasn't a lawyer, but he'd picked up a few tricks from being married to the judge's daughter, not to mention his own sister who used to pound on him pretty good as they grew up.

Having no counter to the "victim" comment that wouldn't inflame the dialogue, Mari decided to provide an answer that simply described the ambivalence she felt, "Murph, I just can't decide. Even though it's not consistent with some of the things I just said, I guess I would like to be with both of you, probably keeping it in two separate worlds, you here, him Below – like those people who have two separate happy families in two different cities that you read about."

"Well, the problem there is that the person who creates the situation is usually screwed up, has to lead a life of deception, is not personally happy, and gets caught and goes to jail because everyone else recognizes its not the right thing to do either. This is Earth, not a flawless existence within One Mind."

Mari threw out, "Well, couldn't we just move more in the latter direction?"

"Certainly you're not telling me being duogamous right now would be a move toward a flawless existence?" He was getting pretty good at sparring by answering a question with a question and wondered if he just invented a new word. Maybe he'd change his name to Socrates Bailey. Even though he was engaging in a little levity with himself to relieve his own tension, he did think his question was fair.

"No."

"Why not?"

Mari was straightforward, "It just doesn't seem right. I just have the wrong vibes, the wrong intuition, about it."

"Me too. So now what?" Slick, the ball was still in her court.

She knew it, but didn't feel it was an unfair move. She ran her hand through her tousled hair, "I don't know, I really don't know. Maybe this conversation should just be the *start* of a process, now that we have agreed to face the problem." She was surprised at how much she had assimilated from Murph. "We can't decide everything tonight. We are both awfully tired. Let's start thinking about it in earnest and talk about it again when one of us has something meaningful to say."

That was all right with Murph. He was just as happy to delay the possibility that they would agree to split up. He loved her, which is why it bothered him so much, and this had been cathartic for him in any event. He took his glasses off, rubbed his eyes wearily and started getting ready for bed.

That night, they fell asleep with their arms around each other.

<<~>>

CHAPTER THIRTY

General Payson "Det" Menard was uncomfortable. He didn't know what kind of weapons the Harvesters had, but felt certain they had to be far in advance of anything the U.C., including the Mantid, could develop, no matter how good the U.C. believed its weaponry was. In the effort to find out all they could about the Harvesters, Murph, working with Pralit, suggested he try to remote view archeological artifacts from the periods when they believed the Harvesters had planted the Mantid, prehistoric man and, ultimately, *Homo sapiens* on Earth.

Murph presented his idea to "The General" and explained that remote viewers could view the past, present or future. At least they said they could and from his personal experience, Pralit was the best of them all, certainly with respect to existing objects and presently-occurring events. He also disclosed that Pralit had, without authorization, been briefly remote viewing those "planting" periods with what he believed was some success. Det just chomped on his cigar and didn't remind Murph it was the U.S. military that had started organized remote viewing research in the twentieth century. There was such a paucity of information about the Harvesters, coupled with Det's pressing need for facts, that he was ready to try almost anything. Knowing Pralit Lofler's reputation, Det authorized "the little mystic guy" to spend some more time at it. They all felt time was extremely scarce, which is why Det carefully controlled its use in relation to various projects

"Det" Menard never failed to plan ahead the best he could. Expense was not considered at this juncture. The only consideration was time, knowledge and results. A positive result from Lofler would most likely result in a lot of archeological activity, which in turn would take time. At least it would require a different type of personnel so he would not have to appropriate that time from much of his existing cadre.

Det instructed Murph to have the Mantid psychic, Teenaan, perform the same tasks independently in an attempt at verification. He knew that referring to Teenaan, or almost any Mantid, as a psychic, although some were clearly more gifted in this area than other Mantid, was either redundant, an oxymoron or ludicrous in relation to Surface people, perhaps even in relation to Pralit Lofler, except the Mantid seemed to have a peculiar block when it came to the Harvesters. Lofler had speculated that the Harvesters either built it into them in some autonomic fashion when they first put them on Earth, or they were simply automatically blocking them now. The latter idea made Det even more concerned about the power of the Harvesters. He made up his mind in advance that if there were a conflict between what that Mantid and the human "viewed," he would go with Lofler.

Pralit got a good night's sleep and then went into his zone as never before. Murph functioned as his monitor. Curiously enough, what Lofler saw was the Sphinx. Although Murph wondered if Pralit had seen the various remakes of that old movie, *The Mummy*, he went with it and several hours later they both reported back to The General.

Murph started, "Pralit says that the Harvesters built the Sphinx, at least we call it the Sphinx now, as a memorial to their seeding Earth with prehistoric man, certain animals and other things. They actually built it some time after they did those things, at a point in time when that area was green and verdant, paying tribute to their early experiments. Later still, they added the headdress to the Sphinx as a monument to the additional seeding of *Homo sapiens*, after what we might loosely call 'prehistoric man' didn't work out as they had planned."

Det's cigar suspended in midair. He swelled up in his chair, leaning toward Lofler's small body, "You've been watching too goddam many of those old Indiana Jones movies on the digivision Classic channel," he growled. "The fucking Sphinx. What the hell. Nobody will believe this."

Pralit leaned forward also, "General Menard, it only matters that you believe it." Pralit's quiet, unintimidated manner was like a shout next to Det's usual gruff reaction.

"Believe what? What the hell does it matter if they built it? What in holy shit does that tell us?" His voice was rising.

Murph interjected, "It's what's under it, Det." Murph and The General had worked together so much in the past few months that the familiarity had become natural. Det's ingrained gruff manner no longer had any effect on Murph. The two had a mutual respect for the other's intelligence and the different abilities they brought to the task. Murph's statement got Det's attention.

Now that he was interested in what Pralit had to say, and having already thought several steps ahead, The General asked quietly, "What is under it, how deep is it, what will it take to get to it?"

"I believe it is a room containing a written record of the Harvesters' activities on Earth relating to those particular times, including a narration of their intent when they performed the various 'seedings'."

"Believe. What the hell do you mean, believe!?" His voice was rising again, "I don't know what it will take to dig under the Sphinx, but it will be a bitch of an undertaking just to keep it from falling in on the excavation, not to mention the time it will take. People will probably die in the effort and the media will have a feast on it. And you're telling me you *believe*!" His face was getting redder than normal, his two front teeth looked bigger than usual and Murph was hoping that cigar was not a Rod because it looked like it was getting ready to shoot out of his mouth right at Lofler.

In Pralit's own quiet way, "I can't do anything but believe, and neither can you, until you dig it up."

"And if nothing's there!?"

"Then I'm wrong."

Det let the air out of his lungs. He knew that Pralit couldn't do any more than tell him what he saw and, knowing he had done all he could do, it would be a waste of Pralit's emotional energy to care what Det did. Still Det pushed, "What assurance do I have that you aren't wrong?"

"Only this." He turned his psychic eyes and looked straight into The General's, "I am not wrong."

Det didn't bother to ask what Teenaan had viewed. It wouldn't matter. He pushed a button and Major Francesco Klitschko appeared. "Klitschko, you are going to dig a hole under the Sphinx. Do whatever these two tell you to do."

Klitschko didn't blink. He knew his job as a soldier was to charge in the direction he was ordered, to do or die and never question the reason why, particularly if the order came from The General, or he would end up wishing he were dead. "Yes, sir!"

<<~>>

CHAPTER THIRTY ONE

When Murph and Klitschko spoke with Jenoor to arrange appropriate logistics for the quickest possible transportation of personnel and excavation materiel to the Sphinx, Jenoor was incredulous that they had not thought of simply shifting it out of phase, and then digging. With The General's permission, Minuum flew the three of them to the Sphinx immediately.

Jenoor stepped out of the craft and put his hand on the great structure. Nothing happened. Jenoor communicated something to Minuum and they flew to a nearby pyramid. Jenoor stepped out of the craft, put his hand on the pyramid and shifted it out of phase, much to the consternation of the people in the area who were already excited at seeing the Mantid craft and Jenoor in person. When the pyramid disappeared, they were bewildered and some dropped to the ground and started praying. In a moment, Jenoor and the pyramid returned to Earth phase. Those praying stopped as suddenly as they started and stared wide-eyed, as did everyone else. The Mantid craft flew back to the Sphinx and Jenoor tried again.

Jenoor returned and told The General that the Sphinx could not be Phase Shifted so they could get under it. Being aware of the Mantid ability at some point, the Harvesters had obviously anticipated an attempt to reach their secrets and had done something which locked the Sphinx in the Earth phase. Det directed Murph to get with Xanthas and work out a public relations campaign for excavating under the Sphinx.

After the experience with the Visitation 1000 media, it had been clear to Det and other U.C. Headquarters personnel that Xanthas would be the perfect public spokesbeing for the United Continents Command. People just seemed to go into a trance looking at her, listening to her, or both, and subliminally accepted anything she had to say, or suggest, as the gospel. Thus, that became her task and she was marvelously effective at it.

Being physically close to her again didn't help Murph's thinking processes. He found himself constantly watching her while she was doing something else. He had to mentally chain himself to the chair to avoid leaning over and brushing his lips against her soft porcelain neck, right below her ear – just for starters. At times his mind was screaming "No, no, no!" to stop himself from completing the motion of reaching out and touching her.

None of this was particularly consistent with his side of the prior conversation with Mari in their apartment, so he decided he'd better talk to Xanthas about the entire issue. Maybe she would bring him to an epiphany, or at least give him some guilty comfort by participating with him in what he had previously decided would be a mistaken choice.

He explained everything he believed Xanthas may not know that had happened between Mari and Jenoor, and between Mari and him as a result, including his recent conversation with Mari and his ambivalent feelings about being monogamous with Mari, which included being duogamous with Xanthas and Mari, and Mari with Jenoor, but no one else, ever.

Murph timidly pushed the question forward, "So, I wondered how you felt about that idea?"

"Are you saying you want to do that, Murph?"

"Well . . . uh, not exactly, I just . . . uh . . ."

In her gentle, direct way, "You want me to commit one way or the other so it will be easier for you to decide."

"Uh . . . yes, I guess so."

Looking directly into his eyes, the violet radiating from hers seemed to suspend his thoughts in midair, "Does the word 'selfish' hold meaning for you?"

"Uh . . . shit. God, I'm sorry, Xanthas, I'm not thinking well. I'm so confused about this whole thing that I'm not thinking about anything but myself."

"Clearly. But, let's carry the discussion out."

His blood pressure jumped. Might she actually consent to this? Holy shit! If she did that, then what would he do? *He'd* still have to decide.

She continued, "Who do I get as my second?"

"Huh?"

"Who do I get? I've never done it with anyone, but under these circumstances, I should get two also. Mari would have two. You would have two. Who do I get? The General would be a great contrast to you. I wouldn't want two exactly the same. Or maybe the President – another great contrast and he would be a lot of fun and not so mean and gruff as The General. Could I switch the second from time to time so long as I kept you? I could get bored. How would it work if I had a baby by one of you? How much time would you like to waste this trip?"

"Okay, okay, I get the picture." As practical as she was beautiful, her grasp of "life" seemed to be advancing exponentially.

"Murph, I love you, and I would love to be with you, permanently, or at least as permanent as this particular lifetime is going to get for either of us, but if you want that to happen, divorce my sister – and then we'll see where it goes."

He was amazed at the meteoric development of her maturity. The ball was still on his side of the net, and properly so, and he still didn't know what to do. At least he didn't know what he was *going* to do. He did know that she *wasn't* telling him to divorce her sister, whom she loved dearly. Whatever happened, the decision about his life had to be his – and Mari's had to be hers, which was consistent with everything he had learned about the Superconscious Dimension and why he was in the Material Dimension right now.

"Thanks, sweetheart." He kissed her gently on the cheek. He knew her approach was the right thing to do and he was grateful for it.

<<~>>

CHAPTER THIRTY TWO

As they had imagined, planning how to dig under the Sphinx was a monumental task. It was further complicated by the fact that, in addition to the Mantid's inability to Phase Shift the Sphinx, the U.C.'s subsurface nanopulse radar imaging equipment was of no use. It must have been a technology well known to the Harvesters, even way back then, because they had effectively done something, created some condition, that made the equipment go berserk and render meaningless results. Thus, the U.C. could not verify whether there was a room under the Sphinx or not. But at least those obstacles were some evidence that Lofler may be right, and they continued to press forward.

Pralit had told them that the "library" was a distance of about five "stories" down. Not knowing how accurate that was, they couldn't just start some distance away from the Sphinx on the oblique and dig on an angle until they reached it, and they didn't have time for trial and error. They had to figure some way to support the Sphinx and start digging downward from the top. Easier imagined than done. Over one hundred of the best structural engineers the United Continents had to offer had been burning up their computers for the past ninety-six hours and hadn't come up with a workable answer yet.

"Mr. Lofler, why don't you just remote view what's on the records you saw down there?"

"Mr. President, while I can view things that are there and get a sense of them, sometimes very accurately, and I did see volumes that seemed to be books of some sort, it is very difficult to remote view numbers and letters with any degree of confidence, and of course, I can't turn the pages. Even if I could, I presume it would be in a language or structure I am not familiar with."

Bronc looked at Murph who nodded confirmation. Bronc looked at Veerphol, Mantid Chief of Habitat, the Mantid Chief Borer and Holemaker as Bronc thought of him, "Can you figure some way to get to it from the bottom?"

"Mr. President, not knowing exactly where the 'library' is, if we did tunnel around somehow and got under the bottom, we would still be removing the subjacent support from under the Sphinx which, without quoting figures, is an extremely heavy structure." By now, Bronc immediately recognized the Mantid mastery of understatement. "Thus, if we were able to do that, we would still need to support the Sphinx just as if we were digging from the top, and we haven't yet solved that problem."

"Well, people jack up houses and just move them off. Why can't you do that?"

Veerphol politely responded, "The mechanical stresses would exceed parameters, Mr. President."

Bronc smiled, "Can you translate that into cowboy terms?"

"It's just too fucking heavy, sir," shot back Det with his usual aplomb.

Undaunted, Bronc continued in his disarming cowboy way, "Well looky here, these Mantid folk are just too goddamned smart and clever and advanced not to be able to figure out an easy way to do this. Now isn't that right, Mr. Veerphol? I think you ought to get some more of your Grey heads together and figure it out – *fast*, or soon, none of us will have to bother." Bronc's gaze tore through Veerphol's head and he looked away, perhaps a first in Mantid history. Bronc's way of getting a defining concept across was more effective than the infamous Det "kick in the nuts" to get someone's attention, which Det had actually done from time to time in his career, referring to them as "testicular incidents."

Veerphol said he would handle it and left quickly. Much to everyone's' surprise, he reappeared about ninety minutes later with three strange-looking volumes, each about two and one-half by three feet and perhaps four inches thick. They were on a small hand truck wheeled in by Major Klitschko whose perpetually stoic military face never changed. All the important players were summoned to the huge conference room, having been told "the library is open." If Veerphol could have, he would have been grinning from ear to ear.

A Grey none of the Surface people had ever seen before was standing next to Veerphol. Mamadou Bennajem, being United Continents Chief of Security, acted like it and barked, "Who the hell is this?!" He put his hand on his weapon.

Jenoor stepped forward, uncharacteristically showing some irritation, "Well, apparently, we do not all look alike. This being is the Mantid soldier, Maartindael, who not only thought up the plan to acquire the 'library,' but willingly experimented with his own life in order to carry it out."

Bronc did smile from ear to ear, "Well, I'll be goldarned, I knew you boys could do it – with the right motivation. How did you do it?"

Veerphol, with new-found confidence, and relief that he had not had to devise a plan to support the Sphinx, spoke, "Well, Mr. President, by way of background, the Mantid have had very unfortunate experiences in the past from Particulating and then re-forming in other than clear space, resulting in a Mantid being stuck in or 'welded' into a solid object through the mutual commingling of energy, atoms and molecules. That is a horrible death, particularly if it doesn't occur immediately.

"Mantid experiences in that regard were similar to the unfortunate experiment the United States conducted in the twentieth century during its World War II when it attempted to alter the molecular structure of a war ship to make it invisible to the enemy, but was unable to control the effect on living beings. After rendering it invisible, when the ship with the crew on board was reconstituted, humans were 'growing' out of the decks and many other unfortunate things occurred. I believe you refer to it as 'The Philadelphia Experiment'."

Bronc, having extensively reviewed those still-classified reports concerning the U.S.S. Eldridge, nodded with sad understanding.

Veerphol continued, "Maartindael felt that instead of having exactly one chance to be right by Particulating so that he could pass through the dirt under the Sphinx and hope, if he guessed correctly, that when he re-formed he would be in the open space of the room, if it were there, perhaps he could try to Phase Shift instead of Particulate, go out of phase and then come back in phase ever so slightly as to be able to determine where he was, but not enough to get 'stuck' if he were not in the room, as had occurred in the other unfortunate Mantid Particulation and re-forming instances.

"Because of those Particulation experiences, we have never tried to move through solid objects while in a partial Phase Shift, only while in a full opposite phase. Maartindael believed that if he were still in the ground when he slightly re-phased, he would either try to determine if he could move through it without harm, or go out of phase again if he weren't irrevocably stuck, then move and come slightly into phase to see where he was, keeping up the process until he had located the room containing the 'library.' "

Bronc interrupted, "I'll be damned, I didn't know there was a difference between that 'Particulation' and 'Phase Shift' stuff. It was all just a bunch of gobbledygook to me. All I knew was that you could disappear and reappear wherever you wanted, and if you had aholt of me, I'd go with you, whether I liked it or not."

"Yes, Mr. President. From Soldier Maartindael's perspective, Particulation turns him into extremely small energy particles so he can pass through solid media for a predetermined distance, then he is completely reconstituted or re-formed in the same phase in which he started. Phase Shifting leaves him exactly the same as when he started so he can think and act while it is occurring, except he is shifting the phase of his vibration so that from the perspective of the solid media, he is becoming invisible or less dense in relation to it.

"In the past, whether Phase Shifting or Particulating, while it may look like we are walking *through* walls, for instance, we are actually Particulating or completely Phase Shifting and re-forming on the other side of the wall after each particle has finished moving through it, but in that case, or the case of going through the Earth to one of our Mantid cities, we know where we are and where the clear space is."

"Damn!" At times when Bronc was impressed, he wasn't particularly articulate or intelligently expressive.

"In any event, we took a craft rapidly to the Sphinx. Maartindael shifted out of phase and located himself where Mr. Lofler said the room containing the volumes would most likely be. When he shifted slightly back into Earth phase, he was a little off and found himself in hard ground. Of course, he did not know if he would be able to move through the ground, or go back out-of-phase from that slight in-phase condition. Being absolutely stationary at that point, Maartindael wiggled the last digit of his left 'hand' as you would call it to see if it would move through the ground. He immediately lost all sensation of that digit and decided to go completely back out of phase if he could. He was able to do so, but was minus his left digit."

He grasped Maartindael's left arm and held it up, showing those in the room, all of whom were hanging on every word, that Maartindael no longer had a left "little finger," leaving one less digit on that hand.

"As Maartindael was able to go out-of-phase and slightly back in, after several tries repeating the process but remaining stationary, he found himself in the room with the volumes, almost exactly as Mr.

Lofler described it. Maartindael went into full phase, took possession of the volumes, went out of phase with them, returned to the Surface and then back to Earth phase – the phase, of course, in which you presently see him and the volumes."

The room burst into spontaneous applause. Murph couldn't tell if Maartindael flushed a little, presuming he could. Bronc spoke quietly to Det who, in turn, whispered to Klitschko. The latter quickly left the room. Bronc spoke to Maartindael, "Soldier Maartindael, I understand you folks have been developing emotions. Were you frightened?"

Jenoor sent Maartindael a thought message to be absolutely candid. Maartindael answered, "Mr. President, to translate into Surface vernacular, which in my training as a Mantid soldier I have studied and also learned from my patrols with U.C. soldiers prior to the Visitation 1000, I was scared shitless." The room roared with laughter.

"Why did you do it?"

Maartindael became completely serious, "To paraphrase one of your great past Surface leaders, whom I have also studied – if not me, who?"

Det and Mamadou Bennajem glanced at one another. Both knew that when the conflict with the Harvesters began, they wanted Maartindael on the President's guard detail. The door to the conference room opened again. Striding back through it, Klitschko handed a small, flat, black container to Det who stepped over to Maartindacl. The room fell silent. "Soldier Maartindael, we don't have a lot of time these days. We definitely don't have time for reports and reviews nor pomp and circumstance. We don't even know if we'll be alive next week. As a result, President Freeman, as United Continents Coordinator, and I, as United Continents Protective Forces General Commander, are jointly and extemporaneously exercising the authority we have to confer the highest military honor the United Continents has to offer. You'll just have to imagine the Surface band, parade grounds and troops. So, hearing no objection from any in this room, on behalf of the United Continents and with its deep appreciation, we hereby award you the United Continents Medal of Valor."

To the repeated spontaneous applause and cheers of all in the room, Dct opened the box and fastened the medal around Maartindael's skinny little neck. Murph was certain he saw Maartindael flush.

Det then went over to the 'library' volumes, broke the clasp on the one slightly larger than the other two and opened it. It was actually a container, not a book. They saw what looked like an eight by twelve inch flat ccd computer screen, some kind of disc player, a power source, a soft looking flat, circular pad surface about ten inches in diameter, and pictorial instructions on how to start the apparatus. They opened the other two volumes which held what appeared to be the discs for the player.

Det spoke to Mamadou Bennajem, "Get three separate digicorders and operators in here and two remote digicorders rolling before we start this thing. No telling what will happen. It might work only once if it works at all." Bennajem had already done various scans on the volumes and had concluded they were exactly what they appeared to be, containing no known explosives, gasses or other harmful devices. The power supply was some type of well-shielded gamma radium technology with an extremely long half life and as a result, shelf life. He knew the U.C. scientists would be almost uncontrollable in their demands to tear it apart for reverse engineering purposes after military intelligence was done with it.

While this computer memory technology was dumbfoundingly advanced by Earth standards at the time it was created, disc technology was now so out of date by Earth standards that it was necessary the pictorial instructions be very clear and simple, which they were. They popped in the first disc and pushed the button. The screen came to life and it was clear that the Harvesters wanted someone to place a hand on the flat pad surface. They all looked at each other, debating who should do it.

Calzaghe Vanderpool tendered, "This could be a device which will instantaneously suck all the information in a person's brain into this computer and transmit it to the Harvesters. Then they will know all our plans and preparations."

Raama responded, "They may well have already done that with their telepathic capabilities. I think they scarcely need this device to accomplish that end. My surmise is that it will be probing the respondent's brain through whatever cellular-transmission, electromagnetic or other technological process it uses, but only for the purpose of communicating with us in the language of the respondent."

Evidencing his respect for Raama's intellect, Calzaghe

Vanderpool recapitulated and agreed.

Then Boudouani Norris, Hoffman Green and Beyer Koon started a general worry-session about what could happen if they were wrong. It picked up steam and paralysis-by-analysis set in.

"Sheeitt!" Bronc walked over and slapped his hand down on the pad.

There was a collective gasp from the play-it-safers in the room, followed by absolute silence from everyone, except for the sound of all staring hard, very hard, at the device.

Det leaned over to Murph and whispered, "Don't look now, but I think Green needs to change his diaper."

No one needed to ask why Bronc did it. They all knew that it had to be done. They were just stalling until someone showed the guts to take the responsibility. Bronc had defined again why he was the world's leader.

Bronc, knowing they couldn't win a war with that kind of waffling, was not happy, "You piss-ant, lab-coated dickheads will still be sitting here staring at this machine while they're burning us to cinders next month! For Chrissake! Start making some decisions that move us in *some* direction, even if you're wrong! Just do the best with what you've got! But do *something*!"

Det loved it.

It dawned on some of the scientists for the first time that this was not simply an intellectual exercise.

Bronc removed his hand and a human-like figure popped up from the round pad-like surface. They assumed it was a hologram, except it was solid appearing, just like an absolutely real miniature person, flesh and clothes, about ten inches tall. It was an attractive blonde female in what could be described as a pilot's jump suit, and it started talking in a pleasant voice.

"Hello. Don't be apprehensive. I'm actually an illusographic representation, an Illusograph, a computer program designed many thousands of your years ago for the sole purpose of leaving a record of what we have done on this planet. We believed the record would be viewed by members of *our* civilization upon return to your planet, but I can see, by the joulergs transmitted from this gentleman's hand into the computer, that you are not members of our civilization, but descendents of those we left many, many thousands of years ago.

"By placing your hand on the pad, it enabled the program to learn how we could communicate with you in terms of your language, its syntax and vocabulary and where you are in relation to the time we left you on Earth, as you call your planet. The program translates from our language into yours, and if you speak to me, vice versa. It is a very sophisticated program and I can converse with you and answer your questions."

Raama's large eyes gazed about the room knowingly.

"However, my knowledge is limited to the time this program was made and I do not know anything about the many thousands of years that have passed since then, except what I have learned and can deduce about your development from the joulergs of the person, Bronc, who placed his hand on the pad. The more people who place their hands on the pad, the more I can learn; thus, the more I can deduce and the more efficiently and intelligently I can communicate with you."

No one else moved to place a hand on the pad.

While she was only ten inches tall, her voice sounded very natural and much larger than that. They finally realized that the sound was coming not only from her mouth, but from the pad surface she was standing on, much as sound would come from behind a movie screen, although they correctly presumed it was not the same technology.

"While I look and feel real and solid, though miniature to you, I am in reality only an illusion of substance, an Illusograph created by a computer program. If you pick me up and move me a short distance away from the pad, I will disintegrate between your fingers and reintegrate back on the pad. The power source of the computer, while strong enough to accomplish the illusion, is confined to the area of the computer and is not universal enough to continue the illusion for any distance.

"In any event, with the exception of my size, I look exactly like the female members of my civilization look, although we have individual differences as you do, based on what I already know and on Bronc's joulergs. We have male members also and I can have one join me now if you would like."

There was a collective "yes" from the fascinated occupants of the room, almost none of whom had diverted their gaze from her since she first appeared. A male appeared next to her, shoulder-length blonde hair, blue eyes, as were hers, somewhat taller and more muscular, also in a pilot's jump suit. From their appearance they both could have been Nordic humans. Bronc, Det, Murph and Lofler looked at each other and muttered in unison with astonished recognition, "The Blondes!"

Having heard them, she continued, "From Bronc's joulergs, I believe that your conclusion is correct. We are the 'Blondes' that people on Earth have sighted through your centuries as we returned from time to time up to the making and completion of these discs, and I conclude from Bronc that we have also returned from time to time after that to check on the progress of our work."

They were beginning to realize that they were witnessing the process whereby all they believed about the Harvesters up to this point was being confirmed. More than one took a deep breath. Those little things looked like such nice people too.

All of a sudden they all started asking questions at once. Det stopped them. "I think it would be wise if I asked the questions in order to conserve time and stay focused. If you have a question, write it down and give it to General Larsen. He will attempt to prioritize them."

Det was not the U.C.P.F. General Commander simply because his personality was very effective motivating combat troops, but primarily because he was very intelligent in a rapid and practical way, particularly thinking on the move when he could hear the reaper counting off the seconds to the Harvest. Boxers would call it "quick feet."

He recognized this may be his only chance to interrogate the enemy, "Have you been programmed to lie to us?"

The female continued, "Do you mean withhold information from you in answer to a question, or to answer it in a way which is misleading?"

"Both, and please provide an explanation with your answer."

"No. We believed we would be communicating with our own kind. Even had we known it would be those we placed here, there would be no reason to be dishonest. We had absolutely nothing to fear from you at the time this program was created, nor at the times it was updated with additional discs when we placed the headdress on the monument. Our technology was so far in advance of yours at those times, that even though you have developed technology exponentially since then according to the joulergs I received, I presume that our exponential factor has, relative to yours, kept us far to the fore, with still nothing to fear."

The occupants of the room looked at each other, recognizing the logical implications of what she was saying despite the arrogance of its content, but no one was even close to giving up.

Det continued, "Why did you come here?"

"Well, at a point after Earth had become capable of supporting life as we know it, which is basically as you know it – you can see how similar we are in appearance – our government determined that if we had individuals who could do all the work in our society that was necessary to maintain it physically and administratively, all the commercial, domestic and governmental labor and administration, our people could devote themselves entirely to developing themselves metaphysically without having their time, energy and thoughts taken up by those more basic physical and administrative tasks related to our existence.

"Additionally, food supplies would get low on our planet at unpredictable periodic intervals due to certain peculiarities of its weather and natural resource patterns. Our government was exploring ways of meeting those needs in the most efficient and economical way possible, and in a way that would preserve our civilization in times of hardship."

"So you decided slaves were the answer?"

"More than that. We desired 'field workers,' as we call the laborers you refer to as slaves, who could also be used as food if that were necessary, and it was clear to us that it would be required from time to time."

From that answer, which put the room in a state of reality shock, it was clear to Det that this "Illusograph" was just laying it out like any computer would. If she were going to lie, she wouldn't have said that. "Go on."

"In the beginning of our visits, at varying times, we put some insects, bipedal beings and other things here that we had developed, some of which were similar to what was already here, but with the potential of becoming more intelligent with time. It was experimental in those days. We did most of the things just to see what would happen, and it couldn't contaminate our planet.

"The original bipedal beings we put here, loosely referred to as 'prehistoric man' by your people, just did not develop enough intelligence, either to do what we wanted or to survive over time. So, at a point we developed and introduced to Earth what you know as *Homo sapiens*, which is what developed into *you*."

Mouths were literally open all over the room at actually hearing from this source the things that Jenoor had been telling them about the Harvesters, plus even worse intentions.

Det knew he was at war now. Slowly, "Anything else?"

"One fortuitous event occurred that gave us a 'bonus' as you would say. We had put some insects here way back in the beginning, and a particular species, which disappeared and we thought had become extinct, developed superior abilities, intelligence and technology, superior to that even of *Homo sapiens*. We were astonished when we unexpectedly picked up their thoughts some eons ago. We immediately realized it would provide us with at least two levels of 'field workers' and also food variety. We are highly telepathic and it was a very pleasant surprise."

Jenoor wasn't surprised at this point to learn he had the ability to become absolutely furious.

Bronc interjected, clearly irritated, "What's your name?"

"I am Lanta and this is Nordine."

Bronc was getting red in the face. There was no trace of his cowboy accent, "Lanta, on Earth we call it slavery and cannibalism, the latter being a type of murder. Both are illegal here these days and have been for some time. Those laws were motivated by the realization that it is just plain wrong. We call them human rights, but for your purposes, let's just call it 'right.' And, frankly, it isn't at all clear to me which of our civilizations is the most advanced. Apparently, you folks were so busy working on this problem that you forgot to work on your metaphysics."

Lanta replied matter-of-factly, "It is just a matter of a civilization's cultural beliefs. Since neither you, even though we look similar, nor the insects, are of our species, we view it no differently than you view using oxen to plow fields or breeding chickens and cows for food. You are smarter and ultimately more powerful than they are, so you do what is convenient, even necessary for you, *and* to repeat, they are not of your species."

Jenoor stepped forward, noting with interest that his emotions had developed to the point where he was getting this upset, "If it is helpful to you, a difference here, Lanta, lies not in the nature of the species, but whether they are beings who are members of a sentient, linguistic civilization."

"By your definition and values. But, the definition and values that ultimately control are those of the most powerful. That was clear even on Earth at the time these discs were made." She paused, "You are one of the insects aren't you?" It became obvious she could see as well as hear and talk. Jenoor did not like her and did not like being called an insect in the way she meant it. He felt like educating her about the fact that he could no longer be properly be referred to as an insect, but he controlled himself with quite an effort and did not respond.

All of her answers continued to be matter-of-fact in a very pleasant voice. She was simply answering inquiries, not arguing, which Det recognized and continued to pursue, "So what do you intend to do?"

"Take you when you are ready."

Another of Det's important attributes was his ability, when he believed it necessary, to suppress reaction to his emotions in highly charged situations and continue to react calmly and think logically in the direction of his goals, "When will that be?"

"You appear to be ready now, based on the plan at the time of this program's creation."

"So when, exactly, will you come for us?"

"I do not know. My knowledge of my people stops at the point this program was created. All I know about events since then is what I picked up from Bronc's joulergs, which is the fact that you think we are coming soon. But I can tell you that after my people collect you and return to our planet with you and the insects, those who collected you will be viewed in our society just as angels from heaven are in yours."

With the exception of Bronc, they had no words to respond to the enormity of what she was saying. For global political reasons, Bronc's almost daily Bible reading was not widely publicized, and many would be surprised at what followed. He leaned over and looked directly into her little blue digital eyes, spitting quotations from the book of Matthew into her attractive little electronic face,

> The . . . labourers are few;
> Pray ye therefore the Lord of the harvest,
> that he will send forth labourers . . . .
> The field is the world;

the good seed are the children of the kingdom;
but the . . . enemy sowed them; . . .
the harvest is the end of the world;
and the reapers are the angels.

The room was silent and Det said quietly to Bronc in an effort to calm him, "She's a computer. She looks real, but she's not. She's just somebody's mental concept turned into energy, closely spaced energy. She's an illusion that appears to think. She doesn't get it, Bronc."

<~We understand, Bronc.~>

There was instantaneous, collective alarm. They had been so fascinated by Lanta that they completely neglected to do anything about shielding their thoughts. They didn't know if it did any good anyway, but they could at least have tried. They all turned and looked accusatorily at Mamadou Bennajem, as if the U.C. Chief of Security should have done something about their thinking. Bennajem, with arms crossed, just raised his eyebrows and cocked his head a little. He felt there was nothing effective that could have been done, and it was clear he wasn't afraid to die.

They waited for more telepathic messages from the Harvesters, but none were forthcoming, so with a few instructions from Lanta, they put in the rest of the discs which gave a fairly detailed illusographic audio-visual history of Earth's seeding by the Harvesters, the development of the "labourers" and the Harvesters' chilling intentions. But it stopped at the time they put the headdress on the Sphinx, which was when they sealed the "library."

<<~>>

CHAPTER THIRTY THREE

In order to make certain the inhabitants of Earth were properly motivated, the security digisticks of that "Afternoon With Lanta" were shown over and over again to a frightened world.

More time passed without attack by the Harvesters and the Earth was ready. At least as ready as it ever was going to be. Surface and Below had all done their best in their respective areas of expertise. The continents had pulled together in an imperfect but unprecedented display of Entrainment and cooperation motivated by fear of extinction, slavery or becoming a meal for an extraterrestrial after a long day in the harvest fields. One could pick any of the reasons. It scared the hell out of a person no matter which one it was.

An interesting byproduct of this Entrainment and cooperation was an increased mutual tolerance and respect for others of differing viewpoints, national and ethnic origins, religions and socio-economic backgrounds. Suddenly, those differences didn't seem nearly as important any more. What was important was human beings, actually *beings*. Many of each kind, Surface and Below, human and former insect, came to realize that there were certain things, the *most important* things, that bound them together. Not just the fear of the negative things, but a realization that whatever the origin of one's species, there were underlying and universal concepts of consciousness related to love, harmony and right-thinking that amalgamated them, that each possessed a development of certain facets of the whole to share with one another. A collective recognition that surfaced was that life without love, in its broadest form, is the antithesis of life.

Thus, Earth's sentient occupants, in the main, became relatively tranquil in relation to one another, but not in relation to "those fucking farmers from space" as Bronc had taken to calling them. The beings on Earth, with eyes to the skies reminiscent of the old news film classics from World War II, had become second-nature familiar with terms coined by the talk PP's, such as "ETC" (Extra Terrestrial Craft), as opposed to "KTC" (Known Terrestrial Craft) which, of course, included the Mantid craft. "UFO" no longer imparted the required specificity. All were constantly and habitually looking up.

Having come to the conclusion it would be useless against the Harvesters to go to a "secret" location, and believing it vitally important to set an example of courage for the world, both Bronc and Det had decided to work primarily in the White House and the Pentagon, respectively, believing they would be among the first to go and there would be little they could do about it no matter where they were. However, the Vice President and other appropriate officials of the United States and the U.C. had been sent to "secure" and "undisclosed" locations around the world for whatever good it might do.

As it ultimately turned out, only Bronc had to look toward the sky. While he was contemplating where all this would lead in a conversation with Det, Jenoor and others in a White House communications room, he was gazing out the window when a mountainous ETC materialized, hovering soundlessly over the White House. For the second time in his adult life, Bronc involuntarily wet his pants. It was here. This *was* it. All the preparation, all the thought, all the emotion crystallized into this one moment which he had hoped, had *prayed*, would never come. And his reaction? – he lost it in his pants.

Det knew there were no atheists in combat, and Bronc knew there were none on the backs of bucking horses or bulls. They waited for a white hot blast, or something similar – they weren't sure what it would be. Bronc thought that at least he would see if there was anything to what Jenoor was saying about the continuation of consciousness, but he would rather find out another way, a way more of his own choosing, or at least have a little more time to think about it. Det walked defiantly to the window and stared at the craft.

Nothing happened. The ETC just sat there like a Death Star out of one of the classic *Star Wars* films. But this was *definitely* no movie, and it didn't have to sit there long before it was surrounded by smaller Mantid attack craft, manned by combination Mantid/Surface crews now under the United Continents logo, waiting for further orders from the United Continents Protective Forces Command Headquarters.

At the same time, and while perhaps it wasn't necessary since the relevant White House security cameras and audio were now being pumped into the Tesla Field digifeed, the entire world was placed on alert, not only all the U.C. military installations, but the world citizenry as well, both Surface and Below, since it was a certainty they would need to be ready for evacuation and civil defense. Training had been intensive, not only for the military defense forces, but also for civilian defense with respect to the mayhem that would inevitably follow.

Initially in accordance with its usual procedures, UniCom tried to communicate with the great hovering craft by digicom radio. "Unidentified flying object in Quadrant 49623, this is United Continents Protective Forces Command Headquarters, please identify yourself."

<~Your digicom radios are not necessary. Your experience, particularly what you have learned from the Mantid, has shown you that if you wish to communicate with us, you need merely think it and contact us through what Jenoor has denominated to you as the Universal Connection. We have your 'radio' technology aboard our craft only because we know that is the way you do it on the 'Surface.' We would suggest that you follow the developmental lead of the Mantid, whom we left there long ago, and merely communicate telepathically with us.~>

Det spoke into the microphone, irritatedly, "That may be appealing to folks of your abilities, but I'm sure you have figured out that if a Surface person did that, the other Surface people wouldn't have a clue what is going on because they would not get the Surface half of the thought transmissions, even though it's pretty clear that everyone can receive your thought transmissions, at least when you want them to. But then again, I suspect confusion among us is your wish." He could perceive no reason to be nice to the "farmers." Everyone knew what they were here for.

<~That is incorrect. We wish you no harm whatsoever.~>

The torpedo-sized Rods inside the Mantid craft had Particulated through the crafts' walls and were hovering next to them outside. There were about three hundred Mantid craft surrounding the great hovering Harvester craft which had a footprint of about three city blocks and was about twenty stories tall. Det had no doubt it was not the mother ship and was small in comparison to it. They had to have a lot of room to take all the slaves back with them. He didn't believe their false assurance for a moment and didn't bother with any questions to try to test their prevarication quotient, which he was sure was considerable.

Det threw out sarcastically, "Sure, pal," as he pressed the attack order on the keyboard after a nod from Bronc. Three thousand Particulating torpedo Rods and the invisible photon module streams from fifteen hundred photon cannons entered the Harvester craft from every angle imaginable. Det, Bronc, and the entire world listening and watching on their digivisions waited for the biggest whumping "kabung" they had ever seen or heard. The awesome craft disappeared without a sound.

The world cheered in unison, but Bronc and Det knew that was not what was supposed to happen. They turned and looked at Jenoor and Teenaan, who knew that *nothing* had happened except that the Harvester craft had disappeared, and not from any Earthly cause. The Mantid psychic, Teenaan, said quietly, "Their consciousnesses are still intact."

<~We could have let the Rods and photon modules pass through and destroy your defense craft on the opposite sides of us, but that is not our purpose.~>

Det shot back over the microphone, "I'll bet it's not. You need as many live bodies as you can get!"

<~We repeat, we mean you no harm.~> Their thought transmissions were calm, quiet and powerfully authoritative.

Raama, an ever curious scientist, ~If you mean us no harm, then you will not mind telling us how you did that and where you are now.~

<~Not at all. We have reached a level of realization about the nature of being *beyond* the knowledge that matter is generated by mind. Our understanding has reached the point that we can produce, alter or 'unproduce' matter simply by changing our thinking. When you fired upon us, we simply changed ourselves, our craft, and the matter you had propelled into it, all of which is energy in various forms, back into its basic format.~>

~What is that?~

<~I trust you know, Raama, certainly Jenoor does – mindstuff.~>

Raama knew the postulate and believed it. He had seen Jenoor demonstrate it to a limited extent in healing other beings and was familiar with the raising of Mari from the "dead," but he had never seen its demonstration carried to this logical extension. He was truly amazed. ~Well . . . where are you then?~

<~In our real, substantial and natural state, that of Superconsciousness which, based on everything we understand, flows from One Mind.~>

"Well, all it means to me is that you are invisible," growled Det.

<~Certainly to material eyes, your eyes, General, which are man-

ifestations of lower, much lower, levels of consciousness. We are not calling you unintelligent. Certain people on Earth refer to the concept as different planes or dimensions of consciousness in order to explain it. You are in the Material Dimension, which is illusory. The illusion is considered to be 'real' only by other parts of the illusion, and you cannot see us because the illusion sees only itself. The matter-illusion is conveniently self-validating. Its validation disintegrates with understanding.~>

"I still don't see you."

<~Perhaps it will help to consider that so long as a child believes it, the boogieman is real and substantial. When the child's level of understanding increases to the point where it ultimately knows there is no boogieman under the bed, that it is simply an erroneous belief, the boogieman illusion loses its apparent reality and thus its power, the putative power given it by the miseducated and misinformed viewer, power given in good faith but in ignorance.

<~We are an extension of that analogy, General. You cannot see us because we have passed beyond your material understanding, and thus beyond material sight. And in contrast to the boogie man, while our material form is illusory, our existence and power will not end with an understanding of that on your part. As beings made of mindstuff, we are substantial because consciousness, or mind, is the natural state and the substance of existence.~>

"Well, as far as I am concerned, you are the *real* boogieman."

<~You will not cooperate with us?~>

"No, we will only fight you . . . unless you will leave."

The Earth held its breath.

<~The circumstances will not allow us to leave. In order to be true to ourselves, we must carry out the mission we came to perform.~>

"Then go fuck yourselves! We'll fight you till it's over one way or the other!"

<~You cannot harm us.~>

The great craft reappeared. Det did not waste any more Rods or photon modules. He just waited. Nothing happened. The craft stayed there for days and did nothing. Det instructed the U.C. Mantid craft to maintain their positions, but neither he nor Bronc knew what to do.

So, when in doubt, convoke a meeting, in this case the United Continents Security Summit, which included Manticon and the related

Mantid underground cities. They had been unanimously declared an underground continent pursuant to, as some called it, the "Atlantis Resolution."

The notice went out for a meeting three days away, and the Harvester ship disappeared again.

CHAPTER THIRTY FOUR

Bronc knew this Summit would be the most important meeting in his life and in the history of the world. He was well aware it could result in the world's decision to fight to the point of total annihilation. The knowledgeable media believed Det would be the key spokesman advocating the ultimate fight, which they presumed the Summit would ratify since surrender seemed anything but a viable option. After the unresolved confrontation at the White House, Bronc correctly concluded that the world population needed a significant boost to its confidence in the U.C. leaders, particularly the leader of the U.C. military. So, Bronc convinced Det to participate in a one-on-one worldwide digivision interview with Cynthia Carole, the world's most respected digivision journalist.

Det had always served without seeking the limelight and consistently refused any interviews longer than short sound bites. This would be the first in-depth look at him the world would have and it was a major broadcast coup for Cynthia Carole. While he would not be able to answer any questions about the Harvesters for security reasons, Bronc, Murph and Det believed it important for Earth to see who would lead them in the battle.

The live interview was taking place in Det's Pentagon office. His broad, tough countenance was resplendent in his military dress and medals. His uniform's headgear with insignia and gold braid was in full view on the desk. The U.S. and U.C. flags behind him were magnificent. The six stars on each side of his collar cast a golden glint into the camera from time to time. He refused to remove the cigar for the interview and Cynthia Carole, not wanting to antagonize this imposing, even ferocious-looking, figure and jeopardize the interview, wisely chose not to make an issue of it. After accomplishing the initial on-air niceties, the interview began.

"General Menard, while most of the public knows little of you, you have earned the post generally considered to be occupied by the foremost military figure in the world through effectively putting down flare-ups of terrorism and illegal, inhumane regimes all over the globe on behalf of the United Continents. The result, for a number of years now, has been relative peace and fairness among the world's inhabitants, even though there may be vehement disagreement over issues. When you are given a set of orders by your Commander in Chief,

Bronson Freeman, how do you perceive your mission?"

Her producers insisted she open with that insipid question. Just by looking at Det, she knew the answer was obvious even if he chose not to speak. He clamped down on the cigar and the answer came out of the other side of his mouth, "My mission is to succeed, to win, to accomplish it, whatever 'it' is. I serve. If I'm told to locate the softest baby's butt, I do it. If it's to exercise military power, I do everything I can to keep from pulling the trigger, but when it becomes necessary, I do not hesitate to annihilate a fifty-thousand-person troop unit to accomplish and insure the proper exercise of freedom. Once the decision is made, I do it and I don't wait until it's too late."

Knowing that Det had never been on DV for more than half a minute at a time before, Bronc had debated at length with Murph about coaching Det on his approach to answering questions. This was an extremely important public relations effort and Bronc wanted him to project the image of the quintessential soldier, the resurrection of Teddy Roosevelt charging San Juan Hill. Murph had finally convinced him not to try to change the "real thing." "Bronc, believe me, the old adage is absolutely true in this case, 'If it ain't broke, don't fix it.' I guarantee you, if you let him be himself, the only possibility is that he will be exactly what you want. Don't confuse the issue by asking him to 'be natural.' He is a 'natural.' Leave him alone." Watching on DV, Bronc was ecstatic.

Cynthia Carole's mind was racing for the interviewer's counterpoint, "What if the only decision that makes sense is to surrender?"

His look was filled with the type of incredulous curiosity he reserved for the illogically inane. She thought for a moment that the cigar was going to pop straight at her, "I've never surrendered. Others have. I have not. I don't intend to."

She wasn't willing to give up either, "Doesn't that beg the question?"

Taking the cigar between his thumb and first two fingers, moving it toward her like a slow missile as he spoke, "If it does, you'll have to live with it. Whenever I've faced it, I've refused and it worked out fine."

Bound and determined she wouldn't flinch, she wondered if she could expose a little of his belly, "Is there a soft part of you?"

His eyes darted back and forth, searching hers. She was looking right at him, trying to read his with the same effort he was making to read hers. No matter what else he saw there, and he saw things that surprised him, he could see she was not going to back off the question. So, as with his other answers, he gave her a straight shot, "Sure . . . I can cry when I think of people not being free to determine their own destiny. Take my freedom and I'll weep. Take it from another and don't allow me to do anything about it and I'll weep harder. *That's* my soft spot."

Bronc could see that quote all over the Tessie. Unbelievable. The speech writers probably couldn't come up with something close to being that good, and it just tumbled right out of Det's mouth. Wahooo!

Judging from his eyes, she felt lucky to get an answer and decided she would get no more on the subject, "Aside from that, you have a reputation of being hard and insisting on unreserved best effort, yet at the same time, you have a reputation for being reasonable."

Det and the cigar seemed happy to be on another subject, "That's why I'm good at what I do. The ones who think I'm unreasonably hard are those who put out reserved effort."

She believed she could push on this one a little more, "What about the ones that are so scared, particularly in combat, that they put out significantly impaired effort? Last century in the Second World War, General Patton is reported to have slapped at least one soldier when that happened."

Impressed that she knew tidbits of military history, the mashed-up cigar came out of his mouth again and the hand with it rested on the desk. The humanity peeking out of his answer surprised her, "They are doing the best they can with what they've got. Some have less than others. I don't slap them. I just try to identify and utilize the ones who perform well even if they are scared. It doesn't matter if they're scared. Almost everyone is. No one wants to die. How they perform under those conditions is what's important." He jammed the cigar back between his teeth, "Now, the ones who make a conscious, selfish decision to let someone else carry the risk, they are slapping material. I'll slap them from now till their next life. I'll slap them into their next life."

Overjoyed at the opportunity to flip the direction toward the unexpected, "Does that last comment imply that you believe in reincarnation?"

He didn't blink or hesitate. With the cigar rolling to the other side of his mouth, "Listen, if all that stuff is true, and if you know your history, which I think you do, then I was Patrick Henry, George Patton and Teddy Roosevelt, and I'm still charging up the hill. I was born the way I am, and you are at liberty to believe in that if you want to, but I'm just too damn busy right now to wonder."

Persevering, "So, do you think you've been a military guy in your prior lives?"

While he appreciated that she didn't give up easily, he knew he did not want this to be the headline sound bite from the interview, and he was infinitely too sharp to be sucked in by the psychology of a second try, "I just told you. If that's true, then it must be the case because the military is what I know and what I choose to do. It's like I said, I do not have time to think about it."

Watching him, she had been fighting the tendency to be mesmerized by his countenance, but she succumbed, "Well, to tell you the truth, the only thing I can focus on is that cigar. It's alive and can think, right?"

Whoops! She said it. It just subliminally jumped out. The fate of the world could depend on this man, and all she could do was blabber about his vivified cigar. The camera zoomed in on his face and the side of his mouth without the cigar slowly broke into a grin, at least she hoped it was a grin, but he said nothing. It was his turn and, knowingly, he wasn't taking it. It didn't bother him in the least. Cynthia was desperately searching for a question to jump-start this suspension of time. Staring at that damn cigar, she'd lost her place in her mental notes, and all she could see was her own obituary – "General suffocates broadcast journalist, live, with silence."

The director whispered "boxing champ" into her ear-dot receiver and, at a loss for a segue, she blurted out, "You were an All Continents Heavyweight Boxing Champ in your earlier days in the military, undefeated in forty-nine fights. What do you think it is in you that accounts for your perfect record?"

Thinking he had a sense of humor because he grinned when she babbled about his cigar, she was expecting him to quip that it was due to the fact that he quit before he lost. He shot back, "Because there is no part of me that thinks I can be defeated. I have absolutely no doubt, none whatsoever, about my ability to win, to accomplish my mission no matter what the odds. I don't fight from the viewpoint of fear of losing, not one molecule of me. What you fear manifests itself sooner or later. That is not an issue I must correct my thinking about. I am not so foolish as to fail to assess, and counter, the risks, but I fight to win – period."

Bronc was jumping up and down in front of his DV with glee.

Finding she had again lost her train of thought because of that exasperating hyperkinetic cigar popping all over while he talked, "Why did you stop boxing?"

"Because I was ordered to."

She pulled her eyes from the cigar and, knowing she could not ask about the Harvesters, tried to focus on a question that wasn't so vapid in this circumstance and might lead to a little more insight. This time intentionally without segue, she pulled out her trademark inquiry, "Tell me about your mother and father."

His eyes narrowed, the cigar stopped and he looked at her for perhaps three seconds, which she was sure was close to half an hour, "My father was military, as was his father and his father's father. My mother was always trying to keep him from overpowering me with his personality, from dominating me so I couldn't think for myself. That's all you need to know." Then, as an afterthought, he growled, "Except I started smoking this cigar just to piss him off."

What he didn't add was that he had a younger brother who couldn't take the pressure of their dominating father. Det always tried to protect him, but his brother took his own life when he was in his teens. He had surrendered.

After recovering from The General using the "p" word in such an important interview, Cynthia decided to continue with the family theme, "Why haven't you married?"

"I am married – to my country, to the continents, to the idea that you should be free to think for yourself and to ask me that question and any other question you want no matter how much I don't care to hear it or answer. I'm married to the idea that I don't have to answer it if I don't feel like it. I'm married to your freedom so long as you exercise it in a responsible way, a way that preserves my freedom. For all practical purposes, I'm married to you and to every citizen like you."

Bronc was dancing around his living room.

Cynthia had been assuming, as with many public figures, Menard had probably been coached nonstop since he agreed to do the interview, but she was keenly drawn to the sincerity and simplicity of his beliefs. This was the type of stuff politicians spouted in political campaigns, but face-to-face it was clear he *really* believed it – and lived it. She'd met a lot of powerful people, but had never met anyone like Det. In her peripheral thoughts during the interview, she had been thinking that both of them were unmarried career people, and it more than crossed her mind there could be some possibilities. She was mesmerized and couldn't help herself. Damn! Right in the middle of this interview, she was wondering what it would be like to be hooked up with this Big Bear, cigar and all.

Catching herself, but indirectly curious, "Do you ever want to have any children?"

"The country and the world are my children. I'll protect them the best way I can."

She looked at him for a moment and then asked the question she knew every viewer was thinking, "Are you for real?"

He leaned forward, clamping on the cigar, the camera focusing from his chin to the middle of his forehead, filling the three-dimensional DV image with his face, the cigar seemingly jutting right into the mind of each viewer, and said in a grizzly, quiet way, "If there's a war, whose side would you like to be on?"

Time was up, the digivision faded to a commercial and the crew started breaking down the equipment. Cynthia Carole decided she'd never get another chance, "General, would you like to have dinner sometime?" She was sure she flushed a little.

He took the cigar out of his mouth and looked at her for a moment, *really* looked at her, not anywhere except right into her eyes, "Tell you what, if we're both alive six months from now, it's a date."

<<~>>

CHAPTER THIRTY FIVE

The world leaders with the absolute decision making power for their countries had been primed and ready for some time to attend a U.C. Security Summit emergency meeting. Bronc had persuaded them to gather in one place with the same reasoning that had caused him and Det to continue working in their respective Washington offices. They agreed it was vital for the leaders to present an aura of fearless leadership. Their "seconds-in-command" were secreted in the "secure" locations around the world. With the help of the Mantid craft, the participants were assembled from across the globe at the United Continents Building in New York City and the meeting started right on schedule.

According to instructions from Jenoor and Teenaan, those in attendance prepared themselves mentally to block their thoughts from the Harvesters as best they could. That primarily consisted of giving themselves a conscious command to continuously block their thoughts, and repeating that command from time to time. For the same reasons, the meeting was also blocked from world viewing. Because the subject was so controversial, the participants were glad to have the excuse since no one thought it would be a good idea to exhibit tense world leaders fighting like ferrets at a time when they hoped to present as united a front as possible.

Bronc convened the meeting and looked around the capacious room, "Well, what do you think we should do?"

"What do you think is going to happen?" Spain's President, Ruvalcaba Vanancio fired back. He, as well as most of the others, was understandably edgy.

"You saw what happened with the Harvesters. Frankly, we don't have a clue," Bronc tossed in reply. "That's why we called this meeting to tap into the intellect of world leadership."

Murph pushed it out of his mind that a meeting to decide the fate of the Earth would begin like this. He'd seen better starts at high school student council. No wonder they weren't sending it over the Tesla. But Murph was certain he knew whose opinion they should be soliciting.

He switched on his microphone, "I think Pralit does . . . have a clue that is . . . ," volunteered Murph.

"Who is Pralit? asked Sondergaard McCoy, Chairwoman of the United Nordic Lands. She knew Murph had risen to some prominence at U.C. Headquarters, but was irritated that he had the audacity to speak up without being asked to do so.

Murph ignored her attitude and explained Pralit Lofler's background and abilities, all the while wondering how a native of her part of the world got the last name "McCoy."

Sondergaard McCoy spoke with disdain, "He can foretell what they intend with this 'remote viewing?' Well, I'd like to hear that." She believed the assembly would laugh Lofler into silence and half-expected a crystal ball to fall from his pocket and roll across the floor as he moved to the rostrum to speak so they all could hear. He did not have a desk at the Summit and, thus, no microphone. While anyone could have provided him with a lip-dot microphone and wireless public-address transmission module smaller than a button, some things never change.

"Mr. President, Madam Chairwoman, I do not claim to always be one-hundred percent accurate, or always close to the score even though I have accurately identified the ball park . . . excuse me, even though I am more-or-less right. But for all meaningful practical purposes, I have been one-hundred percent correct on a number of occasions and I usually am when I feel that I am."

Sondergaard McCoy had no time for fortune tellers and decided to dispose of him with logic, "Mr. Lofler. It is your use of the word 'usually' that concerns me, among other things. No matter what you tell us, we cannot take it as an absolute forecast of what will happen, we can't afford to."

"Yes, Madam Chairwoman, but since no one here seems to 'have a clue' as President Freeman put it, I believe I do."

Realizing that, ultimately, he would be allowed to speak his opinion, she responded, "Well enough, sir, what is it?"

As always, he spoke with a light Indian accent. "The result of my remote viewing procedures is that, in fact, they mean us no harm."

"Hahahahahahahahahahahahahahahahahahaha!" Det could not help his derisive, loud and rude laughter. It was shocking to the others in such a momentous meeting. His gruff voice boomed out, "I'm sorry, Lofler, but I just can't believe it after everything we know to date. How can it be that these demons intend to be nice to us? They are giving us a snow job and they obviously have you snowed, or are able to control your thinking or perception when you 'Connect' with them through the Universal Connection as you call it now."

"General, they can just wipe us out if they want to. I'm sure that ability is a counterpoint to our inability to hurt them. They haven't done anything to us. They did not even harm the defense craft that fired upon them. Isn't that some meaningful evidence for you, wholly apart from my remote viewing?"

As he spoke, the cigar was suspended by some unknown force of Det's passion for his point, "The only thing meaningful about it is my realization that the more of us they kill, the fewer they have to take back." Det paused, "So tell me, what is their plan for the immediate future?"

"They intend to tell us."

"I thought you were not clueless here?"

"General, they would not let me acquire any more information than that they do not intend to harm us and they will tell us what their plan is. They would not allow a deep mind probe."

Det bit down on his cigar and glared.

Sensing Pralit was in the process of burying himself and wanting to hurry it along, "Mr. Lofler, I'm certain you realize that is pretty weak stuff," Sondergaard McCoy put forth matter-of-factly.

"Yes, except for the way I feel about what information they did allow me to access, and I feel very strongly about that."

Murph jumped in, hoping his psychic friend would take the cue to find another approach, "Pralit, it's just not good enough."

As always, Pralit looked at them calmly and, in his lilting accent, continued in his courteous, logical and somewhat formal Indian way, "Mr. President, Madam Chairwoman, Mr. Bailey, the way I see it is this. It is painfully obvious that their technology and abilities are so far ahead of ours that we cannot defeat them, no matter how many flags we wave, and no matter how loud we yell 'Charge' when we engage the battle. They aren't going to sit there doing nothing forever, and if we do resist, when they ultimately defeat us after a fight, the damage to Earth, its population and its infrastructure will be monumental indeed – and we still will have lost."

Pralit continued, recognizing he had captured the entire room's attention from the first, "At that point they will do one of two things. They will either take us to their planet and do as Lanta said, or they will not harm us further, tell us it is too bad we resisted because they did not intend to harm us, which is what they are telling us now, and *then* they will disclose their non-harmful plan.

"Since we have *no* chance to win and will end up in their control anyway if that is what they want, *and* we have the *possibility* that they will not harm us, no one needs my remote viewing or psychic experience to make a logical decision based on the evidence. We should 'cooperate' with them and not get anyone hurt before we do that, because we will end up 'cooperating' with them anyway."

Pralit Lofler had punched Payson "Det" Menard's "blow button." Det could scarcely say the "S" word and each time he did, it sounded like a hand grenade exploding in the middle of a watermelon, "You mean *surrender*, and *surrender* without a fight?"

"If you want to put it that way."

"They intend to take us, work us and then eat us when it is convenient! I'd rather die than do that!" Det seemed to have puffed to twice his size. Some thought he had swallowed his cigar.

Prime Minister Stephane Hilton of the United British Isles was beginning to see the light. In her sterling British accent, "But, General, are you now certain that you are absolutely right? In consideration of the *possibility* that they may not harm us, which you must admit exists and has *some* support in fact, however slight, what sense does it make to engage in a bloody resistance we are certain to lose? This is not an exercise to prove how brave the citizens of the world are. It is an exercise to give ourselves the best chance of coming out of this in a positive way. As I see it, surrender is the only logical choice, albeit a highly emotional one."

Det tossed back, "Frankly, I think a lot of people would rather die than be under their control under any circumstances."

Teenaan timidly spoke, not being able to resist, "I know that you do not think much of my abilities because I, as other Mantid, for the most part have a thought blockage where the Harvesters are concerned. That, by the way, puts us in the same mental-ability boat as most Surface people. However, it seems to me that if the Harvesters have developed the ability they describe to produce matter from mind, and I note there was no mention of it at the time they made the discs, they could just 'manufacture' as much food as they want now, and they wouldn't need slaves to produce anything else. As I recall from my training in Surface culture, and referring specifically to food, that has been done here on Earth before by at least one entity on the Surface, the one you refer to as Jesus who, as you also know, stated that not only will those who come after him do the things he did, but they will do greater works than he did, provided they have the right mindset. Now if the Harvesters have risen to that ability since they made the discs, what motive would they have to take us as slaves or food?"

Det jumped back in, the cigar flying around in his mouth, "Look, the disappearing act could have been done exactly the same way the Mantid do it, by Phase Shifting. The guts of this could be a Wizard of Oz act – speaking of illusions."

Jenoor replied, "Det – he enjoyed the 'familiar' form of address – we had another three hundred craft there out-of-phase. If they came from out of phase or went into it, we would have seen them. Even if they went out of phase after you fired at them, since the Rods and the photon modules were inside their craft at that time, those weapons would have stayed in the same phase as the Harvesters' ship and blown it up. So, their going out-of-phase is not only improbable from all that we know, it would have been impossible for them to do so under those circumstances and not be detected by us. In addition, Mr. Lofler did not mention it, but he has also learned from them that a number of their kind exist almost constantly now in the Superconscious Dimension, materializing only when it is absolutely necessary. If that is the case, it also mitigates against any necessity for food or slaves."

Det's nature wouldn't let him quit, "Well, perhaps they have people back on their planet who are not all as advanced as the ones who are here, and perhaps the ones who are here aren't all as advanced as you think, so an 'absolutely necessary' reason for their materializing here would be to do exactly what their Illusograph, Lanta, talked about. In any event, wherever they are from, its got to be a looooong way from here and I'm sure we will all be dead from old age by the time we get there in any kind of space craft – so we may as well make a fight of it."

Raama had been wondering for some time how they would travel such a distance and keep everyone vital. The minimum distance to any theorized possible Harvester-type life supporting planet outside the Earth's solar system would be so far with any known technology that it couldn't be done in any timely way. Even at the speed of light, the most optimistically appropriate destinations would take tens of thousands of years. He wished he had asked the Harvesters about this issue when he was talking to them the day they had hovered over the White House.

Bronc had heard all he needed to and knew it was time to intervene. In his good natured way, he piped in, "Det, ya'll's a walkin' advertisement for why generals should not be elected President these days – which is why you're not and I am."

Det could see it coming. The Commander in Chief had made his decision.

"Det, they can annihilate us if they want. The only logical decision here is to surrender. As a bare minimum, that will give us an opportunity to talk with them, and when I start talkin', there's no tellin' what will happen. And who knows, maybe the little Indian guy is right."

Pralit took some offense at the characterization, but he also knew damn well he was right.

The final vote was preceded by several continuous days of tumultuous discussion, with a number of fistfights breaking out among dignified people, and was far from unanimous because it barely passed – but it passed. Except for surrender, no one could suggest any other logical way to handle the situation. The opposition's only position, admittedly emotional, was that if the Earth was going to go down, they wanted it to go down swinging – but they lost the vote count.

Informing the public, many of whom, as Det had pointed out, would rather be dead than be under the Harvester's control under any circumstances, would prove to have much more than a tumultuous result.

<<~>>

CHAPTER THIRTY SIX

The decision to surrender was announced and worldwide harmony instantly disintegrated. As if the decision to surrender the Earth to the Harvesters wasn't enough by itself, the Paranoia Purveyors were eagerly the first to get everyone more riled up. Eastman Foster was right in the forefront. He was now auto-translated into every language on Earth and carried by the Tesla Field to every area of Earth to essentially everyone on Earth, since virtually everyone had, as a minimum, a personal digicommunicator.

"Ladies and gentlemen, this unbelievable decision by the United Continents to surrender Earth to the Harvesters can mean only one thing. The high level U.C. Command and the U.C. leaders have made a deal with those Space Reapers to save themselves in exchange for us. The Grasshoppers have to be in on it. They are inside 'plants' by the Reapers who have waited eons for this moment. We have been compromised every step of the way. Do not let them do it. Stand and fight. It is better to stand and die as citizens of Earth than to be Thanksgiving dinners for the Harvesters on a foreign planet!"

Back at the Capitol, Bronc was furious. He bounced his hat off the table, "What the hell is that asshole trying to do! All we'll have is anarchy. There won't be any unity of continents to negotiate with anyone and we'll have to kill half our own people just to give Earth a chance to find out whether or not the other half will survive! Does that jerkoff ever think?!"

"Yeh, I know his picture is in the knowledge bank under 'Dickhead,' Bronc, but we'll have to figure someway to combat him. If we take any measures to silence him, it will only be taken as government-conspiracy proof that he is telling the truth." Murph was thinking as logically as he could and trying to figure out the best way, from the standpoint of public psychology, to counteract Foster who had, unfortunately, regained his influence and had positioned himself to become one of the most influential and powerful public personalities in the world, next to Xanthas as the public spokesbeing for the U.C. Until the decision to surrender, Foster had supported the U.C., but now, not even the threat Jenoor had made to him on the spacecraft's newsbriefing stage deterred him. He was going to ride this charging horse right over the cliff.

Jenoor expressed his concern in the inimitable Mantid style,

"Murph, if Eastman Foster is successful in channeling a large portion of Earth's population into negative mental Entrainment, it can severely delay positive understanding. The more people he converts to negative thinking, the more momentum that erroneous wave will gain. If it gains enough negative valence, it will eventually reach a critical negative mental 'mass' that will produce a highly destructive result. That is a very hard and unnecessary way to learn the truth for those beings practicing that mal-thinking. We must devise a way to short circuit, short-to-truth, this negative thought."

Xanthas, who had been sitting quietly listening to everyone, was about to speak when Major Klitschko burst into the room, "General, I'm sorry to interrupt, but General Tiozzo Cardona has gathered a contingent of South American fighting Stratocraft and, based on the data from the Mantid Foo Fighters that are following them, they are apparently headed here. He will not respond to requests to identify his purpose."

Det handed his digital communicator to Klitschko, "Patch me." Klitschko punched a few keypad items and handed it back. "Tiozzo, what the hell do you think you are doing?"

"Det, you gutless Grasshopper lover, we will give you this one opportunity to either join us or surrender your command. The U.C. supplied these craft to South America and you know they are one-hundred fifty of the finest state-of-the-art destructive machines. You also know the world population is behind me, that we have operatives everywhere, and . . . get these damn Foo Fighters away from me or I'll take it out on you personally!"

In spite of his strong personal feelings, and true to his loyalty to those he served in the chain-of-command in which he functioned, Det had accepted Bronc's and the U.C. Security Summit's decision and he knew his mission, "Tiozzo, you insufferable jerk. You either have a death wish or you are terminally stupid. Those little shiny balls are our eye in the sky and they are looking right at *you*. You know the technology. Those little drones shift in and out of your phase so they can see you and then transmit the information to the Mantid craft that are right with you, probably often out-of-phase. And I'll lay money that your 'operatives' are in the singular, in the form of that talking pecker, Eastman Foster. I can't believe he isn't there broadcasting from your aircraft. No, I can too. He's too chickenshit to take the risk.

"Tell you what, bonehead. I'll give *you* this *one* opportunity to turn around, go back to South America, land and turn yourselves in to our authority, failing which, it has been not-so-nice knowing you, and I'm sorry for the rest of the fools that are with you up there, and I'm particularly sorry for their families."

Cardona's voice crackled from the digicom, "Fuck you very much, Det. Here's your answer."

The Stratocraft were screaming from the stratosphere down toward the Capitol. On Cardona's command, one-hundred fifty strato-weapons officers' brains began to tell their forefingers to start the downstroke on the "Enter" buttons of their firing computers which were programmed to simultaneously fire their full compliment of lasers and missiles at the White House, the Pentagon and the Capitol Building.

Those one-hundred fifty thoughts were never consummated. Minuum, in command of the three hundred Mantid craft following the Stratocraft, had actually been slightly in phase about a mile above the South American contingent, closely scanning Cardona's thoughts. At the point Cardona decided to give the command to fire, Minuum gave her own forces the command to release the Rods. They were on their way when Cardona said the word "Fire." They materialized inside each of the hostile craft and superexpanded just prior to the point the weapons officers would have finished the thought for their forefingers to go into action.

Then there *was* the biggest whumping kabung heard to date over the Capitol, but it wasn't the Harvesters going up, it marked the beginning of Earth's effort to shoot itself in the foot.

<<~>>

CHAPTER THIRTY SEVEN

The "Cardona Incident" set off major flare-ups all over the world and they were becoming worse and worse. There was widespread rioting in the streets, citizens trying to take over government and military installations, and general panic and gnashing of teeth. The negative Entrainment had gained momentum and the positive Entrainment was losing ground. Earth could scarcely surrender if it's inhabitants weren't organized enough to surrender. The situation was becoming catastrophic.

While under no legal obligation to do so in connection with military action of any kind, Bronc had decided that the matter must be put to a worldwide vote, and its citizens could decide their collective fate, based on emotion or logic as they may chose.

Murph and Xanthas were alone in a planning room trying to figure out a public relations strategy for the vote which would be held in less than three weeks. Murph idly said, "Xan, we've got to do something absolutely momentous to jolt the world into the realization that neither the U.C. leaders, the U.C. Command nor the Mantid are subversive, but have made the most intelligent decision toward giving Earth's population the best chance at survival. We have to do something stupendous, shocking and believable."

Xanthas thought for awhile and suddenly got a calm look of understanding in her beautiful eyes, which Murph caught instantaneously since he seldom had his eyes off of her when they were together. He looked at her quizzically and she responded, "I am half Mantid, half human and I'm an 'insider' at the U.C. Command which is accused of trying to save only its own neck. I'm highly thought of, even revered, for my integrity throughout the world. I am the perfect person to do this."

"I know all that. Do what?"

"Something stupendous, shocking and believable that will jolt the world's population to its senses, so it will trust and follow the U.C. leadership."

"Okay. But what is it?" Murph was getting somewhat impatient with Xanthas' vagueness and drumming of her obvious qualifications.

"If I tell even one person it will leak and become totally ineffective."

Murph was tired and didn't want any games. A little annoyed, "Well, how about a general idea."

"I'll explain on International DV that I am all the things we just talked about, that I want the world to clearly understand which is the right thinking and the right leadership, that I love the world so deeply and know it is so critically important for them to follow U.C. leadership that . . . .and then I'll make my point in a way that will definitely get their attention."

"Look, that vagary is not good enough. We are talking about the future of Earth here. There is a decision and command structure. Even if you plan to materialize Jesus, it has to be approved by, as a bare minimum, Bronc."

So she told him.

<<~>>

CHAPTER THIRTY EIGHT

A little over two and one-half weeks later, from the Lincoln Memorial to the Capitol Building, the National Mall and every flat area adjacent to it was overflowing with many more than the number of citizens and media from all over the world that the U.C. had estimated would be there. It seemed that every space with grass or paving of some kind was filled with a person. The crowd did not know exactly what was going to occur, but Xanthas would be appearing live with an announcement she said would change the course of world history and extract it from its present chaos. That was all that was necessary. If it were possible to have a larger worldwide DV and radio audience than the previous Visitation 1000 event, then it was happening.

Murph was watching it on DV in his apartment. He was the only member of the Headquarters inner planning circle who was not at National Mall.

A large, elevated platform had been set up at the Washington Monument. Bronc was introduced first by the U.C. General Secretary, Colombo Martorre. The General Secretary made a safe, politically correct introduction since no one was quite certain how to include the Mantid, and 'Beings of Earth' seemed a little over the top, "Citizens of the world, I present the United Continents Coordinator and President of the United States of America, Bronson Freeman."

After the playing of all the appropriate Pomp and Circumstance type tunes, there was about a fifty-fifty mix of boos and derisive comments versus cheers and wild applause. It was an opinion mix representative of the world citizenry.

As usual, Bronc had on the big white Stetson, "Ladies and gentlemen – Bronc was not always a rigid stickler for political correctness – it is no secret from anyone that since the United Continents Security Summit announced that the most reasonable course of action is to surrender to the Harvesters, approximately half of the Earth's population appears to be vehemently, many violently, opposed to that course of action. This cannot continue. We must end this paranoia and distrust, and decide one way or the other. I'm sure we can all agree, 'no decision' means 'no chance.'

"Thus, as has been scheduled for the last fifteen days, the vote on the most significant global issue we have ever faced will occur tomorrow at noon, World Mean Time. For two hours, all of you will have the opportunity to enter your vote through your digicom units, for or against, at WorldEncryptedVote.ola. Please do not forget to look directly into the digeye in the top of the unit when you press 'Send' so that you may be properly identified. As you know, the record of the vote and the identification are not encrypted in tandem, so your vote remains secret.

"As the votes come in we will have representatives of every faction from every continent monitoring the results, including the media, and including Eastman Foster, so you can be assured there is no fraud. The United Continents will abide by, and enforce, the results. We are the representatives of the will of the people, and whatever the result, the majority have the right to expect those who voted in the minority to abide by the vote. Our only chance is to unite toward a single course of action, whichever you choose and for whatever reason.

"The United Continents spokesbeing, Xanthas – a spontaneous cheer went up from the crowd – has requested an opportunity to make one last statement to the world prior to the vote. As you will come to understand, while the United Continents is arranging this public viewing, Xanthas' comments and actions here today are her own. You must make up your own minds."

Since Xanthas was the U.C. official spokesbeing, the last comment from Bronc left the crowd a little puzzled and the media was buzzing to its audiences about what it might mean, all of them wrong, but when Xanthas walked forward on the platform, with her now familiar face appearing on the giant DV screens erected all over National Mall and the surrounding area, and on DV's and digicoms all over the world, a resounding cheer went up, not only at the Mall, but people cheering everywhere at their screens, projected DV holograms, wall projections, and into the air if they were wearing digiglasses.

It was clear that Xanthas was the most popular, trusted and respected "spin doctress" on the globe, and with good reason, in addition to being more stunningly beautiful, inside and out, than any other known Earthling, a beauty, intelligence and loving kindness that women as well as men identified with, she always told the truth, which actually disqualified her from the title of "spin doctress."

She started, "Hello, my friends . . ."

In unison worldwide, "Hi, Xanthas."

"I am here today to impress upon you that neither the United Continents Command, the U.C. leaders nor the Mantid have made any arrangement with the Harvesters to save themselves at your expense, or at all. Their well-considered decision has been made only with the interests of the population of Earth uppermost in their minds."

There was a lot of murmuring from the crowd and those watching DV screens around the world. No one wanted to call her untruthful, but the large volume of dissenters believed a deal had been made.

"I am aware that probably half of the world does not believe that statement. I do not know how to convince you otherwise, except to point out that I am half human and half Mantid, half Surface and half Below. My interests are allied with both species of beings and with Earth. I love all of you – a cheer went up. I love you so much that I would give my life for you – a louder cheer and reciprocal responses – and that is what I am going to do so that you will understand how important this is, and know the depth of my sincerity and truthfulness."

Confused, the crowd and the rest of the world fell silent, staring very hard at Xanthas, the large DV screens, their little digicom screens, their digiglasses, their in-home DV's, and their DV holographic projections as if that would help them clearly see her meaning. They were paralyzed with disbelief when she pulled the small laser weapon from the pocket of her jumpsuit.

"I am asking each of you, personally, to vote in favor of surrender. Do not let me have died in vain."

The "Zzzzt" of the laser weapon was just a picosecond ahead of the screams of horror uttered by those at National Mall and the rest of the world.

That is, the rest of the world except one. Murph had collapsed, unconscious, onto the floor of his Washington apartment when he saw her lift it to her head. He didn't see what the horrified rest saw, the small wisp of smoke from a pencil-lead sized tunnel, exiting the opposite side of her head as she fell.

Bronc, Det, Jenoor, Murph and Xanthas were the only ones who knew what Xanthas had planned. They had not told Mari. She had simply thought the pressure of the Harvester situation was why Murph and Jenoor were both acting like zombies.

Jenoor, whose intellect was failing him in favor of his newly developed emotions, was having a very difficult time putting into practice what he knew about why beings came to Earth. Experiencing feelings of terrible personal loss generated by his expectation of Xanthas' death, he just could not change focus and elevate his thinking according to his knowledge.

Bronc and Det had wrestled with and accepted the plan and decision as one of those necessary and terrible sacrifices that occur in war when the stakes are ultimate global survival. As leaders and soldiers, they divorced their emotions in favor of the logic that perhaps her life would spare all the others. If not, it probably wouldn't matter anyway.

As Xanthas was speaking, Mari was standing by the platform, distracted by Jenoor who had started to weep. As a result, she did not see Xanthas fire the laser weapon, but she felt a searing pain go through her own head and, looking up, saw her sister fall and watched the smoke rise in slow motion from the little hole.

Thinking someone had shot Xanthas, Mari grabbed Jenoor and shouted, "Help her! Help her! Before she dies! Help her like you did the reporter! Help her, *NOW!*" Her red hair seemed on fire. She was shaking Jenoor and he was not responding. He was just crying deep tears from his huge agonized eyes.

"I cannot."

She was screaming, "Yes you can. Yes you can. Do for her what you did for the reporter! Do it!"

"I cannot. It was her choice."

"What the hell do you mean it was her *choice*?! *DO IT!*"

"I explained, I *showed* to you the choice you made before you came here this time. She said it was *her* choice, and she shot herself."

"You mean you *knew*! Get up there and *save* her. Get up there and do it, *now!*" She was screaming in his face.

He was resigned to the sadness. "I cannot, even if I wanted to. She is dead." He mustered the thought, "to us," but didn't say it.

"What kind of a cop-out is that? Raise her! *Raise* her! You raised me, raise her!"

"You know I did not raise you. I asked and argued, and the Teachers did it. My thinking has not advanced to the level necessary so that I can do what you ask."

"Then ask *THEM*, dammit!"

"It was her choice. They will not intervene here."

Incredulously, "To commit *suicide*?!"

"No. Suicide is an escape from learning, a bailout. It is a foolish and selfish mistake which only delays and repeats the lessons. This is war. Xanthas gave her life in a truly heroic and unselfish way so that many others might continue. There is a vast difference. I'm sure some kind of incredibly difficult, vitally important and momentous choice was implied in her life preview before she ever came here this time."

"You *knew* she planned to do this and you didn't tell me so I could stop it! *Fuck you! You fucker! You stinking fucker! You asshole! You fucking asshole!*" She continued to scream in his face until she went hoarse, but the pandemonium of the crowd drowned her out. Jenoor stood sadly immobile. His tears continued to stream.

CHAPTER THIRTY NINE

Late that night, having stayed with Xanthas' body as long as she was allowed, Mari returned to the apartment she still shared with Murph. Out of a sense of duty and love for Xanthas, she had also been busy helping the U.C. Command hastily plan a period of lying in state and a public funeral, all demanded by millions of electronic d-mails to the Command Headquarters from all over the world. She was haggard and drained. The natural bounce had gone from her hair. All the blood vessels in her body felt like they were filled with an expanding, acidic, radioactive gas trying to blow them apart in unison. Had she not known why, she could have believed she was going crazy.

Murph was still on the floor. He had regained consciousness long before and rolled over onto his back, but had been there for hours recounting in his mind every detail of his relationship with Xanthas, over and over, particularly the minutes he had spent with her after she told him her plan. Murph had just looked at her. It would not register with him that she could be dead. He had just stared at her, but he could not think of an alternate idea. As it sunk in that she meant it and he sensed, for reasons and through processes he could not identify, that it would happen despite anything he did, he began to cry, feeling then as if she were already dead.

She had cradled his head in her bosom as if she were his mother. He was sobbing uncontrollably when she said softly, "Murph. This is it for me. This is why I am here. I see it clearly."

"But you'll be dead," he blubbered. "What'll I do?"

"Murph, I understand it now. The reality of the matter is that my body simply has no life to lose, and I can never die."

Murph was too upset to apply what he had learned to the implications of what she said. His focus was on this plane, right now. He knew she wouldn't be back and he couldn't shift his thinking to any other focus. She held him, sobbing like that, for a long, long time.

He lay there on his apartment floor wondering why he had acquiesced in her plan, whether he should have done something to try to change what had happened, whether he could survive her loss, whether he wanted to survive her loss, where she was now, whether she remembered him, whether he was important to her, whether he would see her again, someplace, somehow, and thousands of other "whethers." He couldn't stop. It was a perpetually moving circle of thoughts and he couldn't break the cycle.

Mari broke it for him. Accusatorily, "Did you *know*?"

He was afraid to tell her. She was the only link he had left to any-thing he considered a meaningful contact with life. He didn't want to lose her too. He didn't answer.

"You weren't there. You *must* have known! There's no other rea-son you wouldn't be there, except that you didn't have the balls to watch it happen." She waited for him to answer. Nothing. "Speak up or I'll take your silence as a 'yes'." Nothing. "You asshole. You stink-ing asshole." She visualized the word "asshole" forming into a wood-en stake driving through his heart as she spoke.

He felt it. He figured it wouldn't be suicide if he just laid there and died, but it didn't work. He was going to have to respond. If he lied, he'd never be able to keep it up in his present mental state, particular-ly under the barrage of emotional questions getting ready to missile out of her mouth. He said very quietly with the sound of total contrition and surrender, "Yes, I knew."

She became unnaturally calm. He wondered if it would be a prel-ude to a front page headline about how a redheaded mad woman had hacked him to death. If she tried, he wouldn't resist. After what seemed like an unnaturally long time to Murph, Mari spoke in an even, meas-ured, possibly compassionate voice which was either like that of a mother who had decided to try to calmly understand her child who had just intentionally tipped over a full punch bowl on the living room floor in front of her bridge group, or the voice of a snapped human turned killer, "Why didn't you tell me."

He responded in the same measured voice, but his tone resulted from emotional confusion and defeat, "I . . . I couldn't. No one who knew could. Everyone felt that your emotional reaction would override any rational thinking – which wouldn't be good with the fate of the Earth hanging in the balance."

Still unusually serene, "Why isn't emotion part of rationality?"

Uh, oh. Here it comes. He knew he wasn't going to win, or even make a dent. No matter how this dialogue turned out, he was going to wish she had already hacked him to death, because she was preparing to do it metaphorically now, and probably with full justification. He didn't know whether to play psychologist, which, with some marvel, he recalled he was, and lead her into a full venting, or to go into some type of a defensive mode, or . . . . Nah, none of that would work. Anything but straight answers would be figured out in two seconds and she'd slice him "frequent, neat and wide."

He tried to push his glasses up, but they weren't there, "Cheez, I don't know, Mari. Maybe it should be. Maybe we *were* wrong. I just don't know. I've been lying here trying to figure everything out for hours, and I can't. The only rationalization I can come up with is the one we came up with in the first place when we decided not to interfere with her plan and not to tell you. And now with Xanthas gone, it doesn't seem like a very good reason."

There was silence for a few minutes. Then Mari looked at him. Her eyes seemed a tranquil deep blue.

"Xanthas is not dead. Things change, but she is not dead."

That was the last thing he expected her to say. He tried to respond, but couldn't.

Mari continued, "I know it. I just *feel* it. I felt it right this instant, just like a little floating leaf whispering through my mind. Her presence, her life force, her consciousness still exists. I know it. I feel it with every essence of me. For what may be the first time, I truly believe that what we have experienced in our hypnotic regressions, that what Jenoor and Xanthas have told us, is *true*."

Her absolute certainty calmed him. Suddenly, he felt the whisper also. He quietly and slowly articulated what he had just realized.

"Death has no power."

"Exactly. It will have only the effect we are willing to give it."

They were both hoping they wouldn't lose sight of this understanding under the barrage of emotions and beliefs that, even right now, were in close competition with those thoughts for the tag of reality.

<<~>>

CHAPTER FORTY

The Paranoia Purveyors had been speechless, meaning that between the time of Xanthas' passing and the vote the following day, they couldn't think of a single remotely plausible negative reason that would be fruitful, for themselves, to present to their listeners.

Eastman Foster actively "supervised" the counting of the votes, which was ludicrous because they were all tallied by computer and his computer knowledge was limited to laboriously retrieving his digital mail; however, he didn't want any of his listeners to know that. Thus, he declared, accurately, but not through his expertise, that there was no fraud in the voting.

The vote was approximately 90% for the United Continents' plan of surrender. There always seemed to be 10% who were against anything.

While the world had voted for surrender in shock over Xanthas' death, few believed the end result would be positive. There had already been a number of foolish suicides by those without the emotional courage to take the only chance they had, by some who stupidly believed they would be joining Xanthas and by some who, believing it a certainty, said they would rather be dead than harvested. A terrified world waited for the Harvesters' next move.

It came soon. With media digicameras humming, a relatively small ETC settled quietly on the White House lawn at the time Bronc had agreed for surrender to the Harvesters. It bore the indicia of the Harvesters on the outside. It seemed like a seed of some kind, but no one was quite certain what it was, and everyone had much more important concerns on their minds.

Four tall human-looking Blondes strode purposefully from the craft toward Bronc, Jenoor, Det and others in the U.C. Command contingent. They did not look or act threatening, arrogant or demeaning in any way. In fact, they looked very pleasant and decent. There were two males and two females, the latter slightly smaller than the males but still in the area of six feet tall, or more. The males were at least six feet five. All were good looking and had athletic frames.

The leader extended her hand to Bronc who was admiring her

incredibly piercing and attractive blue eyes. "Mr. President, I am Combine, the leader of the 'Harvesters,' as you call us."

"Well, ma'am, your own name sure seems to fit with the title we have given your group. What do your people call themselves?" Bronc had on his best snow job manner and smile, but in actuality, there was no way he could sell a used car to thought readers with the skill of his guests.

" 'Harvesters' will be entirely appropriate Mr. President – and 'Combine' also means 'to unite.' Please don't think of this as a surrender. We have come to tend to our garden, so to speak, tend the seeds we planted many eons ago." Immediately after that statement, exactly 7,281 suicides occurred around the world.

She said it with such an engaging, even loving smile, that all Bronc could think of was how he would like to manage her campaign. She'd be a can't-lose politician. If these folks were serious about not hurting us, maybe he could get her to move to Earth, at least acquire residency somewhere, maybe New York, and they could run for something. What a running-mate she'd make. But, he harbored no illusions about why she had come and he was just looking for some wiggle room somewhere while he waited for the scythe to drop. After her last comment, there was no doubt in his mind it was starting on the downstroke, right now.

"Ma'am, you have all the cards in this game, call your next move, please."

As she thought-motioned to one of the Blonde males who had started to take a sheaf of papers from his case, Combine said, "Perhaps it would be more convenient for all of us if we retire to one of your conference rooms so we can sign some papers." The Blonde stuffed the papers back into his case and the media pool rushed ahead of the governmental parties in order to set up the digicameras.

As they walked into the White House, determined to keep his "charming" face on as it was the most positive thing he could think of to do, Bronc mused, "Just think, all of these spacecraft flying around with extraterrestrials and their incredible technology, and we're doing intergalactic business by signing a stack of papers."

She smiled a charming smile. The world, watching wide-eyed, hoped Bronc was doing some good.

When they were seated in the Cabinet Room and the papers had been placed in a fairly thick pile in front of Bronc, with a heavy cover of some material acting as a loose paper weight on top of them, Combine spoke, "Mr. President, if you would be kind enough to sign each one of these papers, we will be able to proceed." At that moment, 9,478 more suicides occurred around the world.

Bronc was certain the stroke of his pen would be his last act, certainly as the leader of a free Earth and probably of his life. With hands as steady as a gyroscope, he reached down and removed the cover from the top of the stack of papers. The remote overhead camera immediately zoomed down to fill the world's DV screens with the contents of that sheet. In addition to the date, it read:

> The Undersigned, who is the elected leader of Earth, being authorized to
>
> do so by a vote of the people, hereby unconditionally surrenders Earth
>
> to the Harvesters,
>
> and agrees, for
>
> and on behalf of all citizens of Earth,
>
> That all citizens of Earth will hereafter, unconditionally,
>
> do as the Harvesters may request, for all eternity.
>
> Bronson B. Freeman
> United Continents Coordinator
> Earth

At that moment, there were 48,492 more suicides around the world. Bronc signed it and, expecting to be vaporized, turned to Combine on his left, smiled and said, "What? You don't want it notarized?"

Amidst gales of laughter from Det who was sitting on Bronc's right and also expecting to be vaporized, Combine stated, "Please sign the rest Mr. President. They are all identical. I would like an original to be given to the head of each country on Earth.

As Bronc was signing the rest, he noted his was the only signature on the document, and he inquired of Combine, "Shouldn't your signature be on this document also?"

She smiled, "It is not necessary. It is signed on behalf of the parties to be charged."

At that moment, there were 72,421 more suicides around the world.

Bronc finished signing. "Okay, now what?"

"I would like to address the citizens of Earth."

"Well, I guarantee, every last one of them is watching you right now, ma'am. Just look into that camera and give them your orders."

"Thank you." She looked directly into the camera and in a calm, conversational, soothing, even loving, but authoritative voice, "Citizens of Earth, many eons ago when we first seeded the Earth with your ancestors, it was our intention to do exactly what our computerized spokesperson, Lanta, told you, and what you have been worried about. We wanted slaves that could double as a food source. Even at the time we did this, it was a matter of great debate within our society; however, the thinking of a group whose name translates as 'Lords of the Harvest' was in the majority, so we seeded Earth, as well as other planets in the universe.

"Since the time we made the discs that produced Lanta and sealed the library that contained them under the monument you call the Great Sphinx of Giza during the ceremony that placed the headdress on that creature, the thinkers in our society who were against seeding and Harvesting subsequently reached a critical mass of consciousness and became the overwhelming thought-valence in our society. Changes mitigating the Harvest have occurred very rapidly since that event and a Neo-Harvest plan has been developed.

"To elucidate, as the being, Jenoor, explained to most of you at the raceway at Phoenix, Arizona, Entrainment is a powerful force because it is the force of mind. Once a critical mass of thinking is reached, it becomes an astonishing force, whether on an individual level or on a collective level. You know, personally, that when your thinking changes and reaches a sufficient level with respect to an idea, you change and begin to effect that idea. All meaningful change commences with thought and, of course, all meaningful action is thought demonstrated.

"The same is true with groups of individuals. When individuals engage in like-thinking concerning the same concept, their like-thoughts build and begin to function as one mind. That mental Entrainment affects the thinking of others. More and more become entrained to the same thoughts and concepts. The Entrainment builds, and once this collective thought reaches a critical mental gravity, an 'Event Proportion' occurs. From that point, Entrainment begins to rapidly attract and affect the thoughts of those whose understandings trail, until at the last, the effect on all seems instantaneous. At that point, the Entrainment of collective thinking is singularly demonstrated. Unfortunately, Entrainment can be negative as well as positive."

Bronc and Det looked at each other wondering where that shoe was going to drop. They had focused on the word "mitigating" at the beginning of her talk in connection with the "new" Harvest plan, and together wondered to what extent these Blonde beasts were actually backing off of their old plan. Perhaps just slaves, but not food. If so, at least the decision to surrender would be partially correct.

Jenoor, however, was beginning to understand where she was going. She was allowing him to receive some of her thoughts.

Combine continued, "That demonstration of our society's elevated thought resulted in the universal understanding that our original concept of the Harvest was wrong."

Bronc leaned over to Det and whispered, "Shit, here it comes. This fan's running silently, but at full speed. Maybe we should duck."

"We have become, literally, your angels from heaven. We have not come to reap your bodies. We are here to fertilize and cultivate what we planted, acts which will be beneficial in connection with the Harvest of your souls."

Almost all in the room were becoming very agitated, and 182,476 more people around the world committed suicide.

"To continue to borrow language from the King James version of the book you call the Bible, from which President Freeman quoted when speaking to our construct, Lanta, an event on the U.C. security digisticks which have been shown on your digitalvision throughout the world, our intention is to eliminate the tares and gather the wheat. This will, fortunately, result in the end of your world as you know it."

Around the world, 436,322 more people committed suicide, including two reporters who left the conference room and retrieved weapons at their respective vehicles.

Bronc breathed out the words, "Fuck me . . ." Det stared at the table wondering if he would at least be able to kill her with his bare hands before they could kill him.

Jenoor, listening to the thoughts she had given him, leaned over to both of them and admonished softly, without bothering to congratulate himself on his informal manner and the colloquialisms he'd picked up from the old movies, "Cool it, and listen to what she has to say."

Combine continued, "Do not be alarmed at the meaning of this which you presently suppose. Your synchronicity is in operation and my words will ultimately become clear to you. We have no present plans to take you anywhere or to harm you physically, unless you attempt to physically harm others first. In that case you will have assumed any risk of harm to yourselves, any at all that may come to you as we or others try to stop you, and of course, that will be as it may be.

"Nor do we intend to force you to do anything, but we implore you to listen to us as we attempt to elevate your thinking by teaching you concepts many of you do not know, or have not thought about in any meaningful way. For certain of your numbers who have thought about these matters with prescience and in great detail, it will validate the direction of their thinking. For all of you, we hope it raises your understanding. Thus, continue your daily lives in peace, and concentrate upon the message we delivered in Phoenix, an aptly named location for such a concept. We will be in touch."

Recognizing they were still alive and no one had yet been vaporized, Bronc turned to her, almost idly, and inquired, "Ma'am, what is that insignia on your craft?"

"It is a seed as you surmised, a mustard seed."

With that, all of the Harvesters and their craft disappeared. The room, and the world, was filled with confused, but relieved, at least for the moment, chaos.

CHAPTER FORTY ONE

Xanthas, having carefully planned her death, was only slightly confused and, in any event, felt no pain. She was floating above the platform at the Washington Monument looking down on the chaotic scene beneath her. She saw her body with the wisp of smoke rising from her head. Then she saw Mari in great emotional distress. She tried to telepathically reach out to comfort her, but Mari was so distraught she was not receptive. Xanthas continued to float away from the scene until she was in a tunnel of energy which seemed fairly dark in comparison to the bright light at the end of it. She was drawn through it rapidly, and was beginning to recall that it had happened to her on a number of occasions before.

As she came out of the tunnel into the light, she felt the loving presence of her Guides, and of her classmate souls and other friends who were not presently in an incarnation. She was ecstatic to know she was home. Then she saw them. Lantard, Remnas, Bina, Inaar, Nalne and the others. They had caused their energy to appear in human form to be certain she would not be confused so soon after returning from Earth. She floated quickly over to them and the energy of their love and friendship intertwined. Oh, how she had missed these pure feelings of existence! She knew Mari, Murph and Bronc would not be there and did not try to locate the small portion of their energy they had left in the Superconscious Dimension while concentrating the rest of it on their present incarnation.

Then Jenoor appeared.

She communicated with him by his Earth name, rather than the soul name he often called himself, ~Jenoor! Did you pass back too?~

He responded in kind, ~Xanthas, having so recently returned, you are still a little disoriented. Recall that I bifurcated my energy and bilocated my concentration. Part of my energy is still concentrated here as your Guide, and part is partially blanked and focused on my incarnation on Earth as Jenoor, all in order to assist you with your Earth incarnation from here, and also to continue my own development with an Earth incarnation.~

It is somewhat unusual for a soul to bifurcate its energy and bilocate its concentration as Jenoor had done, leaving its Superconscious energy in a normally functioning state, but it occurs from time to time for appropriate reasons, particularly when souls want to continue their development on both planes at the same time. Of course, they have to be careful that enough of their energy is directed to the incarnation exercise to effectively deal with its demands.

Usually, when one is engaging in an incarnation exercise such as those on Earth, that soul's energy is almost completely concentrated on the exercise for purposes of continuing and operating the incarnate Earth form in the Material Dimension; thus, that soul's energy in the Superconscious Dimension appears dimmed to the others there and is primarily unaware of surrounding Superconscious circumstances. However, the unblanked portion of a soul's Superconsciousness not projected toward the Earthly exercise, often aptly referred to by incarnates as one's "Higher Self," is available for guidance to material consciousness if the incarnate learns how to gain access to it, primarily by quieting material thoughts, simply asking and waiting for the answer or intuition, presuming the soul's Guides do not prevent the knowledge that could be gained from that particular Connection because it would interfere with the current learning exercise.

Of course, from an Earthly perspective due to their blanking, incarnates in the Grand Illusion generally believe that their material minds originate in the human body, not realizing that Superconsciousness creates and operates them.

It came back to her in a flash. They had discussed all this before she left. The temporary incarnation amnesia was leaving her rapidly now. Jenoor was a more advanced soul than she, and had been her Guide through many incarnations. As she rapidly acclimated, she could easily see the colors of Superconscious soul energy again. When a soul in the Superconscious did not choose to take on a particular form, its concentration of energy just appeared as the hue of its level of understanding and spiritual development. The golden color of Jenoor's soul energy, which also contained light blue flecks, was readily apparent. It was the spiritual energy hue of an upper-level-intermediate soul, which was consistent with his intermediate Guide level. To be a Guide, if one wanted and was otherwise suited for it, a soul had to reach at least a dark-yellowish energy level.

Then she noticed the color of her own energy. When she left, it was a nice shade of spring yellow. A number of incarnations before as a new soul, it had been a bright radiant white, progressing through sunset-reddish shades to that light spring yellow shade she had just prior to becoming Xanthas on Earth. Those changes in color occurred with the advancement of her development, which included her studies in the normal Superconscious environment, such as class and individual discussions with the classmates in her group, some of whom were Mari, Murph and Bronc, and also studies and discussions with her Guides, which included Jenoor, as well as solitary mental work and self examination

Additionally, changes in color came about through development resulting from her periodic incarnations on Earth as an adjunct to the work on certain areas of her spirituality. Clearly she had made incredible strides in her most recent incarnation. She had leaped right through the dark yellow stage and now her energy was just like Jenoor's – gold with light blue flecks!

At that realization, she became somewhat saddened since it meant she had advanced to the point where she would probably be the first one to leave her class, most likely not incarnating as often, and doing much more solitary mental work. She was happy to experience this evidence of her increased development, but would dearly miss being with her group on the same basis they had associated during so much progress.

All had started the class together as new souls and had shared many incarnations together in many different physical states, roles, sexes and relationships in their learning exercises on Earth. Each time upon returning to the Superconscious Dimension, with assistance from their Guides, they would help one another with loving analysis of the spiritual progress of each during the incarnation. Perhaps by becoming a beginning Guide, she could work with the members of her group who were less advanced. She felt both Murph and Bronc could benefit from some extra help.

Having so recently returned from her incarnation, Xanthas was troubled and worried about all those she loved and cared for on Earth, as well as the fate of Earth itself. As with almost all returning souls, she was having a difficult time dissociating her thinking from the "reality" of the occurrences there. She turned her thoughts back to Earth. It was still the night of her "death" there and Mari and Murph were in their apartment agonizing about it. She sent love, life, calmness and understanding. She felt it float like a leaf into their minds.

At the same moment she was experiencing these things, she also felt herself being guided by an intelligent and caring force toward an area she was beginning to remember, the "Readjustment Area" as she called it. She floated into it and felt the substance of her consciousness washed by Superconscious mind, enveloped and bathed by a loving energy that restored and rehabilitated the equilibrium of her thinking to the Superconscious level, including a full Superconscious memory of all her experiences, both in the Superconscious Dimension and the Material Dimension. It placed her Earthly experiences in proper perspective. She felt a mental and emotional healing taking place. She was bathed with unconditional love. She felt at peace.

Floating at the Readjustment Area in that peaceful state, but wishing to make the float to her group so she would feel truly at home, a completely light-blue energy appeared. She knew at once that it was Saba. Saba was her advanced Guide with whom Jenoor worked as Xanthas' intermediate Guide. Xanthas was surprised to see her since it was Jenoor who usually assisted with her group. Saba kept a watchful eye on them, but interacted directly only periodically.

Normally, Jenoor came for her at the Readjustment Area and they would have an extended reorientation and self-evaluation counseling discussion examining whether she accomplished the goals she, her Guides and her group had set before her most recent incarnation. After that, she would be drawn by the force to float to the "Central Station" as she referred to it. Jenoor used to accompany her there, but starting several incarnations before, he had determined it was not necessary.

But Saba was here. She had never come to see her at the Readjustment Area.

~Saba, why have you come? Was I wrong to try to help Earth that way? Was my performance on Earth that poor?~ She knew there would be no retribution. There never was rancor at home for anyone, only a loving, but deeply probing, discussion of what opportunities one missed to act in a more positive way and how that aspect of one's soul could best be improved. Saba had been her advanced Guide since Xanthas had unfolded as a brand-new soul, even incarnating in one of her early human lives as Xanthas' grandmother. They both loved each other very much.

~No, Xanthas, your performance on Earth was so outstanding, and you have developed so much as a result of it, that the color of your energy has advanced enormously, as you can see. The Principal

Overseers have asked the Master Teachers to discuss something extremely important with you, but it means you will be taken out of the usual progression and you will not have much regular contact with Jenoor or me in the Superconscious Dimension, and an even more sporadic contact here with the members of your group.~

Xanthas dismay at greatly reduced contact with her beloved Guides and group was exceeded only by her amazement. She had never had a Superconscious dialogue with even one Teacher, much less have the *Principal Overseers*, who knew the status of every soul, direct their attention toward her, *and* for the purpose of asking the *Master* Teachers to communicate with her! The Master Teachers were so far advanced they had not even created the physical universe; it was those at the level of advancement below theirs, the Teachers, who did it. And it wasn't the Master Teachers or even the Overseers who originated the interest in her, it was the Principal Overseers! Incredible! If she weren't already floating, she'd be floating! She had only thought about the Principal Overseers a few times and they were reputed to be only one level of understanding away from One Mind. She could not possibly imagine what they had in mind for the Master Teachers to communicate to her.

~Saba! What do they want?!~

~*They* want to discuss it with you. Will you?~ It was a request because no one at home was ever forced to do anything.

~Of course! How could I not? To use an Earth phrase, I'm dying to know!~

~Amusing. Do you want to float over there now, or do you want to collect your thoughts first?~

~Actually, that's amusing, Saba. I am thoughts, aren't I? Could I communicate with my group first and see what they think? Well, cancel that thought. You're here, what do you think?~

~It will be a wonderful opportunity to advance your level of understanding. By all means do it.~

~Let's float!~

<<~>>

Mari, Jenoor and Murph were alone in one of the planning rooms. They had been working hard on a campaign to keep world citizens relatively calm until the Harvesters made their next move. There had been no contact from the Harvesters for several days. They decided to take a break.

"Jenoor, where is our baby?"

It took him by surprise. The subject of their relationship had never come up with Murph in the room, and he and Murph had never discussed it, even though Jenoor knew that Murph was aware of it, and Murph knew that Jenoor knew that Murph knew. The thought flew through Jenoor's mind that perhaps he should incarnate as an Earth high-school student at some point. Some aspects of this seemed to be good preparation for that setting.

It was unlikely, however. He had never incarnated in the Material Dimension as anything except a Mantid, just as most souls who incarnated as humans always did so. Most tended to stick with the same incarnation environment, in his case Earth, and after reaching an intelligent sentient level, they generally stayed within the same species, with occasional exceptions if there were a particular lesson that could be better learned otherwise or elsewhere. But, generally, once established, those things do not change so that concentration can most economically be directed toward the current lessons instead of adjusting to an entirely new species and ambient environment.

Jenoor-as-incarnate was intellectually aware of many of these things in his Earthly state. Being a well-advanced intermediate soul, he did not incarnate frequently, and when he did, the usual amnesic level was not necessary for his lessons and, at his developmental stage, could not only hinder his own development, but that of the others with whom he incarnated. Thus, he would retain a fair amount of his Superconscious memory and understanding on the conscious incarnate level, but obviously not all, or, for instance, the Mantid Earthly-mindset and his initial emotional incapacity this trip would not be effective.

Whatever he knew on an Earthly intellectual level wasn't helping him right now, and because Jenoor's Earthly emotions were developing well, he felt very uncomfortable with Mari bringing the subject up in front of Murph. However, Murph's discomfort was exceeded by a certain perverse pleasure at watching Jenoor squirm.

Jenoor stammered, "Well, I . . . uh . . . it's . . ." Murph was start-ing to smile a little. Jenoor continued, "It's . . . doing . . . fine." Murph pushed his glasses up and sat back to watch.

Mari pressed, "Where is it now?"

Jenoor shot a glance at Murph. If Murph jumped at him, he would Phase Shift. "It's in Manticon."

Mari's hair was bouncing and she drilled, "Stop being cute, and you Murph, knock off the smile. Jenoor, is my baby viable yet, and if not, when will it be?"

They rapidly got the picture that this was not going to be a casual conversation. Murph stopped smiling and Jenoor began imparting more information.

"It will be ready to exist outside the container soon. I cannot tell you when because that is truly up to the child."

Mari continued, "When it's out, I want it."

Jenoor responded, "It was always the plan, Mari – that you would spend meaningful time in Manticon with the child. Then, at a point, it would be brought to the Surface for experiences here."

"You don't get it, Jenoor, use your telepathy, I'm that child's mother. It's not going to be raised by a bunch of attendants with me visiting from time to time. It is *mine*."

Either he was bamboozled enough by the situation, or she had become very good at automatically blocking her thoughts, because he could not pick up a thing. Not wanting her to know, he started guess-ing, "Well, Mari, do you mean that you want to come to Manticon and live with me?"

So long as Murph was in the room and the subject was out, Jenoor thought perhaps they should resolve it. He loved her very much, a per-sonal state that leapt into awareness when he was pleading with the Teachers not to let her die. Nothing would make him happier than rais-ing a family with her in Manticon.

None of them were focusing on the effect the Harvester situation might have on what would actually happen.

"You're not Connecting. I am going to be a *single* mother."

For the first time, Murph spoke, "Huh?"

"I am going to be a single mother. My child and I are going to live without either one of you. I can't live with either of you after what you allowed to happen to Xanthas. We *needed* Xanthas here! The *world* needs Xanthas here! You didn't have the common sense, common courtesy, common decency, or even the guts, to let me speak up to try to prevent it or to present an alternate scenario.

"My reality is here, now. My sister is dead so far as I am concerned, and you are primary co-conspirators who helped pull the trigger. I *could not* live with either of you now, and my child is going to live with *me*!" Mari showed no evidence of the calm conclusion concerning Xanthas she had come to with Murph in the apartment on the night of Xanthas' passing.

Perplexed, Jenoor fell back on contract law, "That was not the agreement, Mari."

Murph, equally confounded, chimed in, "Well, Mari, don't you think you and I are even now?"

Mari was burning, "Agreement! Show me that agreement, Jenoor. I'll roll it and stick it right straight up your glove-smooth butt!

"And as for you . . . !" Murph shrank slightly from the onslaught. "*Even*! Screw even! What in hell makes you think what I did equals Xanthas' life? Does it? Does it? Tell me, does it?" She was screaming now. Murph dared not answer and knew there was no answer anyway. Obviously her love for Xanthas was paramount, certainly in relation to Jenoor or himself.

It was also clear to Murph that at least Jenoor wasn't going to get her, and . . . well . . . if all was going to be lost anyway, Murph thought he'd take one last shot. Maybe he could somehow ace Jenoor. Then again, maybe it would be the end of his life as he presently knew it. She was giving every indication she was angry enough to kill them both with her bare hands. He'd seen her like this before, and as that announcer used to say during the old football games they showed on the DV classic sports channels – "Whoa Nellie!"

Murph got ready to duck, "What alternate scenario do you think you could have presented?"

She looked at him with all the emotion she felt his idiocy deserved – infinite contempt, "Since all of you boneheads had come to the conclusion that the Harvesters might be telling the truth, and that there was no way to beat them anyway, why not let *them* handle it? Make it *their* problem. You've become just like a lot of people in government. If your job is to pound nails, you see everything *as* a nail and blindly start hammering on it. But nothing, *absolutely nothing*, can justify your allowing Xanthas to kill herself! You took the easy way out for *yourselves*. There were *other* ways, *other* possibilities, you selfish bastards!"

Murph foolishly threw out, "In your view."

Encouraged by Murph, Jenoor, with equal folly, piped up, "It was her choice."

Both had missed a golden opportunity to remain silent, "You fucking idiots! Stand up, Murph, I'm going to kick you right in the nuts." Murph pitied her brothers when they were kids. He made no move to stand up. She whirled on Jenoor, "And you, I'm just plain going to bust you in half!" Jenoor Particulated through the door. She yelled after him, "You chickenshit son-of-a-bitch! It's a damn sad shame people have been relying on *you* to protect them from the Harvesters!"

Jenoor stood embarrassed in the hall as the U.C. guards and others nearby looked at him quizzically. He was relieved to have the attention focused elsewhere when, shortly thereafter, Murph burst through the door, trailed by a stream of vile epithets.

<<~>>

CHAPTER FORTY THREE

Suddenly, every digicom and every digivision on Earth sounded the alert and automatically turned on to the emergency channel. All over the world, there was the simultaneous sound of people rushing into rooms to watch DV sets, and digicoms being pulled from pockets, purses and other containers, immediately followed by their covers being flipped open, all to view the DV presentations of varying sizes or just to listen if otherwise occupied. This happened both on the Surface and Below, although some Below merely tuned in their minds since it was apparent the Harvesters were not blocking these broadcast thoughts.

Combine's face faded in, "Beings of Earth . . ."

Bronc was thinking that, so far, events had been as good as any old science fiction movie. He was still looking for a spacecraft to land with a big silver robot popping out to systematically fry everyone on Earth who did not buckle under. He expected her next words to be, "Gort, Klaatu barrada nikto."

". . . as I stated when you first saw me, we wish to bring you to a higher level of understanding. Note that since our appearance we have not harmed you in any way. We only wish to help you understand concepts we have learned. It is our desire to accelerate your learning curve before you succeed in annihilating yourselves."

That was a switch, Bronc thought. Talk about George Orwell's "Big Brother," this is "Big Sister." Her manner was pleasant, calm and reassuring. In fact she seemed to radiate a certain charisma from within that made her somewhat believable.

Having received Bronc's negative thoughts and similar thoughts from many others, Combine looked directly out from the screen and stated, "Do not think of me as 'Big Sister' in the Orwellian sense, simply think of me, of us, as your friends."

It had been the U.C. Command's role to protect Earth; thus, the Command's initial and continuing reaction to the Harvesters was one of cynicism and suspicion. However, most humans were as they had been for centuries. If something was spoken by an appealing and charismatic person, it was likely to be believed by the majority, no matter what was presented, particularly if that person said what you wanted to hear. Being a politician, Bronc was very familiar with the concept, particularly as it was demonstrated by Adolf Hitler in the last century. His prayer was that, in addition to being convincing, Combine spoke the truth. He would like to be comfortable relying on the positive statements Jenoor had made to him about her thoughts at the surrender-signing "party," but it was clear, the Harvesters could control what the Mantid received.

She continued, "We want you to know and understand more of the actual nature of things, at least at the level that is important to you now. Almost every religion or other organized system of thought that contemplates the nature of being speaks to an existence of the individual after what you refer to on Earth as 'death.' That is a subject that all of you ponder in one way or another. Some systems do not carry the concept much further than that, while others have an extensive explanation of what occurs, with all levels in between. But few, if any, agree on what actually happens after so-called death or, of course, there wouldn't be different systems of thinking.

"Once you direct your attention to it, if death means the end of life, but there is existence after death, then 'death' is an oxymoron, certainly an illusion. It is *not* the end of you if you continue to exist." She paused, "What is you? If you stop to think about it, that act is the answer. Your consciousness, of course. A number of your philosophers have been telling you that for centuries. They are correct in that regard. Almost all systems that contemplate the nature of being agree that your consciousness continues, no matter what else they may say."

She actually had Bronc interested. He had grown up in a religion that told him he had an existence after he died, and if he did what they told him while he was alive, it would be good, and if he didn't, it would be decidedly bad. However, that didn't go much further than scaring him to death. He tried to do the right thing anyway, not because he was afraid he would be punished later, but because he simply *felt* he should. He sensed that doing right was the only productive way to go. Productive of what, he wondered.

Combine had not hesitated, "If you continue to exist, what does that mean? It means that 'death' is only an event, of some sort, in your continuing existence. An event with no power to terminate your life. It means that your *real* existence is not dependent on a body. Why? Because mind is not material. Because if consciousness never dies, your body does not have a life to lose."

She waited for it to sink in. Bronc was intrigued now and actually eager for her to continue. Beings in and around the world started to settle in, staring at her image.

"The problem most of you face is that there has never been any *scientific* proof of such a continued existence. At least not scientific within the system you have been trained to accept. If it can't be seen and photographed, heard and recorded, measured with instruments or calculated in a mathematical equation, it can't be proven scientifically and, thus, has no reality. As a result, twentieth century Earth volumes such as *Journey of Souls* by Michael Newton, Ph.D., and *Many Lives, Many Masters* by Brian L. Weiss, M.D., which describe life in a spiritual dimension between lives on Earth in narratives recalled through means of hypnotic regression of consciousness by highly trained specialists, are given little or no weight by traditional scientists, even though there are remarkably similar events described by the subjects who had no connection to one another.

"I spoke before of mental Entrainment that pulls thoughts in the same direction – that amalgamation of like thoughts that unconsciously educate most, if not everyone, into a system of believing and acting. The Entrainment of your *physical* science states that there is only *its* system of reality and, thus, reality can only be *proven* and only *really* exists according to its rules and not according to any other paradigm, such as a metaphysical paradigm. Most of you, even though you may evidence many spiritual qualities, have bought into that without even understanding what, or how, it has happened to you, even though your Earthly author James Redfield described some years ago how it occurred over a period of many centuries in his twentieth century volume, *The Celestine Prophecy*, and his related volumes.

"*Physical laws* are your Big Brother. The doctrine of your physical science has precluded the acceptance as *reality* of what I am telling you. If it did not, if its tenets included proving mind, unreliant on matter, as the ultimate reality of existence, it would be putting itself out of business so to speak. Hence, the necessity for the physical-science imperative of entraining your collective thought against that metaphysical concept. A further example of that, in this and the last century, is shown in the consistent disregard by the majority of the scientific and medical community of the work of Dr. Ian Stevenson, a medical doctor who published many scientific papers on past lives, a situation described late in the twentieth century by the Earthly author, Tom Shroder, in his volume, *Old Souls*.

"As I speak, President Freeman is wondering why I am not simply telling you that both constellations of thought, physical and metaphysical, are the basis of reality. He is more comfortable accepting the reality of metaphysical existence if he can have the psychological safety net of the reality of physical existence. As with most of you, physical-science Entrainment is so strong that the physical world is believed more real than, or certainly as real as, any metaphysical existence there may be.

"I am going to conclude today's talk with a question many of you have asked yourselves. If my consciousness and individuality, that is my soul, exists independent of my life on Earth, where was I before I came here and where do I go when I leave? Stated another way, have I been here on Earth more than once, and if so, where am I between times? These questions are important because we will explain to you at a later time that the 'where' of that inquiry is the natural and true reality of existence.

"That is enough for now. I leave you with those thoughts to ponder. I will be in touch again, at the right time." With that she was gone.

CHAPTER FORTY FOUR

Xanthas and Saba floated to the area of the Master Teachers. Saba had seen Teachers and communicated with them before; they were a deep electric-blue energy surrounded by a radiance with purple flecks. But not even Saba had been in the presence of the *Master* Teachers whose deep spiritual-purple energy was surrounded by a radiance with emerald green flecks. Their collective mind generated amazing feelings of peace, love and stupefying awe. Saba and Xanthas felt they could have basked in that feeling forever.

<<~Welcome, Saba and Xanthas.~>> Such a calm feeling of love and protection. <<~Xanthas, we are pleased you have consented to communicate with us.~>>

If she were on Earth, Xanthas probably would have curtseyed. All she could think of was, ~I'm happy to do it.~ She immediately decided that was a dumb thing to say and they'd probably send her away.

<<~Xanthas, you are at no risk of being sent away.~>> Actually, she knew that. There was only kindness in the Superconscious Dimension, even when discussing the deepest improvements one needed to make.

<<~Xanthas, we need your assistance. With very few exceptions, we have allowed events in the universe to take their own course and 'self-determine' the background 'staging' of the learning environment there. That includes all the activities of the Harvesters from their inception to the present. Few trust them and the Harvester's have brought it on themselves. Matters are at the point where most of Earth's inhabitants are not helping the planet in ways that will preserve Earth's environment. It's resources are being used up to produce goods and material comfort. It may not be long in terms of Earth time before Earth's population negatively entrains its own global thinking to the point an Event Proportion occurs which destroys the planet's physical resources. Of course, in order to do that, each person must allow his or her metaphysical focus to become negatively entrained on an individual basis. Each affects the other and it can become a self perpetuating downward spiral that will threaten the continued utility of our Material Dimension classroom.~>>

Knowing that doing anything other than thinking honestly and directly would be futile, Xanthas communicated, ~What can I do? The

Teachers created it, why don't you just have the Teachers change it?~

<<~That would defeat their purpose for creating it and destroy the internal synergy that has built itself there over eons of Earth time. They see significant value in letting Earth's future be as self determining as practicable so that the course of the lessons will not be easily predictable; however, the key word is 'practicable.' From time to time during the course of Earth's history, it has been necessary to intervene to uplift its collective consciousness since, after all, those who need improvement are the ones who choose to go there, and sometimes their collective Entrainment begins to pull too hard for too long in the wrong direction, which is what is happening now. Although the number of responsible thinkers appears to be increasing, it may be too little, too late. We see a distinct possibility that Earth as you generally know it may not survive, which would be an extremely unfortunate waste of teaching resources.~>>

~But, again, what can I do?~

<<~Xanthas, since you are such a rapidly progressing highly-developed soul, and you have recently returned from an Earth incarnation which was right in the midst of the most important recent events on Earth, we are asking you to observe continuing events with us for a while and then, if things do not start changing significantly, help us formulate a plan directed toward reversing the course of Earth's current negative mental Entrainment, a plan which will create a quantum increase in its collective understanding.~>>

Xanthas was apprehensive that her current level of understanding was not adequate, but she also knew that acting the gossamer namby-pamby would bear no results, except possibly foreclose the opportunity to work with the Master Teachers. ~I'll help any way I am able, let's get started!~

Saba was radiant with excitement for her pupil, whom she knew would soon surpass her in understanding.

<<~>>

CHAPTER FORTY FIVE

Time passed on Earth, still without the Harvesters harming any-one. Combine spoke regularly concerning the loving and harmonious living that had come to her home planet through positive Event Proportion changes in its population's thinking.

Systematically undermining the Harvester's efforts was a loose, highly influential group within the population, Earth's mega-entrepreneurs. Instead of inquiring of the Harvesters and the Mantid concerning how they could improve their thinking and life-actions, they only wanted to know how they could increase the bottom line on their corporate financial statements, and almost exclusively concentrated on questions concerning the economics of extensive space travel.

The world's mega-entrepreneurs were keenly aware that if the frontiers of space could be economically opened, there would be a lot of money to be made, initially in mining minerals and other substances from asteroids and other planets and then in sales of merchandise and services to other planetary societies. They were publicly advancing the idea through the concept of acquiring unimagined wealth and prosperity for all. This overindulgent economic mental Entrainment was in clear conflict with the inroads the Harvesters had begun to make in affecting world thinking.

Combine's six-foot Blonde form materialized in Bronc's office.

More than a little startled, Bronc quickly composed himself and smiled his best cowboy smile, "Don'cha think y'all should at least make an appointment, or whistle a tune or somethin' instead of scarin' me half out of my wits like this?"

"I apologize President Freeman, you are right. I won't startle you like this again, but I would like to talk to you about a very important subject."

"Well, you haven't hurt us so far, jus' like you said, so why don't you call me Bronc since I think I'm feelin' a lot better 'bout y'all. It's funny you should appear right now, I've been sittin' here thinkin,' y'all're called the Harvesters, your symbol is a seed and you said you've come to harvest our souls. I'll bet your planet even has a name connected with that somehow. Taking all that into account, what I'm really curious about is – have you had anything to do with the crop circles that have been appearing on Earth at least ever since the last century?" Bronc easily slipped in and out of his colloquial drawl.

Combine paused for what seemed an inordinately long time, almost laughed and winked at Bronc, <~Well, you've got me. I'm afraid our more artistic and playful pilots have been making them for quite some time. We've communicated with them about it on a number of occasions, but it seems there's no stopping them because, quite frankly, no real harm is done. In fact, it appears to raise the level of consciousness and inquiry concerning whether there may be beings not of Earth 'out there,' which we view as positive for obvious reasons. However, I should say our pilots think the Mantid have also made them with their Foo Fighters for whatever reasons they may have had. ~>

"Gol dang, you were just funnin'. Maybe I can get Jenoor's little pilot people ta 'fess up t'their part one a these days, although they don't seem t'joke much. Maybe they had some other reason if they did it. Well, I know you didn't come here to chat about crop circles. It must be somethin' a lot more Earth-shakin' than that, pardon the pun."

"Thank you, Bronc. While our aim is to elevate Earth-thinking toward a more spiritual state of universal love and harmony, a state that synchronistically creates its own supply, there is an extensive thought-valence here that cannot seem to break from its Entrainment of seeing every event only as a positive opportunity to generate revenue. We want to attempt to reeducate the heads of the world's largest entrepreneurial enterprises so that they will understand the possibilities of supplying products and needs of every kind for all, but not based on the goal of revenue production. We want to take *our* version of the Visitation 1000 to *our* planet so they can see other goals and other ways for themselves."

Bronc looked at her and thought for a moment. As usual, his Southwestern drawl faded in direct proportion to the seriousness of his comments, "Ma'am, I have several questions. First, why ask me? You have the power. Why not just take them. Second, based on the little I know about space travel and Einstein's theories, won't we all be dead by the time you get back? And third, what in the hell are you talking about? These CEO's aren't going to shift to a non-revenue producing corporate model. That means not producing a product to sell, and that is so far out of their constellation of thoughts as to be considered mental instability within their circles. It's out of mine too. Free enterprise may not produce perfect results, but it's a hell of a lot better than anything else that's been tried."

"Bronc, come with us and find out about our system, keeping in mind I did not say it was non-product-producing; I said that supply was not based on revenue generation. We are not going to force your entrepreneurs to go to our planet. It is our intent to *lead* them away from a path of negative mental Entrainment which may culminate in destructive results. In the wider perspective, we can't *make* you love one another, and we don't intend to *make* you do anything. What we have done so far, which you erroneously categorize as force, has simply been to get your attention. Any change in thought is up to the world.

"And, Bronc, will you please ask Jenoor to come here before I answer your question about the length of time it will take to travel to our planet. His experience and thought levels will better enable him to understand it and appreciate the fundamentals behind it; thus, he will, hopefully, be of important assistance in explaining anything to you that you may not understand."

Bronc was thinking that she must know Jenoor was in the building and since he was used to telepathic communication, why didn't she just ask him to come in. She smiled, held up her hand to indicate it wasn't necessary for Bronc to say it, and telepathically requested Jenoor to come to the Oval Office. "I was just trying to be polite, Bronc."

Jenoor entered shortly thereafter and he was very curious, as usual.

Combine continued, "The answer to your question, in summary, is that our space travel is analogous to the dynamics of the processes the Mantid utilize for Particulation and Phase Shifting, but it is, of course, different or it wouldn't be merely analogous." She smiled.

Bronc just stared at her, as did Jenoor, although some might argue that Jenoor could do little else. Bronc knew she was trying to be a little humorous for his benefit, and he still wouldn't mind being her campaign manager for something, but he just wanted her to get to the point. While he didn't mind using a little schmoozing salve on her, he recognized it immediately when used on him and didn't want to waste time with it coming from the other direction. He got enough of it with world leaders.

Insofar as Jenoor was concerned, she was blocking her thoughts from him, and it was his curiosity that caused him to be impatient for further explanation.

She spoke at Bronc's level of understanding, "Okay, forgive my attempt at a little galactic humor. Please allow me to describe some background for the explanation of how we travel through space. I'm certain you are aware at this point that all matter is composed of extremely small instances of electrical/atomic energy, plus what you refer to as mostly empty space, not that it is actually empty, but it seems that way. Since our space travel is an advanced form of mental manipulation of matter, it is helpful to examine how the Mantid mentally manipulate matter on a more basic level.

"From the Mantid perspective, they have been habitually Particulating and Phase Shifting for so long, they now believe it is probably genetic. It is not, but it is unconsciously automatic. They no longer remember the mechanics and fundamentals of how they do it; they just think that they want to do it, and it works. Thinking is the key since that's how the energy comprising matter was formed by the Teachers in the first place.

"As an adjunct to explaining what happens when the Mantid Particulate or Phase Shift, the concepts of 'EnergyForm' and 'HarmonicMemory' are our shorthand way of referring to the two complimentary main properties of matter formed from energy. The particular arrangement forming any specific thing or person is its EnergyForm. It stays in that configuration because of its HarmonicMemory for that configuration. Because they are complimentary properties, any change in HarmonicMemory creates a different EnergyForm configuration and vice versa.

"What happens in Particulation and Phase Shifting is not a *creation* of matter, but a relatively minor mental *manipulation* by the Mantid of the matter created by the Teacher's collective mind. For instance, when Jenoor Particulates, he uses the power of his mind to direct a change in the EnergyForm of his own matter. It is a separating, or Particulating, of the atoms and molecules of his EnergyForm into much smaller and more basic energy particles, or strings of energy, that can slip through the empty space of non-particulated or solid forms of matter. After that occurs, he pops them back into their original HarmonicMemory. The atoms and molecules are reformed exactly and *not* rearranged. So, in Particulation, he disables the particular EnergyForm momentarily and then reinstates its HarmonicMemory exactly as it was before.

"In Phase Shifting, the EnergyForm is not momentarily disabled and stays exactly the same, but the vibration of its HarmonicMemory is mentally directed to change to a different phase in relation to the matter surrounding it. Neither Particulation nor Phase Shifting changes the form or function of what is left after the process is finished. The EnergyForm is exactly the same as before."

Jenoor was fascinated, and Bronc was thinking as hard as he could.

"Jenoor's healing of the reporter's body at the raceway was different. It was a manipulation of matter which *changed* her injured EnergyForm by mentally directing a change in its HarmonicMemory to a *rearrangement* of some of the atoms and molecules which comprise her body, a direction that they rearrange back to a healthy body. That is an applied-mind application which humans can learn to demonstrate much more easily than Particulation, and some have already learned it, because it involves much less matter to affect, and thus requires less necessary mental conviction that it will actually work. One's level of understanding determines the strength of that conviction. The result demonstrated validates the level of understanding.

"To recognize how that works is analogous to writing a computer program to cause a particular configuration or action on a three dimensional Illusograph such as Lanta. One needs to understand that the current configuration of one's body matter at any given time is the objective result of that individual's thinking. That is, the program is written mentally by the consciousness of the individual involved and is projected, or manifested, as that individual's body. The way that mental program is written is heavily influenced by the conscious and unconscious programming of that individual's thinking.

"On the most basic level, the universal mental programs and rule-constellations of the universe, such as the laws of physics and physical medicine, were created by the Teachers through collective archetypal Entrainment of material minds to those laws. Subsequently, scientists' discoveries, applications, modifications and additions relating to those laws create additional program Entrainment for material minds. Of course, those discoveries are actually 'creations' which are limited by those scientists' Entrainment to the archetypal laws 'governing' the concepts they investigate. Generally, those scientists do not break that Entrainment cycle with metaphysical understanding of the origins of matter and physics, even though many believe in a higher power. You have a saying, 'The blind leading the blind.'

"A simple example of that Entrainment is aging in humans. Their unconscious Entrainment to the physical 'laws' of aging, either archetypically existing or newly 'discovered' variations that 'educate,' slowly and constantly causes thinking to alter the HarmonicMemory of their bodies in conformity to what is programmed to be a 'natural' progression. As a result, the EnergyForm/HarmonicMemory configuration of their bodies is altered. That alteration in turn affects function.

"When the reporter fell at the raceway, her mental programming told her, as did the programming of those watching, that her EnergyForm should instantaneously be rearranged with a new HarmonicMemory manifesting an injured body. Their Entrainment is that injury is going to occur when one has a severe fall like that, and so it is. It becomes a self-fulfilling prophecy.

"Since all of that is initially created and controlled by mind, Jenoor and the reporter, by creating contrary programming for her thinking, rearranged her EnergyForm back into matter that was a non-injured perfectly functioning configuration, that is, back to the original HarmonicMemory for the arrangement of each energy string, electron, neutron, muon, quark, atom, molecule, cell, etcetera. The result manifested health and harmony. You call that process 'healing', except the programming of medical procedures and a lengthy recuperation as a prerequisite to healing was dispensed with, together with the negative Entrainment that the result of those medical procedures may not be entirely successful."

Speaking sincerely, Bronc interjected, "Ma'am, that is truly fascinating and I want to think about it a lot. I truly do. In fact, I seriously wish you would write it down for me so I can study it when my mind is open. But right now, how do you travel through space?"

She smiled. It was very kind and pleasant. "Thanks for your patience, Bronc. I felt it was important that you have an understanding of that so you can more readily understand how we travel from one place to another in space. I know you are highly familiar with theories of space travel, including the advancements in speed, propulsion and rapid changes in direction made by the Mantid. Their accomplishments are truly remarkable when applied to the EnergyForm level of understanding, which is of course, the Material Dimension. Our space travel is advanced beyond the EnergyForm level and, thus, is only *analogous* to the results, such as Particulation, Phase Shifting or healing, that have been achieved within it."

Bronc and Jenoor were both anxious for her to get to the point.

"Bronc, Jenoor, as I described, the Mantid space travel is predicated on theories of manipulation of matter. As such, it is self-limiting because matter is, inherently, a self-limiting concept. In order to eliminate the space and time factor from travel, which is what concerns you, one must utilize the knowledge that space and time are material concepts relating only to the Material Dimension, being created from mind in the first instance for a limited schooling purpose. It necessarily follows that neither matter nor space nor time is a basic element of existence.

"Recognizing that and utilizing the understanding we have developed, we direct our thinking to stop generating the energy that appears to be our physical manifestation as matter and direct our mental focus to return fully to its native *super* consciousness, to 'mindstuff.' Stated another way, we simply recognize that our true existence is in the spiritual Superconscious Dimension. We stop the thinking that generates and perpetuates ourselves in the Grand Illusion and *allow* our apparent matter to disappear into its natural nonexistence. That is how we disappear from your sight, and as you have seen, it happens instantaneously. It is vastly different from Phase Shifting, Particulation or healing, all of which manipulate matter *in* the Material Dimension.

"However, as true consciousness is not subject to physical laws and, thus, the Superconscious Dimension contains no time, space or mass, there is no place to go in the spatial sense and we do not perform the 'space' travel there. In order to accomplish 'travel' from one place to another in the physical universe, we simply decide on the location where we want to regenerate material mass, that is, where to refocus our thought in the Grand Illusion, and we do so instantaneously, generating material energy and utilizing the same HarmonicMemory for the EnergyForm representing 'us.' In essence, we 'Mind Shift' between the Superconscious Dimension and the Material Dimension and vice versa. So, it will literally take no time at all to 'travel' to our planet since we can affect anyone with whom we are in contact and take them with us."

Reading Jenoor's thoughts, Combine said softly, "Yes, it *is* amazing, Jenoor. As one's understanding elevates into higher dimensions, one begins to realize that all things are possible with mind."

Returning to the original purpose for her visit, Bronc looked at her, "Well, ma'am, I'd like to go to your planet very much but, for obvious reasons, it would not be good form, nor an intelligent move, for me to leave Earth. I can't let Jenoor go either, but I will consent to your taking the Mega Moguls if they want to go since it would be a loss we could deal with if you didn't bring them back. What are you going to call your contingent?"

"Is it necessary to call them anything?"

Bronc was in his element and laying it out for her now, "Combine, *this* world is run by marketing and public relations. You are going to try to convince those Big Buck Business Boys, the Masters of Mogulism and Marketing, to go to a place from whence they may never return. I suspect they function on a level you haven't seen for a long, long time, if ever, in your society, if what you tell me is true. I'm also thinkin' that you are going to need some help from some of us low-lifes in order to get them voluntarily on board, and for some reason I can't explain, except for my intuition telling me that this is a positive synchronicity, which Murphy Bailey and Jenoor have taken great pains to explain to me, I'm going to lend you some of my best people in order to help you get the job done, and to help me construct a plausible public reason for doing it."

Combine smiled a genuine and charming smile, "Thanks, Bronc. Let's call them the 'Quadtrillionaires Club'."

Bronc let out an involuntary burst of laughter, "Combine, you may be functioning on a level unknown to us, but from a marketing standpoint, you're pretty naïve. That's the last thing they want to be called. Trust me on this. I got elected President. Call them something like 'The World Advancement Group,' with a 'mission to open the frontiers of space for the purpose of teaching those on Earth to become peaceful citizens who operate on the principle of universal and loving exchange.' That'll work." Bronc roared with gleeful irony.

It did not take long to convince the founding members of The World Advancement Group to visit the Harvesters' planet, which the Harvesters told them they could call "Reapa." The world's mega-entrepreneurs were so intent on finding out how the Harvesters traveled through space, and whether it would be economical for their purposes, they were more than willing to risk their lives, since they viewed life as scarcely worth living if they missed the next nascent opportunity to make more money than their rivals. For that reason, and with each being allowed to take two aides or advisors, almost all the "aides and advisors" were specialists in some aspect of space travel, interspersed with a few mining geologists.

At the appointed day and hour, the five-hundred members of The World Advancement Group, their one-thousand aides and advisors, senior officials, but not the highest leaders, from the United Continents, including Raama, Veerphol, General Thulane Larsen, Tua Rahman, Mamadou Bennajem, Teenaan and Murph, plus the approximately eight-hundred members of the Visitation 1000 media who had actually made the trip to Manticon, including of course, Eastman Foster, were all assembled again at Phoenix International Raceway.

But this time it was to board a Harvester craft which hovered without sound or motion above them. It was at least twice the size of the raceway complex itself. Combine materialized in the air above the group so they could all see her, and she telepathically asked them to all join hands. They did, she dropped down gently, touched one of them and instantaneously they were inside the craft. The thousands of non-traveling media covering the event at the raceway gasped in unison, as did the rest of the world. A moment later the craft simply disappeared, prompting a second round of gasps from the same gaspers who gasped before.

<<~>>

CHAPTER FORTY SIX

With the globe in a state of seeming suspended animation awaiting The World Advancement Group's return, Mari tracked down Jenoor at the White House. He took a couple of steps backward when she entered the room.

"Don't worry, I won't hurt you, but I want my daughter. Now."

"It . . . it . . . really wasn't in the plan."

"Listen, quit stalling, if you do not bring me my baby, I'm going to bore a hole in that mountain and take her out myself. If I have a problem with you over this, I'll hound your butt 'til the end of time as we know it. I'll get you here, in the afterlife, and anywhere else we may exist or go. You will not get away from me, and presuming this is a spiritual developmental exercise for the soul, I guarantee it's going to be you who learns the lesson. *Give me the baby, GreyBoy!*" Her voice had risen considerably, her hair again seemed to be flaming and she had him backed against the wall.

"Look . . . I . . . uh . . . Oh, shit. Okay." He was stunned that in this time of stress, he had reacted like a human – most notably, Murph. Talk about Entrainment.

"I want to go Below, *now*. Tell Lenaan to get that damn thing out on the lawn."

Not being a fool, he did not inquire if by "thing" she meant the baby or Lenaan's space vehicle. He knew what she was thinking and they Particulated through the wall and then into the craft, which left immediately.

As they went into the Manticon nursery, Jenoor asked, ~How did you know your baby was female?~

Still very unhappy with him and not transmitting with a very kind mental energy, ~ I can *communicate* with her. She's *my* baby and she's half Mantid.~

He had previously observed this emotional and communicatory attachment between Earth-mothers and their Meld babies, whether or not they had let the mothers have physical contact with their offspring, but he had never *felt* it before now. With emotion had come empathy. He began to understand why Mari was so vehement. He instructed one of the Mantid attendants to bring her to Mari immediately.

It was the most beautiful child she had ever seen. She had Xanthas' eyes and porcelain skin. My word. There had to be only two pair of eyes like that ever created in the universe. Only two complexions like that ever created in the universe. Realizing that now there were only one pair of eyes and one complexion like that existing in the universe, and at the same time overwhelmed at the sight of her daughter, Mari started to cry.

Jenoor put his arm around her. She looked at him questioningly. "I *am* the father, you know," he said out loud softly. He understood completely now, and she did not pull away.

Mari cooed at her daughter and Jenoor said, again out loud, "She looks exactly like Xanthas when she was a baby."

~She must, were you there?~

~Yes.~

~You never told me you were directly involved.~

~I was.~

It hit her. She looked up at him in astonishment. ~You're *Xanthas'* father too!~

~Yes.~

~My God! It's *all* in the family!~ She did not know how she felt about that or how to react. She was so happy and satisfied to have her baby in her arms, she decided to think about it later. ~Well, I love Xanthas and miss her so much, and I love this child so much who is her image, I'm going to name her Xanthas.~ She looked at Jenoor to see his reaction. She had become expert at reading even the tiniest Mantid movements.

There was a long pause from Jenoor. ~Mari, I can feel exactly how you feel, but something, some strong intuition, tells me that you should not name her Xanthas for reasons I cannot articulate or even comprehend right now, but I feel to a certainty that you should not do it.~ Since the Earthly portion of Jenoor's bilocated energy in his present incarnation had been blanked to a certain extent, the limited knowledge from his Higher Self came to him exactly as he described.

She looked at him and then closed her eyes, relaxing and opening her mind as Xanthas had taught her to do, flowing into the Universal Connection. In a few moments she opened her eyes and looked calmly at Jenoor, ~You are right. I don't know why either, but the intuition comes to me that Xanthas is not the right name. Xanthas taught me always to listen to that 'still small voice' floating through the corridors of my mind.~ Jenoor understood inherently.

~What are you going to name her?~

~I don't know. It'll come to me.~

Jenoor was hoping she would ask for his input, but knew this was neither the time nor the place to raise the issue, if ever. Mari asked that she and her offspring be taken back to her Washington apartment – from which she had previously expelled Murph.

CHAPTER FORTY SEVEN

The Harvester craft instantaneously re-materialized at Reapa and took its occupants on a short tour of the planet. But for the shapes of the continents and major landmarks, it looked amazingly like Earth, and was approximately the same size, except it was cleaner, less cluttered and seemed more streamlined. The wilderness areas were magnificent, with colors intense, saturated and alive. The populated areas were clean, uncrowded, flowing, peaceful. There was no sense of urban sprawl or 'hectivity.' Everything harmonized and *was* harmonious.

The craft settled in the center of a beautiful, grassy park-like setting in the middle of a large city. Instead of having the contingent exit the craft, it just disappeared from around them and they were standing in the park. It was a beautiful, spring-like day. The birds were chirping – they had beautiful birds – the planet's stars were shining, the temperature was perfect. There was a sense of calm.

Combine was again suspended above them so all could see her. <~I will take any questions now. I know I can transmit to all of you telepathically, but you cannot do so for each other. So, please address your questions to Sigmache who will instantaneously relay them telepathically to all of you, as if the questioner were transmitting to you directly. Think of it as a mental public address system. Sigmache will select the individuals, and you may speak or think your questions.~>

Eastman Foster was, of course, first to blurt out a question, predictably negative, "Is this some kind of a mind trick? We got here too fast. How do we know we aren't all hypnotized and still back on Earth?"

<~Mr. Foster, in a very broad sense, everything that has happened in your life so far has been mental; however, I assure you this is not a trick, and, consistent with your level of understanding, this is real. You are *not* hypnotized and you *are* on Reapa in your full Earth consciousness. Our planet is in a different galaxy than Earth, but the same physical universe. I could tell you where it is, but it is so far away from Earth, the answer would be meaningless to you. Suffice to say that if you were travelling by even the most advanced Mantid methods, the distance and time it would take would be incomprehensible, even to them.~>

"Well, if this isn't a trick, why is this so much like Earth? You could have hypnotized us and then either taken us to someplace on Earth with which we are unfamiliar, or we are just in a trance someplace imagining all this." He knew all the digicorders were humming and he was making his best show to maintain his contrarious image.

<~We did not do that. You know you are not on Earth because you have already tried to locate yourself with the Tesla Field locator on your digicom and received no reading, nor can you pick up any of the usual Earth transmissions. If you believe you are merely lying hypnotized and this is not as I said, take the laser weapon you have secreted in your digicamera bag and buzz yourself in the foot. Set it on maximum penetration. We will wait.~>

Unmasked. He did nothing.

<~However, I will explain why this is so much like Earth. When the Teachers created the physical universe, the Earth was not the only place in this dimension for souls to incarnate as part of their education to advance and learn the lessons of existence. There are many places, with different levels and kinds of existence. All you have to do is make calculations from your Drake Equation to get an idea of how many. In any event, Reapa was created with an atmosphere very much like Earth's, or, actually, it is the other way around because our planet has been around much longer than Earth, and, as you may have surmised from what you know about us, we have survived some very foolish decisions as a planetary population. We made many similar mistakes to that of Earth and, fortunately, corrected our collective thinking to a positive mental Entrainment on a planet-wide basis and did not destroy our ecosystems and ourselves. We were not only 'trashing' our environment as you might say, but 'trashing' ourselves spiritually. The two are interrelated.

<~At a point in our planetary development, either as happenstance or as a matter of planning in the Superconscious Dimension, and we believe it is the latter, planetary political and spiritual leaders incarnated who slowly started a turnaround in our thinking until positive Entrainment valence reached the point where changes happened very rapidly on a physical and spiritual front. We have touched on this before in our recent contacts with you on Earth. One of the results is that we no longer want to enslave you or dine on you. Perhaps you believe that now since you are still alive and still free. Now, we only

want to help you advance, which is entirely proper for us to do by the way, both for your sakes and for ours. In fact, that may well have been a basic underlying reason for the creation of such similar planets – a training ground for the spiritual advancement of both of us.

<~As a matter of collateral interest for the more spiritually-minded among you, keep in mind that when souls incarnate in their training, they usually incarnate in the same general place or on the same planet, and usually with members of their own Superconscious Dimension classrooms or related Superconscious classrooms, in order that their training may have a certain continuity. Thus, it is not likely that you will have any "intuitive leakage," directed or unintentional, relating to Reapa, nor is it likely that there will be soul-mates between our two populations; however, there are exceptions to that general rule if it is appropriate for one's development.~>

Recovered from his minor humiliation, Eastman Foster wouldn't let loose, "Well, is there some way you can physically prove to us that this is not Earth. It sure looks, smells and sounds like it from where I'm standing."

<~Yes. Will all of you please hold one of your hands out, palm up, so I may create a piece of smoked viewing glass to give to each of you. When I do, use it to look at what you would call your sun.~>

They did so and a piece of smoked glass materialized on top of every palm. Each looked at the "sun" through it. Sounds of amazement and "I'll be . . ." with a variety of words following, were heard throughout the crowd. They saw the outline of two discs which gave the impression of being partially pushed into each other.

<~As you can see, while our 'star' appears singular in your peripheral vision, it is not one but two. They are both smaller than your sun, one smaller than the other, the larger further out and behind the other from our perspective, both together approximately equaling the mass and heat of your sun. They revolve around one another, and our planet rotates on its axis as Earth does, but orbits them at a constant relative point which always gives us the perspective you see. Not only are all three always in the same relative position to one another, but Reapa was planned at exactly the right point in the ecosphere of our two 'suns' to support life as you are familiar with it.

<~Since the pattern of light falling on Reapa originates from two different sources, it covers more than half of Reapa at once, and since our planet, which is approximately the same size as Earth, rotates on its axis slightly faster than yours, our days are shorter and our climate is much milder and more pleasant overall without wide swings in temperature.~>

Bonacai Shallo, Chairman of the Board and Chief Executive Officer of MultiScore.ola, the largest multi-national holding corporation on Earth, involved in every highly-profitable consumer product, industry and service known on Earth, could contain himself no longer, having visions of not only mining asteroids and planets for minerals, but developing Reapa into a vacation resort paradise, "Madam President . . ."

<~I am Combine . . .~>

"Madam Combine . . ."

<~Just 'Combine' will do.~>

His calm manner and silver-haired, tanned, fit, pleasant good looks, punctuated by steel-blue eyes, masked his impatience and quadruple "Type A" personality. He wanted only to ask his questions and get the answers quickly in order to make his decision. But he knew that political or spiritual – whichever, it didn't matter to him – leaders such as she could not be addressed with abrupt indifference, the latter being his customary treatment of corporate employees and business persons whom he felt he could crush.

He paused with a smile that must have caused an undefined anxiety among the parents of his high school prom dates. His arrogance refusing to fully accede and believing she would view his manner of address as one of respect, "Ms. Combine . . . I am anxious to know, as I am sure others here are also, how we can produce products that meet the needs of others and, inherent in that concept, how we can transport those products, or the raw materials for them, economically through space." He did not include in his question the tag line related to his ultimate goal, "with maximum profits for the company and, thus, for myself."

Even though Shallo had hired several remote-viewing organizations for the purpose of attempting deep-mind-probe corporate espionage, and even understood some things concerning how that worked, the process through which Shallo was transported to Reapa still hadn't sunk in. Nor had it registered that he was being disingenuous with a dead-level mindreader.

Combine responded, <~Mr. Shallo, I have already explained to you, and you have experienced, how we travel through space. I think it will take a marked increase in your understanding in your current lifetime to be able to Mind Shift soon, but since we both originate from the Superconscious Dimension and certain Harvesters are able to do it, it is clear it is *also* achievable for you – at some point – and it should be a collective goal of Earth's population because the understanding which produces that knowledge and ability is your true goal.

<~But, as always, your primary thoughts are on revenue generation. We want to show you supply which does not need to result in, and is not motivated by, revenue generation. We want you to see the achievable possibilities and, hopefully, motivate you to start working toward them as your primary goal at this point in your development.~>

Salivating in his patronization, "Yes, Ms. Combine. We are all very interested. Hopefully, the manner of your space travel can be explained in greater detail to the advisors who accompany us." Ordinarily, he would have tried to cut a deal with her only for his conglomerate; however, he presumed that learning their manner of space propulsion and travel, not to mention the cost of the craft, would be an astronomical undertaking requiring a vast economic conglomerate of the conglomerates. "And, of course, we are anxious to commence the learning curve."

<~Good. Our intent is to open your eyes and your minds. Let's get started. I want to show you a few things.~>

Murph was thinking that while he was no mindreader, Bonacai Shallo, CEO, had certainly not fooled him, and Murph didn't think it was because he had professionally counseled heads of high-pressure businesses who were trying to prop up their personal show while their internal mental infrastructure was collapsing. He understood Shallo purely because it was just plain obvious to anyone who bothered to pay attention to the world at large.

From Murph's personal standpoint, as well as that of the other non-business personnel there, he was very anxious to see what Combine had to demonstrate concerning a non-revenue method of supply. While he understood it was economics that seemed to be making Earth go around these days, that same principle appeared to be killing it. There had to be a better way in the long run.

Crofton Nimrod, CEO of the second-largest conglomerate on

Earth, blurted out, "Listen ma'am, you didn't bring us here to convince us that communism or socialism works did you? Those ideas tanked a long time ago."

Combine laughed a wonderful laugh, <~No, Mr. Nimrod. Come with me, you won't believe this if you don't see it, and I predict Mr. Foster will claim he doesn't believe it anyway.~> Eastman Foster wasn't sure whether or not he should be offended.

On cue, they all touched hands and Combine touched them. Instead of being instantaneously in the spacecraft, they were hovering, as a group, in the same way Combine had hovered over them. It was very strange to them, but effortless and fun. They all felt like the super-heroes they had wished they could be as children. It was a great perspective from which the media could shoot their digicorders. Recognizing their enjoyment, Combine "flew" them slowly over the city to their next destination.

They found themselves transported into, and hovering in, a very large warehouse grocery facility. There did not seem to be any customers, just blonde, blue-eyed employees waiting, presumably for Combine. They were not surprised or shocked at seeing over two thousand people hovering in the air watching them. To the contrary, they were happy that the observers had arrived.

Leaving Sigmache to keep them airborne, Combine descended from the group and went to a very clean work area with large stainless steel pallets on supports about waist high. On one pallet was a single loaf of bread, wrapped.

A tall, blonde, blue-eyed man was standing next to the pallet, <~Ladies and gentlemen, this is Zupance who manages this food distribution facility. Zupance, what is the bread for the day?~>

<~Fourteen grain today, Combine.~> It was clear Zupance was proud of his choice, and happy. He stepped back slightly as Combine approached the pallet.

Combine placed her hands on the loaf and closed her eyes for a few moments. Somewhat slowly, like a fade-in on a digiprogram, the entire pallet filled with identical loaves of bread about ten loaves high. Combine asked Eastman Foster and others to take a loaf from anywhere in the stack, taste it and pass it around. It was the best bread they had ever tasted.

Foster finally found his tongue, "What the hell happened?"

Combine smiled kindly at him, <~Mr. Foster, do you recall our discussions concerning the origination of energy as being produced by mind, and further, matter being mind's arrangement of that energy through its thoughts concerning what that arrangement should be? In short, that matter is the objective manifestation of our thinking?~>

"Yes, I do."

<~That is all I did. I went directly from the source to the manifestation, eliminating the usual intermediate steps. The usual Entrainment you are familiar with is planting seeds, watering, harvesting, separating the grain from the chaff, grinding the meal, leavening, baking, wrapping, and so on. Throughout your history, those have been necessary intermediate steps in achieving the result because that is the set of rules for physical function to which you entrained your thinking in order to make bread; however, those steps all flow from the same mental principle I demonstrated. The difference is that you do not yet understand how to accomplish what I did, nor do you understand the Entrainment etiology of the intermediate steps you have performed on Earth.~>

"I'm not sure I follow the intermediate step part."

<~By 'intermediate' steps, I mean that the process of grain being planted, growing, and so on is nothing more than mental Entrainment of everyone on Earth. Those intermediate steps are part of the physical 'laws' created by the Teachers concerning the functioning of matter, which they also created. They are perpetuated by incarnates through basic archetypal thought Entrainment, originally implanted by the Teachers, which is functioning on the deepest of human unconscious levels.

<~But they are not *the* basic *principles* governing *existence*, they are just the basic laws governing *material* existence, an existence which has been *constructed* temporarily and, as such, is not eternal. According to those so-called laws, bread does not occur unless seeds are planted, watered, harvested, ground, etcetera. In short, I have just penetrated part of that Grand Illusion for you.

<~When your level of understanding concerning how that artificiality occurs and continues rises to the level of demonstration of the principle, you can change what you have been entrained and educated to believe is the unchangeable, and you can create matter. The principle in both cases underlies how the reporter at your raceway was

healed and how I made the bread from what seemed to be nothing. *It is thought made manifest.* With the bread, I simply replicated the EnergyForm of the 'bread of the day', the original of which was made in the 'conventional' manner by the occupants of Reapa.~>

"Why don't *they* just mentally make the bread? You know, have people like that Zupie fellow do it."

<~Because 'they' have not yet the level of understanding which, for instance, I have. Different members of the Harvester community function at different levels of understanding and, as a result, the number of dimensions in which they can function are likewise limited, as well as the level of their demonstrations.~>

"Can you expand on that?" a somewhat puzzled reporter interjected, to the relief of most.

<~Some Harvesters function on the same level as most of you right now, with one fundamental difference. They have an abiding belief, actually they *know*, that their demonstration of mastery over the 'matter-principle' is accomplished by reversal of previously fundamental thought-patterns, just as you are certain you can learn the rules of a new game. They know they can achieve mastery by improvement through appropriate education, study, right-thinking, right-doing, elevation of their thought and practice. Their progress is measured and proven by their incremental demonstrations, which usually start out small.

<~Please make an important note for your viewers and listeners here. When I just used the term 'matter-principle,' I used the word 'principle' in relation to matter in its sense of an accepted rule of action, rather than its sense of a fundamental truth. A very important distinction in the progress of this understanding is that the laws of physics are an accepted rule of action, but are not a fundamental truth. They were artificially created at the level of understanding upon which the Teachers function, taken only to the level of detail that the Teachers believed necessary, operate only in the Material Dimension, and then only to the extent of one's Entrainment and belief that they will continue to do so.~>

They were all concentrating as hard as they were able, but for different purposes. Some were beginning to appreciate the import and magnitude of what she was saying. The Mega Moguls and most of their "aides" were waiting for space travel secrets to slip out. And the

PP's were just waiting for something to take a pot shot at.

Combine continued, knowing her comments would return on digi-sticks to be broadcast over and over on Earth, <~Presently, the 'low-est' level at which individuals function on Reapa is *always* treating others in the same way one wishes to be treated. That way of life is a manifestation of a principal of existence, the fundamental truth of unconditional love. It is the springboard for 'thinking right' and 'doing right' from which all remaining levels of understanding arise.

<~Based on what I have described, I think you will agree that the base-level of thinking on Reapa is, unfortunately, much higher than the base level demonstrated by the beings on Earth. Conversely, the high-est level at which Harvesters presently function is the level I am on. That is stated as a matter of fact, not pride. I'm certain I have a long way to go.~>

"To go where?" inquired a young, thoughtful and curious reporter.

<~To fully understand and *demonstrate* the nature of my relation-ship with One Mind.~>

There was a brief silence among all, engendered by a momentary intuity of, or at least a wonder about, each's final destination.

Combine continued, <~My level is the smallest group of Harvesters, but it gains new additions periodically. Our small group is at a level of understanding that has risen beyond the limitations of material thinking. We primarily function in the dimension of Superconsciousness where the laws of physics have no use, meaning, reality or even apparent reality. Members of our small group no longer incarnate for periods of separate material lifetimes, but we continue a relationship with the material universe, particularly Reapa, and we Mind Shift, 'pop in and out' as you might say, as needed to assist on Reapa from time to time, and we also to try to help others like you raise their level of understanding.~>

For a multitude of reasons, some had become fascinated, some discomfited, and others could not see how this subject could make them any money.

<~We retain the same material identity each time we see a need to incarnate in the Material Dimension and when we are finished, we Mind Shift back to the Superconscious Dimension at will, Transpiring from a matter-based 'reality' to a consciousness-based reality. Of course, reincarnating with the same material identity has not

been traditional with souls of the Earth school, nor do they go back and forth between dimensions at will; however, we understand there may be another exception there soon. In any event, regardless of one's learning environment, a fundamental truth to keep in mind is that we have all originated from the same source. We are still, and always will be, part of that source, and each individual's purpose and goal is to increase understanding and demonstration of the existence which unfolds from One Mind. Each individual's progress flows from understanding.~>

The same young reporter, "What do you mean an exception soon?"

Kindly, <~What is your name?~>

"Kellie. Kellie B'Lee, Commerce News Service."

<~Well, Kellie, I'm not at liberty to comment beyond that, but if and when the exception occurs, there will be no doubt in your mind that it has.~>

Kellie was tempted to press further, but considered herself fortunate to be on this trip and did not wish to wear out her welcome with Combine. From what she had seen of the Harvester leader, she was certain the discussion of that subject was over, even though Combine had reacted to Kellie's interruption in a kind and considerate manner.

Combine pressed on with her original discussion, <~While different Harvester individuals function at different levels of understanding, I am the leader only because one is necessary for our interaction with you. Among ourselves, it is not necessary. Everyone acts in accordance with the same universal loving principles I have alluded to. Harmony of thought, feeling and action is the result. Those of a higher understanding share it with others who exercise their best effort to make positive use of it.~>

Kellie couldn't contain herself, "Don't you ever disagree?"

<~Not any more, Kellie. When everyone is sincerely trying to increase understanding in a truly unselfish way, with a recognition – initially through intuition, then belief, then understanding – that only good flows from One Mind, and because that Mind *is* everything that is unfolding, there is not a problem, only enlightenment which results in peaceful action.~>

Kellie still couldn't resist her own inquisitiveness, "Why do you say 'intuition'?"

<~Because that is usually how it comes to you first. Those hundreds, even thousands, of unconscious observations, and the messages whispering to you from the hollows of your mind, telling you the course.~>

They all just stared at Combine, with some thinking what an amazing thing if the unselfish action she spoke of was the primary motivation on Earth, also recognizing that Earth had a long way to go to Entrain its thinking in that direction until it reached an Event Proportion which would Entrain the thinking of all.

Combine continued the press, <~Now, those functioning on the primary levels in our society pursue a level of thinking which you might over simplify and refer to as continuous positive thinking. No one here engages in negative thinking any more, nor are they irrational 'Pollyannas' as you might call them. Their right-mindedness stems from an understanding that the way they think affects themselves, individually, and affects their life experiences. In turn, their collective positive-valence individual-thinking is an Entrainment that effects beneficial results in the societal-planetary arena.

<~This understanding is proven in its demonstration. Look around you. This is a clean, healthful, happy, loving, sharing planet. It got this way because of the way its occupants think, which affects the way they act, and that effects results. As you know from what you have called the 'Lanta Discs,' it wasn't always this way. It literally started changing one thought and one act at a time until, at some point, an Event Proportion was reached.~>

Someone called out, "What happens when you get sick?"

<~In terms of health, at the more basic levels of thinking here, individuals now understand that they have been unconsciously entrained through archetypes, and consciously entrained and educated on how to be sick. As a minor example, in our past, as I know in yours, once a new illness or condition was publicized, many more seemed to get it than ever before. 'Fad illnesses' and 'fad conditions' are terms that have been used in your society. It was all a result of well-intentioned negative education, not only on a conscious level, but on a most basic subconscious negative Entrainment level. Once a cure was discovered, people were relieved of those conditions to the extent their thought entrained to the cure. One of your physicians who recognized the effect on physical health of thought processes outside physical laws

was Dr. Deepak Chopra who authored his perception of those dynamics in the late twentieth-century volume, *Quantum Healing*.

<~The laws of the various physical sciences in our world are exactly the same as yours. They were intentionally created that way by the Teachers for the entire Material Dimension. To imbue those laws with apparent validity and effectiveness in the physical universe, the Teachers also created concurrent archetype mental Entrainments that functioned at Event Proportion levels from the beginning of matter. Even the simplest and tiniest building blocks of matter were infused with basic levels of material intelligence in order to perform within the material rules set up by the Teachers. Dr. Chopra recognized a basic intelligence in cells and chemicals. Because these rules or physical laws have a mental genesis, they can be altered by mind, and matter can be 'taught' to respond accordingly. As you have learned, we have referred to it as HarmonicMemory and EnergyForm. One result of this was that additional medical events were periodically created by well-meaning materially-oriented scientific and medical minds on our planet through the discovery of additional 'laws,' or a new 'understanding' of existing laws. Material diseases and conditions arose and were perpetuated by that Entrainment and, it follows, the same was the case for their material cures. At least until our thinking developed to its current level.

<~As you know, that dynamic is still true on Earth presently. New conditions appear and new cures are discovered for old conditions on your planet constantly. They appear to be the operation of physical laws about which one is gaining increasing knowledge, but the reality is they are thought-created material compositions being 'discovered' and 'cured' by materially-oriented minds. They have no significance or meaning beyond that given to them by the Entrainment of the occupants of the matter-based world.

<~It is the Grand Illusion and its progeny. Simplified, without intending to demean those who do it, make up a disease, make up a cure – a collective super-hypochondriacy, sustainable only by the strength of the Grand Illusion's thought Entrainment, perpetuated in large measure in your planet by DV commercials, news reports, and health and science programs.

<~That is one of the primary reasons a learning soul is blanked prior to a material incarnation on your planet or elsewhere in the

Material Dimension. If not, the laws of physical science would lose their apparent reality. But once an incarnate starts to perceive how it works, that individual can begin to change it through mind. The Teachers have never discouraged that because it is a facet in a soul's development. Thus, as a result of the elevation of our base-level thinking, our societal mental Entrainment commences on a much higher level of understanding than Earth's, and it is not necessary that our 'blanking' be as extensive as it generally is for most of you.~>

To the relief of those who were exhausting themselves trying to open their minds to the concepts she was presenting, and to the relief of others who didn't care to think that deeply, the interest in food resumed, "So, does all of your food come from you replicating it like you showed us?"

<~Well, the replication comes from those of us functioning on that level of understanding. Generally, others make a few of something that's needed and then we replicate enough to meet the need at that time.~>

"Why don't you just create it instead of having someone make it first?"

<~We are not at the level where we can create on that scale without an EnergyForm template to begin with. We are not on the level of the Teachers.~>

Hoping to generate a controversy, Foster interrupted, "Can you clone living beings?"

<~We have not tried.~>

Foster was incredulous, "Why not?"

<~Due to our rapid health advancements, there has never been a need. You have done it on Earth to have spare parts for diseased or malfunctioning organs. Others have made desperate efforts to continue living through either freezing or replication of oneself, believing existence otherwise ends if not perpetuated in the 'reconstituted mannequin,' not understanding the illusory nature of material life.

<~Long ago, compared to you, we ceased to have need for medical practitioners as you customarily think of them. Our healers are mental practitioners and they teach that anyone and everyone can ultimately learn to do it, beginning with simply deciding to change the direction and perception of their thought from the physical to the metaphysical.

<~Our understanding as a planetary society has risen to the level where we are able to mentally reorganize the energy of any portion of our physical selves which appears to be malfunctioning. Depending on a person's level of understanding, she does that either individually or with the help of someone with a higher understanding, a mental practitioner, who assists her to elevate and focus her thinking to the necessary level. To the extent one is not ready to participate in that type of assistance, the mental practitioner helps 'heal' that individual with positive mental Entrainment through the positive force of the 'healer's' thinking, if the recipient is willing to receive it. Either method rearranges the atoms and molecules of the one in need. It changes the EnergyForm and, thus, the HarmonicMemory of its energy, just as occurred in Phoenix with Jenoor and the reporter.~>

That sounded pretty good to Foster, particularly if he could get the results with little effort. "So once a person decides to change focus from the physical to the metaphysical, does it happen quickly?"

<~Ordinarily not. People do not usually change their material thinking and focus all at once. Because of the negative Entrainment and rules of thinking one commences with, it is a process of developing new habits of conscious and unconscious reaction, which is accomplished through education and practice, usually starting with small demonstrations and working up, though there are individual differences with every soul.

<~Even though every soul who incarnates on Reapa has been subjected to blanking just as you, metaphysical thinking is now much easier in our society because we have had so many years of shifting our emphasis from the physical to the metaphysical. Thinking primarily metaphysically, instead of primarily physically, is socially acceptable here on a planetary-wide basis, which facilitates exploration and demonstration of the principles I describe. Earth has started, but has a long way to go to accomplish societal Entrainment in this area. However, it will have an opportunity to arrive at the point of that Event Proportion if its population does not annihilate itself with material prosperity first. And the latter, of course, is what we are trying to help you prevent.~>

Still not close to comprehending all the information that had been made available to him, but calculating that "living forever" could be a "good deal," Foster inquired, "So, does anyone here ever die?"

<~Mr. Foster, we have been explaining on Earth over the past months, and clearly demonstrating by inference from events you have witnessed, that physical death is not a watershed incident in the course of being, except to indicate that the purpose for one's present incarnation is over. From that perspective, people here only 'die' when the current lesson is finished. In addition to the familiar reasons for incarnation, I should note that sometimes the lesson's emphasis is not for the soul who passes back to the Superconscious Dimension, but is for someone else or a group of other persons.~>

Kellie B'Lee piped up, "Which explains why some young, innocent children, or innocent victims of some other occurrence, seem to bear a lifetime of affliction or pass prematurely, all without an apparent meaningful reason."

<~Yes, dear. You clearly understand the idea. They have volunteered to be victims. Of course, particularly when it is an extended affliction, it can also be a lesson for the soul experiencing it as well as for others.~>

Eastman Foster chimed in, "Well, I'm not sure I do. If everyone knows this, why is anyone here?"

<~This is a school, Mr. Foster. Intellectual knowledge of the principle and the understanding necessary to demonstrate it are two different things. For instance, you have a basic knowledge of the principles of mathematics and have sufficient understanding to work out certain problems of algebra and geometry, but you have not developed the understanding to do calculus even though you know it exists. The reason, of course, is because you have not had the necessary education and practice, the necessary elevation of your thinking and understanding in order to demonstrate it.

<~The same kind of foundation is essential with metaphysical education and demonstration. One starts with smaller, easier demonstrations and works her way up. As understanding and practice continue to increase, so does the magnitude of the demonstrations, and the cycle continues upward.~>

Bonacai Shallo was interested in a different subject, "What do you pay the people who create the template products you replicate and what do you sell them for? They can't possibly make any meaningful money just producing one loaf of bread for you to replicate. Or do they do the marketing of the replicated bread and get a cut of the proceeds?"

But for the fact that Shallo had just provided a segue into a main purpose for the trip, his obvious and pathetic disinterest in the conversations that had occurred to this point might have offended Combine had she been a less-developed soul.

<~They are not remunerated in the manner you have in mind. As on Earth, different people here have differing talents for producing different items or educating and helping others in certain ways. When someone needs something, right-thinking leads that person to the synchronicity which provides it, and it is given without charge. In turn, those who receive provide their particular skill to others who come to them in the same way. It is an amplification of those wonderful coincidences of supply and spiritual abundance which appear in every right-thinking being's life, whether on Earth, on Reapa or elsewhere. It is a demonstration of what you refer to as the 'Golden Rule.' Each person here focuses on giving, and as a result, each receives.

<~We still produce crops, goods and services, but in a synchronous, spiritual, sharing way. Our physical needs are easily met. This abundance is a result of our current spiritual development. Continually improving metaphysical understanding is the present goal of life here. Mental attention is focused on that goal and not on the accumulation of wealth and objects in an attempt to generate the feeling of security. Individuals here *are* secure, but as a result of improvements in their thinking, and not as a result of physical accumulation created by the free enterprise system as you practice it on Earth. Need is met here as it arises and no one is apprehensive that it will not be. If fact, now they *know* it will be. We call it the 'Natural Enterprise System.' It creates peace. And all this has happened as a result of changes in our thinking.~>

Eastman Foster's eyes lit up, "So I could just sort of sit back, take it easy and let everybody else do the work. Hey, what a life!" By now, many people in the group had pegged Foster as a self-perfected idiot.

<~ Not at all, Mr. Foster. This system is based on right-thinking, not selfish-thinking, and once the Natural Enterprise stage is reached, individuals have realized that their goal is to improve metaphysically, not acquire physically, and they work with great happiness and enthusiasm toward elevating their thinking to higher levels of consciousness, higher levels of understanding and demonstration, higher planes. It becomes a joyful labor of love to follow this bliss. No thoughts such

as yours occur on this level. But in terms you can relate to, the Natural Enterprise System demonstrates the positive meaning of, 'What goes around, comes around.'~>

Foster could not think of any antithesis to articulate. The best he could do was wonder why she incarnated when it was obvious she didn't have to do any of that stuff and didn't need anything physical. Why bother? She'd gotten hers. He had forgotten she knew his thoughts, which he had no idea how to shield.

<~Mr. Foster, we incarnate and help because we can, and because we are continually working mentally to rise to higher levels of understanding. We do it because for Reapa, and for Earth, it is the right thing to do at this time. It is not a matter of getting and hoarding. Love is not love until you *give* it away – unconditionally.~>

With his customary lack of finesse, Crofton Nimrod blurted out, "Hey, Reapa really *is* either communist or socialist isn't it?"

Through the groans of the crowd, Combine communicated, <~No, Mr. Nimrod, as we touched on before, those systems were short-lived and failed quite some time ago on Earth. While they seemed like a nice idea to some at the time, they failed in their demonstration for two primary and equally important reasons. They were based on a *compulsion*, either legally or by force, that *required* one or more segments of a society to provide for others, and they lacked a core of *spirituality*, evidenced by their compulsory nature. We are showing and describing a system to you that is the *voluntary* provision by each individual for others, arising out of metaphysical development.~>

Shallo did not want Nimrod's asinine remarks to cause this opportunity to slip through his fingers, "Ms. Combine, none of this would work on Earth because we don't have anyone who can replicate objects, unless you plan to stay there and do it, so we do need to learn economical space travel, and economical methods of producing more, both on Earth and in space, in order to meet the increasing physical needs of our population, so they can concentrate on their mental development."

<~Mr. Shallo, the point I am trying to make is that there is a system existing in the physical universe that supplies through a method other than the constant over-utilization of natural physical resources with its resultant depletion and pollution, and the constant striving for economic and political power with its concomitant poor utilization of

time and thought. I am trying to change your mindset. I hope to do this by showing you what *can* be accomplished, that is, that metaphysical thinking can ultimately meet your physical needs. As they are inter-connected, you can work on both goals at the same time with one thinking-paradigm. 'Two birds with one stone' as you say. Perhaps not reaching this scale in the next few years on Earth, but thinking in that direction can start – with just one thought and its demonstration, then another and another and . . . . You get the idea.~>

"Well, Ms. Combine, in the meantime, I think we need to know about space travel."

Although a few of the business contingents and their scientific "advisors" started contemplating the example of Reapa, most entre-preneurs subscribed to "Shallo-think" and they were a viable and mighty force.

<<~>>

CHAPTER FORTY EIGHT

Mari loved the name she had chosen for her baby and was cooing to Yasmaere softly. There was a knock on the door of her apartment, ~It's me,~ transmitted Jenoor. Yasmaere smiled. Mari knew it wasn't gas. She could receive Yasmaere's transmissions, which at this point were primarily emotional, and it was clear Yasmaere recognized the individual signal-line of Jenoor's consciousness.

~Well, Particulate in,~ she responded.

~We had a deal I wouldn't do that here.~ More and more, Jenoor had begun to think in Surface language.

She opened the door. Now highly experienced at recognizing the difference in Mantid facial expressions, she could see Jenoor's eyes light up when he saw Yasmaere and she handed the bundle to him. He made soft, un-Mantid-like noises to his daughter and she responded with her own. Mari smiled at the scene. Not too many months ago, this would have been science fiction. Incredible! Mom, dad and daughter, and not even from outer space. Some day she had to write a book.

Mari's personal digicom sounded. It was Murph. He had been back from Reapa for several weeks. "Mari, can you give me a hand. Bonacai Shallo and his ilk are whipping people into an economic profit-frenzy. They have formed a large number of new corporations for space exploration and exploitation, and the stock market is going crazy with the public snapping up those new stock offerings. The moment the stock is sold, it is resold until now the average multiple of the initial price is about 700 unicredits to one, even though there are no earnings and are not likely to be in our lifetimes. Making a buck has become the overriding focus of most of the world, and if the economic substance is not there, they'll fantasize it."

Murph continued. He sounded worried and even a little panicked. "The public is completely losing sight of what Combine has been trying to convey to them. The frantic attempts to create new spacecraft and new space fuels will result in more employment, but also significantly more pollution of all types and depletion of natural resources, not to mention a further stagnation in spiritual development. Most of the population is focusing on material acquisition far beyond anything remotely necessary for comfort, convenience or even luxury. As usual, the Shallo-thinkers are shooting for the bottom line, no matter what the accompanying damage. We'll drive ourselves into extinction before anything spiritually meaningful ever happens."

Jenoor had been reading the conversation. Transparently, ~He obviously needs help right away to plan a public relations counterattack. I'll watch the baby.~

Mari saw his small happy smile at this opportunity to spend time alone with Yasmaere. Mari's attitude had softened over the weeks as it became clear how much Jenoor loved the baby. Softened not only towards Jenoor, but towards Murph who clearly loved Yasmaere just as much – she presumed not only because the child was hers, but because Yasmaere was a stunningly beautiful baby who was the miniature image of Xanthas.

Murph continued, "Do you know where Jenoor is? We need him too."

"He's here and he's going to watch Yasmaere, Murph."

Murph's jealousy pangs started running up his back, but he knew he shouldn't act like a jerk. He blocked his thoughts from Jenoor, "Well, can you come right down?" At least he could see her, and his reason was "legitimate" for a change.

"Sure, I'll be right there." She kissed Yasmaere goodbye. Jenoor was hoping for one too, but it didn't happen.

Mari, who had taken on the job of U.C. spokesbeing since Xanthas' death, sat in Murph's office listening to his discourse, continuing where he had left off on the phone, "We have to figure out a way to get the world's attention. We are losing them. I think that many understand intellectually what the Harvesters are saying, but they are making no attempt to live it. If anything, world thinking seems less elevated on the whole than it was before the Harvesters got here. The Shallos and Nimrods of the world have everyone whipped into a profit frenzy, not to mention the fact that most of the people don't trust the Harvesters no matter what they do or say.

"They all want to make a killing and not have to work any more. They want discretionary time one-hundred percent of the time so they can do whatever it is they want and they don't care how they get it or how it affects anyone else. They think money and constant recreation will bring them the sense of peace they all long for, and once they have that, then they will work on their spirituality."

"Well, the Harvesters have had some effect. There is an increasing minority of responsible business heads as well as other types of people out there who are trying to do something positive."

"But, clearly not nearly enough, Mari. Think of something brilliant."

Mari mused, "Well, the only thing I can think of is that we're going to need a Second Coming in order to get the rest of the world's attention. Even if that could happen, I'm not certain the world is ready for it. You'd think the Harvesters would have had a more prolonged and widespread effect on positive world thinking after they scared the crap out of everyone like that and then took the media to Reapa, but the vast majority have still ignored the *real* long-term gains for the customary, familiar short-term money and accoutrements. They've made no progress at all. Those people need to redefine upward mobility."

Murph pushed his glasses up, "Well, our job is psychologically-effective public relations, so let's do it the best we can."

Mari tossed it into his lap, "Where do you suggest we start? I think a basic hurdle we have to overcome is the deep-seated public distrust of the Harvesters. There was a lot of initial negative emotion generated toward them and it's still clearly around – negative mental Entrainment as Jenoor or Combine would say."

Murph was pensive for a moment. Not sure whether he was being facetious or not, "For starters, how about praying?"

Reflecting on where to begin, Mari was not being facetious, "Well, I know Xanthas insists that Superconscious forces always arrange events for our benefit. All we have to do is take advantage of it by not interfering, and listen for that small quiet voice in our minds. Let's still our minds and try it."

"Do you mean meditate or pray?"

"You can call this anything you want and I'm sure it would be effective, just as lots of other methods would be, but Xanthas teaches me that you can get to the still place simply by deciding to. It's not something that happens to you, it's something you do. I just quiet myself and count to three slowly. With each count I direct my consciousness to elevate higher and higher into the Superconscious Dimension and I imagine my conscious energy moving upward into that dimension. It's amazing. I actually get a different feeling as my consciousness moves up into it. Many times I get a little shiver up my back when I reach it. Then I just ask those who assist me to help me with the problem, or if I have no problem, I just ask them to let me know anything that would be beneficial. Xanthas says they're my Guides, as well as others in the Superconscious Dimension who love me and help me. Then, I just let my mind float up there. Usually an answer or a beginning point that makes a lot of sense comes to me."

"Do they talk to you?"

"It's just in the form of a thought or feeling that comes to me, an intuition that I know is right, seemingly from nowhere. It just pops into my mind, but it has happened so often since I started doing it that I know I'm getting help, just the right help, just the right amount and just when I need it, even though it may not have been what I imagined before I started. I simply have to be still and let it work."

Murph, of course, was familiar with many forms of meditation because of the nature of his profession and his long friendship with Pralit Lofler. He reflected, "You know, I've never thought of what you suggest as a form of praying."

"Well, Xanthas says that what you are doing is communicating with One Mind because you are not interfering and are letting yourself be a part of that flow. It's a recognition that you are a part of its unfoldment, that it expresses through you. All you have to do is let it happen and listen for it." It flitted through Mari's thoughts that she had been referring to Xanthas in the present tense.

"Okay. Let's try it."

They both got more comfortable in their chairs and closed their eyes. After a few minutes, they weren't sure how many, their eyes popped open and they looked at each other.

"Are you thinking what I'm thinking?" said Murph with a delighted smile.

Mari was smiling too, "If you are thinking that we should take advantage of the world's love for Xanthas and engage in a campaign of what she said, thought, would probably say or would probably think, then we are."

"Yesssssssss!" He jumped up and did a touchdown dance.

They enthusiastically started the creation of the "Xanthas Returns To Your Hearts" campaign.

<<~>>

CHAPTER FORTY NINE

Donacai Shallo and Crofton Nimrod were at the head of the gargantuan conference table which seated the Joint Boards of Directors of Multiscore.ola and Largess.ola in the secure conference room protected on the outside like a military fortress. It was swept for eavesdropping devices prior to the beginning of, and constantly during, every meeting. Additionally, the directors did their best to block their thoughts from the Harvesters, the Mantid and any other telepathic beings, known or unknown, as well as from the mercenary remote viewers employed by rival corporations. They were trained in this as best they were able by their own mercenary remote viewers.

Shallo had offered Pralit Lofler enormous sums of money to "consult" with Uniquire.ola, the joint venture formed by the two mega-companies, but Lofler was very blunt when replying that he did not wish to retard his spiritual development by embarking on an excessive material-accumulation quest, and he advised Shallo to get his head out of his vault, start listening to the Harvesters, take advantage of what he saw on Reapa and recognize that abundance was a natural byproduct of spiritual development, not a substitute for it.

Pralit had delivered that message in a one-on-one meeting with Shallo. There was something about Pralit's conviction, the complete absence of being intimidated in the presence of the most powerful economic personality in the world, coupled with the soul streaming out of Pralit's eyes directly at Shallo, that non-plussed the normally unflappable mogul. After that, Shallo did not attempt to recruit a Mantid "consultant" for that purpose since his only hope was to reach one through Lofler. Shallo was too insensitive to realize that even if he could contact a Mantid citizen for that purpose, it would be futile since, even though many of the Mantid were still wary of the Harvesters, the Mantid were simply too far advanced on the metaphysical scale to provide Shallo any assistance, much less think his goals were important.

Shallo opened the meeting, "We've got most of the public beating the drums for space exploration and 'development.' He smiled an avaricious smile. But we are not getting the information we need. The Harvesters have no intention of giving up their space travel secrets, the Mantid aren't going to disclose their technology or contract to fly for us, and the government won't cooperate by disclosing what it knows, which I presume is considerable. One of the biggest problems, aside from that annoying little bastard Pralit Lofler, is Murphy Bailey and his wife – she is still his wife isn't she? It's that damned couple's 'return-her-to-your-hearts' PR campaign about that gorgeous dead Xanthas. Given enough time, it could be very effective. We don't want that to happen.

"We need enough organized public enthusiasm and sentiment to politically force the U.C. government to impose a world-wide tax to fund this enterprise. The money from the stock offerings isn't going to be enough. I'm directing our best public relations man, Mesne Fecre, to counter that 'return-to-your-heart' crap and convince the public that a 50-50 joint enterprise between Uniquire.ola and the United Continents, with U.C.'s share of the profits to be paid *directly* to the U.C. citizens instead of the U.C., is the intelligent course. We'll get a double-whammy because they can use the money to buy more of our stock. If necessary, we need to force a world-wide vote on this issue and, in all events – and at all costs – *win*."

Mesne Fecre was a greasy, unkempt, pock-marked slob with no conscience. Referring to him as a sociopath would be complimentary. That's why Shallo loved Fecre's work. He would do anything, say anything, broadcast anything and print anything to mold public opinion. Whatever he believed would work is what he did, without regard for anyone or anything. He was paid millions by Shallo and the money was meaningless to Fecre, as was clear by his appearance. He defined his self worth by accomplishing the task set before him – no matter what. Shallo often joked that his motto was "follow your anti-bliss."

The directors set about in an interminable debate concerning the focus and approach Fecre's public relations campaign should take, each one trying to sound more erudite, cunning and resourceful than the last. Fecre left the meeting on the pretense of going to the bathroom and never returned.

"Meany" opened the door to his luxury condo on the 44th floor of his well-guarded and secured building, stepped around the multitude of possessions he had dropped on the floor at a point in time anywhere from that morning to six weeks before, and picked up his secure code-scrambling digicom. He barked a password and then the name

"Slicer." When he heard the answer at the other end, he said, "This is Meany. Are you on your secure digicom?"

Slicer emitted one of those unhealthy chuckles that sounded like small mucous-covered chunks of things made from his sickening constitution were coming up to evaporate onto anything within three or four feet. Even Fecre was glad he was insulated by his digicom as Slicer responded in his usual derisive manner, "Feces Boy, who gets it this time?"

"You remember how I described the thought-guard procedure?"

"Yep."

"Do it."

"I always do it. Don't want no fuckin' aliens pickin' up my thoughts. I'd get executed for what's inside my head. You too."

"I'm having delivered the names, addresses and pictures of a man and a woman. I understand that from time to time they are together in the woman's apartment. See that they are together in eternity. I don't care what you do with her kid. I've got a couple of my people on them. The next time they are both in her apartment, you'll get the usual signal. It shouldn't take long to get there from your place. Do it quick and quiet. My best guess is that they will be there tonight, so stick around. My people will be dropping off the info, building maintenance uniform, key cards and identification card shortly."

"No sweat, my man. It will be fast and silent, just like all the other times, but no two-for-one on the price."

"You'll get the call. Be ready and be fast. Make it look like a burglary gone bad." Fecre cut it off, yawned, farted, and went into his bedroom to nap.

It was late that evening when Murph dropped Mari off at the apartment, which was now her apartment. Feeling particularly charitable, she invited him up for some coffee. "You can see Yasmaere and maybe we can come up with the key word for our next catch phrase." They went up, Mari paid the sitter and filled the coffee maker with "Special Creativity Blend." Slicer's digicom had already been signaled and he was on his way.

Murph was in Yasmaere's bedroom silently staring at what he felt was the most innocent sight in the universe, a child as beautiful as

Yasmaere – sleeping. Slicer was outside the apartment door, happy that Fecre had sent him a quadruple X uniform to squeeze his slimy, fatty bulk into. He was just about to ring the bell when Maartindael materialized on his left side and Lenaan on his right. He was startled, but at 6'8" and 432 voluminously porky pounds he quickly regained most of his composure upon noting the gray beings were quite small in relation to him. However, he was still a little perplexed because even though he had seen Jenoor and a few other Mantid on DV, they weren't around in public much since few Mantid, other than those most necessary, spent any time on the Surface. He had never seen one in person.

Reacting the only way he knew how, he growled, "What do you two little bug-eyed fucks want?"

"We want you to give us your razor and go with us to the appropriate authorities." Maartindael made the statement calmly even though now that he was developing emotions, he resented being called "little."

Towering over them, Slicer grinned widely with his outsized, unevenly gapped, green and gray teeth, some of the spaces clogged with portions of at least his last three or four meals, "I'm fixin' ta cut those big grapes right outta yer melon heads 'n have me a little snack."

His razor had barely cleared his shirt pocket when the Zzzzt! from Maartindael's laser weapon put a small-diameter tunnel in his head and his porcine bulk melted into the floor as he sank straight down. ~Too slow, Blubber Boy.~

~That was not very loving. You could have just paralyzed him with your mind,~ Lenaan thought reproachfully.

~No, pilot friend. This one needs a little more classroom time and I think this is within the parameters of incarnation unpredictability.~ He opened his small mouth and emitted a soldierly "chuckle" he had been working on. It sounded like a cross between a cricket and a turkey gobble, but he was satisfied with it. Lenaan touched Slicer and all Phase Shifted just as Mari opened the door, thinking she heard some kind of noise. Seeing nothing, she closed it and called quietly to Murph that the coffee was ready.

A short time later, Mesne Fecre awakened from his nap to see Combine, Jenoor, Maartindael and Lenaan standing at the foot of his bed. He shoved with his feet so that he was in a sitting position against the headboard and at the same time tried to reach for his chromed laser weapon on the nightstand. His arm wouldn't move.

"Don't bother Mr. Fecre, you will not be able to move your arm over there," said Jenoor calmly.

Try as he might, Fecre could not move his arm or do anything else except sit there. He was becoming very frightened, "Are . . . are . . . you going to kill me?"

Jenoor, even more calmly, "That choice is up to you Mr. Fecre."

His pores seemed to be oozing oil rather than perspiration. "Wha . . . what do you wwwwwwant? His breath was coming in short, fat pants.

"We want you to cooperate with us."

While Slicer had been too arrogant to guard his thoughts, Fecre was too scared to guard his, and they all knew that consistent with his sociopathic personality, he was prepared to look them straight in the eyes and say anything they wanted to hear until they had gone away, and then he would do what he wanted, that is, what he felt was in his best interest. Jenoor nodded to Maartindael whose soldierly ways had educated him to respond in exactly the right preemptive way to situations in which lack of appropriate motivation could be an obstacle.

Maartindael stepped forward, reached out, and wrapped his long gray digits around the middle finger of Fecre's right hand, covering it. When he opened his digits, Fecre's middle finger was gone, Maartindael having Particulated it and left it in the ether.

Mesne Fecre's breath started coming in large panicky gasps. "Where's my finger! Where the hell's my finger!" he screamed.

Maartindael leaned closer, his immense orbs looking right into Fecre's little beady eyes and he said softly, "It's gone, Meany, and it's never coming back. That was just to make certain we have your attention. We are going to give you some instructions and if you ignore them, or don't follow them well – and I am going to be the sole judge of how well you do – the next thing to go is your 'Thing.' Get it?"

The smell coming from Fecre now was close to unbearable. His eyes seemed to have gone from beady to almost as big as Maartindael's, but not nearly so peaceful. They appeared about ready to blow out of his head while the flesh around his neck was flapping as he nodded vigorously in the affirmative. They all knew he would now listen and follow because, as usual, his sole thought was to save his own skin, literally.

CHAPTER FIFTY

Even with Mesne Fecre subtly sabotaging the Uniquire public relations spin efforts by reporting to Murph everything he learned or was going to do, and by cooperating with the Mantid psychic, Teenaan, to engage in a remote-view deep mind probe so that Teenaan could surreptitiously witness the Uniquire meetings through Fecre without detection, the U.C. wasn't able to neutralize the growing shift in collective Entrainment toward unicredits mania, driven by the perception of Uniquire space travel and development as the provider and savior of abundance.

The U.C. Command was extremely concerned that a negative Event Proportion would be reached, with a figurative black-hole event horizon sucking in and extinguishing Earth's resources in a futile effort to construct the necessary space-travel capability, all in order to acquire what Bronc referred to as "a whole bunch of nothin'."

Bronc was sitting in the Oval Office pontificating to Mari and Murph, "Most people just aren't getting it. They're selling their homes and businesses and putting all the money into Uniquire.ola shares. It won't be payola. It'll be flopola. When that star goes into supernova and burns out, they'll have nothing. They just won't listen and are totally unrealistic. The Mantid are not going to provide their technology. And even if they would, much of it is based on physics and light-speed concepts which, while far in advance of our technology, is light-years behind the Harvesters'. It wouldn't come close to accomplishing what is needed in terms of the rapid, economical space travel necessary to produce the imaginary profits Shallo is dangling in front of those poor, misled, pie-in-the-sky stupes. Instead of calling it 'blue sky fever,' they should rename it the 'milky way syndrome.' Uniquire will use the funds to build mammoth machines and create exotic fuels, none of which will accomplish what they want, and will never have a prayer of doing so."

"And if their understanding ever lifts them to the dimension of the Harvesters' space travel, they will know that what they are doing now is foolish and totally unnecessary."

They all looked at each other and then around the room. Seeing nothing, Murph was about to tell Mari he didn't think imitating Xanthas' voice was funny in the least, though he couldn't imagine how she could do it, when Xanthas materialized a few feet away. No one moved. Each wondered if the stress and gravity of the situation had finally shoved them over the edge. They wanted to believe so much, but it was impossible.

Finally, not caring who thought her a fool, Mari sprang from her chair, weeping from the feelings of her loss and loneliness, and propelled herself at Xanthas, not knowing if she would appear the mentally unstable simpleton when she threw herself through the apparition and into the wall. Her tears became those of joy as her arms wrapped around Xanthas and she felt the familiar warmth and unconditional love radiating from her. Xanthas held her tightly, pressing her cheek against Mari's and stroking her hair lightly. Murph and Bronc just stared, tears running down their faces, unable to do anything but try to comprehend what was happening.

Mari stepped back, incredulous, "Is . . . is . . . it really you? I . . . I know its you, but you seem somehow different, in a better way if that's possible. I can't explain it. You seem lighter, maybe . . . maybe more translucent, like you are illuminated from inside. You just radiate something."

"Mari, I've been in the Superconscious Dimension, studying and doing a great deal of mental work in order to elevate my understanding. What you see is a material manifestation by my Superconsciousness, but I have not returned in the usual way, and my incarnation here *is* illuminated with a brighter light of understanding. As my Superconscious Guide, Saba, thought just before I left, 'I am candescent with the light of truth and love.' Perhaps it would be easier to understand if I said there is simply more of the latter in the mix."

Bronc was the most befuddled of the group. He sputtered, "I just don't get it. You're dead. In a day-long, world-view public ceremony, *I* closed your casket and helped push it into the crematory furnace, and forgive me, you are dead, d-e-a-d. *I* helped retrieve and seal your ashes in a golden urn and we presented them to the Mantid. I just don't get it." He continued to stare at her in disbelief and shake his head.

Xanthas transfixed him with a look of joyous acceptance, "Bronc, you've been listening to what more enlightened beings have been saying, but I don't think you've allowed yourself to fully understand and accept it because it's not within the usual envelope holding your ideas. You must think outside material thoughts if you are to advance beyond them. You know that within that envelope, you've been taught that matter, your brain, generates mind, and we've discussed on several occasions that it is just the opposite. Mind generates matter, and not permanently at that."

Bronc thought over what he had been trained to think from birth. Then he introduced the thoughts that had been presented to him since he first met those in the room, coupled with the things he had witnessed since that time. Still in awe, "Xanthas, this may seem like a silly question, but where is your soul?"

Murph didn't think it was a silly question and finally managed to speak, "Yeah. I'm not sure I get it, Xanthas, does your soul just jump in and out of your body, or any body a being is incarnated in for that matter? What's the deal?"

Xanthas stood there holding Mari's hand, "Murph, Bronc, your soul and mind, that is, your true consciousness, is not confined in nor does it emanate from your material body. Soul emanates from One Mind – and you know the name you have for One Mind doesn't matter. One Mind is infinite and forever, that is, eternal; thus, its qualities are too. Analogizing to limited material concepts since that is basically what you have to work with – in the same sense as a star's individual rays are part of the star and inseparable from it, individual expressions of the infinite are one with it cannot be separated from it into detached finite parts. The Grand Illusion is finite because it is temporary. It is self evident that the infinite cannot be stuffed into the finite. Thus, your soul, which is the expression of One Mind's consciousness, is not in that part of the Grand Illusion which is projected as your material body. Soul is not in matter any more than the sculptor's consciousness is in her sculpture. Soul is unaffected by whether matter exists or not. Vaporize a digivision receiver and the waves from the main transmitter still exist.

"Your Superconscious concentration, the blanked portion of which is your material mind, is merely focused on the matter construct for the purpose of the exercise, operating the puppet so to speak. But the puppeteer is not the puppet nor is the ventriloquist her doll, and to say that soul or consciousness, which *is* life, is in matter is to say that the ventriloquist's doll can operate itself. Those who have a limited perception and understanding believe the puppet or the ventriloquist's doll has a life of its own as a result of its apparent activity, but it is illusion. It has no more reality than Lanta, the aptly-named Illusograph."

"Well, are you saying in a real polite way that I'm not very bright?" Bronc seemed a little indignant.

Love emanated from her, "No, Bronc, your material perception was purposefully limited when you came here for your current learning exercise. That's one of the reasons it's very difficult for you to engage in new ways of thinking."

"Well, what is the purpose of my current learning exercise?"

Her love continued, "Bronc, you know that's for you to learn. You're a naughty boy for trying to tease it out of me. If it would be better for you to learn it by the telling, you wouldn't be here for the experience."

Bronc's face got red at the "naughty boy" observation. He hadn't heard it since he was a child and he looked a little sheepish. "Well, wherever you came from just now, and I'm positively glad you're here, why are you here?"

Mari, who understood and sensed more from her sister than either Murph or Bronc, chimed in innocently, "Have you come back like . . . like . . . well, you know? I . . . uh . . . if you were listening in on us a few days ago, I was kind of kidding when I was talking to Murph about a Second Coming, but that's pretty much what we need."

Xanthas seemed to change into almost pure light and said quietly, if not obliquely, "Whether or not you receive the message I have come to bring, and then act upon it, is up to each of you."

At the enormity of the implication, Mari, Murph and Bronc all started crying again. Bronc got up and hugged Xanthas. He felt like he was in his mother's arms. He wondered if it had anything to do with other incarnations. Murph, still frozen to his chair, could only visualize Xanthas as the poet Shelley's phrase, ". . . the white radiance of eternity."

<<~>>

CHAPTER FIFTY ONE

At Mari's urging, Xanthas had quietly returned with her to the apartment to visit Yasmaere and spend some time together. With Xanthas holding Yasmaere and cooing to her, Mari was trying to figure out what their relationship was. Jenoor was the father of both Yasmaere and Xanthas, and Xanthas was Mari's sister, both having the same mother, but Xanthas' was the product of fertilization in vitro with Jenoor's sperm, and the fertilized egg had been genetically manipulated after that in an attempt to implant the unnecessary and non-existent E-gene among other things, and . . .

Xanthas, communicating in a more intimate manner than speech, thought gently, <<<~It does not matter, sister. We are all from the same source and all trying to get to the same place.~>>> Yasmaere smiled at the passing feeling of her aunt's – sister's ? – thoughts.

~You're right of course. I was just musing. Xanthas, what happened that caused you to come back, and what are you going to do?~

Xanthas described her Superconscious Dimension experiences after she dispatched her physical body at National Mall. When she got to the point in her meetings with the Master Teachers where they first presented the very unusual idea of her coming back to Earth in the same manifestation in which she left, she transmitted to Mari a thought constellation that let Mari relive it with her as if she were there as an observer:

<<<< ———————————- >>>>

Xanthas, communicating to the Master Teachers, ~What do you think I can do?~

<<<~Xanthas, we have intervened in Earth's affairs in the past with Jesus, Buddha and other great and diverse leaders of thought who subsequently elevated the collective thought Entrainment on Earth to an extent that shifted the world paradigm back to a positive valence from the negative direction in which incarnate students, who are imperfect by definition, had taken it. You are the appropriate intervenor for this time.~>>

It occurred to Mari that mental communication had its advantages. She wasn't sure if she could have gotten that first sentence out on one breath.

Xanthas continued, ~Buddha? Jesus? I . . . I . . . ~

<<~Do not be concerned. You, just as Buddha and Jesus were, are a developing soul. You will be trained and your understanding will rise to the appropriate level before returning to Earth. There you will continue to develop, as they did, but you will be far in advance of the souls presently there and will be able to teach and demonstrate much that will reverse the negative Entrainment there now. Earth's population is too distrustful of Combine and her group. It will take you to reverse the valence.~>>

~But . . . but . . . I know so little in comparison to Jesus and Buddha, it will take so long for me to advance to that level, won't Earth be lost by that time? Won't it take many incarnations?~

<<~You are still too soon from Earth. You know the passing of events here bear no relation to time. Time is a material concept unknown to eternity. No time is here, only opportunities to think. The occurrence of many events here may be equal to a few seconds, many years or no time at all on Earth, depending on the necessities of development. You also know that incarnation is only an adjunct to your development, and many souls in the course of their improvement do not incarnate often and some not at all. Certainly souls who reach the stage of Superconscious development you will achieve seldom incarnate again, if ever. But *you* will.~>>

~Will . . . will . . . I be able to talk to Jesus and Buddha about this?~

<<~Only indirectly.~>>

~Why is that?~

<<~At the point you fully understand the reason, you will be able to communicate directly with them.~>>

Mari was in awe at virtually being there with Xanthas as it happened, ~So, then what?~

<<<~I studied intensely with the Master Teachers and others to raise my consciousness to the necessary level.~>>>

~Wow. You are incredible. It hasn't been all that long.~

<<<~Translated into Earth time, it could also have been eons. In

the spiritual dimension, it is not relevant.~>>>

Mari was entraining to Xanthas' thoughts. It felt wonderful. Excitedly, ~So, did you get to communicate with Jesus or Buddha?~

<<<~Only indirectly so far.~>>>

~Why not directly, particularly if you are coming to raise consciousness as they did?~

<<<~Mari, I am just beginning to understand the explanation. It would not be appropriate to articulate it now.~>>>

~Well, did you talk to One Mind?~

Xanthas smiled at Mari's persistence, <<<~Mari, One Mind is in us all, and we are one.~>>>

Mari's curiosity was insatiable, ~Well, how far is it from the Superconscious Dimension to Earth?~

Xanthas' love was unwavering, <<<~Mari, it's not distance, it's planes of understanding. What you perceive as distance is levels of thought.~>>>

~Then explain the concept of 'floating' to different places in the Superconscious Dimension.~

<<<~When we 'float' in the Superconscious, it's a 'figure of thought' and we don't actually go anyplace, of course. There is nowhere to go in a three-dimensional sense. One Mind is everywhere and we move in the mental dimension by shifting the focus of our thoughts.~>>>

Mari looked at her for a long time and let Xanthas' radiated joy and love consume her. Then they exchanged thoughts long into the night concerning Xanthas' preparation and undertaking, and, at Mari's insistence, how Mari could help her.

<<~>>

CHAPTER FIFTY TWO

The next morning, Jenoor and Murph were unsure why they had both been summoned together to Mari's apartment for a meeting. It was highly unusual. Any meeting they would attend together would be in the government complexes and not here. They were not comfortable with each other in jointly-attended private settings. While Murph and Jenoor understood the necessity of working together for the sake of the United Continents, Murph did not take kindly to Jenoor's participation in Mari's infidelity, and, conversely, Jenoor's emotional development caused him to feel terrible for interfering with the ultimate in human trusting relationships in such an intimately rending way. Bonds they did share were their love for Yasmaere and their common rejection by Mari as the objects of her intimate affections.

Perhaps Mari and Xanthas wanted to have a private official meeting with them. Almost no one knew about Xanthas' return and it probably did make sense for the four of them to meet at the apartment. Jenoor hadn't even seen Xanthas yet, although she had communicated with him telepathically since her reappearance and explained its reason. Jenoor's Earthly presence, unaware of his bilocated energy in the Superconscious Dimension as Xanthas knew it would not be appropriate to tell him, was very happy that she was back. His material mind had succumbed to the idea she was dead, or certainly never accessible to him again in this lifetime. Jenoor arrived at the apartment and warmly embraced his oldest daughter, marveling at her luminosity.

With the four of them in the living room, Jenoor, having learned to relieve slightly uncomfortable situations with a little humor, looked at Xanthas and said for all to hear, "Well, I guess I raised you right." No one laughed. He'd even included a double entendre, at least to him, and signaled it was a joke with a little chortle. He concluded he needed to work on his timing.

Much to Murph's and Jenoor's confusion, Xanthas excused herself saying she needed to clear her thoughts and went to a different part of the apartment to work mentally.

After she left, Mari came right to the point, "I am going to help Xanthas full-time."

Murph and Jenoor looked at each other. Murph said it, "Why did you have to call us here to tell us that?"

Her sky-blue eyes seemed to lock on both of them at once, " 'Full-time' means I will be going with her everywhere she goes on Earth, doing whatever I can to help her fulfill her purpose. 'Full-time' means that I won't be here unless Xanthas is here, which may be seldom and will most likely always be unpredictable. 'Full-time' means that I do not want to disrupt Yasmaere's life any more than necessary and do not think it is appropriate that I take Yasmaere with me. Leaving her here will keep her physical environment intact and I am able to communicate with her telepathically, including emotionally.

"In short, 'full-time' means that it will be necessary for you two to take care of Yasmaere full-time. That doesn't mean that you hire a nanny. That means that until Xanthas' work is finished and I return, you two move in here together and at least one of you is with Yasmaere all the time as paterfamilias so that she receives as much loving physical contact as possible. That is unless one of you doesn't want to do it."

Indignant, Jenoor shot out, "Well, *I'm* her *father*."

Murph jumped on the end of that line, "Well up yours, I'm her stepfather and she's *my* wife's daughter. I've learned enough about incarnation to know that Yasmaere chose her life situation before she came here, and it darn well included me – which you can plainly tell because I am a principal player here. I love her just as much as any of you, and I'm damn well entitled."

She had played them as if she were the famous jazz artist Junior Claybrown working his double-bass, "It's settled then. You two need to move in right away because Xanthas and I will be leaving soon."

Jenoor and Murph looked at each other with mouths slightly open. Jenoor thought of the old movies and television shows the Mantid had studied – particularly those based on the two males referred to as the "Odd Couple." Their eyes briefly signaled each other that they knew they'd been jointly had, and they wouldn't have it any other way under the circumstances. Neither wanted the other to be the sole caretaker, neither could do it full time, neither believed they had a prayer of talking Mari out of her decision, and both would rather have Mari accompanying Xanthas than anyone else they could think of except themselves, and that wasn't going to happen.

<<~>>

CHAPTER FIFTY THREE

With only the U.C. inner circle having knowledge of Xanthas return, Mari and Xanthas started traveling around the Earth in non-material form for the purpose of observing the general demeanor, goals and mental attitude of its inhabitants. Mari liked the way she and Xanthas traveled. Xanthas would not even have to touch her and they simply arrived wherever they wanted to be. It had nothing to do with the Mantid Phase Shift, so they did not have to be in a slightly in-phase condition in order to see what was going on. They could observe totally unobserved. Mari believed she knew many of the basic explanations about why that worked, and why all the other things like healing worked, but she still couldn't seem to do any of those things herself and wanted to learn.

Shortly after the beginning of their travels, she had asked Xanthas to help her learn how to do some or all of the things she had seen Xanthas, Combine and Jenoor do.

<<<~Mari, I refer to the underlying principle, which you have heard Jenoor and Combine describe, as the "Mind Effect Principle." Note that I am referring to 'effect' with an 'e.' The Mind Effect Principle is applied by activating correct thinking and eliminating erroneous thinking. To say it in a broad way, the demonstration of this right thinking effects health, harmony, abundance and happiness, and negative erroneous concepts fall away into their natural nonexistence.

<<<~Briefly stated, you manifest what you think. In the Material Dimension, the *intellectual* comprehension of the Mind Effect Principle is only the starting point on the continuum of *understanding* which results in increasing levels of *demonstration* of the power of mind over matter. Those demonstrations help create the feeling of *knowing*, the feeling of absolute certainty that you possess the truth. Begin in small ways. Start simply, by replacing negative thoughts with correct ones. You can, and should, do this with any issue or situation, such as lack of anything, disharmony with respect to anything, the negative of anything.

<<<~Actively *think* to yourself that, in the Material Dimension, you are the material objectification of thought that does not have to include any negative idea or process of ideas. *Think* that, as the objectification of your thought, you can be perfectly and harmoniously functioning. Refuse to let any negative thought have effect with regard to

you. No physical condition or negative emotional condition has any 'reality' for you unless your thinking generates that 'reality.'

<<<~Apply the principle to health. For instance, when you see an advertisement on the DV or your digicom that it is the time of the year to have a cold or the flu, don't accept it as a fact of life and merely hope it doesn't happen to you. Don't passively submit to the common Entrainment of how these maladies are transmitted and what they will do to you. If you do, that's why it happens. You do it to yourself. Negative thinking means you are not utilizing the Mind Effect Principle. Actively command any persistent negative thought to, 'Drop away into your natural nonexistence.' The power is yours. You can *decide* not to be sick or upset. It can only be a part of you if you choose to accept it.

<<<~Replace the negative concept with the positive concept in your thinking and objectify it. It is important to avoid wishing something bad doesn't happen, because it focuses your mind on the negative. *Decide* to be healthy and harmonious. Visualize *only* the healthy status occurring in your body or the harmonious status occurring in your life, and direct that it be the case, now. While working your way up the continuum of demonstration, it is quite acceptable to visualize the removal or repair of a negative condition, utilizing techniques such as Jenoor used with the reporter at the raceway, but always end only with the positive, and command that status to be the case within you.

<<<~It isn't limited to health issues. It works on personal and interpersonal issues too. If you are having a problem with disharmony in your life in general, for instance with abundance in all its forms, whether supply, friendship and love, enthusiasm, or in a particular situation with another person, help yourself in the same way you would use this principle if you were physically injured.

<<<~To do that, utilize the Mind Effect Principle and see the energy of the negatives, or of the negative people, rearranged in a positive way. Visualize the positive of the situation as you would like it to be, and direct that all the atoms, molecules – or 'mindecules' if you prefer – and energy relating to the situation, those with whom you interact, and you, be arranged and rearranged in accordance with your positive visualization, *now*. Mentally say to yourself, 'I direct that it occur, *now*. I push the 'enter' button, *now*.'

<<<~Then, think right and do right, listening for the messages that

will come to you in the form of positive intuition from your Guides and others who love you. Recall that you originated from the Superconscious Dimension and *know* that interested, loving forces will always arrange events for your benefit. But you must assist the process, not interfere with it. Discard negative thoughts and command them to drop away. Follow the intuition you receive. You'll know it. It will just *feel* right. Keep doing that on a consistent basis and the world you experience will change. You will be 'healed' in that way, just as you would be physically, because the Mind Effect Principle is exactly the same in all instances.

<<<~To the extent that you correctly know and do this to the point you have no more *fear* of a negative result, you will triumph and demonstrate the principle. To the extent you are reducing that fear with correct thinking, the negative result is reduced accordingly. The demonstrations will accumulate and build. It is not a pass or fail proposition. It's a continuum. You didn't learn how to play the piano overnight, and even when you were practicing and striking the wrong notes, that didn't change the principle of harmony. But as you practiced, you got better and better at demonstrating the principle of harmony, and your fear of an occurrence of discord continually dissipated. The effect was self-reciprocating and self-reinforcing, and all the time, the control of the result was with *you*. It was not out of your hands. The difference of the Mind Effect Principle from the example of the piano is that *everyone* has the aptitude to ultimately demonstrate this principle of being, perfectly. The more you practice, the better you get. At the core level of the material mind, you are retraining your Entrainment.

<<<~Not only fear, but any form of selfishness, anger or similar negatives can interfere with the demonstration. That's why it's important to think right and do right. Of course, as with anything, as you gain experience in the application, you will tackle situations that previously you lacked the confidence to address, if those situations ever occur. One of the benefits of recognizing that your thoughts effect your experience is that if your thinking is appropriate, many negative 'possibilities' never materialize.~>>>

As a result of those teachings, early on in their "travel and observation" period, which was taking several months, Mari began to practice changing the habitual ways in which she thought, changing the

Entrainment that things were always going to happen in a certain way and that the laws of physical science, coupled with the laws of chance, were the immutable laws of existence.

She found that because she had been so accustomed to believe that a certain effect must necessarily follow a certain cause, or that some things just happened by chance with or without cause, she constantly had to monitor her thinking in order to reject thoughts and images that would produce, or validate, negative results, and replace that negative validation with thinking that produced the opposite. The more she did it, the more it worked. The more it worked, the more her life was filled with positive, healthful, abundant, harmonious and loving experiences, and the negative ones seemed to drop away, to simply evaporate. They didn't go anyplace. They simply disappeared, like a flame when it is deprived of fuel.

She saw that the Mind Effect Principle isn't just positive thinking or mere denial of the negative, although that is often an important preliminary step. It is based on the recognition and understanding of the nature of material existence. Xanthas helped her by making an analogy to simple mathematics. In essence, it is the difference between accepting or rejecting whether or not $2 + 2 = 5$. If one knows certain facts are true and correct, then erroneous facts are rejected and have no effect. Even if incorrect facts are taken as true and an erroneous result seems to manifest itself, that doesn't change the principle of mathematics, and the problem can be rethought to arrive at the correct result.

So, Mari would practice immediately replacing erroneous thoughts and images with the correct view. It helped that she had the experience of seeing Jenoor demonstrate the principle, and that, through Xanthas' transmission of thought constellations to her (which was like being able to read a book, see a movie and experience the related emotions all at once), she had the recreated experience of being with Xanthas' during her communication with the Master Teachers in the Superconscious Dimension, plus her own "near-death" experience in Manticon. Those experiences and her immediate and amazing personal experience of being in a non-material state while "traveling" with Xanthas helped raise her material consciousness and understanding concerning the nature of matter and the nature of existence to a new level, and her demonstrations confirmed it.

As Mari continued to learn, Xanthas told her she would come to understand that the demonstration of this particular principle of being, the Mind Effect Principle, does not *substitute* something for a malady or a negative situation. It develops into a knowing that the negative has *no* power – unless you make it *apparently* so. Thus, for instance, the Mind Effect Principle is not a substitute for a flu shot, it is a recognition and demonstration of its lack of necessity.

Xanthas also explained that in the beginning, it is helpful to use the visualization approach that Jenoor had demonstrated at the raceway with the young reporter in order to help *un*-make the apparent reality of a situation. Thus, if her fear of getting a sore throat from some "exposure" interfered with her understanding of the principle involved, and she felt she was becoming ill, then either on the simplified representation of herself or on her body, she could visualize white purifying and restorative rays on her throat, extending all through her and filling her with white purifying light expanding out from her body for a foot or so, and then direct the change in her atoms, molecules and energy consistent with that healthy result, as Jenoor had shown at the raceway. Or if she felt she were in or entering a situation where she might be exposed to illness, or any other negativity for that matter, she could visualize a white light protective field around her and through her, visualizing herself as being unaffected by the exposure or negativity with the only occurrence being health and harmony in the situation, and mentally direct that result. Mari could do those things, coupling them with a mental review of the underlying principle that what one thinks is what will be manifested, until she no longer needed the visualization aid. Then, simply engaging in a higher level of appropriate thought would be sufficient. It was becoming clearer to her that the natural homeostasis of being is harmony, abundance and happiness in all their forms, and if one does not negatively interfere, consciously or unconsciously, with that state, the manifestations in one's experience default to that positive status.

Xanthas explained that while it may not work instantaneously, depending on Mari's level of understanding and lack of fear, as she applied it and it started to become effective for her, it would often reduce the severity or length of the symptoms or negative situation in which she had mentally acquiesced, or which she had created for herself. The more stubborn things seemed to be, she must meet them with correct thinking underpinned by continuous and greater resolve. Of course, at some point it would become as automatic and unconscious as her current incorrect thinking and responses were now, and the resultant harmony would manifest itself in her experience "automatically." She would have succeeded in retraining her mental Entrainment. Xanthas underscored that so long as Mari worked at improving in this learning process, harmony would occur more and more frequently and, for instance in health issues, Mari would feel the need to rely on material remedies less and less.

As Mari worked diligently at elevating her understanding and demonstration, certain questions would enter her mind and she always asked them, ~Xanthas, I'm having a little difficulty. Sometimes it seems I make such an effort at seeing the true non-material nature of existence that I don't recognize the Superconscious forest because all the material trees are in the way. How do you know when you *know*?~

<<<<~From the feeling. There will not be any doubt in your mind. When you *know* you have possession of the truth, a different energy and perception radiates from within you.~>>>>

~Which is why *you* luminesce.~

<<<<~Yes, to human eyes. Because once understanding progresses and thinking elevates toward the natural non-material nature of existence, the material effects evaporate proportionably. The 'density' inherent in matter-based thinking lessens as the consciousness of natural spiritual existence fills the vessel of thought and dilutes material perception. One starts to glow with the inner light of the truth of being. At a point in understanding, one is no longer visible to material eyes, and Transpirates to a higher plane of consciousness.~>>>>

Mari's limitless thirst for spiritual knowledge was exceeded only by the joy of learning it, ~Okay, tell me if I've got it. As my understanding advances, that is, as my thinking becomes more flawless, the *manifestation* of my thinking becomes more flawless and, as a result, my physical body becomes more healthful, as well as my experience becoming more abundant and harmonious. Then, I begin to realize that the way of thinking that manifests a physical body is *super*natural, and the way of thinking that manifests only a loving spiritual consciousness is the actual, true, *natural* way of thinking. As this way of thinking and understanding elevates and becomes more predominant, I become more radiant and translucent with the light of knowledge and understanding. That process can continue until a material body disappears as a manifestation of my thought, and thus, it disappears from material sight. At that point, the demonstration of my understanding has reached the juncture where I have Transpirated to another plane, the Superconscious Dimension.~

Xanthas didn't answer. They both knew Mari had it.

During their months of travel and observation, Xanthas often caused Mari to materialize (Mari could not do that at will herself) to perform certain tasks in connection with their mission, but Xanthas had not yet materialized for anyone else to see. Her observations made it clear that it was important to plan her materialization for maximum impact since the individuals in the world who truly practiced the 'Golden Rule,' by whatever name, as the guideline of their lives were a clear minority. Some in the majority paid lip service to it, and others ignored it altogether.

The majority in the world, in many different ways and for many different reasons, still failed to realize that the correct unfoldment of abundance flows from the practice of unselfish spiritual qualities and not from an all-consuming quest for the personal acquisition of funds, assets, power and control. It was obvious that the entrained mindset of the majority of the world's human citizens still needed to be changed and, of course, the change had to commence with the thoughts of individuals.

Nor were the Mantid without the need for development. While, in varying and often higher degrees than those on the Surface, a much larger percentage of the Mantid at least intellectually understood the principles Xanthas would return to teach and reinforce, Jenoor represented the highest development of their thought, and most were not at his level of understanding or demonstration.

Mari arranged with Bronc for Xanthas' first public reappearance to be at an enormous public gathering near Paris, at the Lois Fields, an immense man-made outdoor meadowland amphitheater and woodslike family entertainment complex that would accommodate over 1,000,000 people and media, one of the main attractions of which was a prodigious early twenty-first century roller coaster named Cap'n Bob that had been preserved and transferred to the site. Naturally, the event would be broadcast worldwide. This would be followed by similar events all over the world so that as many Earth inhabitants as practicable could see Xanthas in person, including an event scheduled for Manticon.

CHAPTER FIFTY FOUR

During Mari's and Xanthas' absence, Jenoor and Murph found that taking care of Yasmaere was a joy, not a chore. Both of them usually communicated telepathically with Yasmaere, but seldom telepathically with each other. Without discussing it, they each felt that telepathic communication between the two of them was too close a contact under the circumstances of their past history relating to Mari, even though they had genuinely, if not reluctantly, adopted a spirit of cooperation, interest and mutual goals in relation to Yasmaere.

One day, Jenoor arrived at the apartment just as Murph had finished playing an educational game with Yasmaere. She had mastered the available games through the six-year level and had started on the seven-year level.

Jenoor looked at the game Murph was putting back in the box and mused, "Man, she's run out of the six-year games already? Soon there won't be anything left to play with her." He loved to use those terms like "man" and living with Murph had given him the opportunity to habitually talk like one of the Surface guys, although there was no way a Mantid could look macho yelling "fumble!" at the DV screen. He didn't like chips or beer either.

Murph speculated, "Yeah, you know if there get to be a lot more children like this as our cultures mingle, you and I could develop a whole line of educational games for them and make a bundle. In fact, we could open a whole series of social clubs around the world for the purpose of the 'eligibles' meeting. Once the ladies find out how you guys are built where it counts, we'd be the unicredit barons of the solar system. Shallo would be asking us for loans. We're right on the cutting edge of this whole damn thing!" Murph was getting excited.

"I'm not sure that Xanthas or Combine would think that is the right focus, Murph."

"Whadda'ya mean?" Murph was starting to become a little defensive.

"Well, presuming that at least one, and perhaps both, of those ideas would perform a worthwhile service and fulfill a true need, the focus should be on the service, performed in a positive and responsible way. That should be a prime goal, not the generation of as many unicredits as possible for any reason."

"Well, in my visit to Reapa, I don't recall Combine saying that there was anything inherently wrong with the free-enterprise system."

"That's correct. The point she made is that for the Harvesters, it is no longer necessary at the level of development they have reached. Their security, abundance and sense of personal worth no longer comes from the drive to amass as much money as possible. Combine is the first to say that didn't happen overnight, and I certainly acknowledge that if it happens, it won't happen overnight on Earth either.

"But to start, people need to change their minds to the view that it is the focus on unselfish service that is most important. The rest would flow from that enterprise. We would gradually convert from a profit system toward a Natural Enterprise System of unconditionally providing to others according to one's talents and skill, others requesting only according to their legitimate need, and in turn providing to others, and so on. It will work, but to get there, minds must voluntarily elevate and change one at a time until the cumulative positive Entrainment reaches an Event Proportion. And you know once that happens, the minority remaining will ultimately and irresistibly become entrained. Even if none of us reach the replication level of Combine until the far future, the appropriate combination of the free enterprise system with the Natural Enterprise System, along with the attendant elevated thinking that accompanies it, will substantially move the world in the opposite direction from its present course of environmental and spiritual destruction."

Murph easily acquiesced, "Yeah, you're right and I'm wrong. Right idea, wrong ultimate goal."

"Well, I'd be interested in thinking about the social club idea, and if it's worthwhile, how to perform that service properly – just as it would be important to design the educational games properly."

"It'll never end, will it, Jenoor."

"What?"

"The responsibility of helping others."

"Not just responsibility toward other beings, but responsibility to Earth, and beyond that to the rest of the universe. It is a continuing process, and flows from each of us developing our consciousness in the right direction and keeping a constant vigilance to see that we do so. After awhile it ceases to become a responsibility and becomes a joy. Every system of right thinking confirms that is the enlightened path to where we all want to be."

It just flashed out of Murph, "Is that the path you followed when you fucked my wife?"

Jenoor was stunned at the unexpected question concerning the subject he believed they had both voluntarily buried, but which always flitted around the surface of their thought no matter what else they were talking about. He also flashed with anger at the use of the "f" word in juxtaposition to Mari, "I certainly wouldn't demean my wife by the use of that word as related to her."

"Well, she's not your wife and from my perspective, you *fucked* her." Murph's voice was not raised, but it was intense and he didn't give a damn right now about how uncomfortable Jenoor felt. In fact, he believed he just saw him swallow kind of hard.

Jenoor had, but not from apprehension. It was motivated by his resolve to tell it like he saw it. He dropped his colloquialisms and lapsed into his pedantic style, "Well, from my perspective, several things happened, not the least of which is that, from an Earth standpoint, I fell completely in love with Mari and was *making love with* her, not doing what you said. Secondly, Mari and I both *chose* to produce an interbeing baby *before* either of us came here. We have both penetrated back into the Superconscious Dimension enough to understand that at this point. Thirdly, from a personal view, I have subsequently developed to the point where I feel terrible about the way what I did has contributed to the way you feel, and I suspect that was also part of the plan worked out for me.

"However, that's mitigated by the knowledge that, from what Xanthas told me of your past incarnations, you are receiving an educational development here that you sorely need and I presume you consented to in some fashion. So, I guess all I can say is that maybe things are working out according to our grand general plan, probably one we all worked on jointly before we got here this time."

Murph didn't know what to say, particularly because that was consistent with everything he had learned from his patients and from his discussions with Xanthas, even though he didn't like it and wished he had a perfect little existence here – but then of course, what would be the point?

<<~>>

CHAPTER FIFTY FIVE

Counting the media, there were more than a million people at Lois Fields. For the past two months, the world population had been bombarded with announcements in all media forms that an event unprecedented in the history of the planet would take place on this date, an event more momentous than the arrival of the Harvesters. The media had no idea what it was, but since it was the U.C. making the announcements, many of which were done by Bronc himself, no one believed it should be ignored, particularly in light of the recent past which had revealed the Mantid and then the Harvesters. Additionally, and for some more to the point, the U.C. was paying for those advertising spots instead of requesting them as a public service and, of course, the speculation was a field day for the media, legitimate and PP. None of their conjecture was anywhere close to the events that were about to occur.

On the appointed day, the Incredibly Curious Million, as the media had dubbed them, were at Lois Fields at Paris. The rest of the world, Surface and Below, were tuned in through every electronic device extant on Earth. The Tesla Field surrounding Earth seemed to be humming from the usage generated by this event. Combine, sitting in her spacecraft not far above the field's perimeter, perceived its glow. The field transferred electrical energy on nanowaves to the devices demanding it, taking an enormous amount of nuclear energy to power it, and Combine was lamenting the unbelievable amount of nuclear waste being generated at various "stations" around the world in order for this "progress" to be available.

The Harvesters had been contemplating sharing their energy secrets with Earth, but wanted to see significant advancement in the spirituality of Earth's inhabitants in order to have some comfort that the information would not be misused. Combine regretted that she had not been able to lead the Earth to accept the degree of higher understanding the Harvesters were making available, but most of its inhabitants were simply too suspicious of them, too greedy, too foolish or too highly entrained to other ways of thinking to recognize the opportunity offered. She prayed that Xanthas was the key.

With the crowd settled, a musical group named "Greek Phil" finished playing and Mari walked out on the stage of the amphitheater. Every big screen throughout the "Lowey," as the Lois Fields complex was affectionately called, was being watched intently. Those in attendance not watching the big screens were looking at their portable digicoms or into their digiglasses. Below, those Mantid who had requested the procedure, which lasted only a few minutes but was somewhat painful, mentally directed the molecules altered in their eyes for that purpose to receive the transmissions. It was a convenient offshoot of their highly developed picomolecular technology, one of many advancements they had not yet shared with the Surface.

Mari's voice and red-haired countenance were now familiar to the world as a result of taking over the U.C. spokesbeing duties. She had been seen in the announcements for this event many times each day by every being on the planet, almost as much as Bronc, and more than Jenoor. The Incredibly Curious Million became absolutely quiet as Mari walked to the center of the stage. They had no idea what major occurrence to expect, but since the Harvesters had not hurt them when they could have, most did not think anything life-threatening was going to happen, and perhaps it would be an announcement that would simplify all their lives. They believed it probably would be if it was this momentous. World optimism had changed, if not its spirituality, and in a sense they had not contemplated, they were going to be right.

Mari, who seemed to be more radiant in person than in her announcements on DV, introduced Bronc and Jenoor, with whom the world were familiar and who actually didn't need to be introduced, but a certain formality was expected if this was to be a genuine watershed occasion.

Bronc spoke. Unusual for him, he seemed kind of radiant also, "Beings of Earth, as you know, we've been through a lot together. First, the public appearance of the Mantid, the preparation for the coming of the Harvesters under extremely extenuating circumstances, the death of Xanthas and the surrender to the Harvesters. They came and not only have they not harmed us, the Harvesters have tried to help us in many ways, spiritually and physically. Unfortunately, most of the world has not seen the deeper meaning of these events. Combine has tried to bring this home to you, but most see only an opportunity for profit, believing that is the path to, and the definition of, abundance. I want to remind you of the words the Harvesters presented to us in the beginning, words we ignored because we were so frightened."

The words were displayed in a large hologram over the stage and superimposed over every DV transmission for all to read as they heard Xanthas' unmistakable voice recite them.

"Love is the immovable object of being. Expressing uncondi-tional love is the irresistible force of reality. The immovable object and the irresistible force are harmonious because they are one and the guiding principle of everything that flows from One Mind, which is the spirit of all. This is the truth of life and the substance of soul."

Eastman Foster, who had been chosen as the "color" man for the broadcast by Mari at Xanthas' direction because he was the best known skeptic, started whining into his microphone for the benefit of his live audience that was, once more, almost every being on the planet, "Oh, for crying out loud, they have given us all this ballyhoo, spent all this money, assembled over a million people here and taken up the time of everyone else on Earth in order to have an inspirational meeting. And what a sleazy trick to have digitized Xanthas' voice to speak the Harvester's words. Isn't this just like government bureaucrats? Have these people no shame or sense of decency?"

Foster was at his indignant, unctuous, insinuating best when Xanthas' radiant form materialized between Bronc and Mari. She spoke softly, "We all need to learn the deeper meaning of these words if Earth is to survive and if we, individually and collectively, are to advance spiritually."

If it were possible, the crowd was more silent than just before Mari had originally begun to speak. They were simply in shock. But not Eastman Foster. He shouted outrage at what he considered the sleaziest device he had ever seen used in a public relations campaign. Picked up by his microphone, a small electronic dot glued just above the "Cupid's bow" of his upper lip, he screamed that obviously what the U.C. had done was acquire the Harvester's illusographic technolo-gy to try to trade upon the world's love and grief for Xanthas.

Foster bellowed from his position next to the stage, "Let me up there! Let me run my hand right through her digital body! What a cheap, crappy trick! Let me up there!"

The crowd, all of whom had their digicoms tuned to his narrative, was now in an uproar. Xanthas raised her hand and, instantaneously, it fell silent, "Please come up, Mr. Foster." Her voice was as lovely as ever. Some didn't care if it was an Illusograph. They were just happy to see and hear her again.

Mamadou Bennajem bent down and with his powerful arm lifted Foster onto the stage as if he were a bag full of cotton puffs. Foster walked quickly toward Xanthas, preparing to whip his arm through her digital form and expose this trashy scheme to the world. He could see his ratings out of sight after this. Det stepped quickly from the shadows and took Foster's arm, gripping it very tightly. He placed the forefinger of his other hand over Foster's microphone and said quietly into the broadcaster's ear, his cigar bouncing up and down against Foster's neck, "Look, Foster, you asshole, I don't care what you do or say just so long as you don't do it in a way that harms her. So if you are planning to punch through her, don't, or two things will happen to you. You will have the worst testicular incident I've ever delivered, and it will be the *last* time you use this particular arm." From the pain, Foster was certain he would see the burly Det's fingerprints the next time he took off his shirt.

Always concerned for his own welfare first, and confused that Det Menard was acting like she was real, he continued at a slower pace until he was next to her. She sure as hell looked real. God, she was beautiful. Before he could decide whether or not to stick his hand through her, she invited him to examine the scar on her head left by the laser weapon. He had been at the autopsy. The only part of her body that had been exposed then was her head and he had seen the damage, but not even at the autopsy had he ever been this close to her and certainly had never touched her.

Something was happening to him he couldn't explain. It was just something radiating from her. His thoughts seemed to be changing. He couldn't bring himself to reach out. Somehow he did not feel worthy. He couldn't understand it, but he just couldn't bring himself to do it. Xanthas leaned over and whispered close to his ear. She had a wonderful scent. She told him that he must touch her, he must examine her. It was for all those watching. He must do it and then express his honest opinion.

He was weak in the knees and perspiring heavily. He and Xanthas filled the DV screens. He looked out at the sea of expectant faces. He could hardly think. His hands were visibly trembling. Again she told him he must. He reached up and touched her hair. He almost passed out, but forced himself to part it and look at the scar. She told him to pinch her midsection. She was wearing a sheer white gown like he had seen in the old paintings of the Greek goddesses. He could feel the heat of her firm flesh as he gingerly put his hand against it and lightly squeezed. He could not speak.

She told him to put his arms around her and hug her to make certain she was alive. He said he couldn't. She commanded him. He put his arms around her and knew then he had never felt loving warmth before. He was melting into it. She moved him back gently and looked into his eyes. He fell weeping onto his knees and begged her to forgive him. She bent down and kissed him on the forehead. He was sobbing uncontrollably and the security forces carried him from the stage.

As the world watched with its collective mouth open, including the little "o's" made by the Mantid mouths, the DV rapidly replayed the scenario over and over from every possible angle and every lens setting from wide to extreme close-up. Xanthas certainly looked real and if *Foster* had been reduced to a blubbering, sobbing mass, she had to be real, but they just couldn't understand it. How *could* it be?

No one at the Lowey had made a sound for several minutes. They were just staring and wondering. Xanthas, of course, knew what they were thinking, "I am going to pass among you now. I want as many of you who can to touch my hands so you will know that I have returned." With that she rose and floated just over their heads, reaching down to briefly touch their upstretched hands. They looked into her eyes as they did so and many fell immediately to their knees and began praying in whatever way they were accustomed. Those who did not simply stood there looking after her, overwhelmed by the feeling that had engulfed them, not only from her touch, but just being near her.

She floated over to a well-known young woman, Kimberly Kimbeaux, who was seated in a wheeled chair due to an injury several years earlier in a spectacular widely-digivised Olympic snowboarding accident. She had been brought to the Lowey on this sunny day by her husband, Dan Salem, a free-lance writer and digiographer covering the event, so they could spend the remainder of the day enjoying the adjoining parks.

Trailed by the media pool which had been allowed to follow, Xanthas settled gently in front of her, "Kimberly, hold out your hands." Xanthas' presence having dissolved all fear, the young woman did so, transfixed by Xanthas' eyes and at this moment grateful she had only been paralyzed from the waist down. Xanthas took her hands and said, "Kim, you do not need this chair any more." Kim had known it from the first touch and immediately rose, stepping away from the chair. Without thinking, her husband dropped his digicam and rushed to embrace his wife. The surrounding crowd and the world-wide DV audience gasped simultaneously and shed tears of awe.

The conviction of the world's inhabitants that Xanthas had returned was exceeded only by their wonder.

<<~>>

CHAPTER FIFTY SIX

After the Lowey, Xanthas and Mari embarked upon a campaign that visited all the major cities in the world, including Manticon, and many lesser ones. Xanthas wanted as many of Earth's inhabitants as practicable to see her in person. It was a relatively simple task for Xanthas, Mari and the media pool because Xanthas simply transported all of them and their equipment instantaneously to the next appearance. Those visitations were broadcast throughout the world. Not only were her several daily visits to various areas a ritual to watch, but there was a never-ending fascination with the healing of mental and physical problems that occurred and with the subsequent interviews of those she healed.

Next to Mari, Eastman Foster had become Xanthas' most visible and ardent disciple, having been unanimously selected by the media as its color man for her visits following the "rebirth" of his thought at the Lowey. The media not only trusted him now, they felt they were getting information from a source as close to, and as familiar with, Xanthas as they were going to get. They still hadn't realized that all they needed to do was listen to Xanthas.

Xanthas told her audiences that one of her primary goals on this round of visits was to ". . . develop a critical mass of understanding among you that a core principle of being is to express and *receive* unconditional love, letting it out and letting it in, to paraphrase your wonderful Surface professor, Morris Schwartz, described in the little twentieth century volume, *Tuesdays with Morrie*, by author Mitch Albom." She wanted that critical mass to affect the consciousness of others, creating a subliminal harmonic empathy of unconditional love that would influence the formation of their thoughts in a positive way, analogous to logic influencing reasonable minds, but more simply and properly described as love influencing conduct. Mari easily recognized it now as positive Entrainment.

After the conclusion of her world tour, another planet-wide message from Xanthas was scheduled to be delivered by her at the Lowey. This time, one and one-half million beings squeezed onto Lois Fields and the surrounding parks, including many Mantid who were themselves an object of curiosity as most had not seen them in the "flesh" so to speak. Many beings had to be turned away. The logistics were phenomenal, but well-handled, and more than before, it was a sea of bodies as far as one could see. Xanthas stepped onto the stage and the crowd not only fell silent, most fell to their knees.

Xanthas spoke forcefully, "Do not worship me! Get up. Get up now before I speak another word!" Puzzled, they rose. Again she spoke firmly, "Do *not* worship me. Have reverence and gratitude for *your* ability to increase your own understanding and raise the level of your thinking to the level at which I am now – and have reverence and gratitude for your ability to surpass my current level.

"You *already* have this power. *Each* of you. It is *your* abundance, it is your account filled with unicredits. Draw them out! They are yours for the claiming. In order to demonstrate this wealth, you only need understand and put into practice the procedures that open the vault. *You* must *do* it. Just do it! You must practice changing your thinking daily, one thought at a time. You can *choose* what you think. That will effect what happens. If you make a mistake, *forgive yourself*, and continue aright with the very next thought. I may set the example, but you must do the rest. This is what I have been teaching you. Listen. I will summarize it once again, only.

"From your present material plane of thinking, in order to arrive at an increased understanding of the true nature of the highest source during your journey in the Grand Illusion, constantly raise the thoughts in your Earthly mind toward thinking right and doing right. This will continually increase the abundance of all kinds manifested for your benefit in the Grand Illusion, first as a result of changing your beliefs and then as a result of higher and higher levels of understanding of your relationship to the highest source, One Mind. Demonstrate your changed beliefs and understanding in increasing increments until you *know* the truth that the Grand Illusion *is* only illusion.

"Arrival at that enlightenment will necessarily include the understanding that *the journey* to it *never existed*, that you have *always* been a part of and at the highest source, the only source, the only true existence of all – which is One Mind, the substance of existence. The *natural reality* is that you *are* pure consciousness, One Mind's perfect, unblemished, continuous, joyous unfoldment and expression. The expression of this consciousness is the manifestation of unconditional love, the substance of soul. We are individual, yet inseparable from this expression because we *are* the expression. One Mind is in us all. One Mind is all of us – continually unfolding in its perfect way."

A young man in attendance, Tracy Glass, looked at his sister, Wendy, and his wife, Amy. In turn, Wendy looked at her husband, Sean McFire. Simultaneously, each thought, 'I want to get it, but I'm not sure I get it.' Their thoughts echoed those of many individuals at the Lowey, and around, even in, the world.

The unspoken thoughts did not escape Xanthas, "I know many will appreciate an analogy."

Tracy leaned over to Amy and whispered, "Man, she must be reading my mind." Wendy, in turn, leaned over and whispered softly to her sibling, "Of course she is."

Xanthas smiled and continued, "Let's presume you are in south Oakland . . ." Sean's mind jumped, 'Perish the thought.' Xanthas glanced in his direction as she finished the sentence, ". . . and you want to get to San Francisco." Sean's mind smiled 'All right!' Xanthas' eyes twinkled in his direction, "So far as you can remember, you've never been there, but you hear it is wonderful because if you go there you will never want to be anywhere else, which is good, because once you go there, you *will* never be anywhere else."

Her last statement definitely caught everyone's attention.

"Someone points out that the path is through Oakland and then across a very long bridge with a number of lanes. You have to go by driving a car and you don't seem to be the world's greatest driver. Additionally, you have to change cars after every block, some of which are long and some short. Before getting another car, it is necessary for you to go to school to work on improving your driving skills. Even though you have studied hard in-between cars, you find that each car you start not only has a different speed, which is always too slow from your perspective, but it has different equipment and requires that you drive it in a different way, plus the fact that you always seem to have a hard time remembering your previous lessons. So, every time, it seems like you are starting over again, even though you are not.

"Not only is there a learning curve to driving each car once you get into it, but you can't see clearly through the windshield and you must constantly stay focused while you are driving because the way is not always well lit, the road often bumpy and there are many distractions. Further, your car gets much better mileage if you put in a special energy additive, but you must learn to generate it while you are trying to do everything else. All of this often impairs your progress and causes you to slow down, stop or make the wrong turn, all for reasons you can't seem to fully understand.

"You also have passengers in each car. Some are helpful, and some distract you from your driving. You have to change passengers every time you change cars. All of this enhances the feeling that you are starting over every block and you tend to lose sight of the fact that if you just keep driving your car to the best of your ability under the circumstances, you will be making progress on your journey and not be wandering aimlessly. When the journey gets rough, if you can figure out where they are and then take the time to listen to them, there are individuals along the route who will help point out the way.

"But, no matter how much you may want to, you are not able to exit the other end of the bridge until you understand everything you need to know in order to properly fuel your car and drive into San Francisco expertly and by yourself. Because at that point, you can only enter one at a time.

"So, from your perspective on this journey, it seems to take a very long time. But you persevere, stay focused and at last you are on the bridge. In order to reassure yourself, you keep looking back at Oakland to see how much progress you have made. Oakland gets further in the distance and, at a point, you realize that you need to choose exactly the proper lane for your car in order to get off the bridge, but you are not entirely certain you are seeing things correctly.

"Then comes the moment when you *know* you have learned and consistently practiced everything necessary to enable you to understand how to see the way clearly. As a result, you can *only* see clearly, which causes you to choose the correct path. You exit the bridge and enter San Francisco.

"You feel marvelous and part of every good thing, which is everything in San Francisco because it is a perfect place. You realize that at some point, your car disappeared from around you. So you turn to look back at the bridge and Oakland. They are not there. The last thing you learn about your journey is that they *never were there*. You have *always* been in San Francisco."

Xanthas floated over the crowd. Glowing with the spiritual hue of understanding, she seemed more effulgent and more transparent than ever. She was so bright that some could scarcely look at her.

She addressed the world, <<<~ I will leave you now to your journey. You have always had the tools to successfully complete it. Constantly think the right thing and do the right thing. Stand ever-vigilant at the vestibule of your thoughts. When in doubt, always do what you *feel* is right. The spirit of unconditional love can never be separate from you. Tune your material consciousness to it. Practice it. Demonstrate it. *Raise Your Consciousness!~>>>*

With that, she Transpirated from material sight.

The crowd was buzzing with discussion, not immediately realizing she had Transpirated from the material to the Superconscious Dimension, her mission on the Earth plane of consciousness completed.

Tracy looked at his companions, "I think I get it."

Amy said gently, "Of course, changing cars is changing lives. The special energy additive is love, unconditional love. The passengers are the people in your life. The choices in life do not always seem clear. The ones who help show you the way are your Guides. The journey takes a long time and a lot of incarnations."

"Well . . . what did she mean that when you arrive in San Francisco and turn around you can't see the bridge or Oakland off in the distance? I mean, you're right there. Unless there's the humongo of all fogs, you'll be able to see it."

Wendy's mental view was unobstructed, "Tracy, its all an *illusion*. It's like having a vivid dream that seems real. It's not. The events in it never happened. You've actually been snug in your little beddie-bye all the time."

"My bed?" He lovingly kidded his sister.

Amy put her hand on his arm, even though she knew he knew, "You've been in San Francisco from the beginning." She kissed him on the cheek.

Sean lit up. "Wait, wait, I got it! It's like you are standing in the perfect place to be, but you can't see it and don't know it because it seems like there *is* this humongous fog."

Tracy chimed in, ". . . and the fog *is* the material world."

Sean jumped back in, ". . . and the more you understand and practice the real nature of being, its like your elevated thinking radiates heat that starts to dissipate the fog. The more heat you radiate, the more fog that's dissipated and it has less and less effect on your perception. Once the fog is gone, you see clearly it was an illusion and you have actually been in the perfect place all along without realizing it."

Tracy, ". . . or, it's like trying to look through a dirty window pane that impairs your vision of the other side. Once you clean it, you can see without distortion."

Wendy, knowing they understood, "Let's let the kids play in the park for awhile and go home after that."

Amy added softly, ". . . and think about it some more."

Tracy added enthusiastically, ". . . and then, like Xanthas said, do it."

Wendy put her arm around her brother as they all walked off. The kids mimicked her, putting their arms around each other as they went toward the park.

CHAPTER FIFTY SEVEN

Back in the Superconscious Dimension, Xanthas floated alone with her thoughts. She had not noticed the color of her energy when the Superconscious portion of Jenoor's bilocated energy floated up to her.

~Xan, that was marvelous. You started a sea-change in Earth consciousness. Almost everyone seems to be contemplating the meaning of your words and how to practice them in small and large ways. The demonstrations of your healing power and your ascension before the eyes of the world has propelled their thought and motivation upward.~

<<<<~Shame on you, Jenoor. You know that is not *my* power. It's the power of One Mind. It's the ability that flows in all of us and can be demonstrated by each of us at every level of thinking in a way that reflects the level of advancement of our thought.~>>>>

~Sorry. I guess I'm like everyone else no matter what level we're at. I tend to worship the more advanced person who demonstrates what I know instinctively is right, but that I'm still working on to fully understand. I lose sight that it's the *principle* being demonstrated that is the key element, not the demonstrator. I need to concentrate on the message, not the messenger.~

<<<<~It is very easy to think the messenger is the most important element because that is the most concrete thing observable. We lose sight of the fact that the *message* is we are each capable of equaling and exceeding the messenger's demonstration, and that *is* our purpose no matter what level of consciousness we are on, including right here in the Superconscious.~>>>>

~By the way, did you know that your energy color is spinning through lots of different hues? It's hard to describe.~

Indeed, Xanthas' color was rapidly revolving among several compositions – emerald green with multi-colored flecks, a multi-colored radiance with trillions of colors, the hue of the Overseers, the hue of the Principal Overseers, and something more than that which neither had words for at the moment. They were both stunned, as was Saba who had floated in.

Saba had not actually seen Xanthas in the Superconscious Dimension since she had agreed with the Master Teachers to study for her return to Earth. Saba was very excited and interjected, ~Xanthas, this is incredible, your hues are evolving beyond the Principal Overseers! I'm so curious. Were you able to talk with Jesus and Buddha before you went back to Earth? If you did, what did they say?~

<<<<~Saba, I could not talk with them or with a number of other spiritual leaders like them. It is impossible for any of us here.~>>>>

Both Saba and Jenoor were somewhat confused and incredulous. Saba, while highly advanced compared to many souls in the Superconscious Dimension, was still roughly in the middle of the advancement of understanding for the Superconscious plane.

Saba queried, ~I don't understand. Wouldn't souls like Jesus and Buddha be at the top of this plane, right next to One Mind?~

<<<<~Saba, this plane is part of the journey. It is a level of understanding above the Material Dimension. But not even the highest level of understanding in the Superconscious Dimension is the final level of understanding. I know you witnessed my last talk at the Lowey. The same principle applies here as it does in the Material Dimension. The principle is constant and does not change whether you are in the Material Dimension or the Superconscious Dimension. It is the same for everyone, with results according to each's level of understanding. That includes Jesus, Buddha and everyone else, whether or not one functions as a spiritual leader.

<<<<~Since most in the Grand Illusion are not prepared to accept only thoughts as a message from 'nowhere,' a messenger within the illusion is necessary to present the message to the illusion. Jesus, Buddha and other great spiritual Earthly advisors were souls projected as material manifestations within the Grand Illusion in order to convey those of One Mind's thoughts that were shining through the fog. But, keep in mind that just as the sun is not part of the fog, One Mind's thoughts are not part of the illusion, and just as the sun is seen imperfectly through the fog, One Mind's thoughts are imperfectly interpreted within the illusion through the language of the illusion, and the message may either not be accurate, not accurately perceived or both to varying degrees. That includes the Superconscious Dimension as well as the Material Dimension.

<<<<~Those souls you have perceived as Jesus, Buddha and other great spiritual leaders have not only Transpired from the material plane of understanding, they have also Transpired from the Superconscious plane of understanding. Their *works* remain in those

dimensions, but they will not return to either dimension. They cannot return. From the perspective within those dimensions, those spiritual leaders understand too much.~>>>>>

Saba and Jenoor just floated blankly, trying to fully comprehend what she was communicating.

Saba, disappointed, ~I always believed that at some point I would get to communicate with them directly here. I've so been looking forward to it. What is it they understand too much of? How do you communicate with them indirectly?~

<<<<<~I communicate indirectly the same as anyone else here does, including the Principal Overseers, I examine their works, letting their real meaning, the wisdom and understanding of One Mind, which shines through in spite of the apparent fog of the illusion, flow into me, *be* me. I do not interfere with it by interpreting it in terms of thought constellations manufactured only within the illusion by our Superconscious-plane consciousness. As one on Earth would quiet the chatter of material thinking, I quiet Superconscious thinking so that only One Mind's thoughts are left. I clear a path through the fog so to speak. On Earth, one's understanding must rise above material thought patterns in order to achieve the Superconscious level of understanding. Here, it is the same principle and process to lift understanding from the *apparent* Superconscious level of existence to that of One Mind, which is possible because One Mind is actually, and naturally, all there is.~>>>>>

Jenoor collected his thoughts, ~You are referring to 'apparent existence' when referring to the Superconscious Dimension? I understand the illusion and nothingness of the Material Dimension which was created from this plane, but you seem to be communicating that not only is material existence an illusion, but Superconscious existence is also.~ If Jenoor had a physical countenance in this dimension, his eyebrows would be up and his eyes wide with incredulous query. Saba's mouth would be wide open.

<<<<<~That is correct. The Material Dimension is part of the Grand Illusion and the Superconscious Dimension is another level of it. Just as the Material Dimension, the Superconscious Dimension has no more reality than the example of $2 + 2 = 5$. With the elevation of my understanding, now I clearly see, I know, I *possess* the Truth as a natural part of my being. The Truth is filling my consciousness, One

Mind is my only real consciousness, *the only* true and natural consciousness. In terms of the journey through the illusion, I understand that the Superconscious Dimension too is merely Oakland to the picopower, and I'm about to step off the bridge into a San Francisco to the infinite power, which is definitely the final place, actually, the *only* place.

<<<<<~In the ultimate place of *the* Truth, there is nothing that needs improvement. *Perfect* being is the only existence and experience. It never began, never ended and has never been less than perfect. There has been no journey from imperfection to perfection. The perfect state of One Mind is *all*. It *always* has been. It *always* will be. That leaves room for nothing else. There *has never* been anything else.~>>>>>

<<<<<~The truth of being is spiritual, and the substance of soul is One Mind, that life which consists of the continuous, harmonious unfolding of unconditional love pursuant to its perfect principle.~>>>>>

All of the Principal Overseers, Overseers and Master Teachers were in attendance now. They had seen it happen before and it always helped renew their enthusiasm and elevate their understanding.

Xanthas told them she loved them. Having separated the tares from the wheat, she had completed her Harvest of Illusion.

Her radiance changed to the hue of unfettered and unconditional love and she Transpirated from their plane of understanding and, thus, from their view.

<<~>>

CHAPTER FIFTY EIGHT

She was in the Divine Dimension, the only dimension, that state which is all and unaware of a Grand Illusion. No thought was present to turn back to say goodbye to the Superconscious Dimension. As a characteristic of its natural nonexistence, it was never there.

The unfolding thoughts of One Mind's infinite consciousness inseparably expressed her as the real nature of being. As the activity of One Mind, she was one with it in that state which is abundant, peaceful, loving, secure, complete and all. That perfect state in which she always had been. The only existence.

They have their exits and their entrances;
And one man in his time plays many parts,

As You Like It
William Shakespeare

<~>

Within you right now
is the power to do the things you never dreamed possible.
This power becomes available to you
just as soon as you can change your beliefs.

Maxwell Maltz, M.D.

<~>

Man can learn nothing except by
going from the known to the unknown.

Claude Bernard

<~>

One Mind,
Thank you for thinking of me.

gcw

To arrive at the highest source,
Journey through the illusion.
Raise the illusion to higher levels of belief and understanding.
Demonstrate your understanding in increasing increments
until you know the illusion is just that
and the journey never existed.
You are always at the highest source
and part of it.
You are its perfect unblemished unfoldment and expression.
You are its expression of love.
God is in us all.
God is all of us.
We are God's idea
inseparable from the thinker.

gcw

<~>

Synchronous occurrences seem separate events conjoined
from the viewpoint of the observer,
but they are one with their source,
constantly unfolding from it.
Never beginning and never ending,
this manifestation occurs according to the
principle of truth and love.

gcw

ABOUT THE AUTHOR

George C. Wallach,

the product of a "right-brained" mother and "left-brained" father,

is a successful attorney morphed to author.

The combination of his spiritual-healing oriented mother

and medical-logic oriented father

resulted in a writer with the union of thinking and introspection

that produced this unusual book describing

a belief system for

a logic-oriented spirituality and nature of being.

<~>

Readers may contact the author through
www.harvestofillusion.com

www.ingramcontent.com/pod-product-compliance
Lightning Source LLC
Chambersburg PA
CBHW020332180626
46812CB00001B/159